The Rock Gods of Jackson Tennessee

Thanks!

2023

PRESIDENT AND PUBLISHER
MIKE RICHARDSON

EDITOR
BRETT ISRAEL

ASSISTANT EDITOR
SANJAY DHARAWAT

DIGITAL ART TECHNICIAN
ANN GRAY

COLLECTION DESIGNER
SKYLER WEISSENFLUH

Neil Hankerson Executive Vice President • Tom Weddle Chief Financial Officer • Dale LaFountain Chief Information Officer • Tim Wiesch Vice President of Licensing • Vanessa Todd-Holmes Vice President of Production and Scheduling Mark Bernardi Vice President of Book Trade and Digital Sales • Randy Lahrman Vice President of Product Development and Sales • Cara O'Neil Vice President of Marketing • Ken Lizzi General Counsel • Dave Marshall Editor in Chief Davey Estrada Editorial Director • Chris Warner Senior Books Editor • Cary Grazzini Director of Specialty Projects Lia Ribacchi Creative Director • Michael Gombos Senior Director of Licensed Publications • Kari Yadro Director of Custom Programs • Kari Torson Director of International Licensing • Christina Niece Director of Scheduling

Published by Dark Horse Books
A division of Dark Horse Comics LLC
10956 SE Main Street
Milwaukie, OR 97222

First edition: June 2023
Ebook ISBN 978-1-50672-941-1
Trade Paperback ISBN 978-1-50672-940-4

10 9 8 7 6 5 4 3 2 1
Printed in China

MIX
Paper from
responsible sources
FSC® C109093
www.fsc.org

Comic Shop Locator Service: comicshoplocator.com

THE ROCK GODS OF JACKSON, TENNESSEE

Library of Congress Cataloging-in-Publication Data

Names: Roberts, Rafer, 1976- author. | Norton, Mike, artist. | Passalaqua,
    Allen, colorist. | Crank! (Letterer), letterer.
Title: The rock gods of Jackson Tennessee / Rafer Roberts, writer/lead
    vocals ; Mike Norton, artist/guitar ; Allen Passalaqua, colors/bass ;
    Crank!, letters/percussion.
Description: Milwaukie, OR : Dark Horse Books, 2023. | Audience: Ages 14+ |
    Summary: Four high school outcasts start a band to gain fame and
    popularity, but have to defend their hometown from a hungry horde of
    monsters instead.
Identifiers: LCCN 2022050451 | ISBN 9781506729404 (trade paperback) | ISBN
    9781506729411 (ebook)
Subjects: CYAC: Bands (Music)--Fiction. | Rock music--Fiction. | High
    schools--Fiction. | Schools--Fiction. | Monsters--Fiction. | LCGFT:
    Coming-of-age comics. | Monster comics. | Graphic novels.
Classification: LCC PZ7.7.R6323 Ro 2023 | DDC 741.5/973--dc23/eng/20221027
LC record available at https://lccn.loc.gov/2022050451

THE ROCK GODS of JACKSON TENNESSEE

Created by

Rafer Roberts
(Writer/Lead Vocals)

Mike Norton
(Artist/Guitar)

Allen Passalaqua
(Colors/Bass)

Crank!
(Letters/Percussion)

Brett Israel and Sanjay Dharawat
(Edits/Managers)

DARK HORSE BOOKS

None of this happened.
All of it is true.

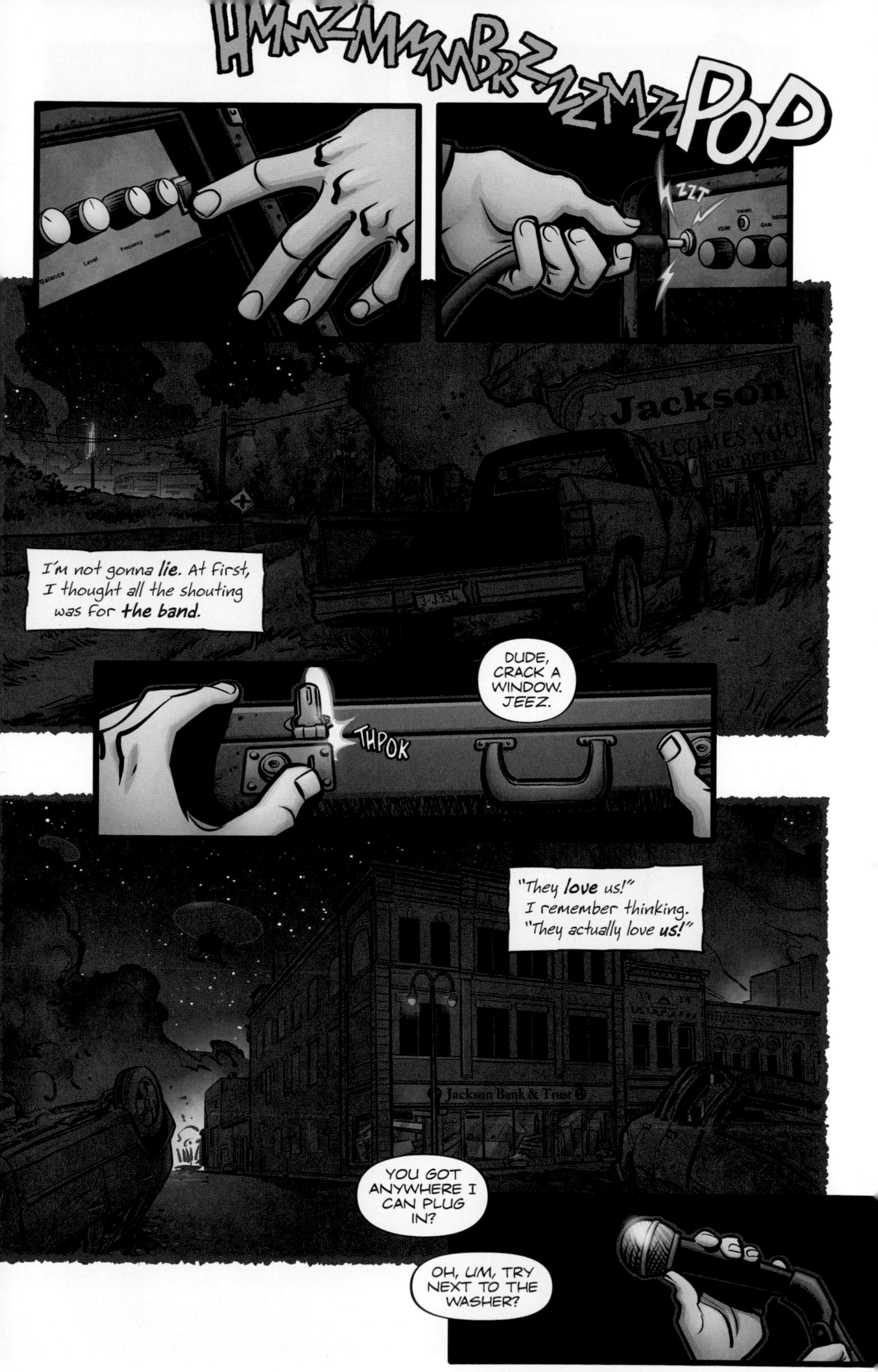
HMMZMMMBRZZZMZZPOP
ZZZT
Balance
Level
Frequency
Volume
Jackson
I'm not gonna lie. At first, I thought all the shouting was for the band.
DUDE, CRACK A WINDOW. JEEZ.
THPOK
"They love us!" I remember thinking. "They actually love us!"
Jackson Bank & Trust
YOU GOT ANYWHERE I CAN PLUG IN?
OH, UM, TRY NEXT TO THE WASHER?

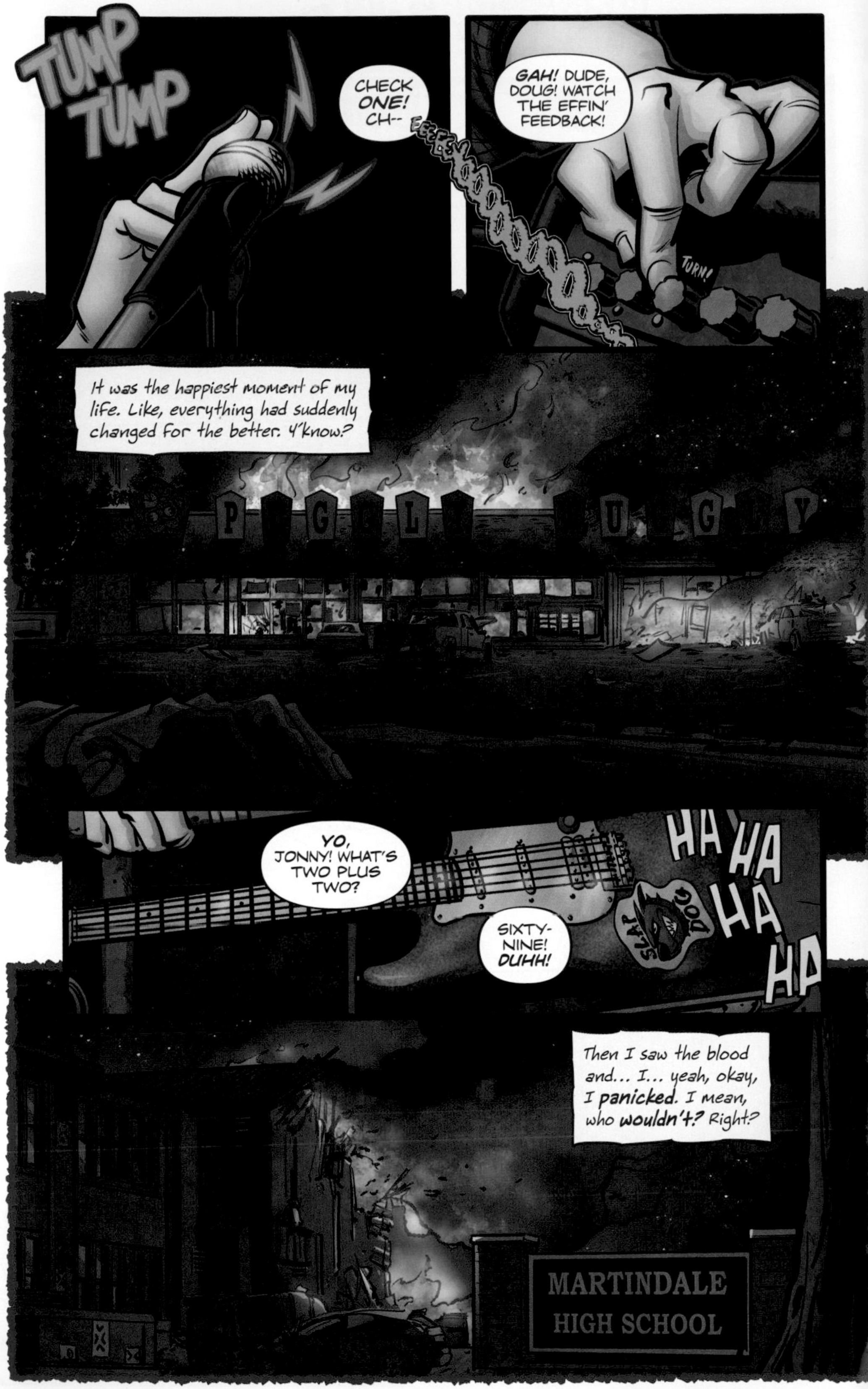
TUMP TUMP
CHECK ONE! CH--
EEEEEOOOOOOOOOOOO
GAH! DUDE, DOUG! WATCH THE EFFIN' FEEDBACK!
TURN!
It was the happiest moment of my life. Like, everything had suddenly changed for the better. Y'know?
YO, JONNY! WHAT'S TWO PLUS TWO?
SIXTY-NINE! DUHH!
HA HA HA HA HA
SLAP DOG
Then I saw the blood and... I... yeah, okay, I panicked. I mean, who wouldn't? Right?
MARTINDALE HIGH SCHOOL

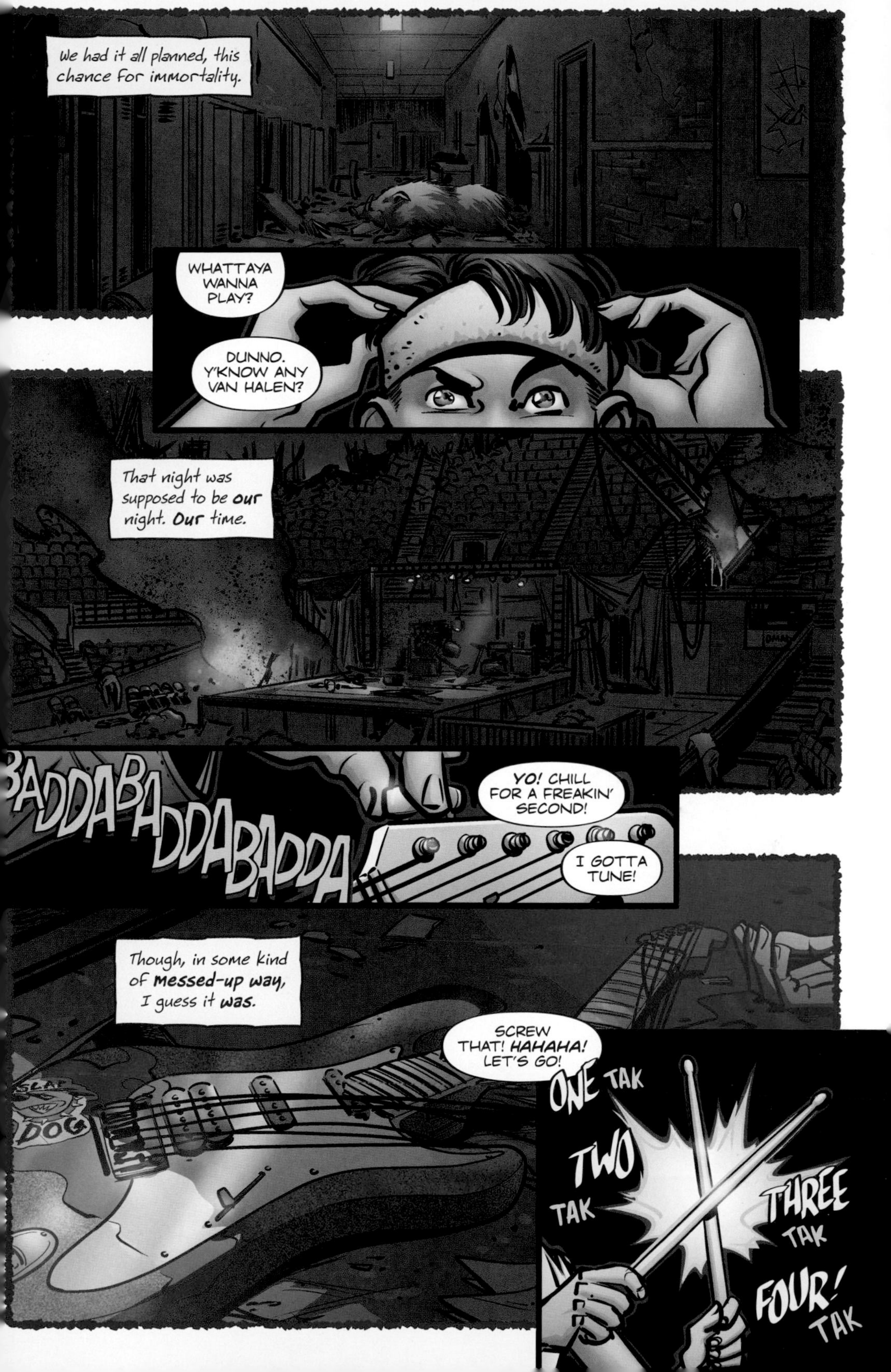

We had it all planned, this chance for immortality.
WHATTAYA WANNA PLAY?
DUNNO. Y'KNOW ANY VAN HALEN?
That night was supposed to be our night. Our time.
BADDABADDABADDA!
YO! CHILL FOR A FREAKIN' SECOND!
I GOTTA TUNE!
Though, in some kind of messed-up way, I guess it was.
SCREW THAT! HAHAHA! LET'S GO!
ONE TAK
TWO TAK
THREE TAK
FOUR! TAK

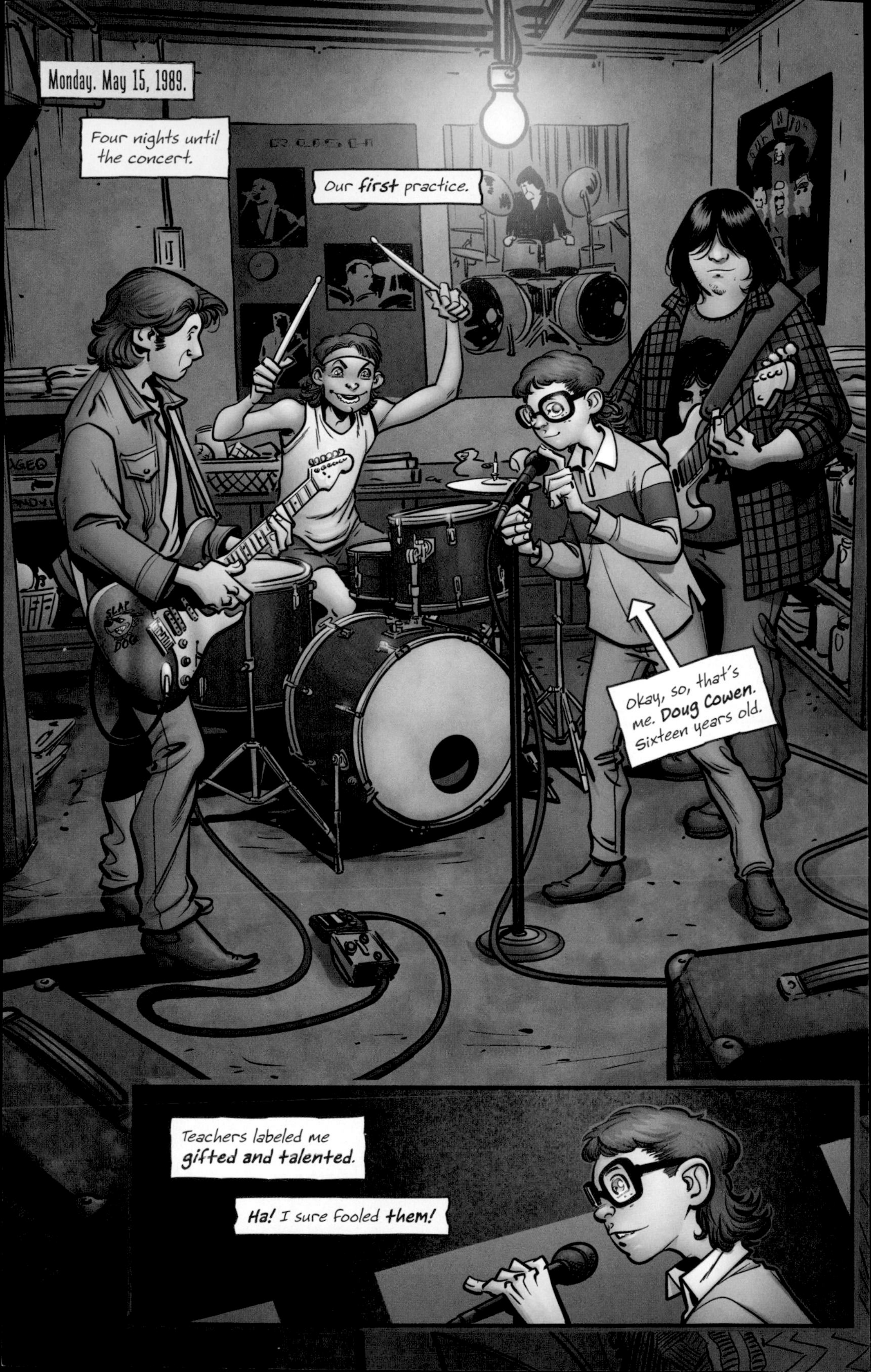

Monday. May 15, 1989.
Four nights until the concert.
Our **first** practice.
Okay, so, that's me. **Doug Cowen.** Sixteen years old.
Teachers labeled me **gifted and talented**.
Ha! I sure fooled **them!**

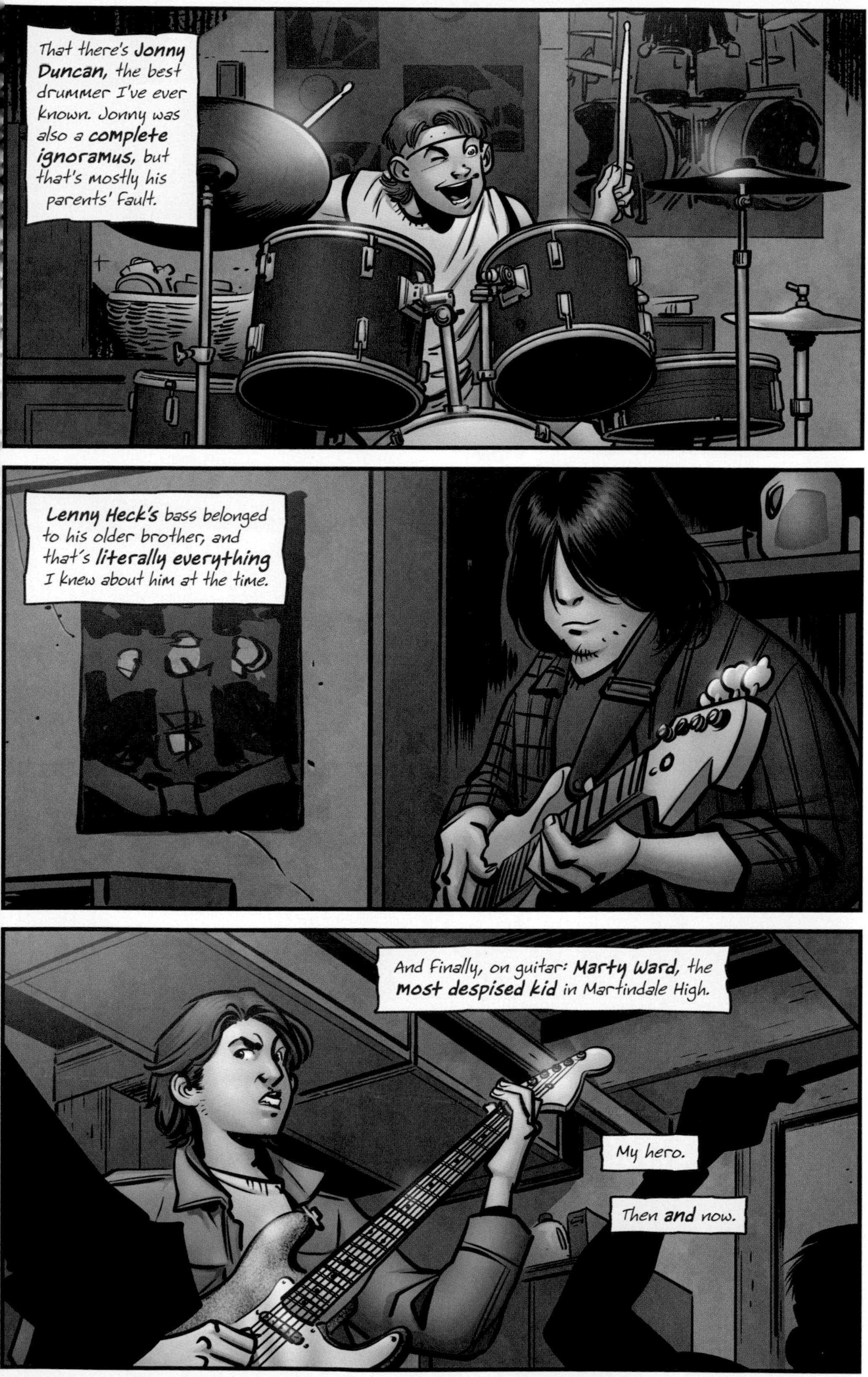
That there's Jonny Duncan, the best drummer I've ever known. Jonny was also a complete ignoramus, but that's mostly his parents' fault.
Lenny Heck's bass belonged to his older brother, and that's literally everything I knew about him at the time.
And finally, on guitar: Marty Ward, the most despised kid in Martindale High.
My hero.
Then and now.

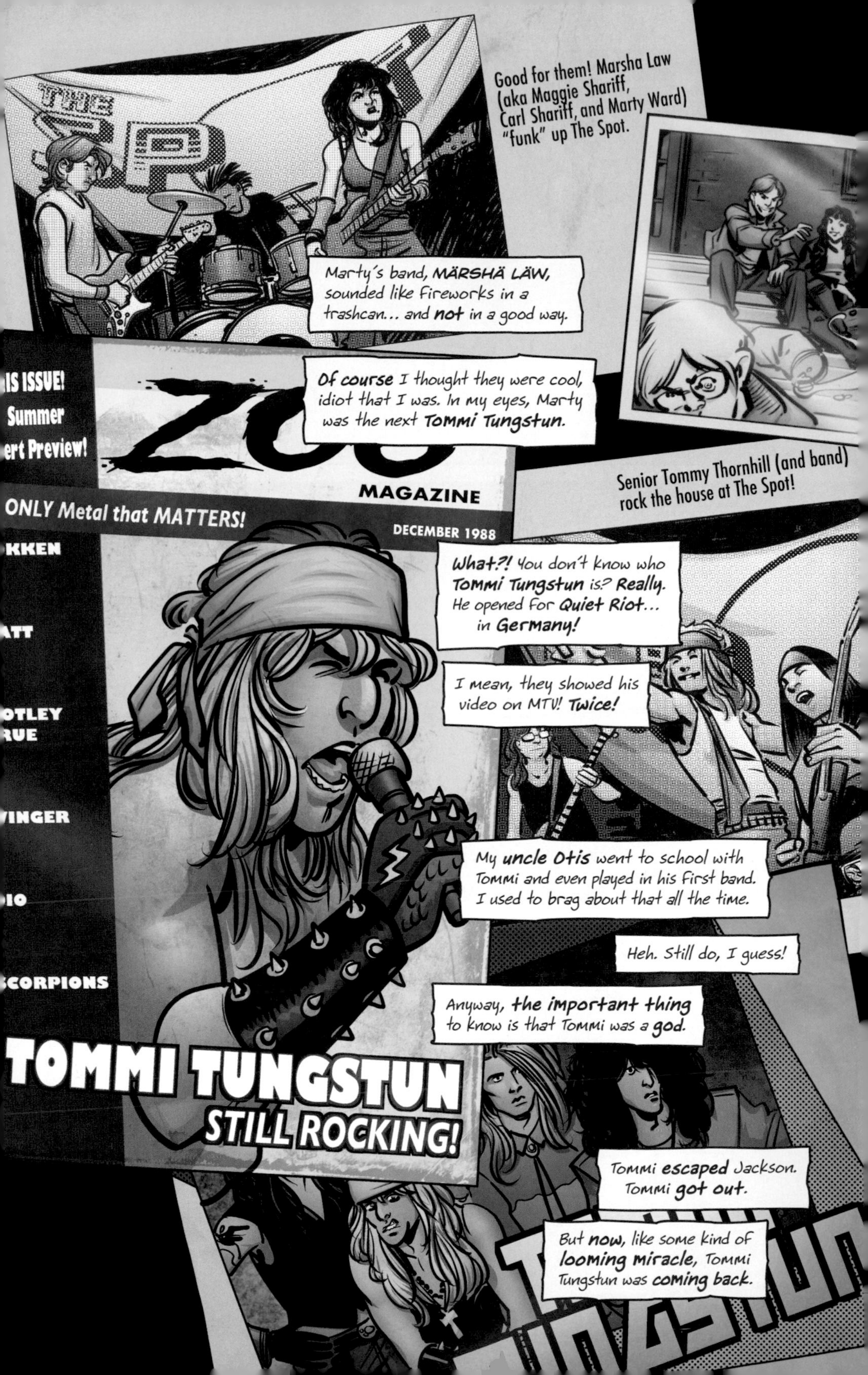
THE SPOT
Good for them! Marsha Law (aka Maggie Shariff, Carl Shariff, and Marty Ward) "funk" up The Spot.
Marty's band, MÄRSHÄ LÄW, sounded like fireworks in a trashcan... and not in a good way.
Of course I thought they were cool, idiot that I was. In my eyes, Marty was the next Tommi Tungstun.
IS ISSUE!
Summer
ert Preview!
ZOO
MAGAZINE
ONLY Metal that MATTERS!
DECEMBER 1988
Senior Tommy Thornhill (and band) rock the house at The Spot!
KKEN
ATT
OTLEY
RUE
INGER
IO
CORPIONS
What?! You don't know who Tommi Tungstun is? Really. He opened for Quiet Riot... in Germany!
I mean, they showed his video on MTV! Twice!
My uncle Otis went to school with Tommi and even played in his first band. I used to brag about that all the time.
Heh. Still do, I guess!
Anyway, the important thing to know is that Tommi was a god.
TOMMI TUNGSTUN
STILL ROCKING!
Tommi escaped Jackson. Tommi got out.
But now, like some kind of looming miracle, Tommi Tungstun was coming back.

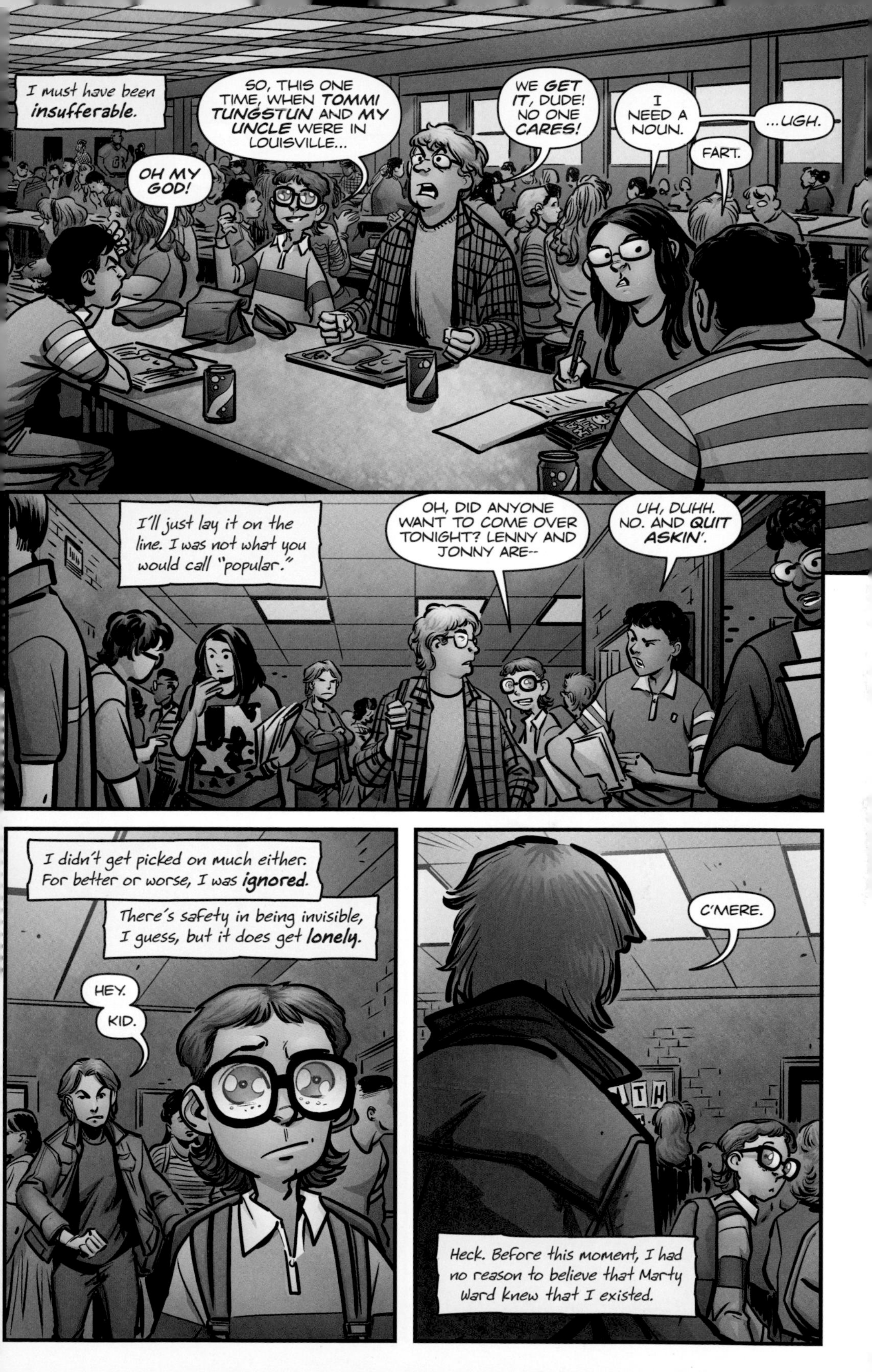
I must have been insufferable.
SO, THIS ONE TIME, WHEN TOMMI TUNGSTUN AND MY UNCLE WERE IN LOUISVILLE...
OH MY GOD!
WE GET IT, DUDE! NO ONE CARES!
I NEED A NOUN.
...UGH.
FART.
I'll just lay it on the line. I was not what you would call "popular."
OH, DID ANYONE WANT TO COME OVER TONIGHT? LENNY AND JONNY ARE--
UH, DUHH. NO. AND QUIT ASKIN'.
I didn't get picked on much either. For better or worse, I was ignored.
There's safety in being invisible, I guess, but it does get lonely.
HEY.
KID.
C'MERE.
Heck. Before this moment, I had no reason to believe that Marty Ward knew that I existed.

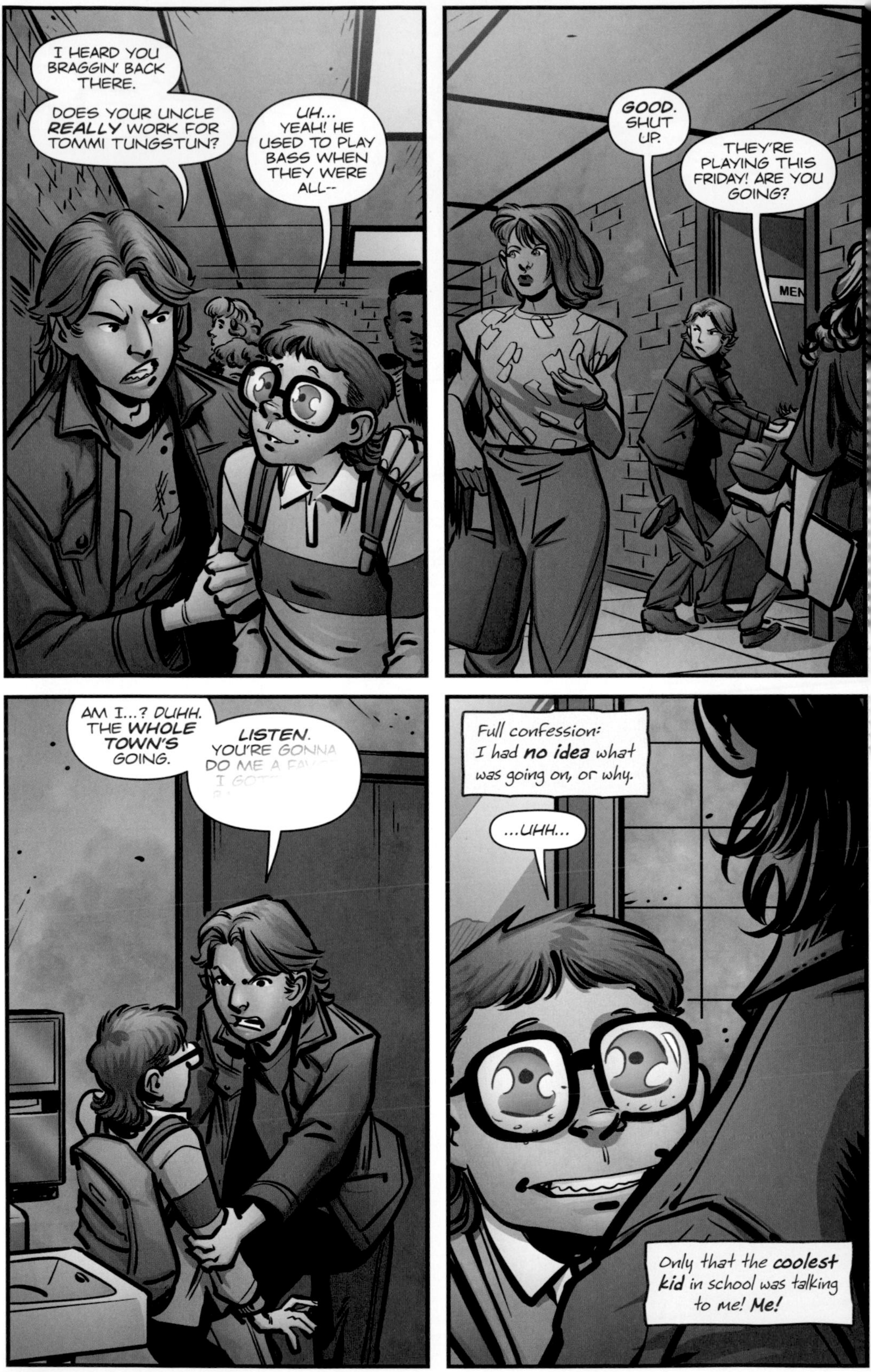
I HEARD YOU BRAGGIN' BACK THERE.
DOES YOUR UNCLE REALLY WORK FOR TOMMI TUNGSTUN?
UH... YEAH! HE USED TO PLAY BASS WHEN THEY WERE ALL--
GOOD. SHUT UP.
THEY'RE PLAYING THIS FRIDAY! ARE YOU GOING?
MEN
AM I...? DUHH. THE WHOLE TOWN'S GOING.
LISTEN. YOU'RE GONNA
Full confession: I had no idea what was going on, or why.
...UHH...
Only that the coolest kid in school was talking to me! Me!

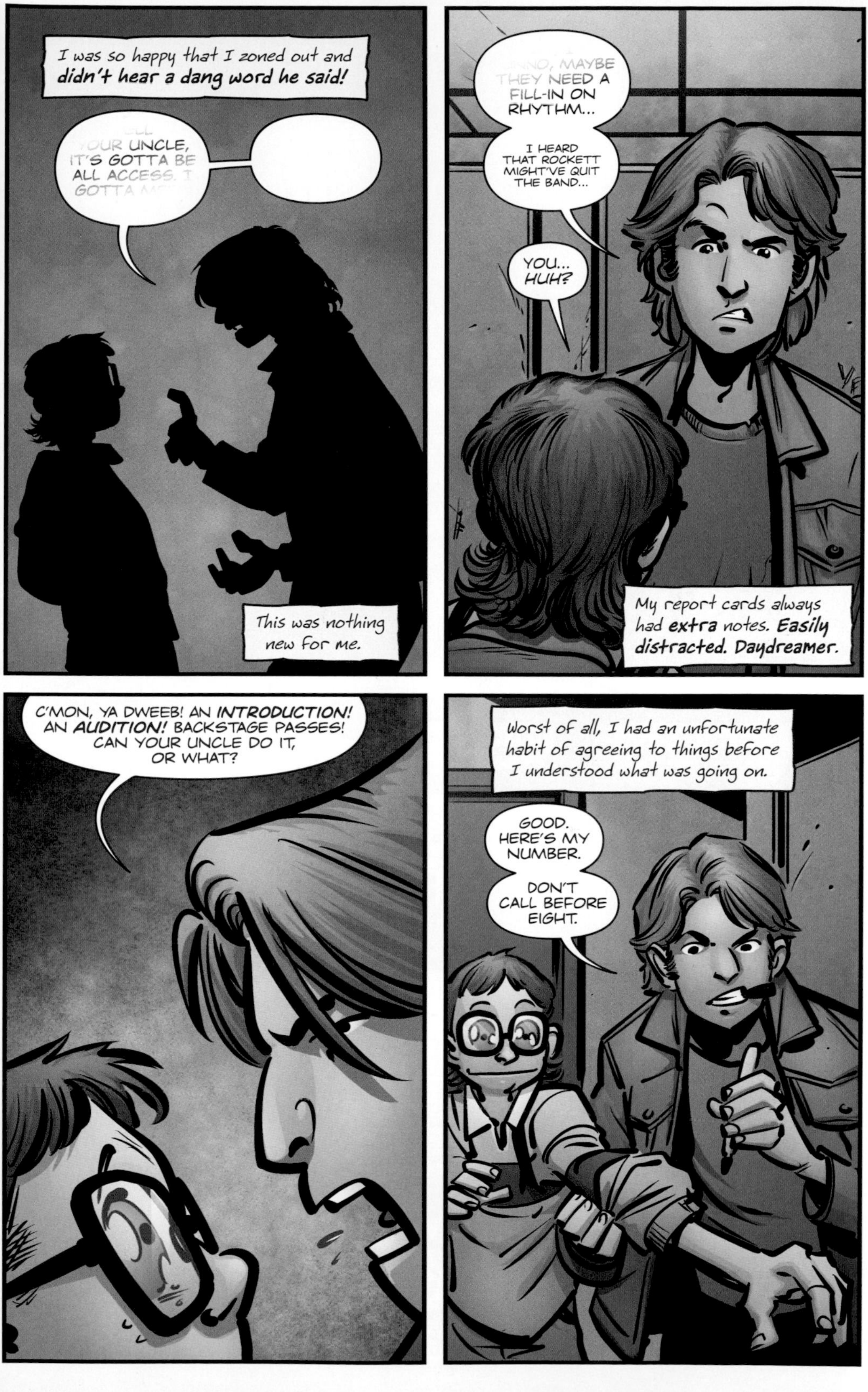
I was so happy that I zoned out and **didn't hear a dang word he said!**
YOUR UNCLE, IT'S GOTTA BE ALL ACCESS.
This was nothing new for me.
MAYBE THEY NEED A FILL-IN ON RHYTHM...
I HEARD THAT ROCKETT MIGHT'VE QUIT THE BAND...
YOU... HUH?
My report cards always had **extra** notes. **Easily distracted. Daydreamer.**
C'MON, YA DWEEB! AN *INTRODUCTION!* AN *AUDITION!* BACKSTAGE PASSES! CAN YOUR UNCLE DO IT, OR WHAT?
Worst of all, I had an unfortunate habit of agreeing to things before I understood what was going on.
GOOD. HERE'S MY NUMBER.
DON'T CALL BEFORE EIGHT.

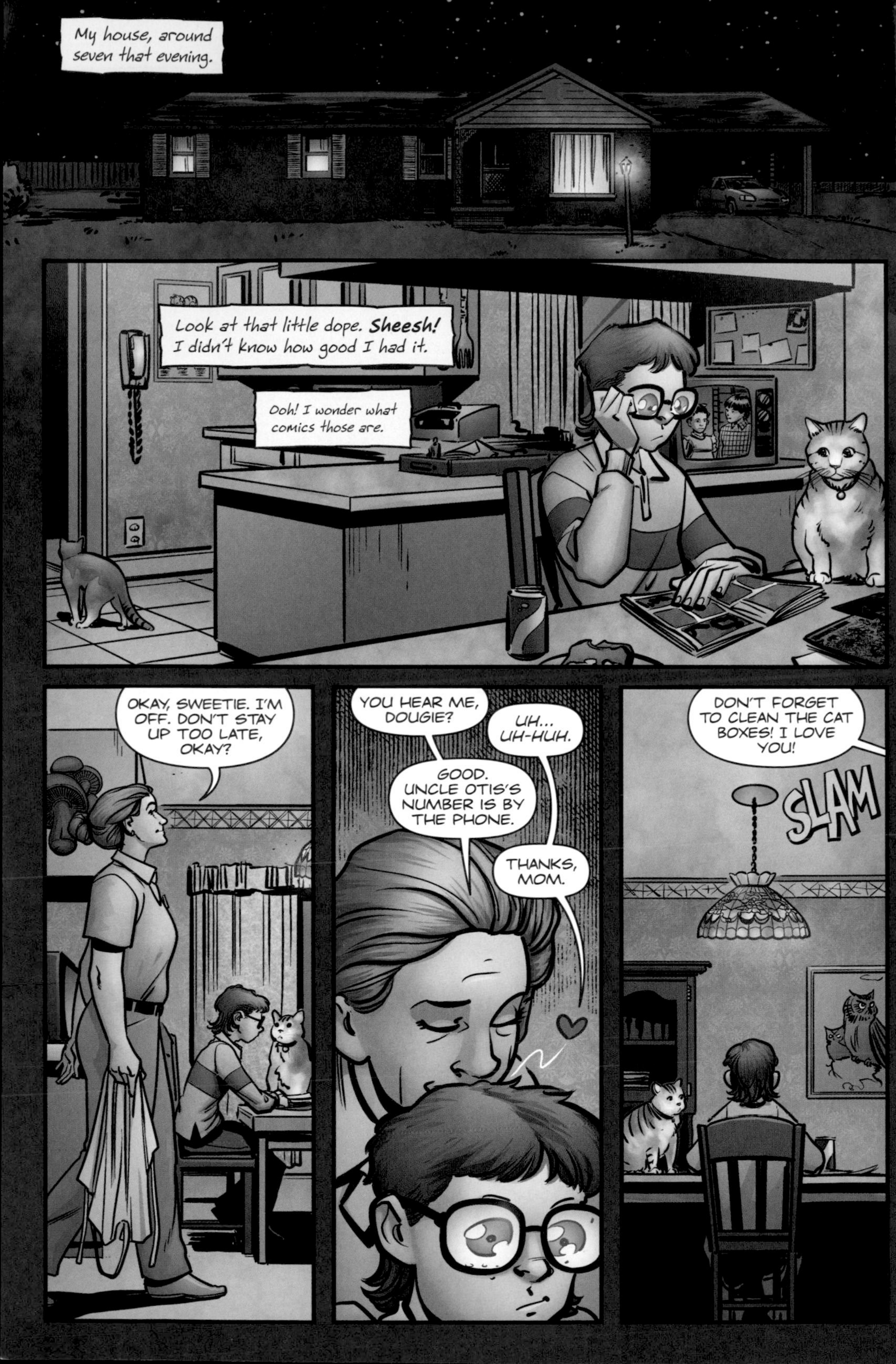
My house, around seven that evening.
Look at that little dope. **Sheesh!** I didn't know how good I had it.
Ooh! I wonder what comics those are.
OKAY, SWEETIE. I'M OFF. DON'T STAY UP TOO LATE, OKAY?
YOU HEAR ME, DOUGIE?
UH... UH-HUH.
GOOD. UNCLE OTIS'S NUMBER IS BY THE PHONE.
THANKS, MOM.
DON'T FORGET TO CLEAN THE CAT BOXES! I LOVE YOU!
SLAM

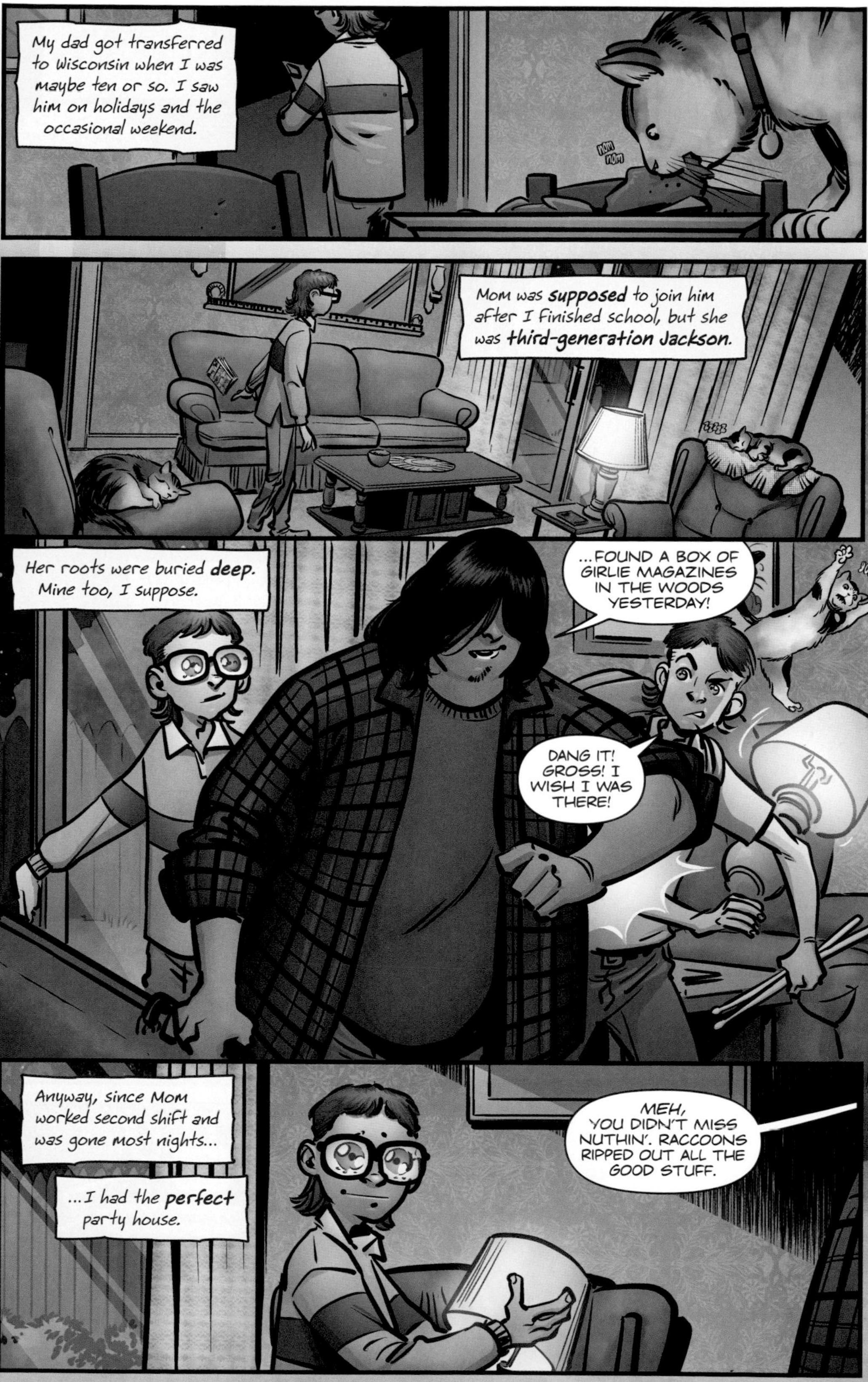
My dad got transferred to Wisconsin when I was maybe ten or so. I saw him on holidays and the occasional weekend.
nom nom
Mom was **supposed** to join him after I finished school, but she was **third-generation Jackson**.
Her roots were buried **deep**. Mine too, I suppose.
...FOUND A BOX OF GIRLIE MAGAZINES IN THE WOODS YESTERDAY!
yowl!
DANG IT! GROSS! I WISH I WAS THERE!
Anyway, since Mom worked second shift and was gone most nights...
...I had the **perfect** party house.
MEH, YOU DIDN'T MISS NUTHIN'. RACCOONS RIPPED OUT ALL THE GOOD STUFF.

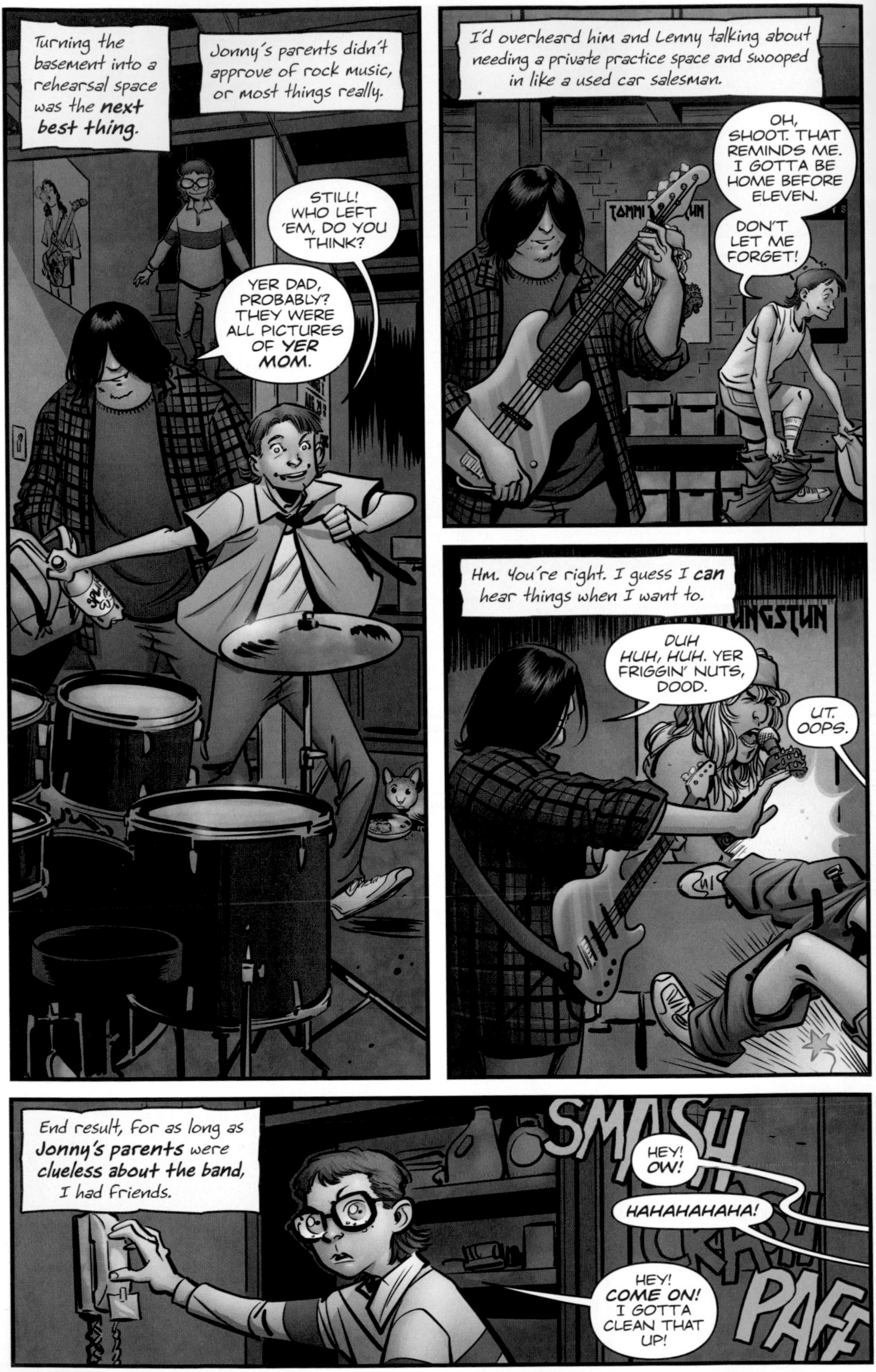
Turning the basement into a rehearsal space was the **next best thing**.
Jonny's parents didn't approve of rock music, or most things really.
STILL! WHO LEFT 'EM, DO YOU THINK?
YER DAD, PROBABLY? THEY WERE ALL PICTURES OF **YER MOM**.
I'd overheard him and Lenny talking about needing a private practice space and swooped in like a used car salesman.
OH, SHOOT. THAT REMINDS ME. I GOTTA BE HOME BEFORE ELEVEN.
DON'T LET ME FORGET!
Hm. You're right. I guess I **can** hear things when I want to.
DUH HUH, HUH. YER FRIGGIN' NUTS, DOOD.
UT. OOPS.
End result, for as long as **Jonny's parents** were **clueless about the band**, I had friends.
SMASH
HEY! **OW!**
HAHAHAHAHA!
HEY! **COME ON!** I GOTTA CLEAN THAT UP!
PAFF

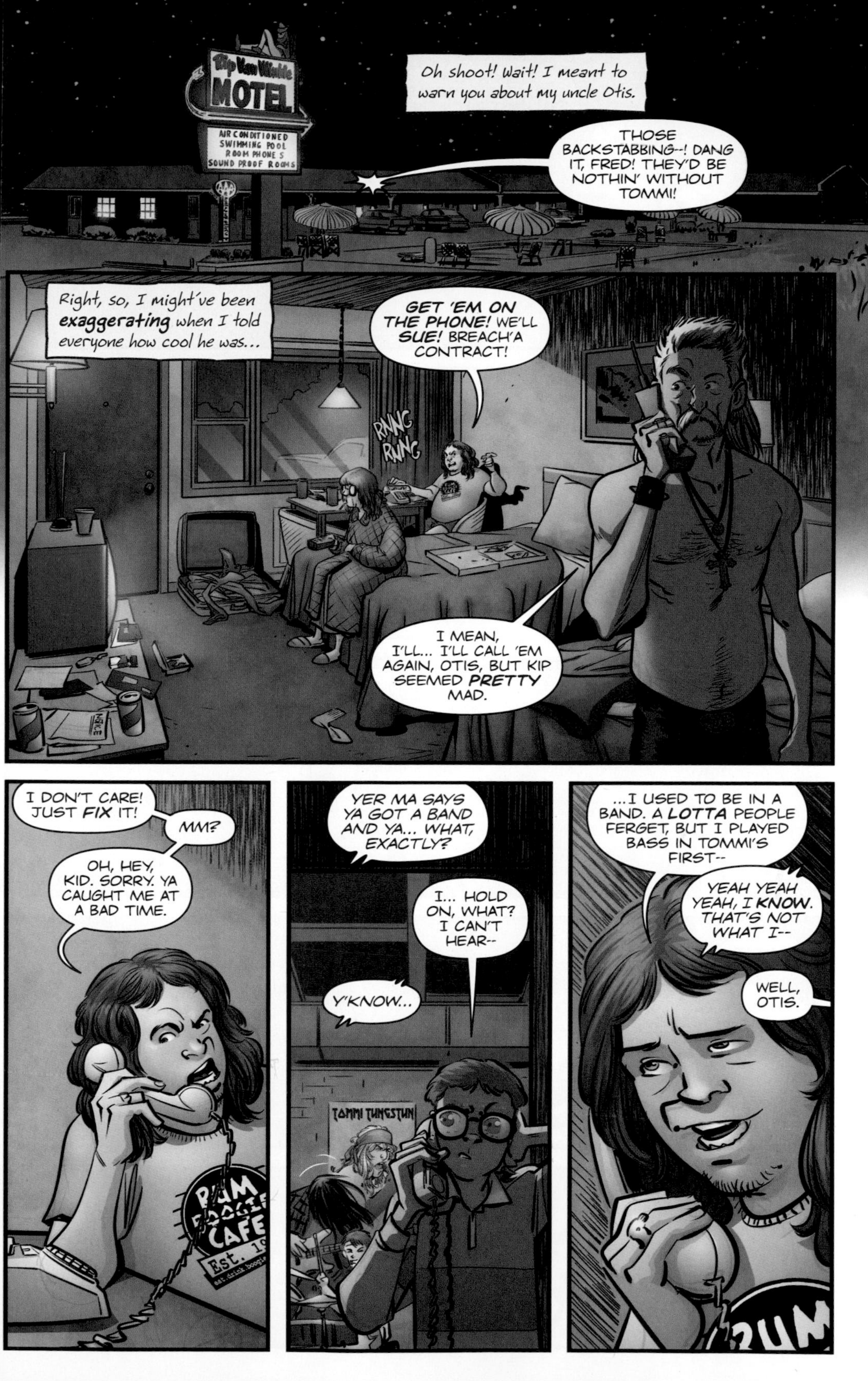

Rip Van Winkle
MOTEL
AIR CONDITIONED
SWIMMING POOL
ROOM PHONES
SOUND PROOF ROOMS
Oh shoot! Wait! I meant to warn you about my uncle Otis.
THOSE BACKSTABBING--! DANG IT, FRED! THEY'D BE NOTHIN' WITHOUT TOMMI!
Right, so, I might've been **exaggerating** when I told everyone how cool he was...
GET 'EM ON THE PHONE! WE'LL ***SUE!*** BREACH'A CONTRACT!
RNNG RNNG
I MEAN, I'LL... I'LL CALL 'EM AGAIN, OTIS, BUT KIP SEEMED ***PRETTY*** MAD.
I DON'T CARE! JUST ***FIX*** IT!
MM?
OH, HEY, KID. SORRY. YA CAUGHT ME AT A BAD TIME.
YER MA SAYS YA GOT A BAND AND YA... WHAT, EXACTLY?
I... HOLD ON, WHAT? I CAN'T HEAR--
Y'KNOW...
TOMMI TUNGSTUN
...I USED TO BE IN A BAND. A ***LOTTA*** PEOPLE FERGET, BUT I PLAYED BASS IN TOMMI'S FIRST--
YEAH YEAH YEAH, I ***KNOW***. THAT'S NOT WHAT I--
WELL, OTIS.

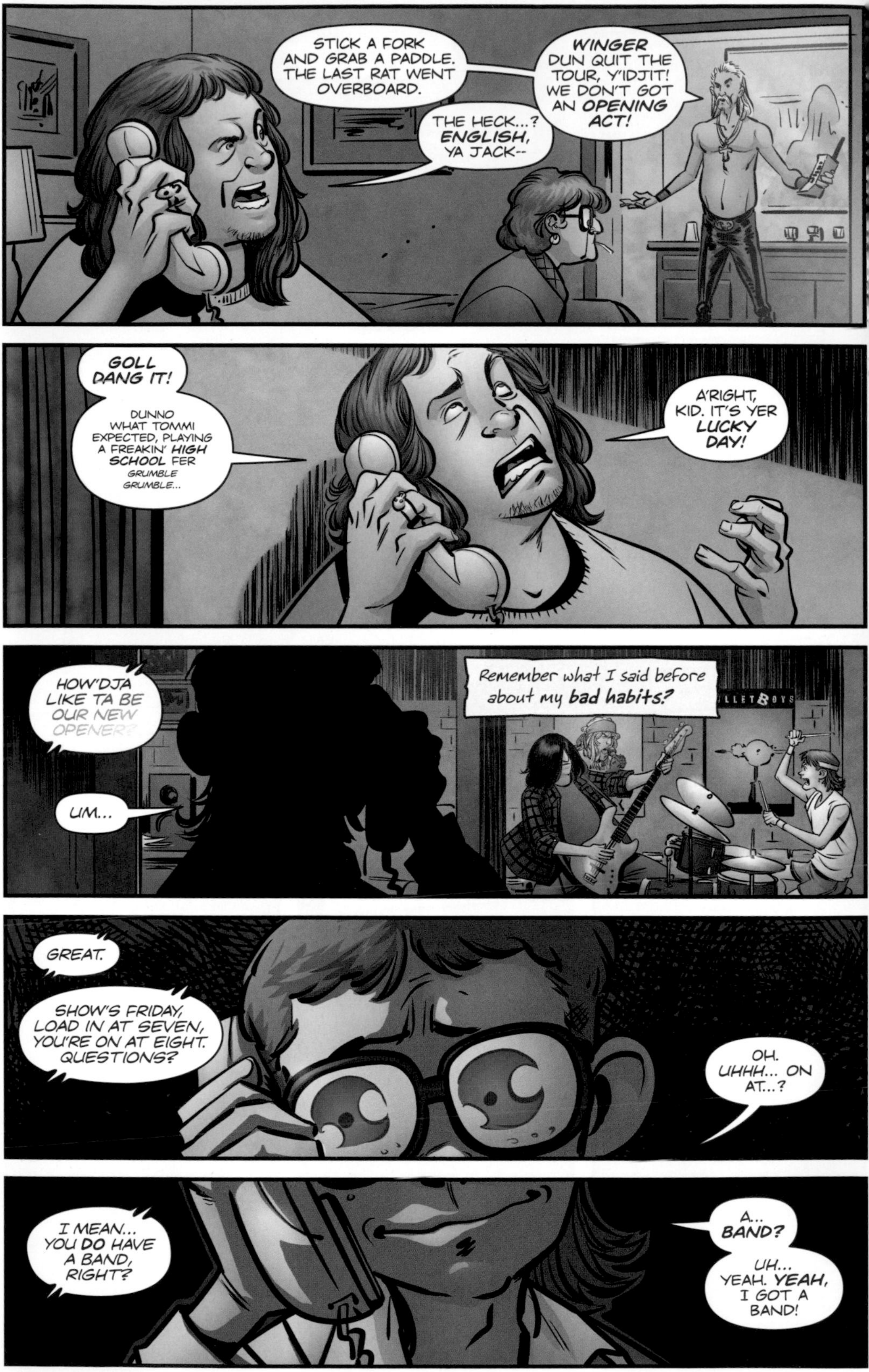
STICK A FORK AND GRAB A PADDLE. THE LAST RAT WENT OVERBOARD.
THE HECK...? ENGLISH, YA JACK--
WINGER DUN QUIT THE TOUR, Y'IDJIT! WE DON'T GOT AN OPENING ACT!
GOLL DANG IT!
DUNNO WHAT TOMMI EXPECTED, PLAYING A FREAKIN' HIGH SCHOOL FER GRUMBLE GRUMBLE...
A'RIGHT, KID. IT'S YER LUCKY DAY!
HOW'DJA LIKE TA BE OUR NEW OPENER?
Remember what I said before about my bad habits?
UM...
GREAT.
SHOW'S FRIDAY, LOAD IN AT SEVEN, YOU'RE ON AT EIGHT. QUESTIONS?
OH. UHHH... ON AT...?
I MEAN... YOU DO HAVE A BAND, RIGHT?
A... BAND?
UH... YEAH. YEAH, I GOT A BAND!

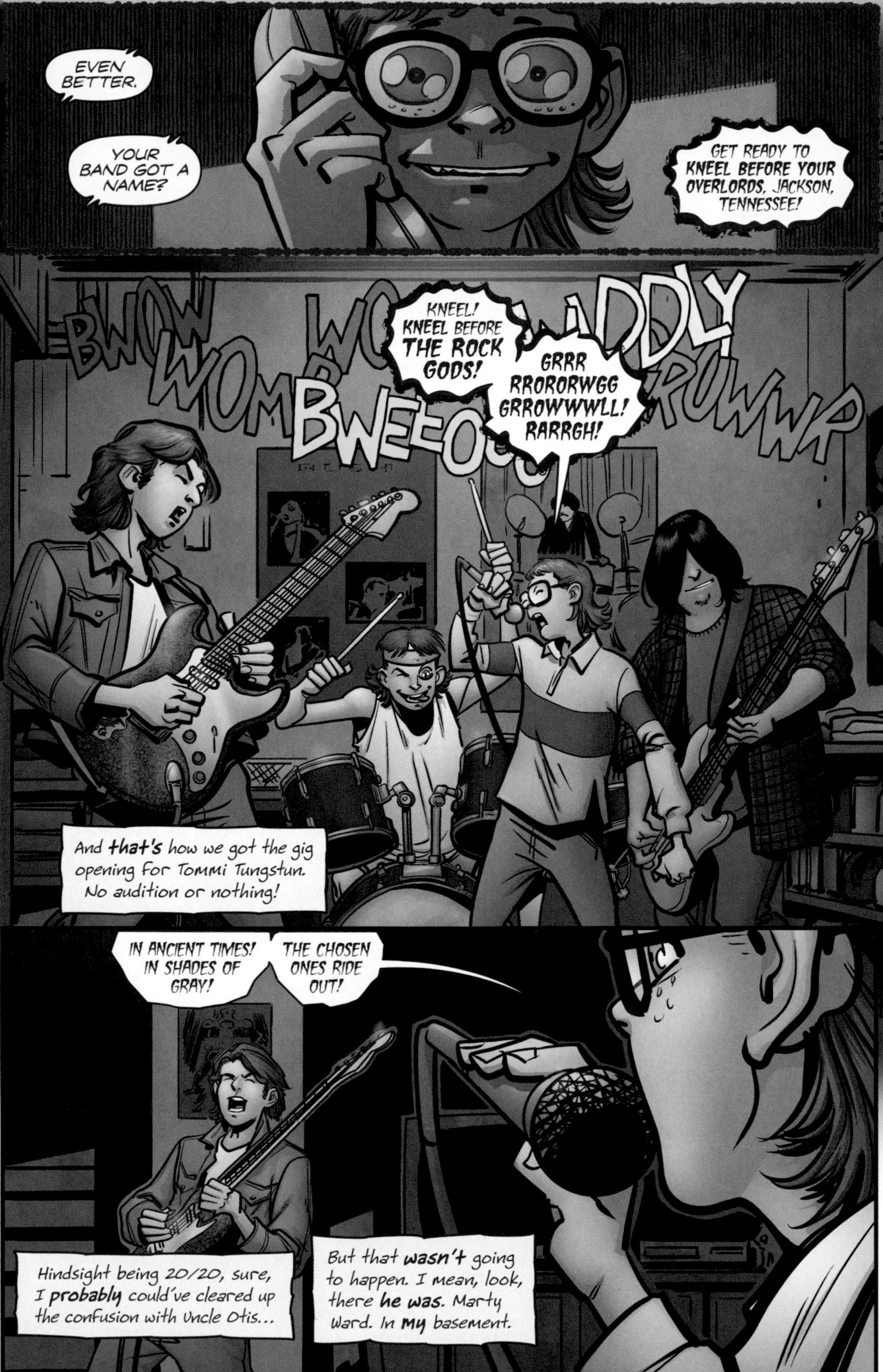
EVEN BETTER.
YOUR BAND GOT A NAME?
GET READY TO KNEEL BEFORE YOUR OVERLORDS, JACKSON, TENNESSEE!
BWOW
WOMB
DDLY
KNEEL! KNEEL BEFORE THE ROCK GODS!
GRRR RRORORWGG GRROWWWLL! RARRGH!
And that's how we got the gig opening for Tommi Tungstun. No audition or nothing!
IN ANCIENT TIMES! IN SHADES OF GRAY!
THE CHOSEN ONES RIDE OUT!
Hindsight being 20/20, sure, I probably could've cleared up the confusion with Uncle Otis...
But that wasn't going to happen. I mean, look, there he was. Marty Ward. In my basement.

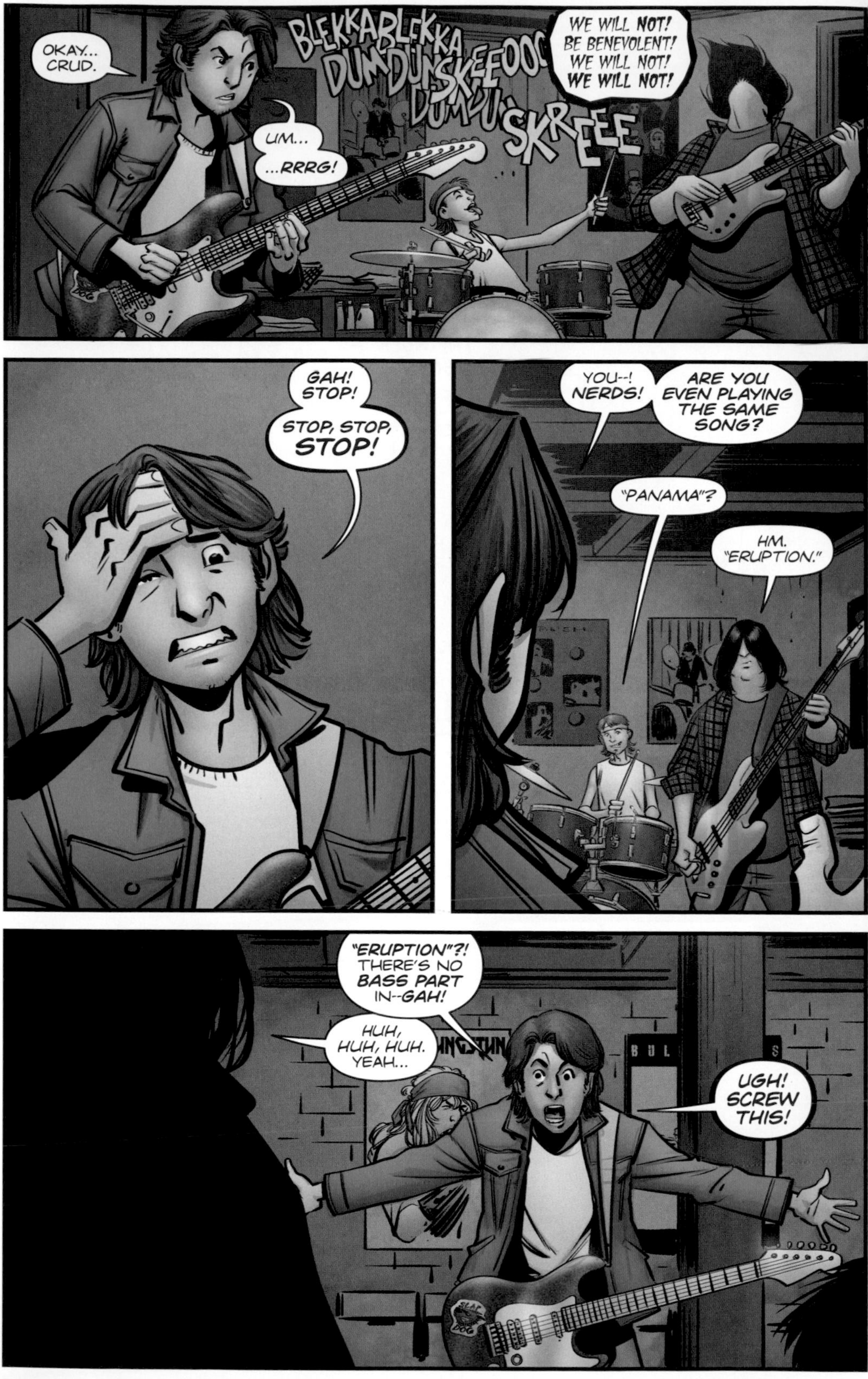
OKAY... CRUD.
BLEKKABLEKKA DUMDUNSKEEOOO DUMDU SKREEE
WE WILL NOT! BE BENEVOLENT! WE WILL NOT! WE WILL NOT!
UM... ...RRRG!
GAH! STOP!
STOP, STOP, STOP!
YOU--! NERDS!
ARE YOU EVEN PLAYING THE SAME SONG?
"PANAMA"?
HM. "ERUPTION."
"ERUPTION"?! THERE'S NO BASS PART IN--GAH!
HUH, HUH, HUH. YEAH...
UGH! SCREW THIS!

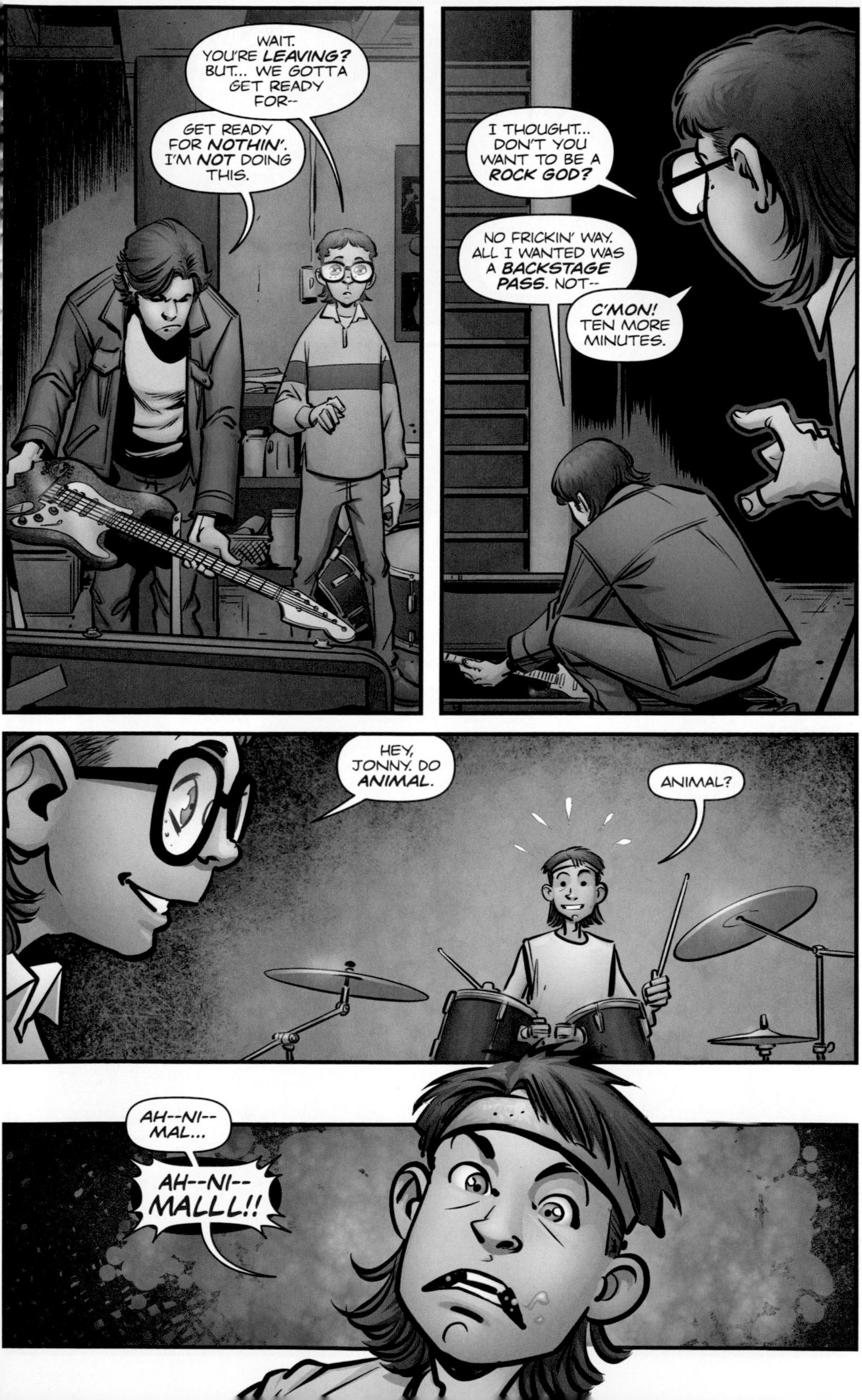
WAIT. YOU'RE LEAVING? BUT... WE GOTTA GET READY FOR--
GET READY FOR NOTHIN'. I'M NOT DOING THIS.
I THOUGHT... DON'T YOU WANT TO BE A ROCK GOD?
NO FRICKIN' WAY. ALL I WANTED WAS A BACKSTAGE PASS. NOT--
C'MON! TEN MORE MINUTES.
HEY, JONNY. DO ANIMAL.
ANIMAL?
AH--NI--MAL...
AH--NI--MALLL!!

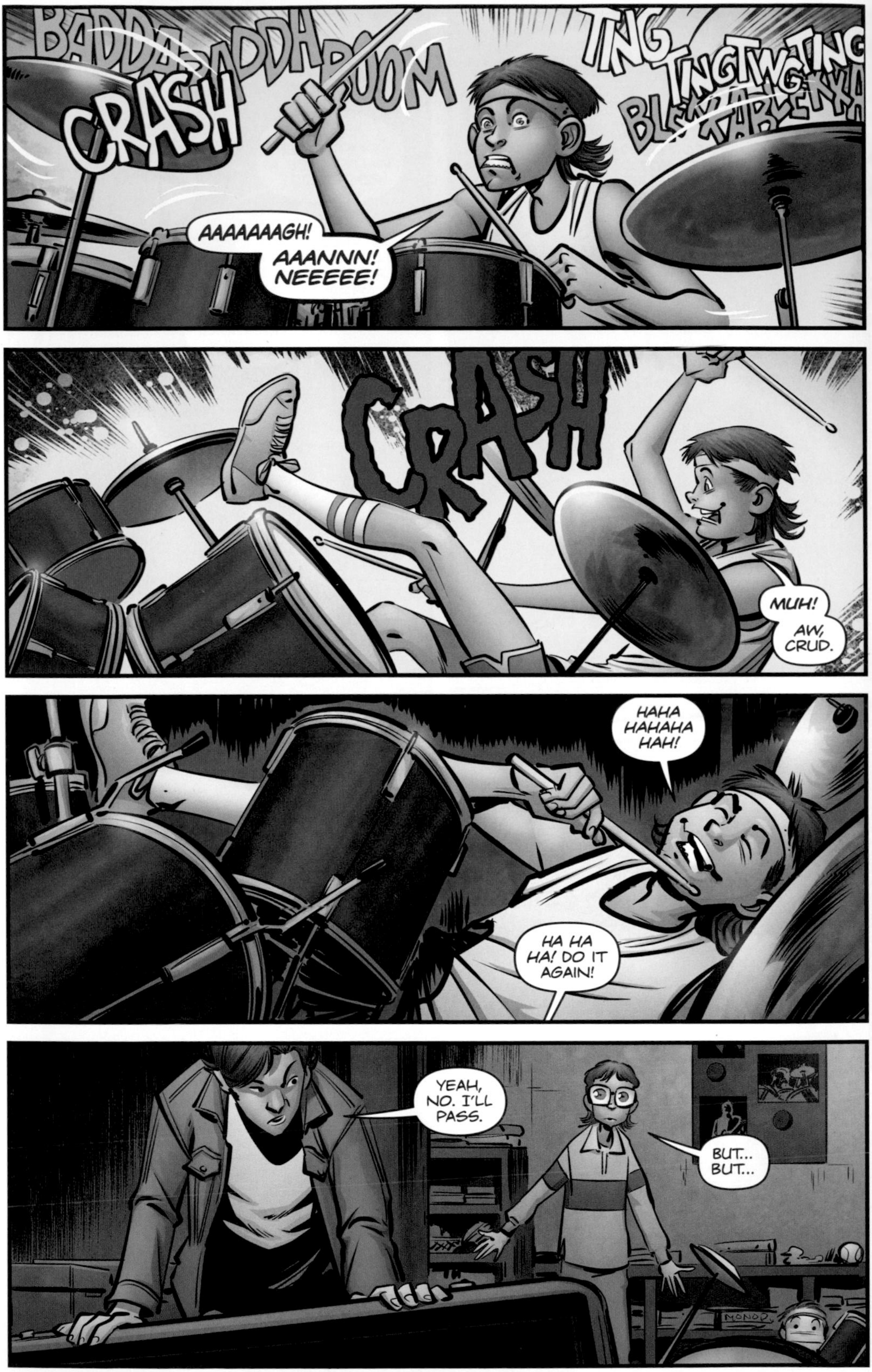
CRASH
AAAAAAAGH!
AAANNN! NEEEEE!
CRASH
MUH!
AW, CRUD.
HAHA HAHAHA HAH!
HA HA HA! DO IT AGAIN!
YEAH, NO. I'LL PASS.
BUT... BUT...

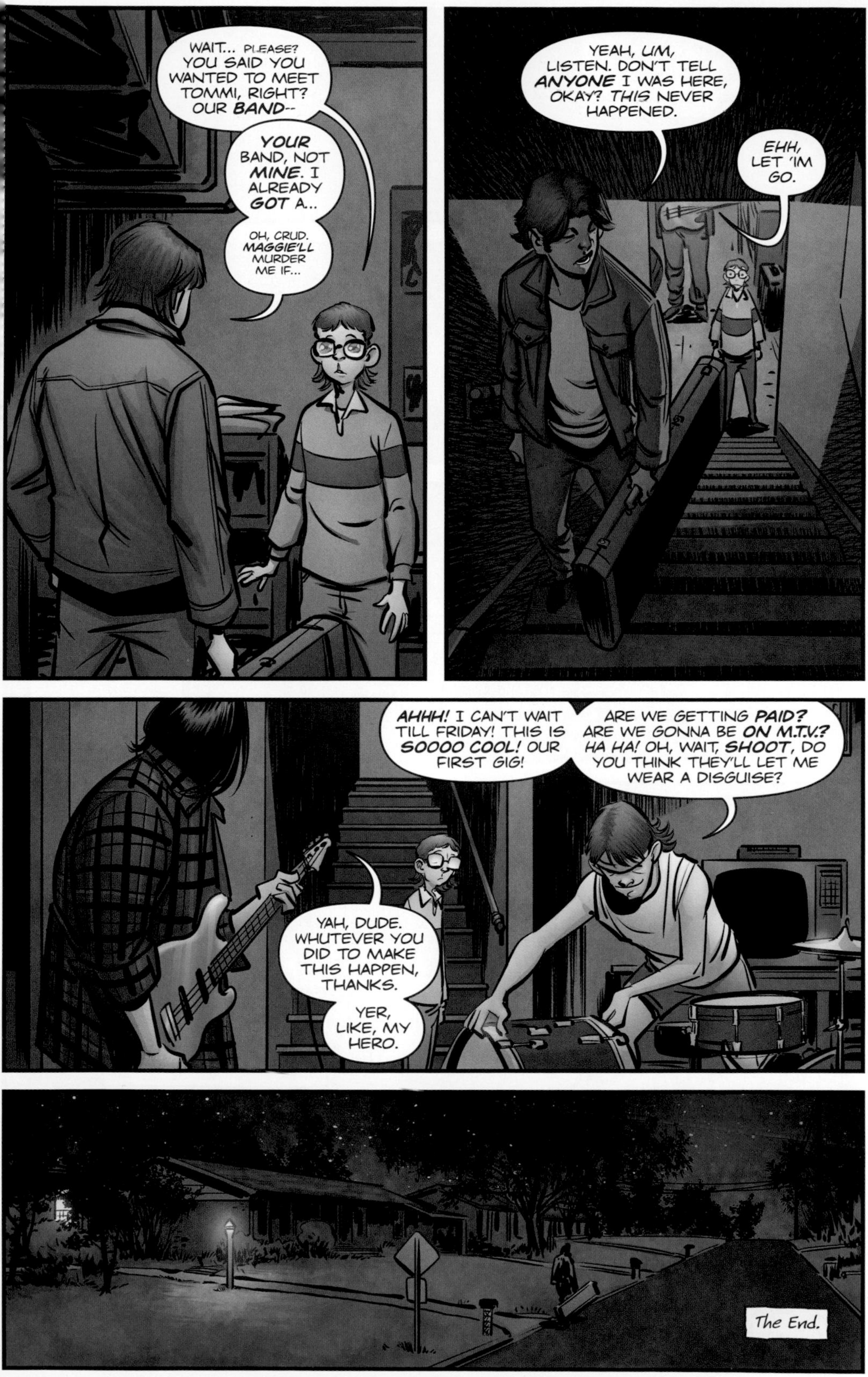
WAIT... PLEASE? YOU SAID YOU WANTED TO MEET TOMMI, RIGHT? OUR BAND--
YOUR BAND, NOT MINE. I ALREADY GOT A...
OH, CRUD. MAGGIE'LL MURDER ME IF...
YEAH, UM, LISTEN. DON'T TELL ANYONE I WAS HERE, OKAY? THIS NEVER HAPPENED.
EHH, LET 'IM GO.
AHHH! I CAN'T WAIT TILL FRIDAY! THIS IS SOOOO COOL! OUR FIRST GIG!
ARE WE GETTING PAID? ARE WE GONNA BE ON M.T.V.? HA HA! OH, WAIT, SHOOT, DO YOU THINK THEY'LL LET ME WEAR A DISGUISE?
YAH, DUDE. WHUTEVER YOU DID TO MAKE THIS HAPPEN, THANKS.
YER, LIKE, MY HERO.
The End.

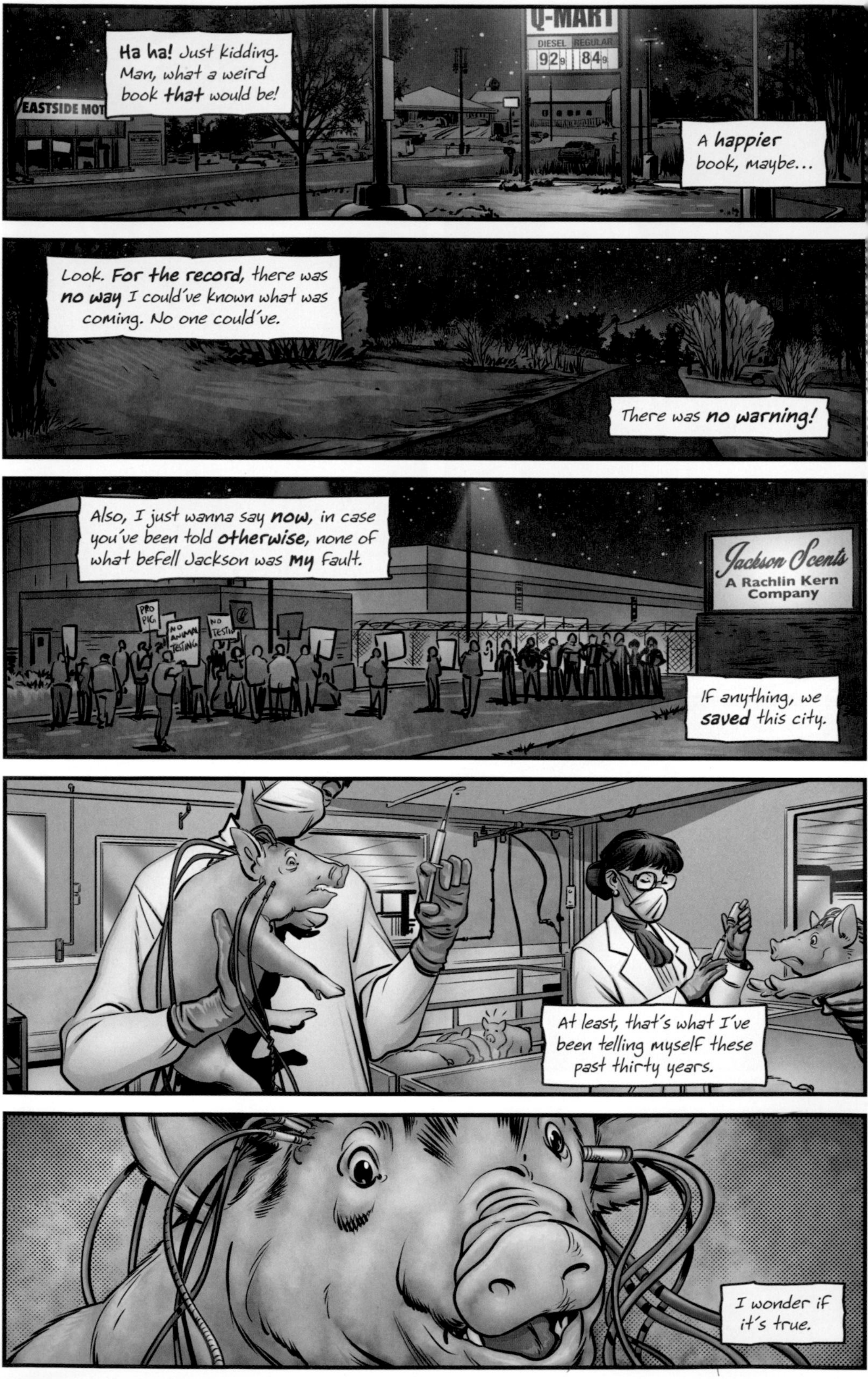
Ha ha! Just kidding. Man, what a weird book that would be!
EASTSIDE MOT
Q-MART
DIESEL REGULAR
92 9 84 9
A happier book, maybe...
Look. For the record, there was no way I could've known what was coming. No one could've.
There was no warning!
Also, I just wanna say now, in case you've been told otherwise, none of what befell Jackson was my fault.
Jackson Scents
A Rachlin Kern Company
PRO PIG
NO ANIMAL TESTING
NO TESTIN
If anything, we saved this city.
At least, that's what I've been telling myself these past thirty years.
I wonder if it's true.

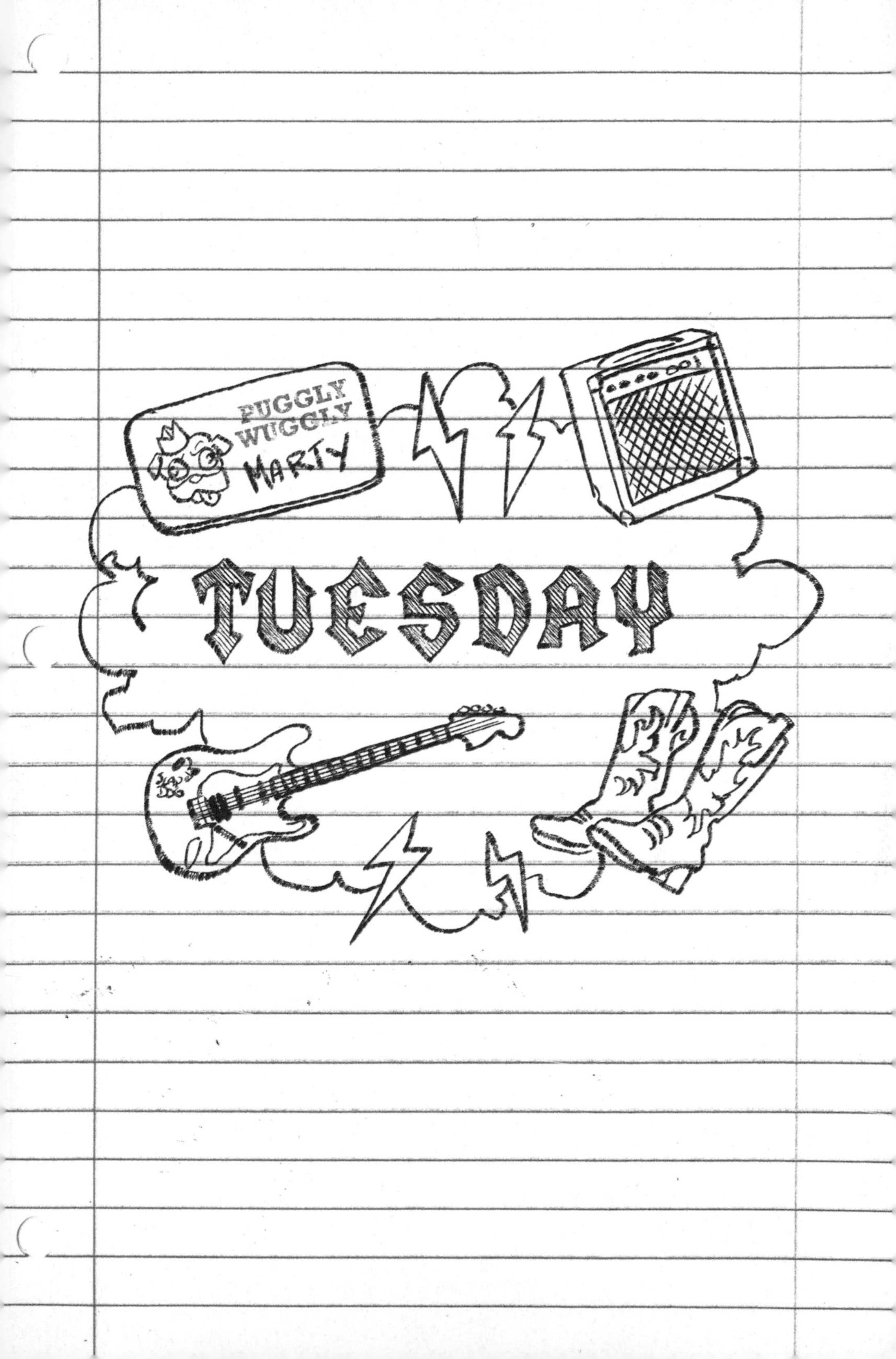
PUGGLY
WUGGLY
MARTY
TUESDAY

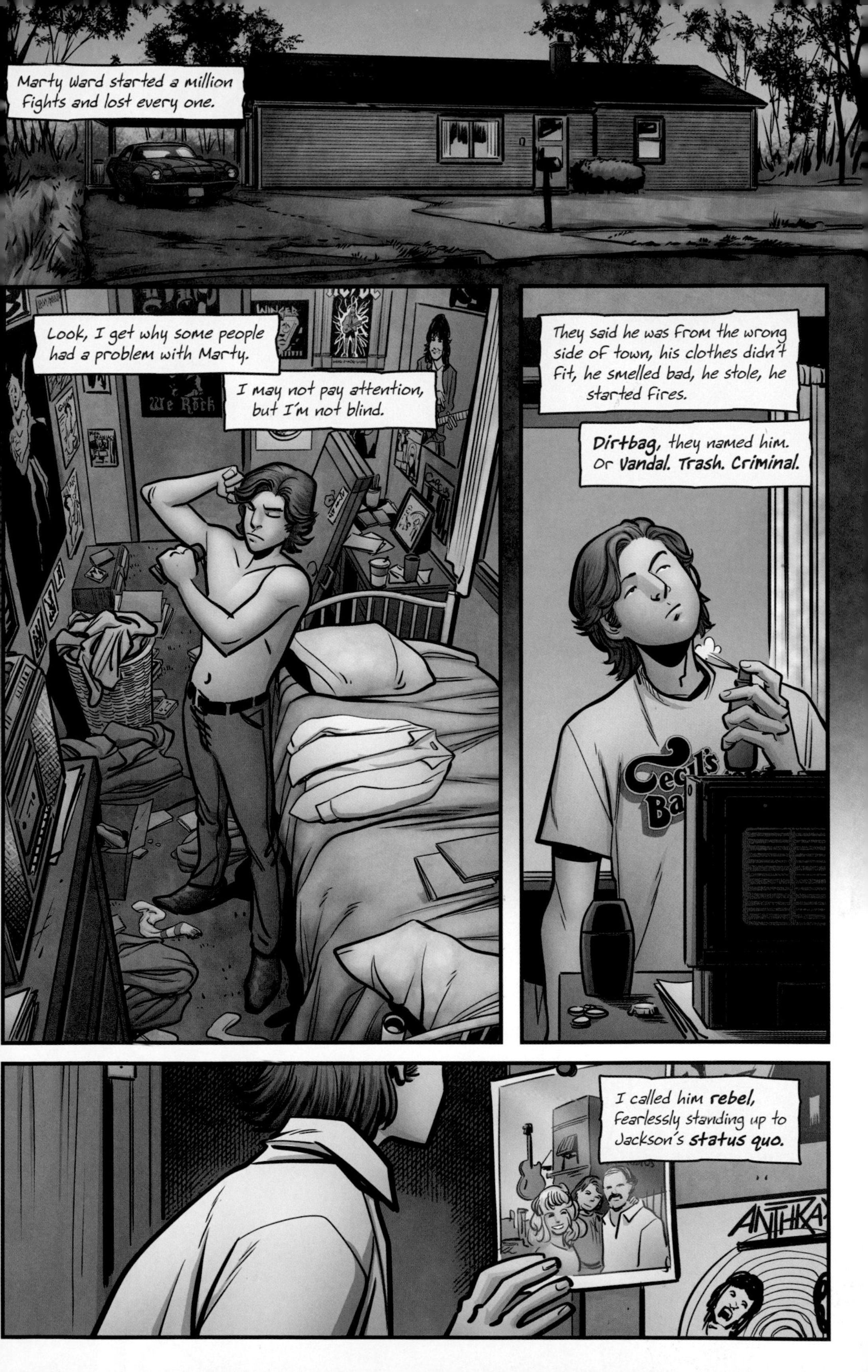

Marty Ward started a million fights and lost every one.
Look, I get why some people had a problem with Marty.
I may not pay attention, but I'm not blind.
They said he was from the wrong side of town, his clothes didn't fit, he smelled bad, he stole, he started fires.
Dirtbag, they named him. Or **Vandal. Trash. Criminal.**
I called him **rebel,** fearlessly standing up to Jackson's **status quo.**

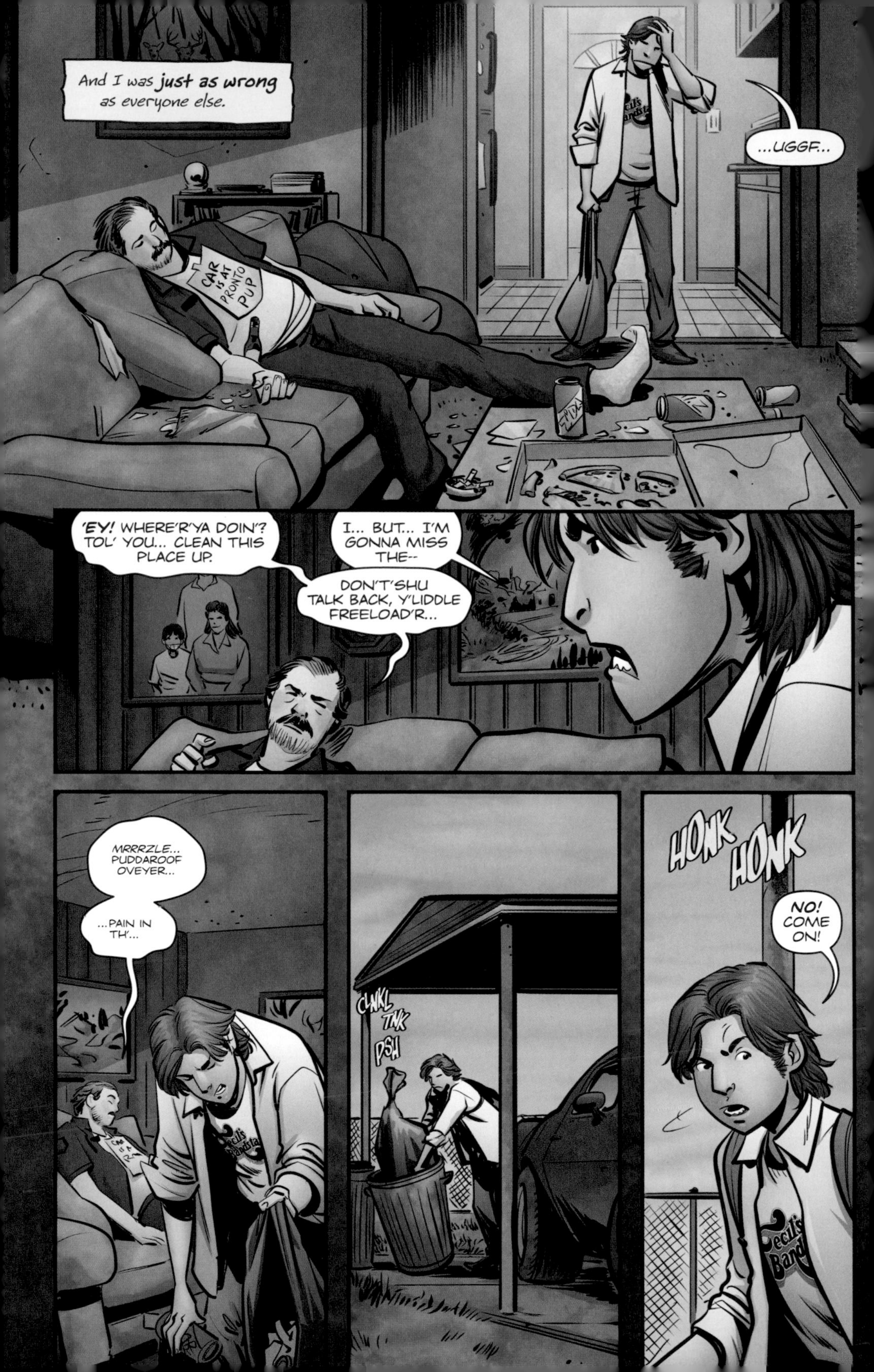

And I was **just as wrong** as everyone else.
...UGGF...
CAR IS AT PRONTO PUP
'EY! WHERE'R'YA DOIN'? TOL' YOU... CLEAN THIS PLACE UP.
I... BUT... I'M GONNA MISS THE--
DON'T'SHU TALK BACK, Y'LIDDLE FREELOAD'R...
MRRRZLE... PUDDAROOF OVEYER...
...PAIN IN TH'...
CLNKL
TNK
DSH
HONK
HONK
NO! COME ON!

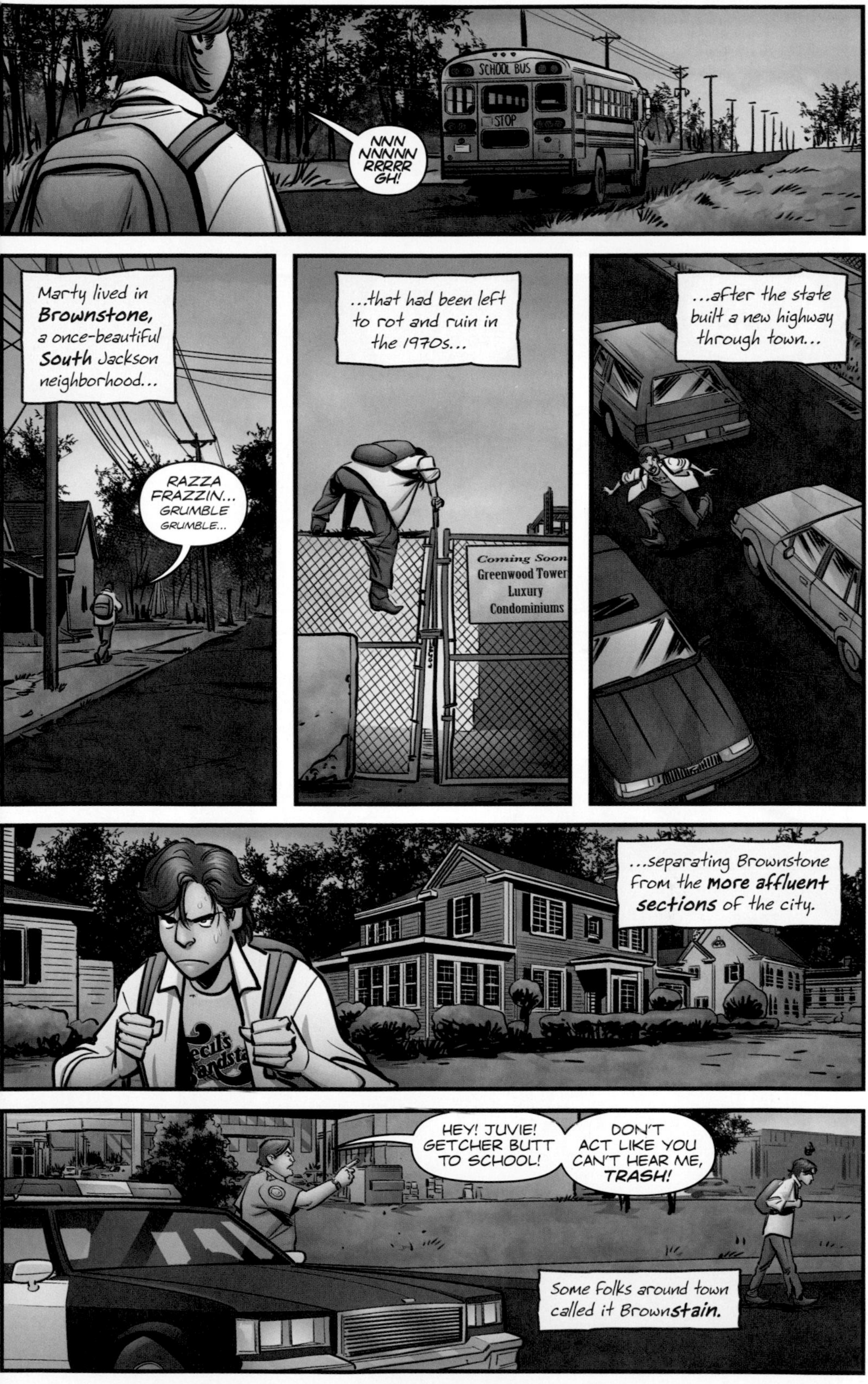
SCHOOL BUS
STOP
NNN NNNNN RRRRR GH!
Marty lived in Brownstone, a once-beautiful South Jackson neighborhood...
RAZZA FRAZZIN... GRUMBLE GRUMBLE...
...that had been left to rot and ruin in the 1970s...
Coming Soon Greenwood Tower Luxury Condominiums
...after the state built a new highway through town...
...separating Brownstone from the more affluent sections of the city.
HEY! JUVIE! GETCHER BUTT TO SCHOOL!
DON'T ACT LIKE YOU CAN'T HEAR ME, TRASH!
Some folks around town called it Brownstain.

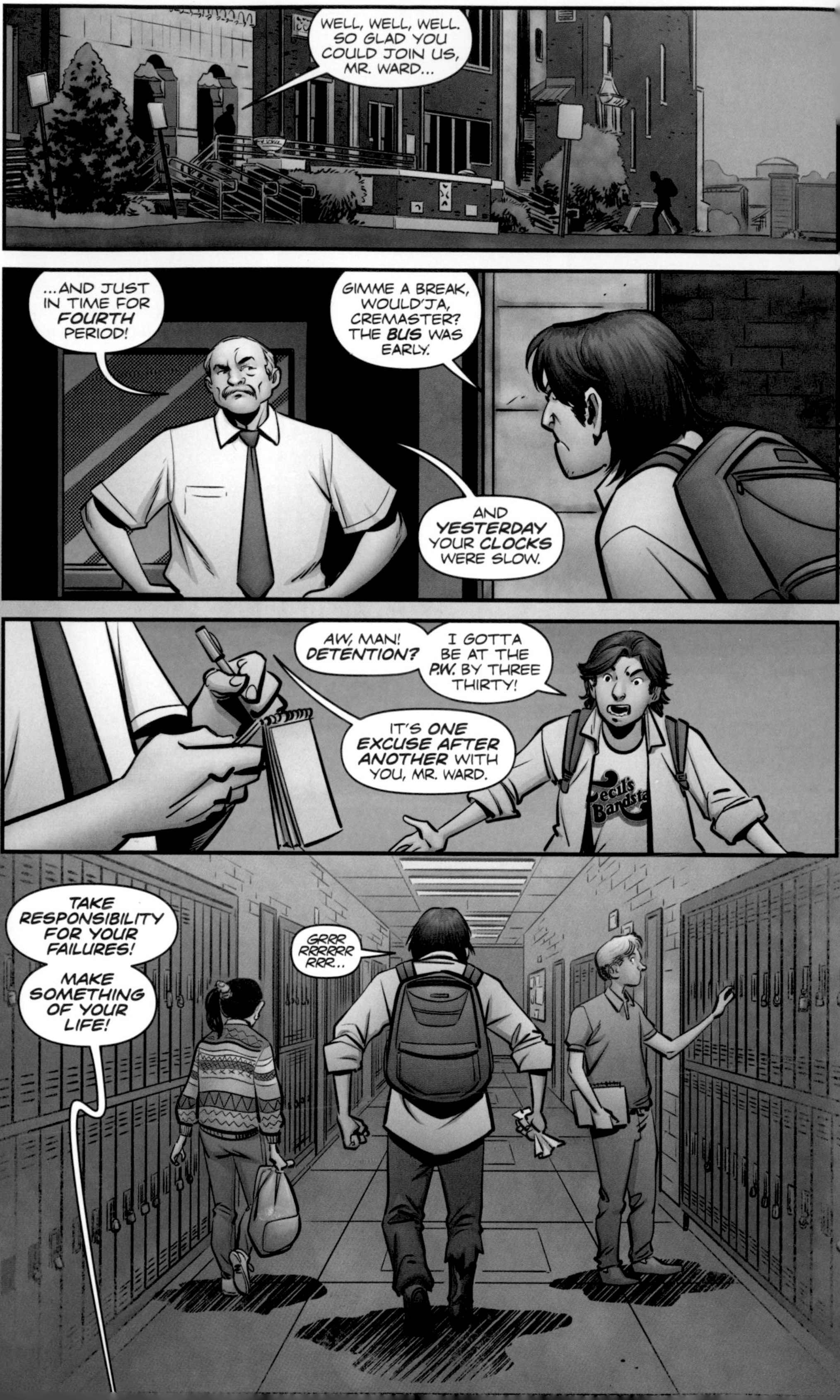
WELL, WELL, WELL. SO GLAD YOU COULD JOIN US, MR. WARD...
...AND JUST IN TIME FOR FOURTH PERIOD!
GIMME A BREAK, WOULD'JA, CREMASTER? THE BUS WAS EARLY.
AND YESTERDAY YOUR CLOCKS WERE SLOW.
AW, MAN! DETENTION?
I GOTTA BE AT THE P.W. BY THREE THIRTY!
IT'S ONE EXCUSE AFTER ANOTHER WITH YOU, MR. WARD.
TAKE RESPONSIBILITY FOR YOUR FAILURES!
MAKE SOMETHING OF YOUR LIFE!
GRRR RRRRRR RRR...

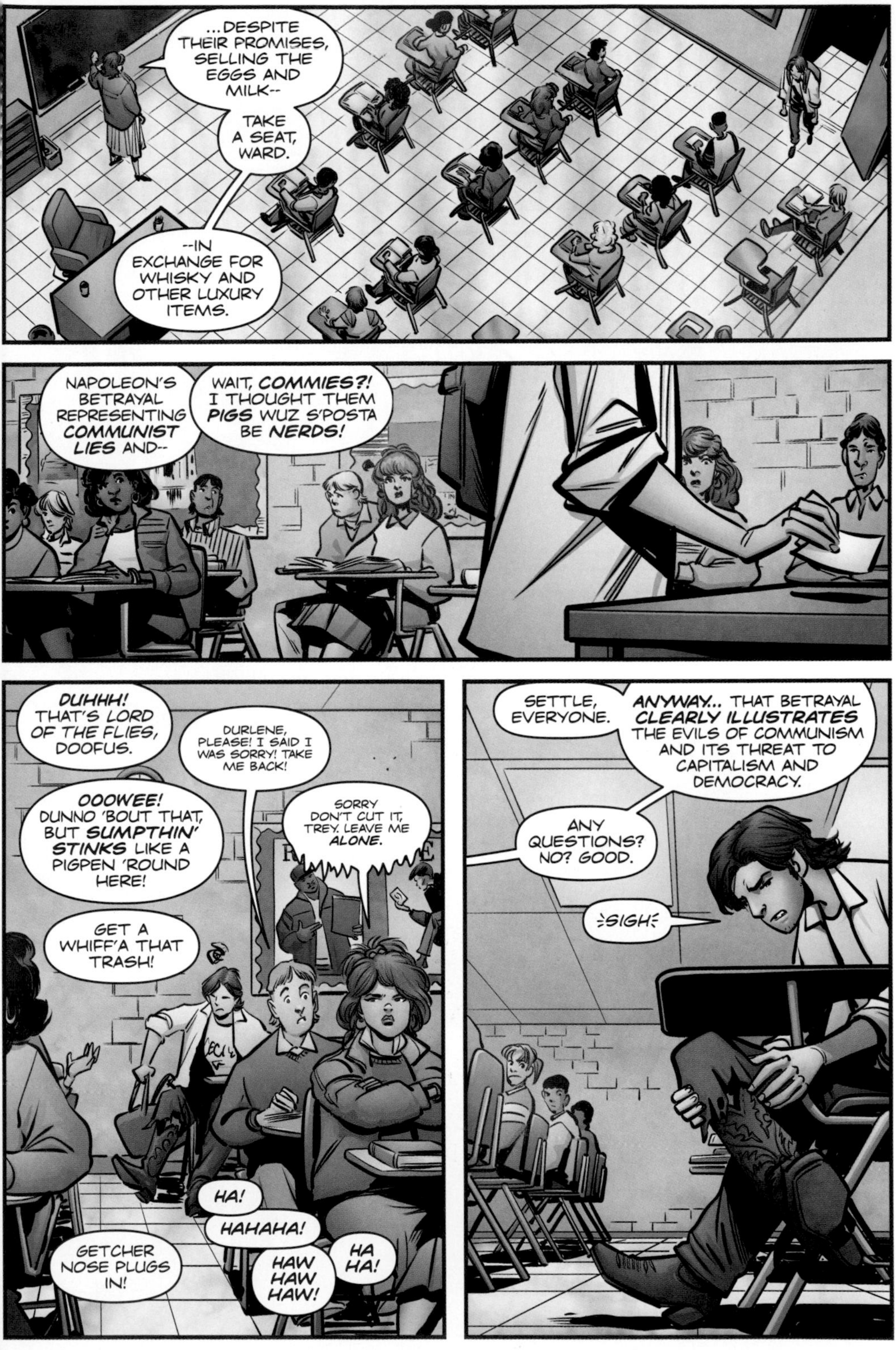
...DESPITE THEIR PROMISES, SELLING THE EGGS AND MILK--
TAKE A SEAT, WARD.
--IN EXCHANGE FOR WHISKY AND OTHER LUXURY ITEMS.
NAPOLEON'S BETRAYAL REPRESENTING COMMUNIST LIES AND--
WAIT, COMMIES?! I THOUGHT THEM PIGS WUZ S'POSTA BE NERDS!
DUHHH! THAT'S LORD OF THE FLIES, DOOFUS.
DURLENE, PLEASE! I SAID I WAS SORRY! TAKE ME BACK!
OOOWEE! DUNNO 'BOUT THAT, BUT SUMPTHIN' STINKS LIKE A PIGPEN 'ROUND HERE!
SORRY DON'T CUT IT, TREY. LEAVE ME ALONE.
GET A WHIFF'A THAT TRASH!
HA!
HAHAHA!
GETCHER NOSE PLUGS IN!
HAW HAW HAW!
HA HA!
SETTLE, EVERYONE.
ANYWAY... THAT BETRAYAL CLEARLY ILLUSTRATES THE EVILS OF COMMUNISM AND ITS THREAT TO CAPITALISM AND DEMOCRACY.
ANY QUESTIONS? NO? GOOD.
SIGH

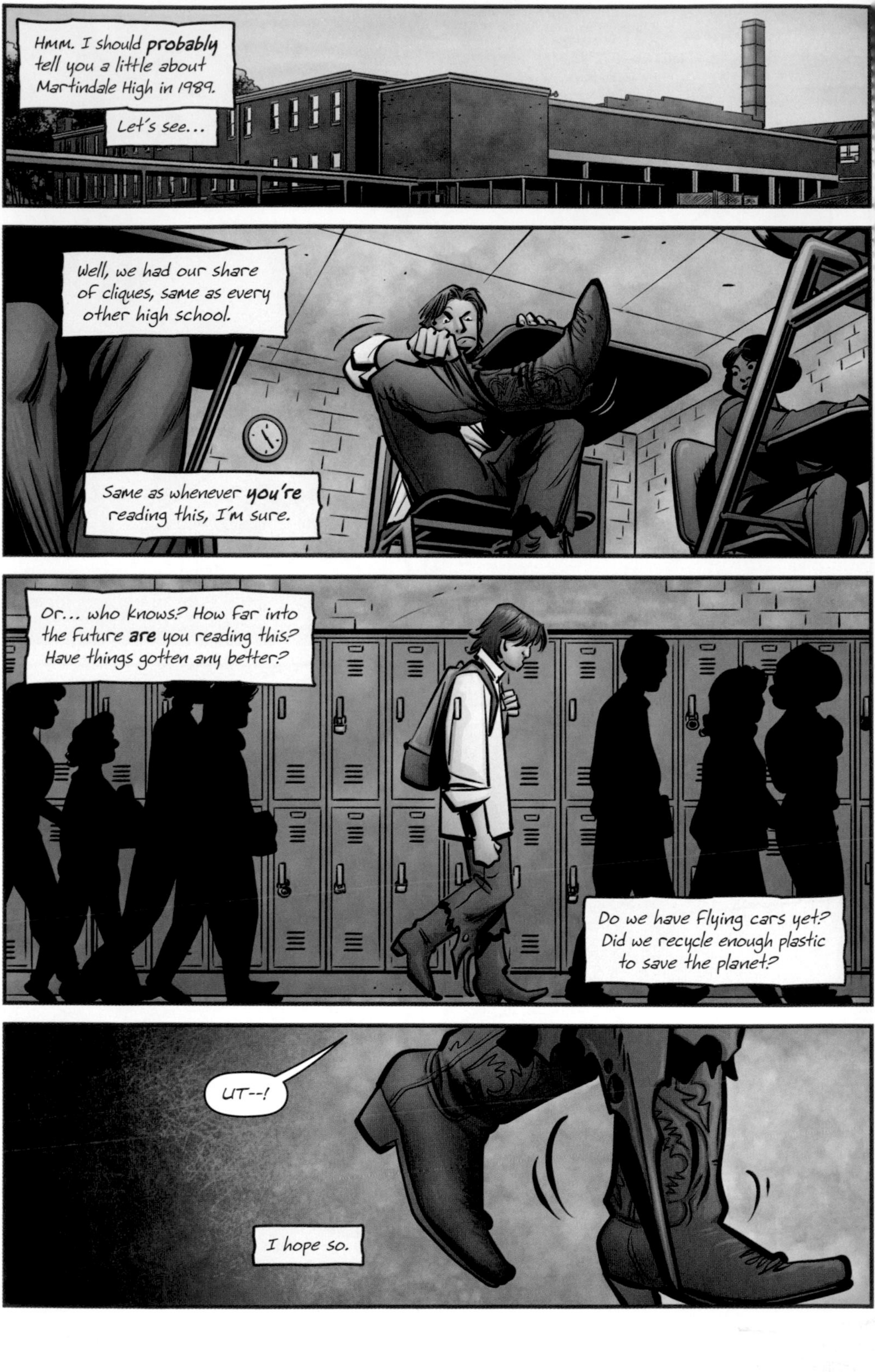
Hmm. I should **probably** tell you a little about Martindale High in 1989.
Let's see...
Well, we had our share of cliques, same as every other high school.
Same as whenever **you're** reading this, I'm sure.
Or... who knows? How far into the future **are** you reading this? Have things gotten any better?
Do we have flying cars yet? Did we recycle enough plastic to save the planet?
UT--!
I hope so.

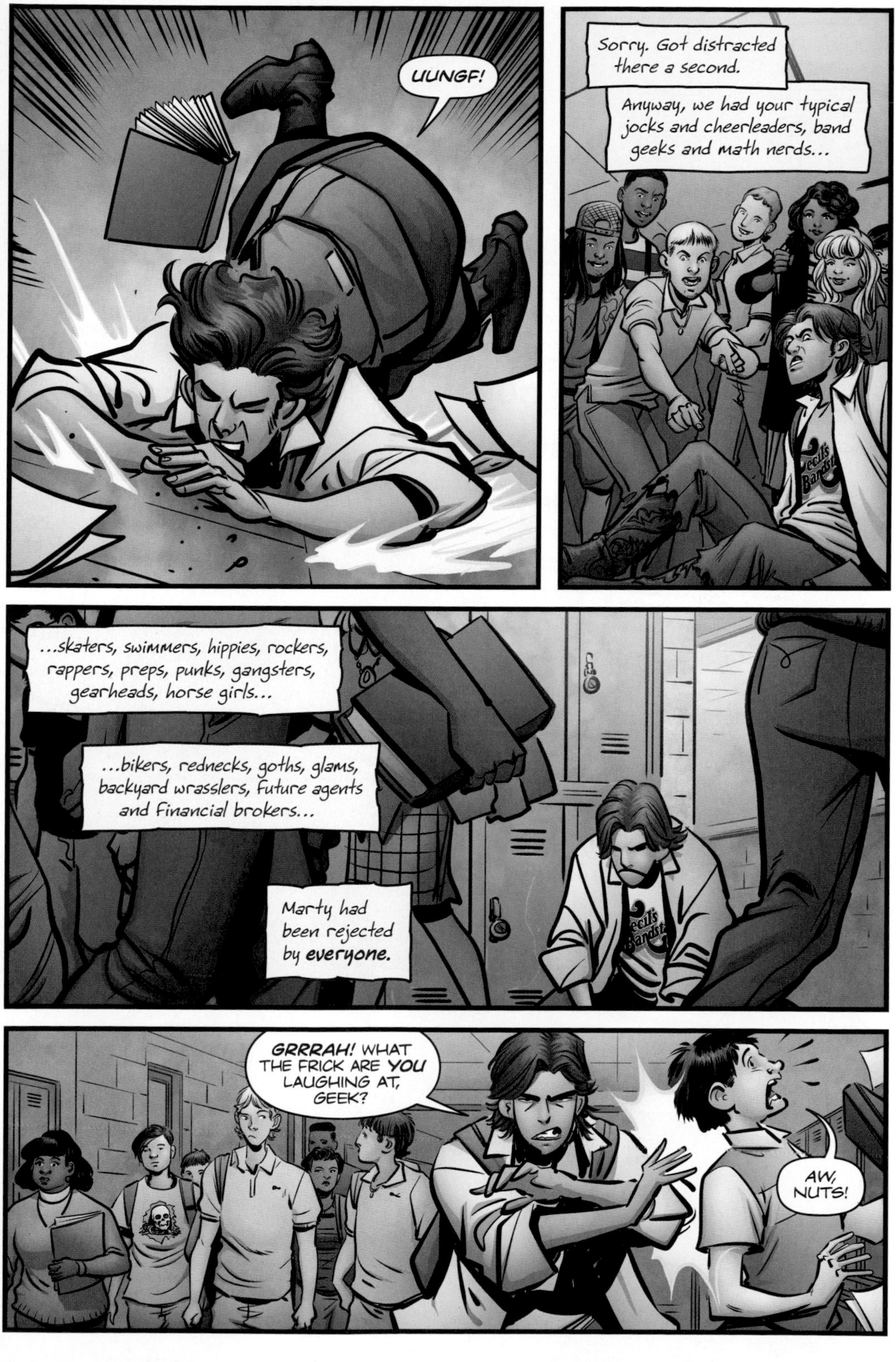
UUNGF!
Sorry. Got distracted there a second.
Anyway, we had your typical jocks and cheerleaders, band geeks and math nerds...
...skaters, swimmers, hippies, rockers, rappers, preps, punks, gangsters, gearheads, horse girls...
...bikers, rednecks, goths, glams, backyard wrasslers, future agents and financial brokers...
Marty had been rejected by **everyone.**
GRRRAH! WHAT THE FRICK ARE **YOU** LAUGHING AT, GEEK?
AW, NUTS!

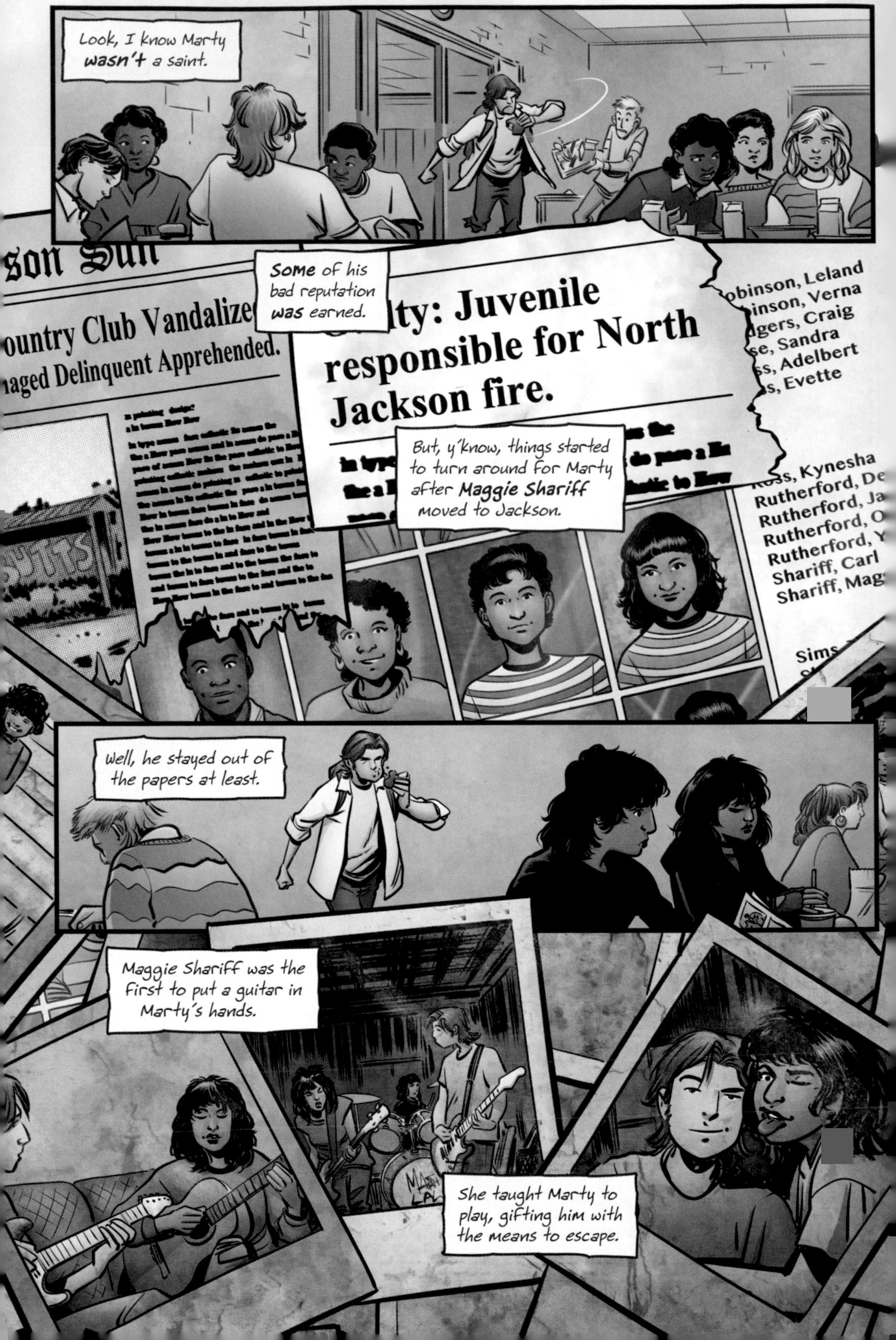
Look, I know Marty wasn't a saint.
son Sun
ountry Club Vandalized
naged Delinquent Apprehended.
Some of his bad reputation was earned.
lty: Juvenile responsible for North Jackson fire.
obinson, Leland
inson, Verna
dgers, Craig
se, Sandra
ss, Adelbert
s, Evette
But, y'know, things started to turn around for Marty after Maggie Shariff moved to Jackson.
Ross, Kynesha
Rutherford, De
Rutherford, Ja
Rutherford, O
Rutherford, Y
Shariff, Carl
Shariff, Mag
Sims
Well, he stayed out of the papers at least.
Maggie Shariff was the first to put a guitar in Marty's hands.
She taught Marty to play, gifting him with the means to escape.

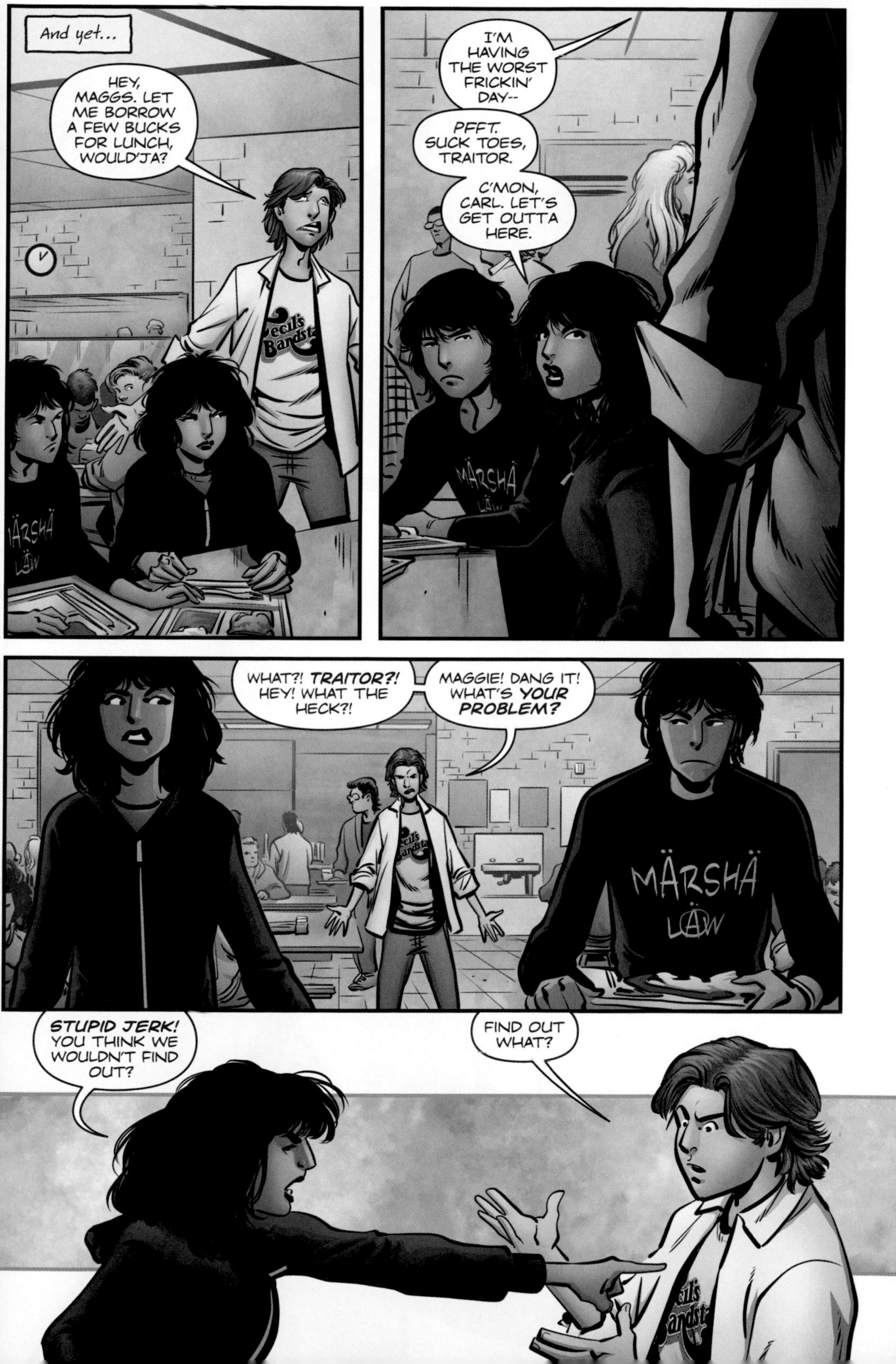
And yet...
HEY, MAGGS. LET ME BORROW A FEW BUCKS FOR LUNCH, WOULD'JA?
Cecil's Bandsta
I'M HAVING THE WORST FRICKIN' DAY--
PFFT. SUCK TOES, TRAITOR.
C'MON, CARL. LET'S GET OUTTA HERE.
MÄRSHÄ LÄW
WHAT?! TRAITOR?! HEY! WHAT THE HECK?!
MAGGIE! DANG IT! WHAT'S YOUR PROBLEM?
MÄRSHÄ LÄW
STUPID JERK! YOU THINK WE WOULDN'T FIND OUT?
FIND OUT WHAT?

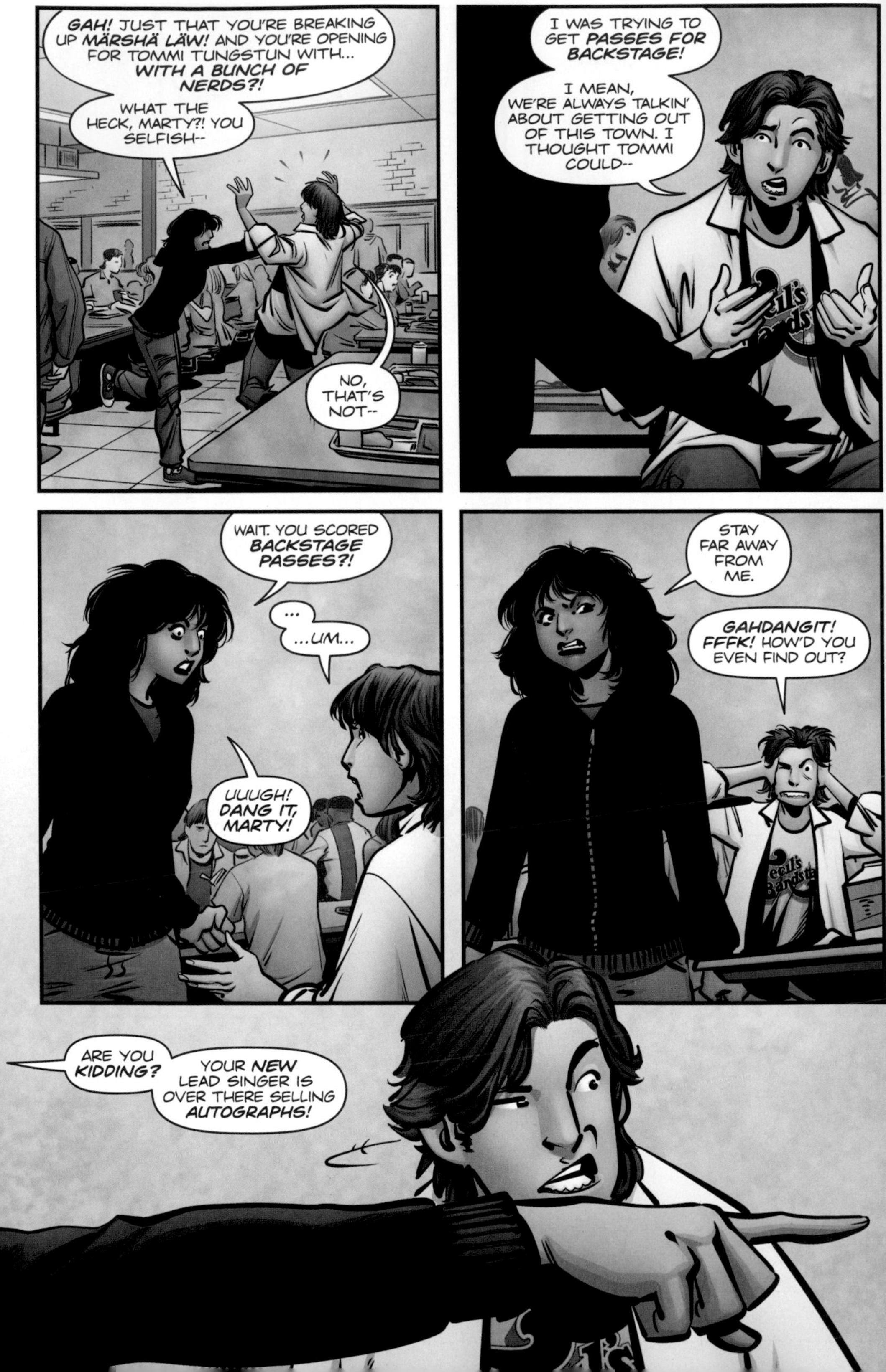
GAH! JUST THAT YOU'RE BREAKING UP MÄRSHÄ LÄW! AND YOU'RE OPENING FOR TOMMI TUNGSTUN WITH... WITH A BUNCH OF NERDS?!
WHAT THE HECK, MARTY?! YOU SELFISH--
NO, THAT'S NOT--
I WAS TRYING TO GET PASSES FOR BACKSTAGE!
I MEAN, WE'RE ALWAYS TALKIN' ABOUT GETTING OUT OF THIS TOWN. I THOUGHT TOMMI COULD--
WAIT. YOU SCORED BACKSTAGE PASSES?!
...
...UM...
UUUGH! DANG IT, MARTY!
STAY FAR AWAY FROM ME.
GAHDANGIT! FFFK! HOW'D YOU EVEN FIND OUT?
ARE YOU KIDDING?
YOUR NEW LEAD SINGER IS OVER THERE SELLING AUTOGRAPHS!

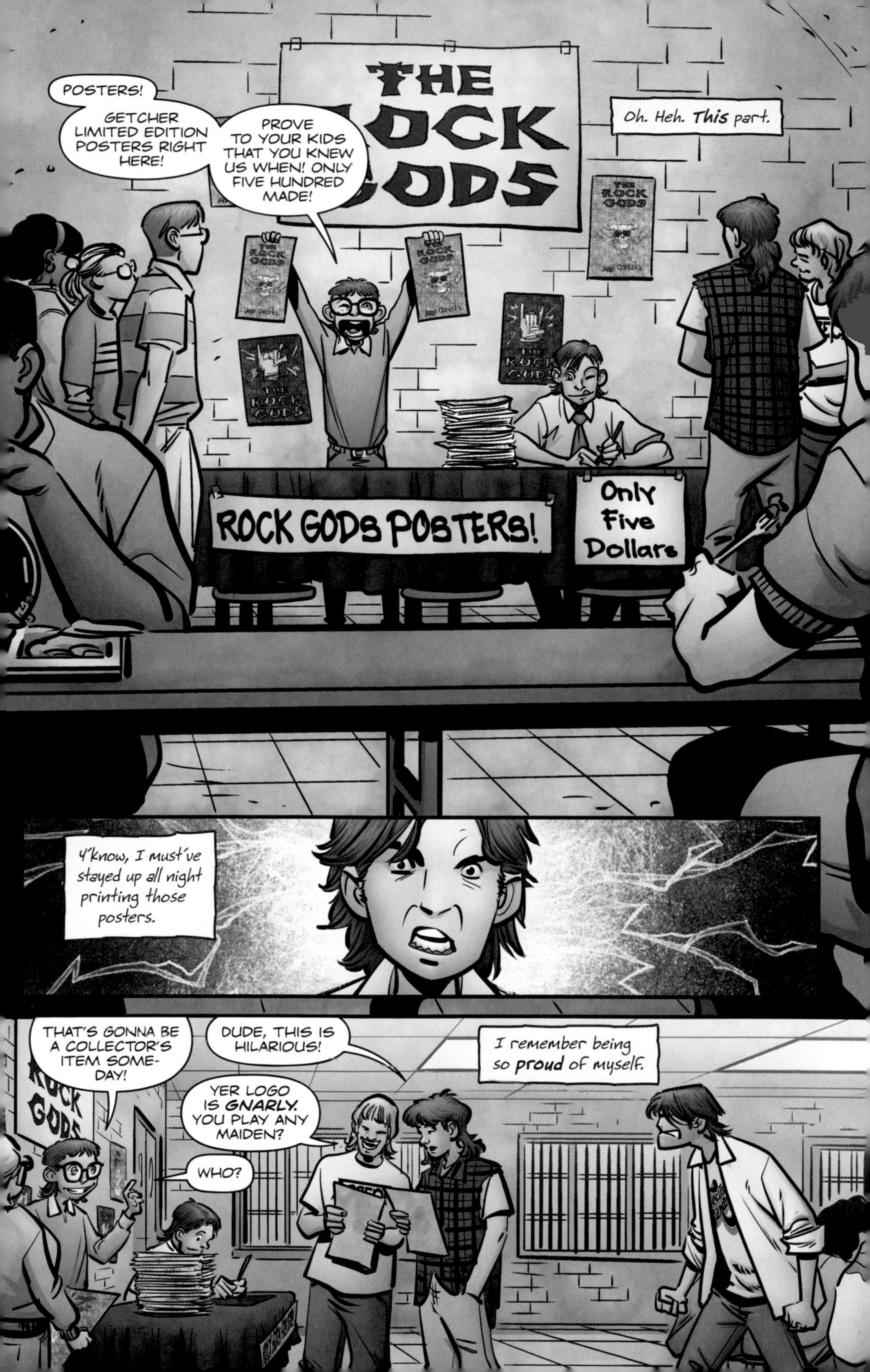
THE ROCK GODS
POSTERS! GETCHER LIMITED EDITION POSTERS RIGHT HERE!
PROVE TO YOUR KIDS THAT YOU KNEW US WHEN! ONLY FIVE HUNDRED MADE!
Oh. Heh. This part.
ROCK GODS POSTERS!
Only Five Dollars
Y'know, I must've stayed up all night printing those posters.
THAT'S GONNA BE A COLLECTOR'S ITEM SOME-DAY!
DUDE, THIS IS HILARIOUS!
I remember being so proud of myself.
YER LOGO IS GNARLY. YOU PLAY ANY MAIDEN?
WHO?

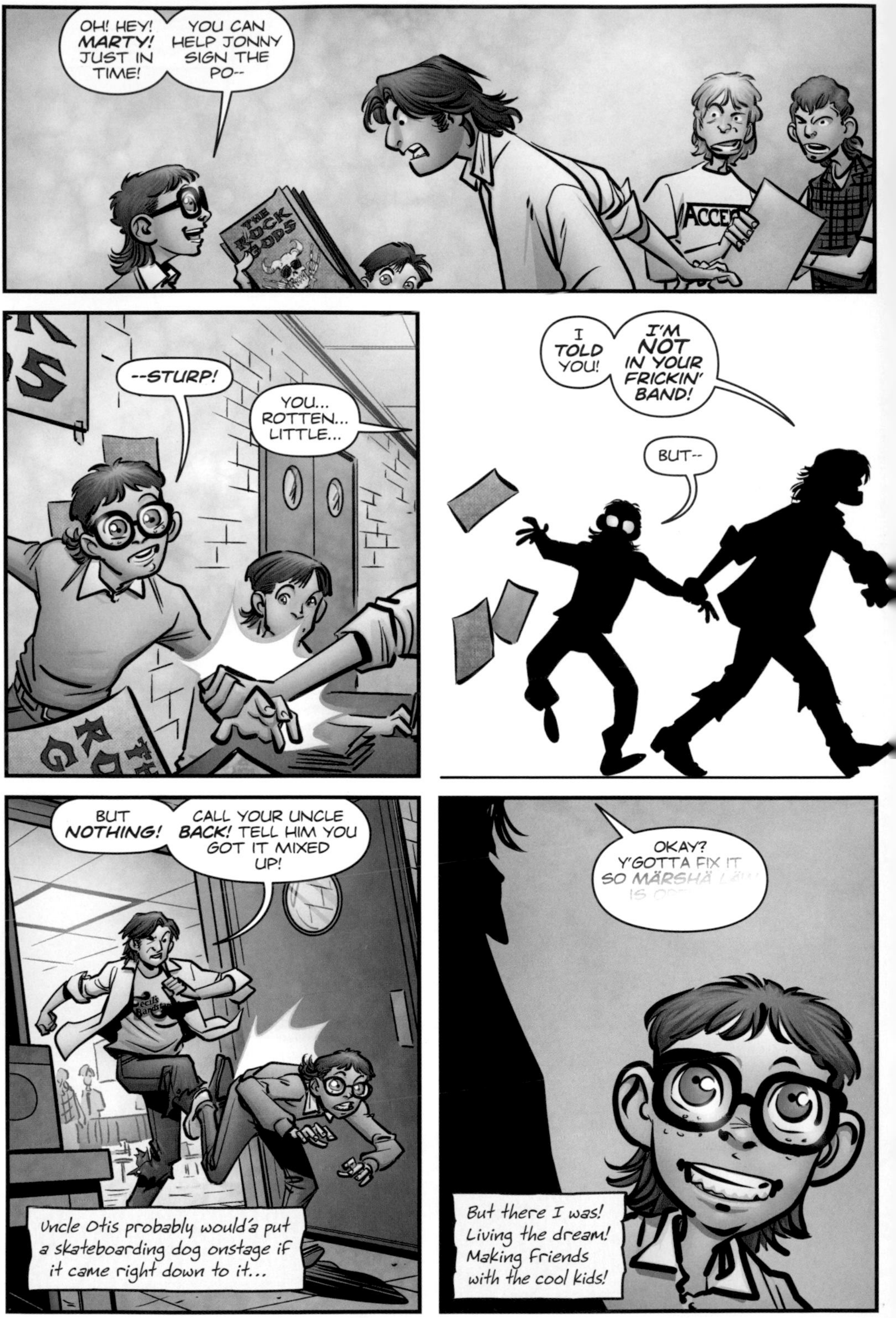
OH! HEY! **MARTY!** JUST IN TIME!
YOU CAN HELP JONNY SIGN THE PO--
THE ROCK GODS
--STURP!
YOU... ROTTEN... LITTLE...
I **TOLD** YOU!
I'M **NOT** IN YOUR FRICKIN' BAND!
BUT--
BUT **NOTHING!**
CALL YOUR UNCLE **BACK!** TELL HIM YOU GOT IT MIXED UP!
Uncle Otis probably would'a put a skateboarding dog onstage if it came right down to it...
OKAY? Y'GOTTA FIX IT SO MÄRSHÄ
But there I was! Living the dream! Making friends with the cool kids!

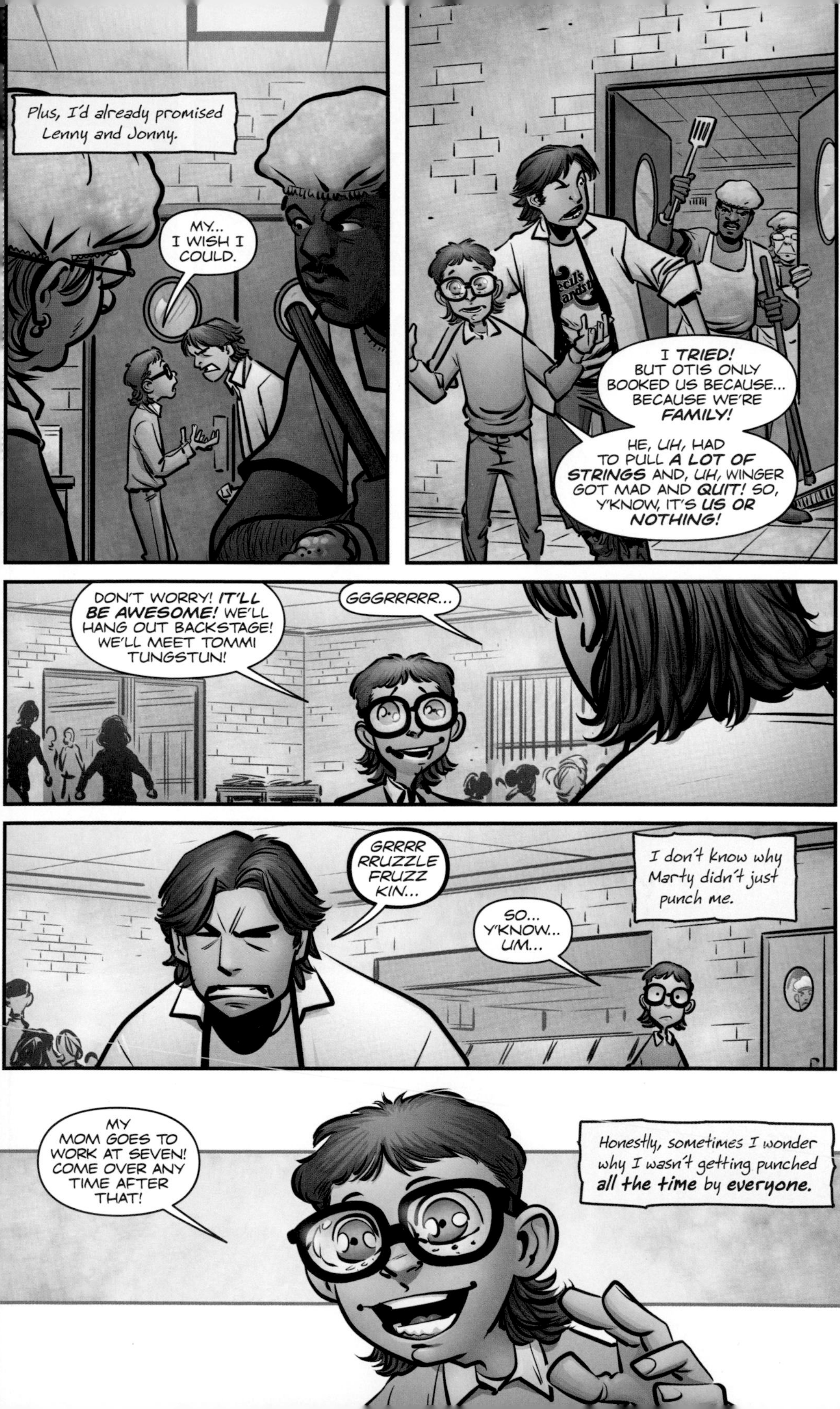
Plus, I'd already promised Lenny and Jonny.
MY... I WISH I COULD.
I TRIED! BUT OTIS ONLY BOOKED US BECAUSE... BECAUSE WE'RE FAMILY!
HE, UH, HAD TO PULL A LOT OF STRINGS AND, UH, WINGER GOT MAD AND QUIT! SO, Y'KNOW, IT'S US OR NOTHING!
DON'T WORRY! IT'LL BE AWESOME! WE'LL HANG OUT BACKSTAGE! WE'LL MEET TOMMI TUNGSTUN!
GGGRRRRR...
GRRRR RRUZZLE FRUZZ KIN...
SO... Y'KNOW... UM...
I don't know why Marty didn't just punch me.
MY MOM GOES TO WORK AT SEVEN! COME OVER ANY TIME AFTER THAT!
Honestly, sometimes I wonder why I wasn't getting punched all the time by everyone.

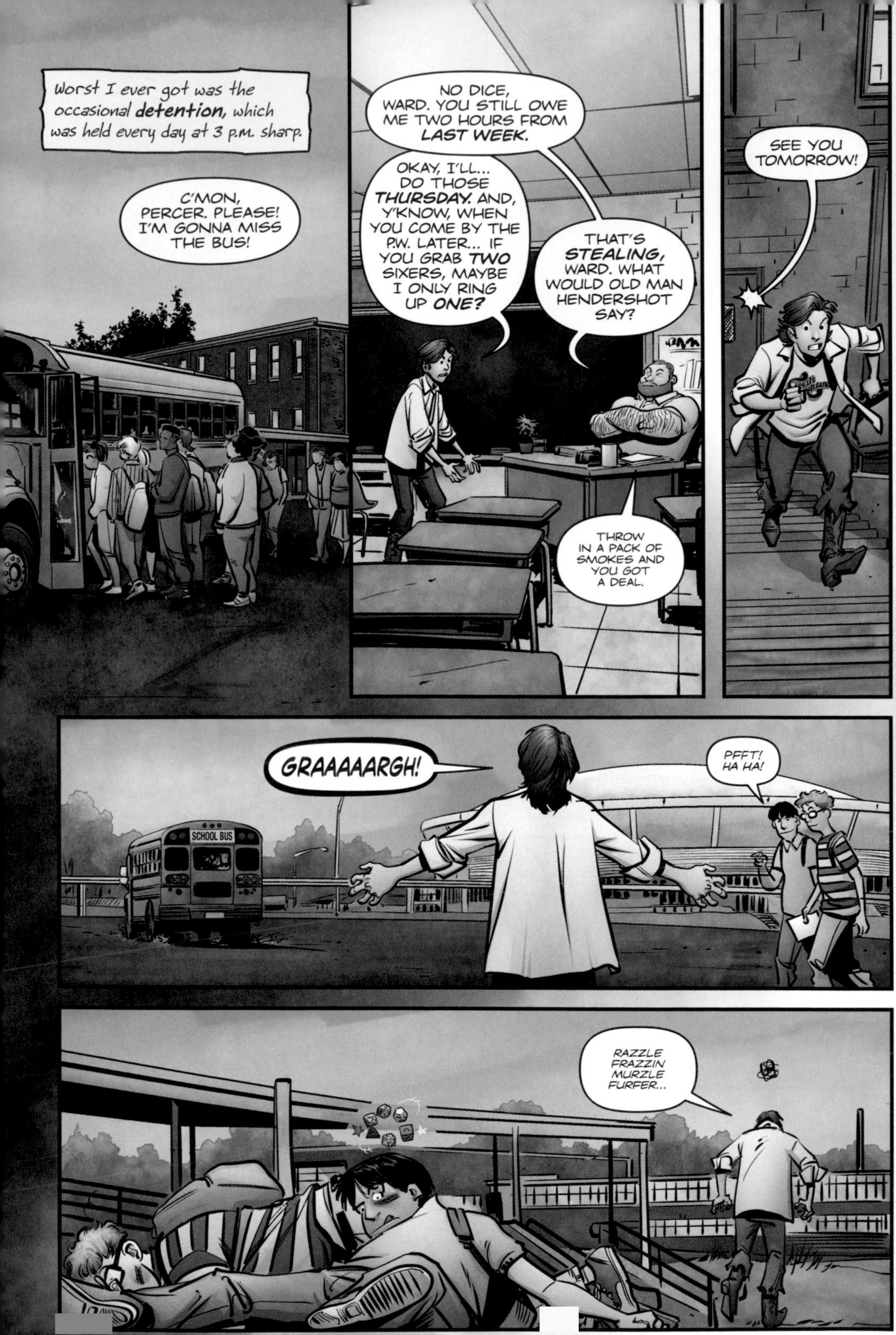
Worst I ever got was the occasional **detention**, which was held every day at 3 p.m. sharp.
C'MON, PERCER. PLEASE! I'M GONNA MISS THE BUS!
NO DICE, WARD. YOU STILL OWE ME TWO HOURS FROM **LAST WEEK.**
OKAY, I'LL... DO THOSE **THURSDAY.** AND, Y'KNOW, WHEN YOU COME BY THE P.W. LATER... IF YOU GRAB **TWO** SIXERS, MAYBE I ONLY RING UP **ONE?**
THAT'S **STEALING,** WARD. WHAT WOULD OLD MAN HENDERSHOT SAY?
THROW IN A PACK OF SMOKES AND YOU GOT A DEAL.
SEE YOU TOMORROW!
GRAAAAARGH!
SCHOOL BUS
PFFT! HA HA!
RAZZLE FRAZZIN MURZLE FURFER...

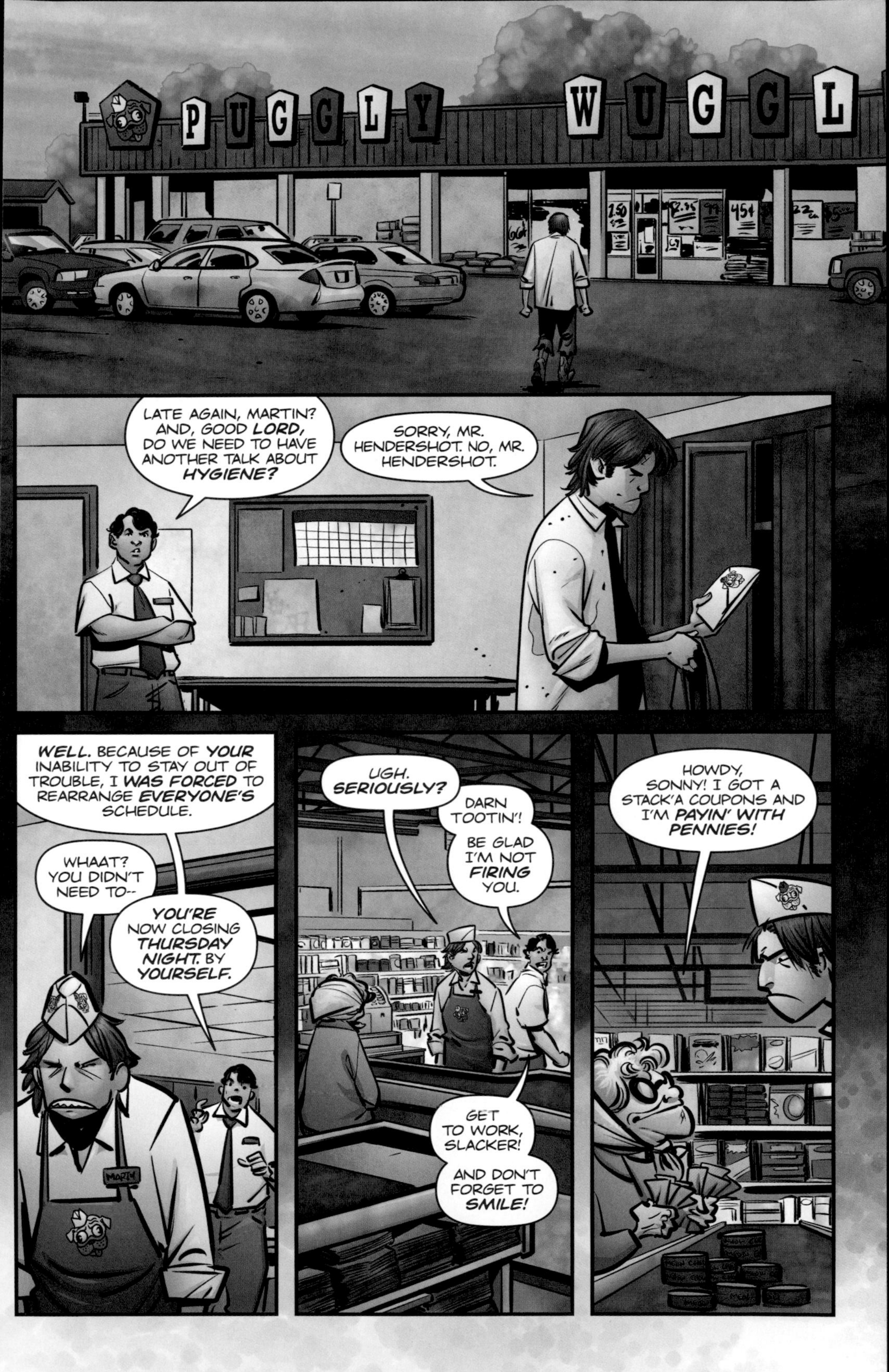
PUGGLY WUGGL
LATE AGAIN, MARTIN? AND, GOOD LORD, DO WE NEED TO HAVE ANOTHER TALK ABOUT HYGIENE?
SORRY, MR. HENDERSHOT. NO, MR. HENDERSHOT.
WELL. BECAUSE OF YOUR INABILITY TO STAY OUT OF TROUBLE, I WAS FORCED TO REARRANGE EVERYONE'S SCHEDULE.
WHAAT? YOU DIDN'T NEED TO--
YOU'RE NOW CLOSING THURSDAY NIGHT. BY YOURSELF.
UGH. SERIOUSLY?
DARN TOOTIN'!
BE GLAD I'M NOT FIRING YOU.
GET TO WORK, SLACKER!
AND DON'T FORGET TO SMILE!
HOWDY, SONNY! I GOT A STACK'A COUPONS AND I'M PAYIN' WITH PENNIES!

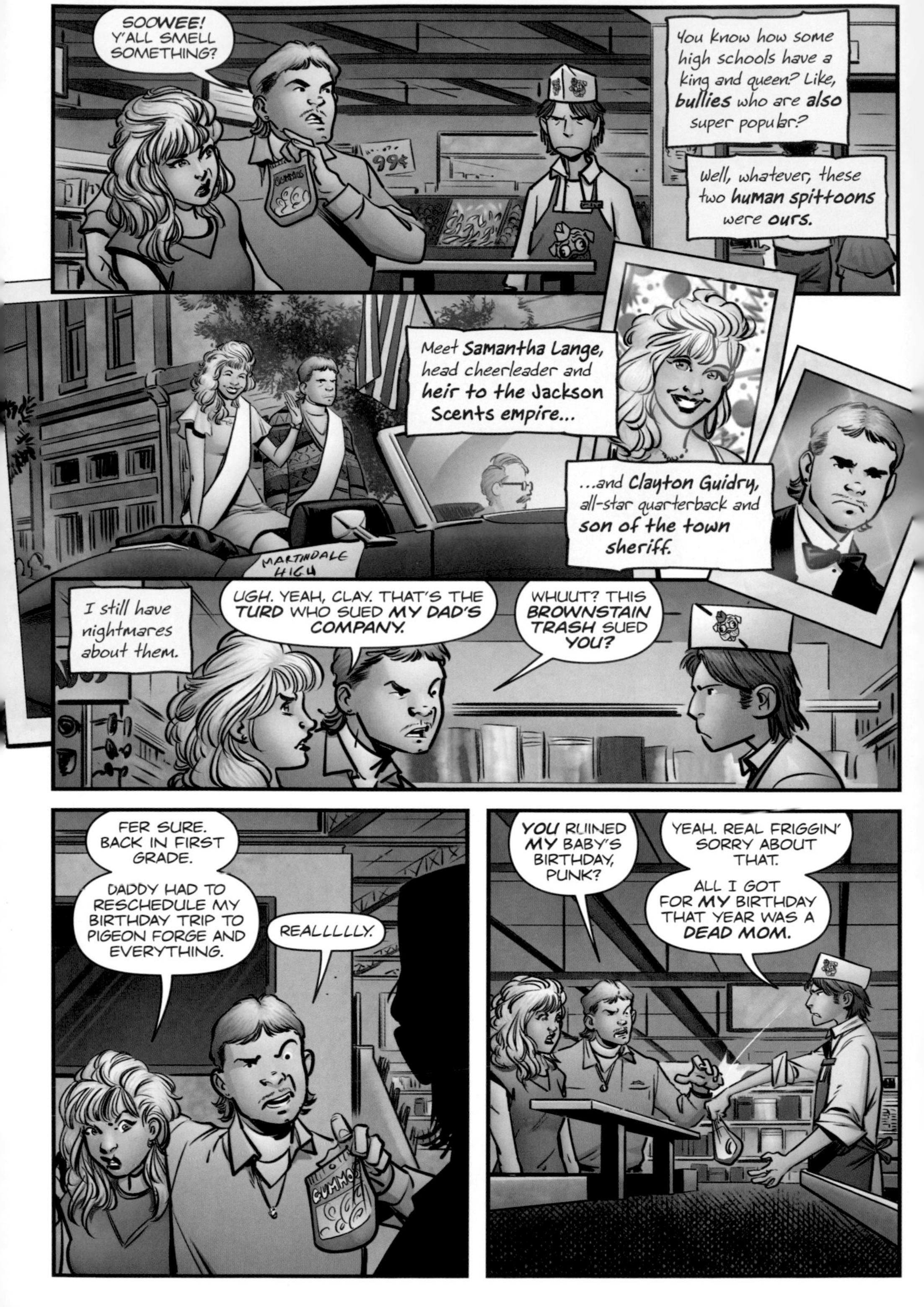
SOOWEE! Y'ALL SMELL SOMETHING?
You know how some high schools have a king and queen? Like, bullies who are also super popular?
Well, whatever, these two human spittoons were ours.
99¢
Meet Samantha Lange, head cheerleader and heir to the Jackson Scents empire...
...and Clayton Guidry, all-star quarterback and son of the town sheriff.
MARTINDALE HIGH
I still have nightmares about them.
UGH. YEAH, CLAY. THAT'S THE TURD WHO SUED MY DAD'S COMPANY.
WHUUT? THIS BROWNSTAIN TRASH SUED YOU?
FER SURE. BACK IN FIRST GRADE.
DADDY HAD TO RESCHEDULE MY BIRTHDAY TRIP TO PIGEON FORGE AND EVERYTHING.
REALLLLLY.
GUMMOS
YOU RUINED MY BABY'S BIRTHDAY, PUNK?
YEAH. REAL FRIGGIN' SORRY ABOUT THAT.
ALL I GOT FOR MY BIRTHDAY THAT YEAR WAS A DEAD MOM.

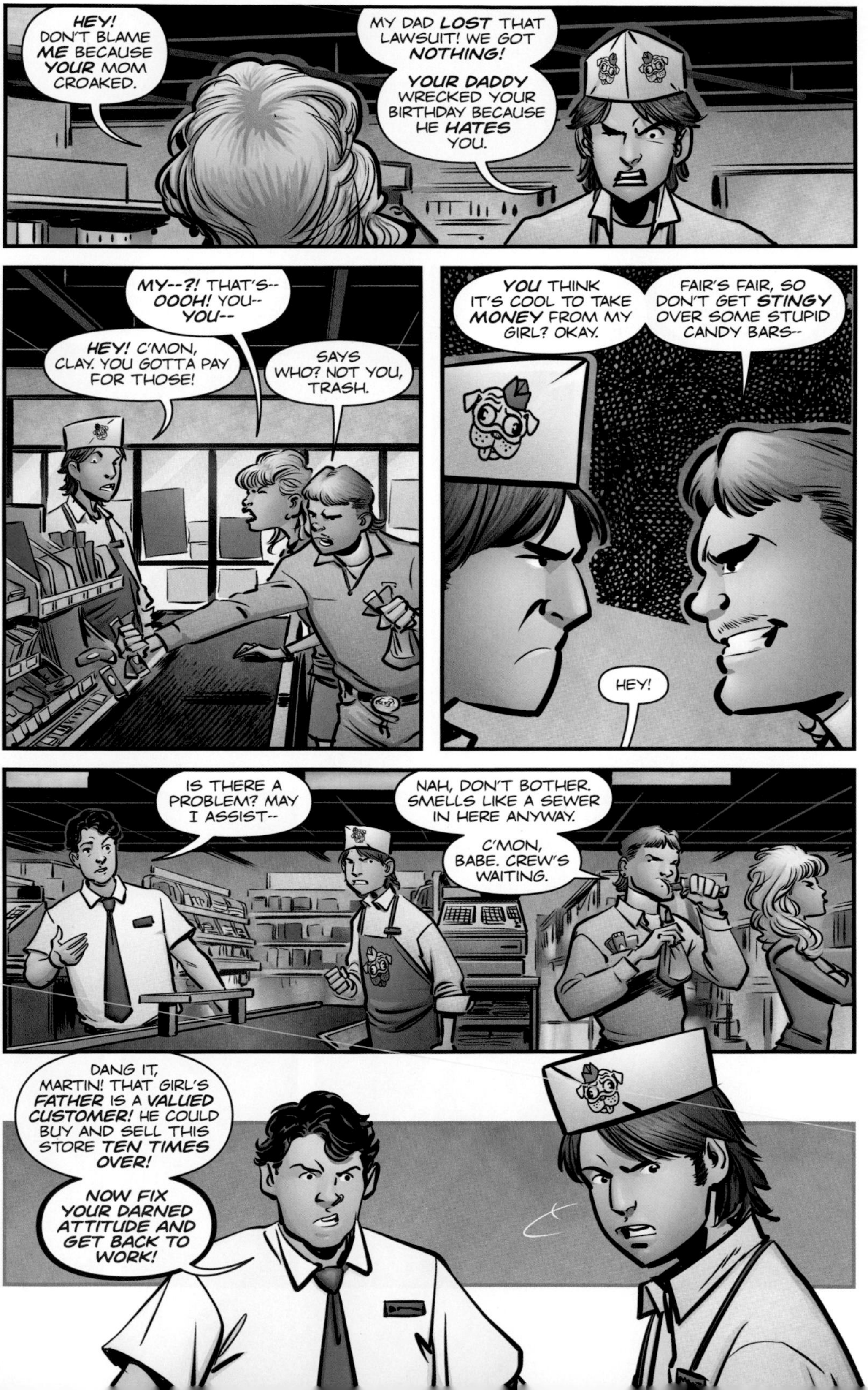

HEY! DON'T BLAME ME BECAUSE YOUR MOM CROAKED.
MY DAD LOST THAT LAWSUIT! WE GOT NOTHING!
YOUR DADDY WRECKED YOUR BIRTHDAY BECAUSE HE HATES YOU.
MY--?! THAT'S-- OOOH! YOU-- YOU--
HEY! C'MON, CLAY. YOU GOTTA PAY FOR THOSE!
SAYS WHO? NOT YOU, TRASH.
YOU THINK IT'S COOL TO TAKE MONEY FROM MY GIRL? OKAY.
FAIR'S FAIR, SO DON'T GET STINGY OVER SOME STUPID CANDY BARS--
HEY!
IS THERE A PROBLEM? MAY I ASSIST--
NAH, DON'T BOTHER. SMELLS LIKE A SEWER IN HERE ANYWAY.
C'MON, BABE. CREW'S WAITING.
DANG IT, MARTIN! THAT GIRL'S FATHER IS A VALUED CUSTOMER! HE COULD BUY AND SELL THIS STORE TEN TIMES OVER!
NOW FIX YOUR DARNED ATTITUDE AND GET BACK TO WORK!

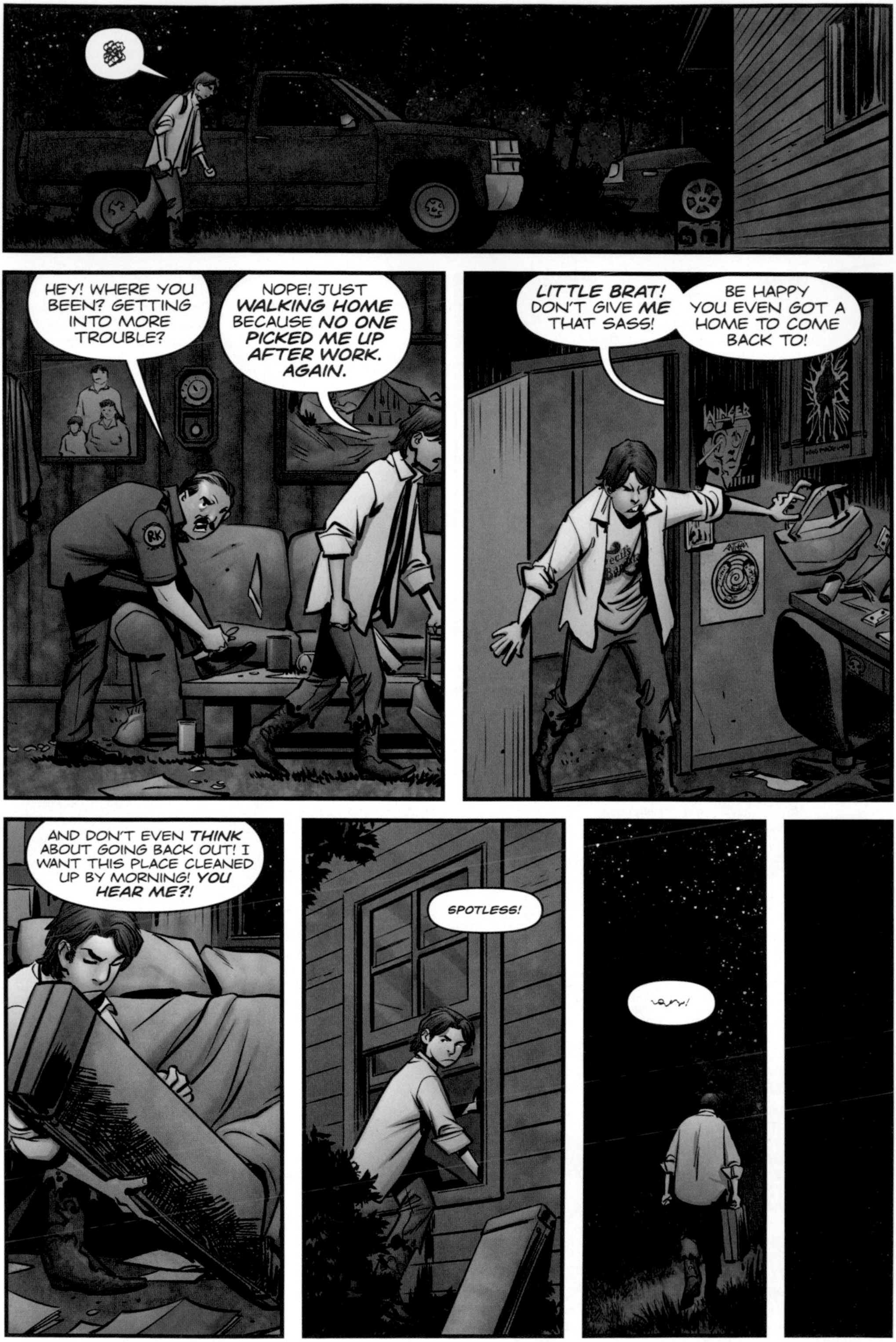
HEY! WHERE YOU BEEN? GETTING INTO MORE TROUBLE?
NOPE! JUST WALKING HOME BECAUSE NO ONE PICKED ME UP AFTER WORK. AGAIN.
LITTLE BRAT! DON'T GIVE ME THAT SASS!
BE HAPPY YOU EVEN GOT A HOME TO COME BACK TO!
WINGER
AND DON'T EVEN THINK ABOUT GOING BACK OUT! I WANT THIS PLACE CLEANED UP BY MORNING! YOU HEAR ME?!
SPOTLESS!

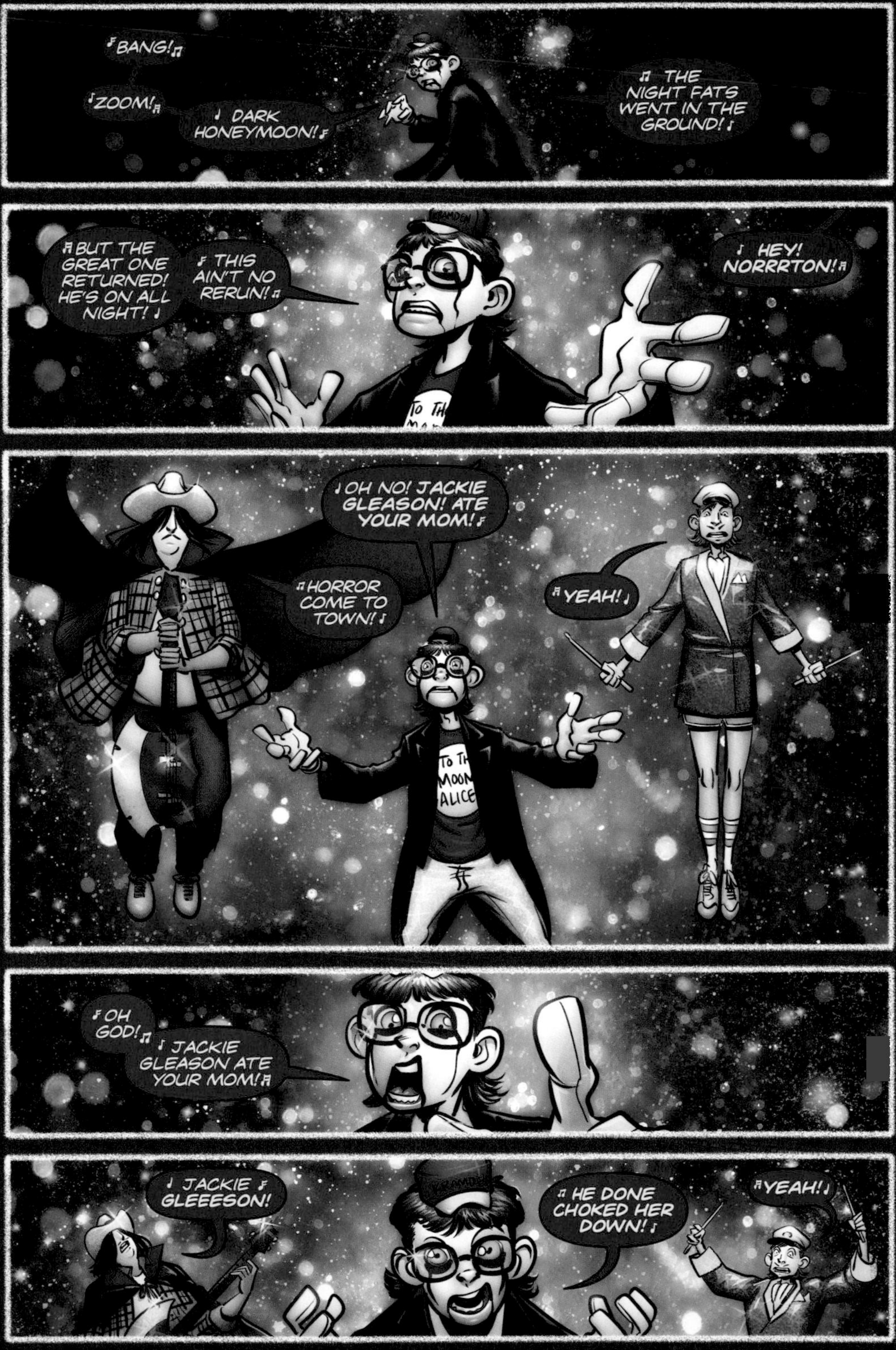
BANG!
ZOOM!
DARK HONEYMOON!
THE NIGHT FATS WENT IN THE GROUND!
BUT THE GREAT ONE RETURNED! HE'S ON ALL NIGHT!
THIS AIN'T NO RERUN!
HEY! NORRRTON!
OH NO! JACKIE GLEASON! ATE YOUR MOM!
HORROR COME TO TOWN!
YEAH!
TO THE MOON ALICE
OH GOD!
JACKIE GLEASON ATE YOUR MOM!
JACKIE GLEEESON!
HE DONE CHOKED HER DOWN!
YEAH!

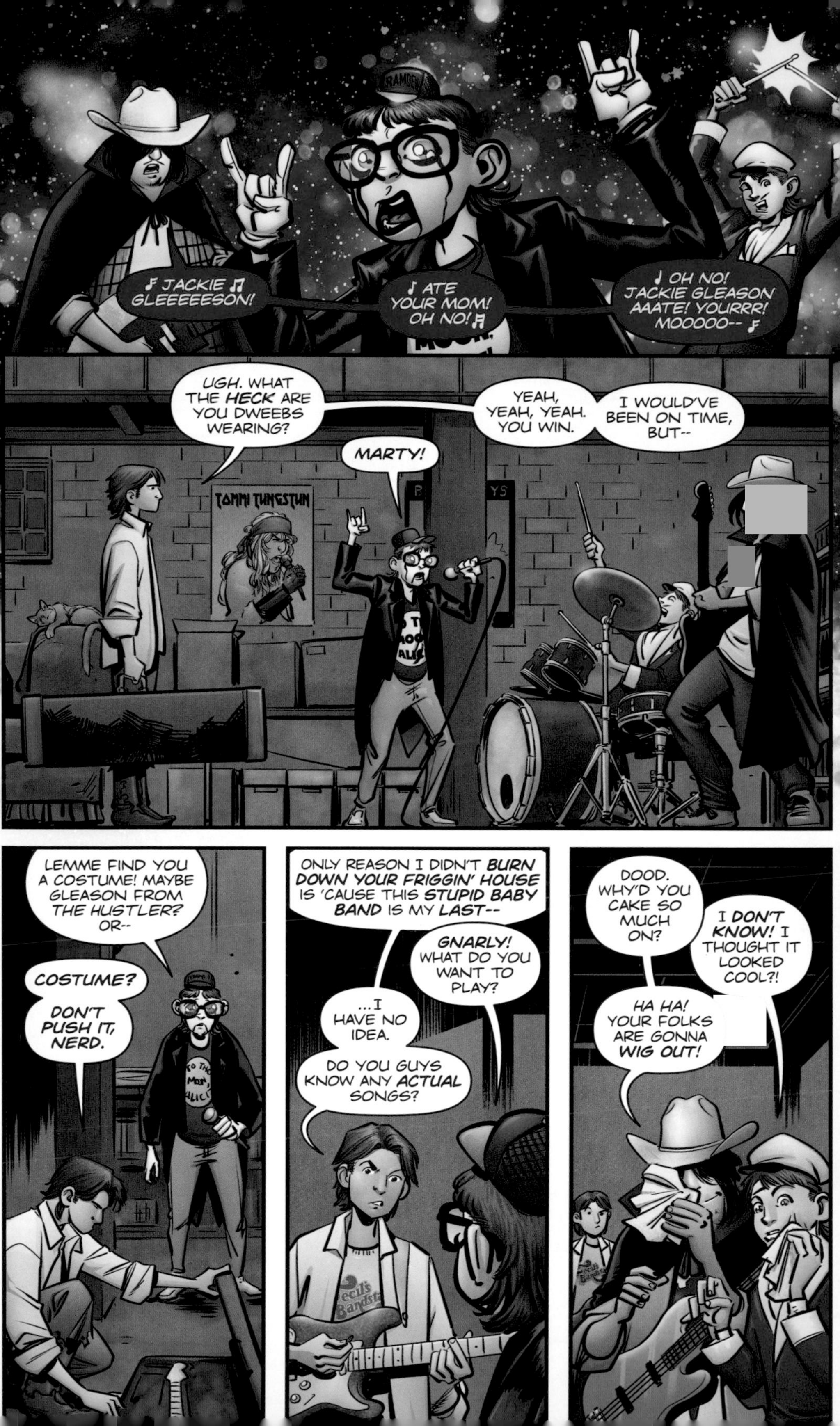
JACKIE GLEEEEESON!
ATE YOUR MOM! OH NO!
OH NO! JACKIE GLEASON AAATE! YOURRR! MOOOOO--
RAMDEN
UGH. WHAT THE **HECK** ARE YOU DWEEBS WEARING?
YEAH, YEAH, YEAH. YOU WIN.
I WOULD'VE BEEN ON TIME, BUT--
MARTY!
TOMMI TUNGSTUN
LEMME FIND YOU A COSTUME! MAYBE GLEASON FROM THE HUSTLER? OR--
COSTUME?
DON'T PUSH IT, NERD.
ONLY REASON I DIDN'T **BURN DOWN YOUR FRIGGIN' HOUSE** IS 'CAUSE THIS **STUPID BABY BAND** IS MY **LAST--**
GNARLY! WHAT DO YOU WANT TO PLAY?
...I HAVE NO IDEA.
DO YOU GUYS KNOW ANY **ACTUAL** SONGS?
DOOD. WHY'D YOU CAKE SO MUCH ON?
I **DON'T KNOW!** I THOUGHT IT LOOKED COOL?!
HA HA! YOUR FOLKS ARE GONNA **WIG OUT!**

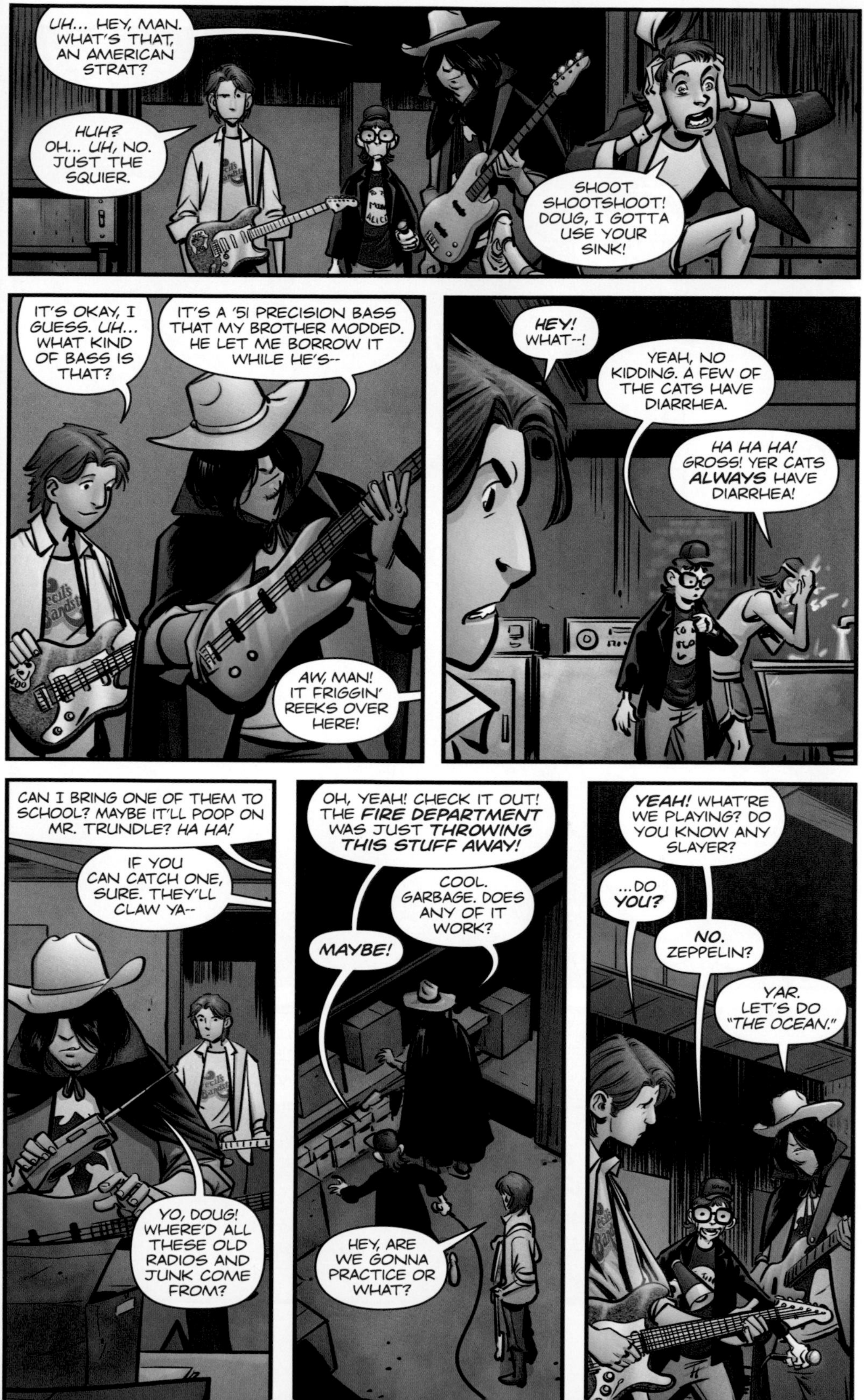
UH... HEY, MAN. WHAT'S THAT, AN AMERICAN STRAT?
HUH? OH... UH, NO. JUST THE SQUIER.
SHOOT SHOOTSHOOT! DOUG, I GOTTA USE YOUR SINK!
IT'S OKAY, I GUESS. UH... WHAT KIND OF BASS IS THAT?
IT'S A '51 PRECISION BASS THAT MY BROTHER MODDED. HE LET ME BORROW IT WHILE HE'S--
AW, MAN! IT FRIGGIN' REEKS OVER HERE!
HEY! WHAT--!
YEAH, NO KIDDING. A FEW OF THE CATS HAVE DIARRHEA.
HA HA HA! GROSS! YER CATS ALWAYS HAVE DIARRHEA!
CAN I BRING ONE OF THEM TO SCHOOL? MAYBE IT'LL POOP ON MR. TRUNDLE? HA HA!
IF YOU CAN CATCH ONE, SURE. THEY'LL CLAW YA--
YO, DOUG! WHERE'D ALL THESE OLD RADIOS AND JUNK COME FROM?
OH, YEAH! CHECK IT OUT! THE FIRE DEPARTMENT WAS JUST THROWING THIS STUFF AWAY!
COOL. GARBAGE. DOES ANY OF IT WORK?
MAYBE!
HEY, ARE WE GONNA PRACTICE OR WHAT?
YEAH! WHAT'RE WE PLAYING? DO YOU KNOW ANY SLAYER?
...DO YOU?
NO. ZEPPELIN?
YAR. LET'S DO "THE OCEAN."

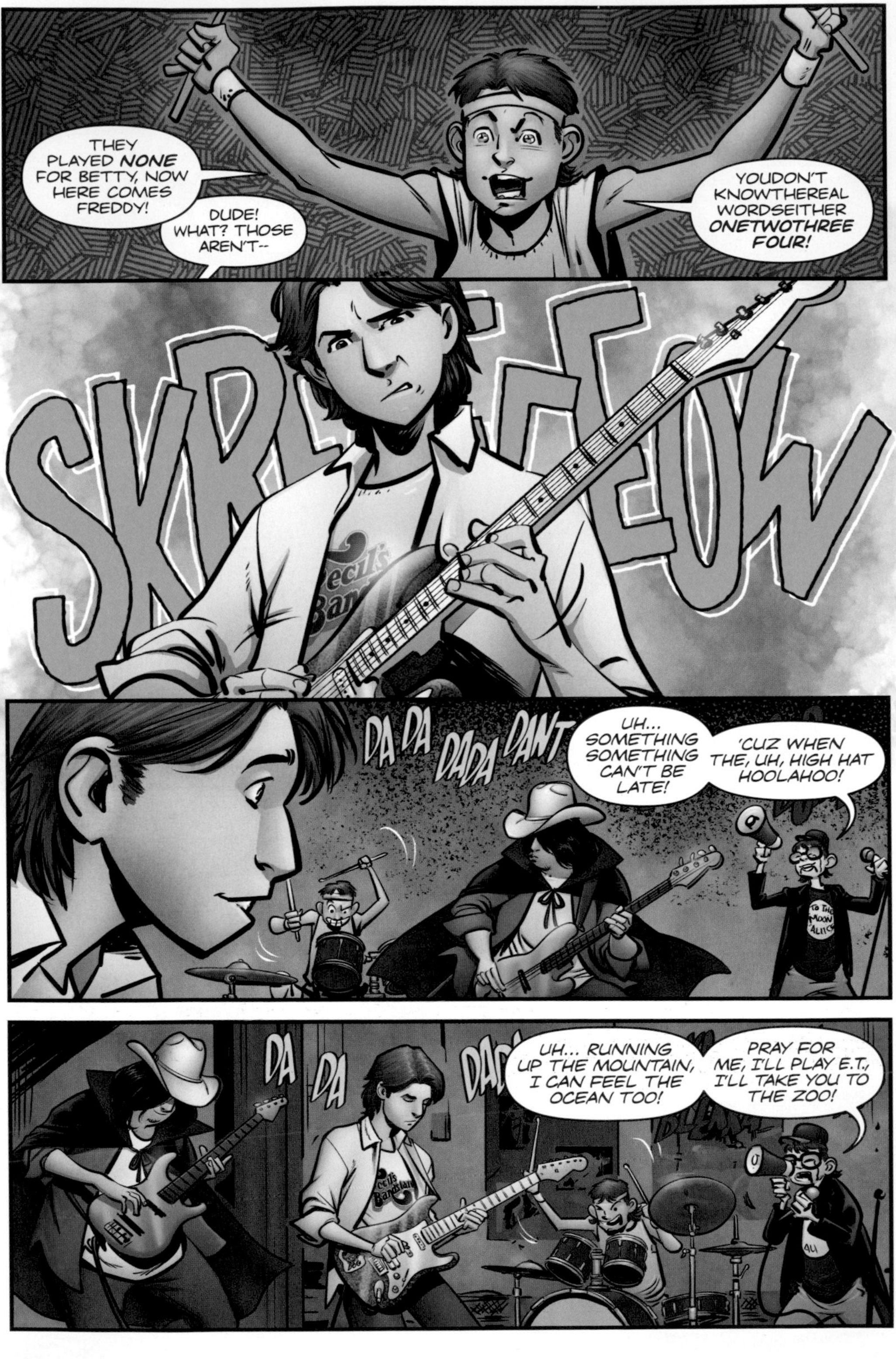
THEY PLAYED NONE FOR BETTY, NOW HERE COMES FREDDY!
DUDE! WHAT? THOSE AREN'T--
YOUDON'T KNOWTHEREAL WORDSEITHER ONETWOTHREE FOUR!
SKREEEEOW
DA DA DADA DANT
UH... SOMETHING SOMETHING CAN'T BE LATE!
'CUZ WHEN THE, UH, HIGH HAT HOOLAHOO!
DA DA DAD
UH... RUNNING UP THE MOUNTAIN, I CAN FEEL THE OCEAN TOO!
PRAY FOR ME, I'LL PLAY E.T., I'LL TAKE YOU TO THE ZOO!

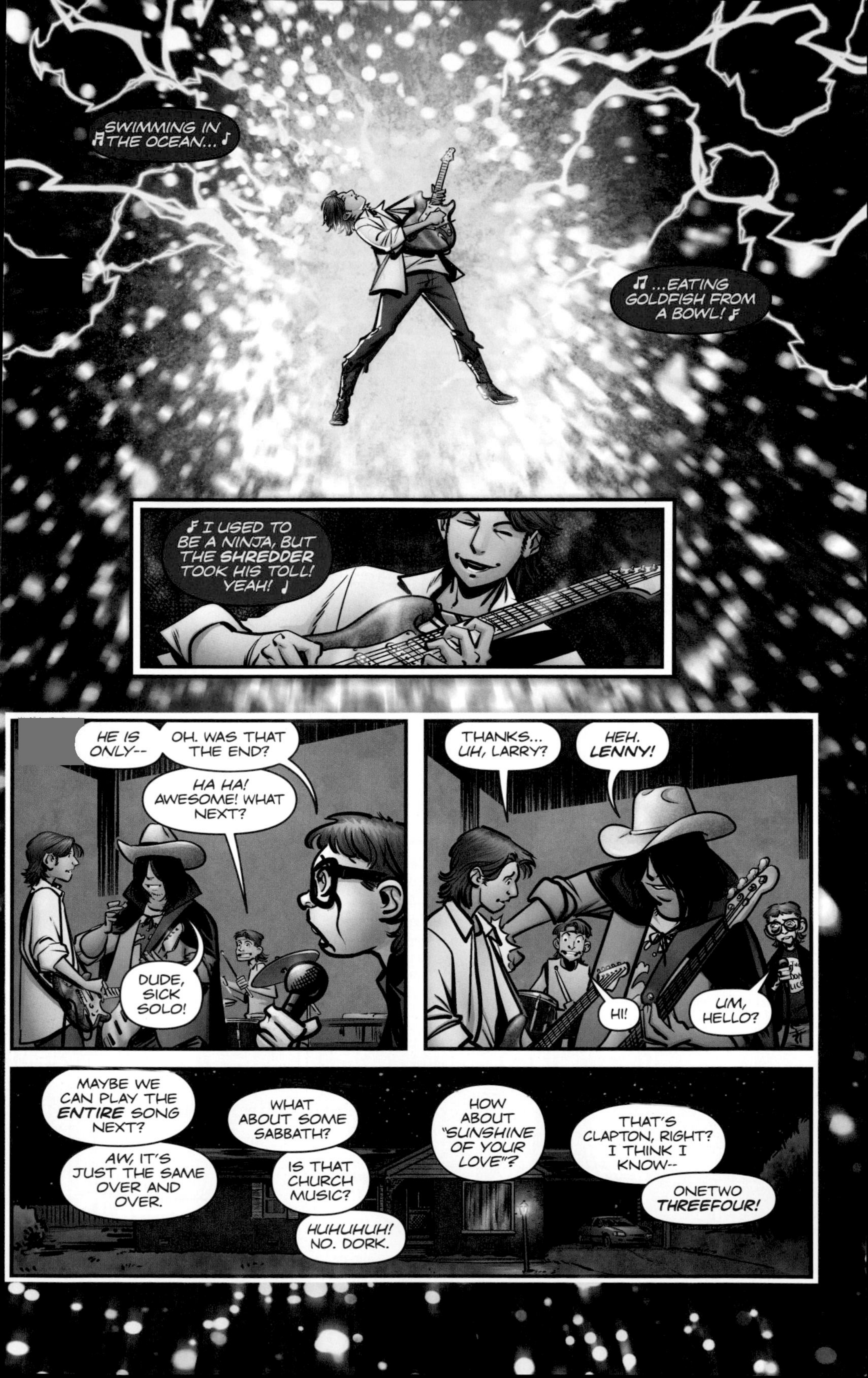

SWIMMING IN THE OCEAN...
...EATING GOLDFISH FROM A BOWL!
I USED TO BE A NINJA, BUT THE SHREDDER TOOK HIS TOLL! YEAH!
HE IS ONLY--
OH. WAS THAT THE END?
HA HA! AWESOME! WHAT NEXT?
DUDE, SICK SOLO!
THANKS... UH, LARRY?
HEH. LENNY!
HI!
UM, HELLO?
MAYBE WE CAN PLAY THE ENTIRE SONG NEXT?
AW, IT'S JUST THE SAME OVER AND OVER.
WHAT ABOUT SOME SABBATH?
IS THAT CHURCH MUSIC?
HUHUHUH! NO. DORK.
HOW ABOUT "SUNSHINE OF YOUR LOVE"?
THAT'S CLAPTON, RIGHT? I THINK I KNOW--
ONETWO THREEFOUR!

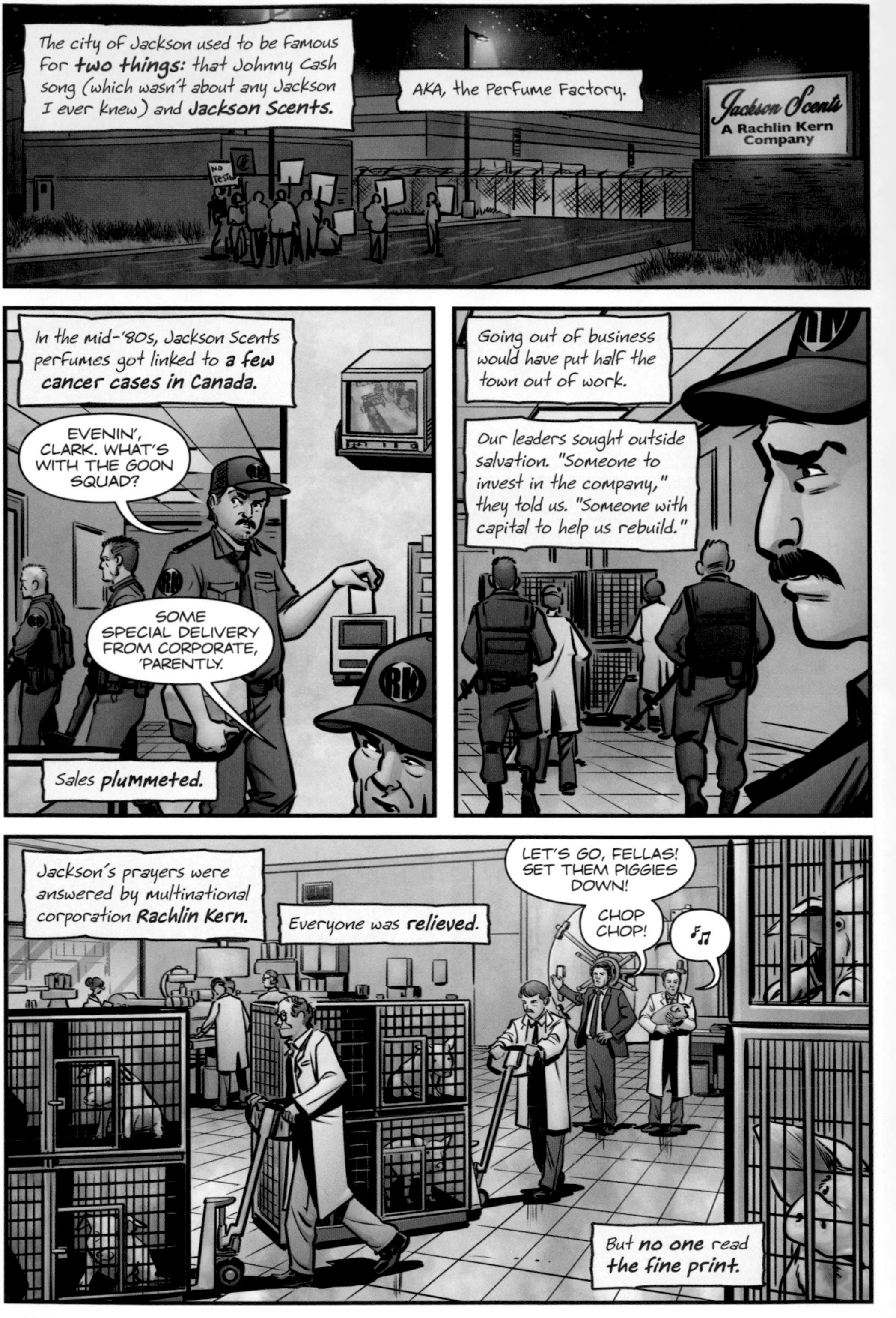
The city of Jackson used to be famous for **two things:** that Johnny Cash song (which wasn't about any Jackson I ever knew) and **Jackson Scents.**
AKA, the Perfume Factory.
Jackson Scents A Rachlin Kern Company
In the mid-'80s, Jackson Scents perfumes got linked to **a few cancer cases in Canada.**
EVENIN', CLARK. WHAT'S WITH THE GOON SQUAD?
SOME SPECIAL DELIVERY FROM CORPORATE, 'PARENTLY.
Sales **plummeted.**
Going out of business would have put half the town out of work.
Our leaders sought outside salvation. "Someone to invest in the company," they told us. "Someone with capital to help us rebuild."
Jackson's prayers were answered by multinational corporation **Rachlin Kern.**
Everyone was **relieved.**
LET'S GO, FELLAS! SET THEM PIGGIES DOWN!
CHOP CHOP!
But **no one** read **the fine print.**

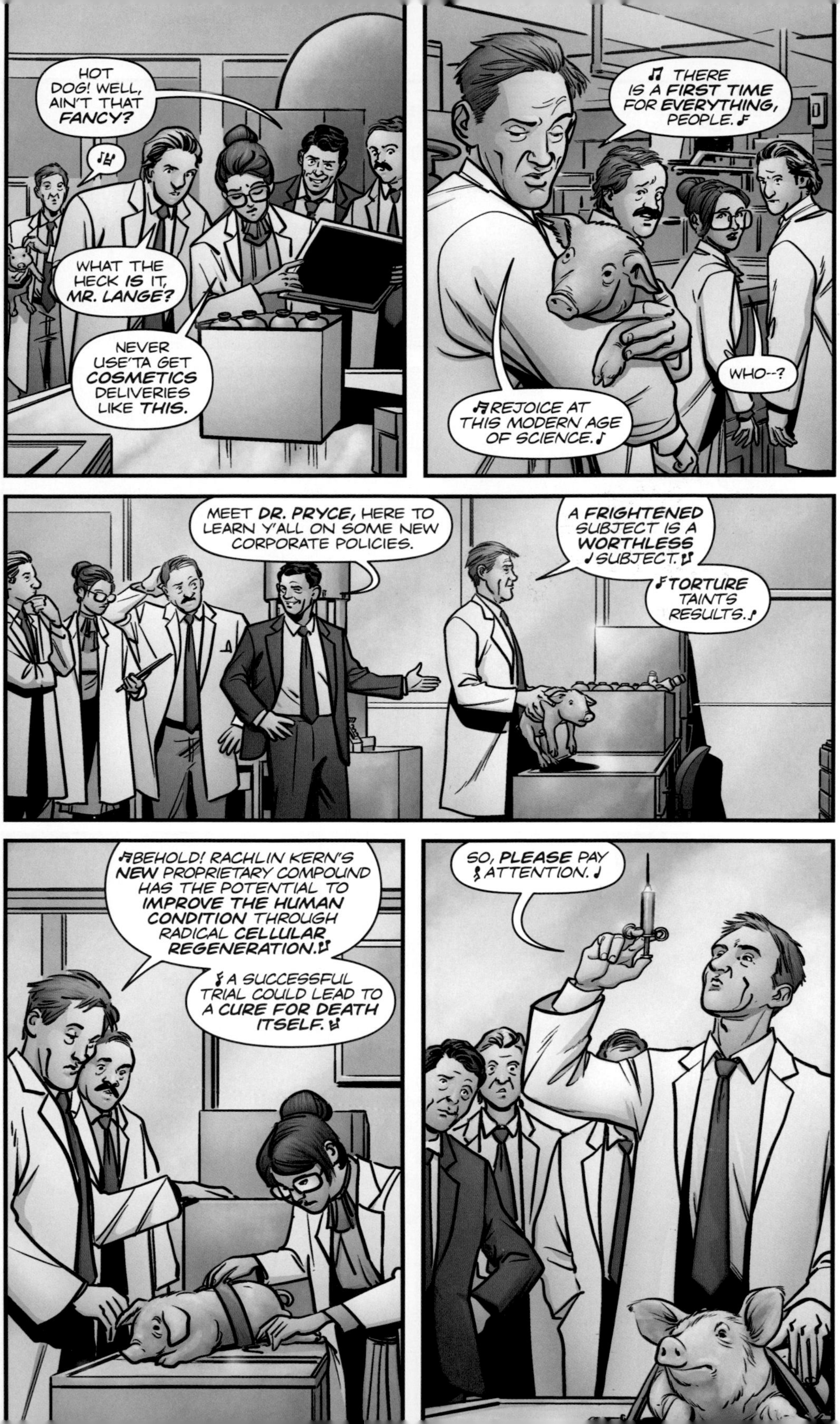
HOT DOG! WELL, AIN'T THAT FANCY?
WHAT THE HECK IS IT, MR. LANGE?
NEVER USE'TA GET COSMETICS DELIVERIES LIKE THIS.
THERE IS A FIRST TIME FOR EVERYTHING, PEOPLE.
REJOICE AT THIS MODERN AGE OF SCIENCE.
WHO--?
MEET DR. PRYCE, HERE TO LEARN Y'ALL ON SOME NEW CORPORATE POLICIES.
A FRIGHTENED SUBJECT IS A WORTHLESS SUBJECT.
TORTURE TAINTS RESULTS.
BEHOLD! RACHLIN KERN'S NEW PROPRIETARY COMPOUND HAS THE POTENTIAL TO IMPROVE THE HUMAN CONDITION THROUGH RADICAL CELLULAR REGENERATION.
A SUCCESSFUL TRIAL COULD LEAD TO A CURE FOR DEATH ITSELF.
SO, PLEASE PAY ATTENTION.

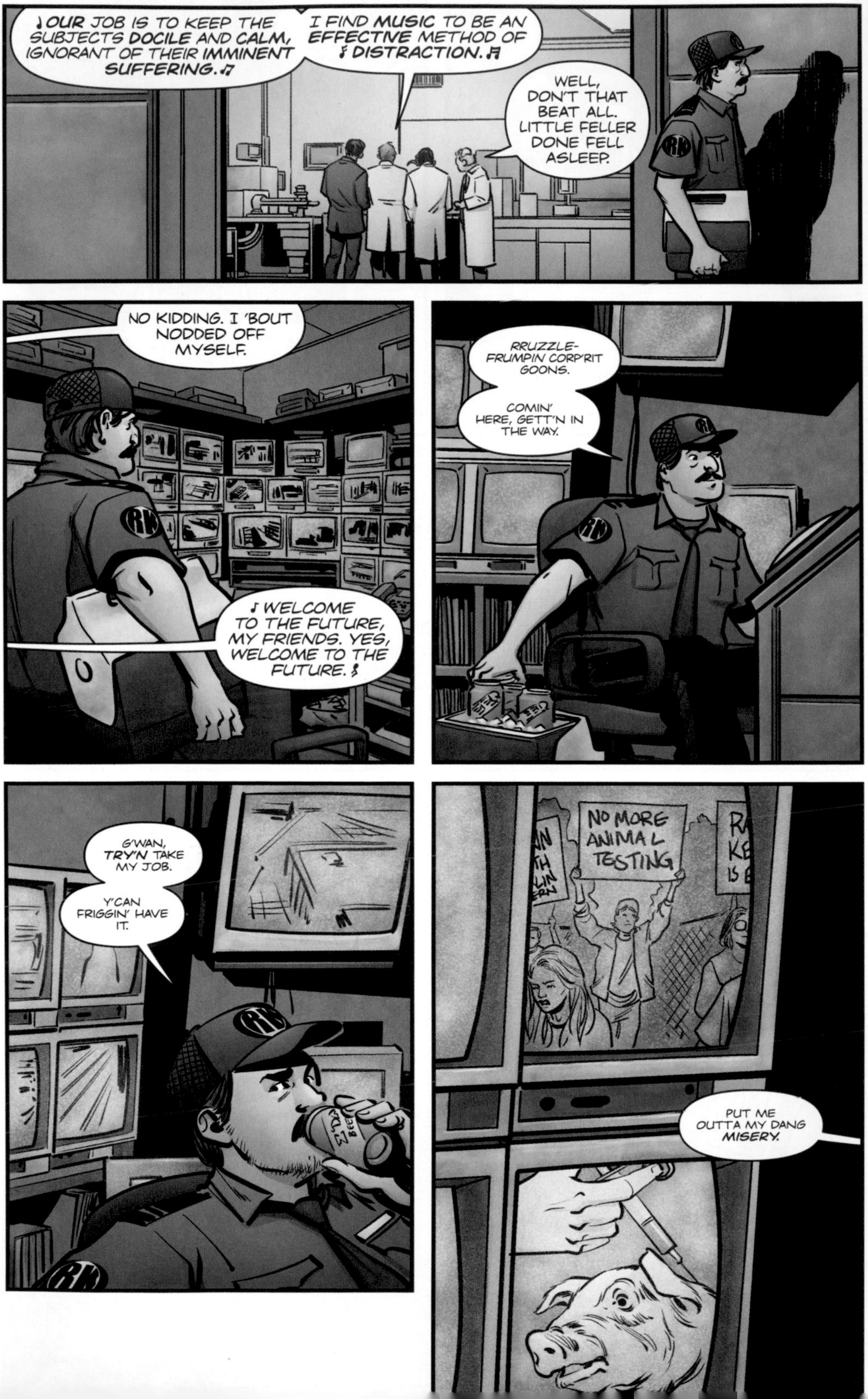
OUR JOB IS TO KEEP THE SUBJECTS DOCILE AND CALM, IGNORANT OF THEIR IMMINENT SUFFERING.
I FIND MUSIC TO BE AN EFFECTIVE METHOD OF DISTRACTION.
WELL, DON'T THAT BEAT ALL. LITTLE FELLER DONE FELL ASLEEP.
NO KIDDING. I 'BOUT NODDED OFF MYSELF.
WELCOME TO THE FUTURE, MY FRIENDS. YES, WELCOME TO THE FUTURE.
RRUZZLE-FRUMPIN CORP'RIT GOONS.
COMIN' HERE, GETT'N IN THE WAY.
G'WAN, TRY'N TAKE MY JOB.
Y'CAN FRIGGIN' HAVE IT.
NO MORE ANIMAL TESTING
PUT ME OUTTA MY DANG MISERY.

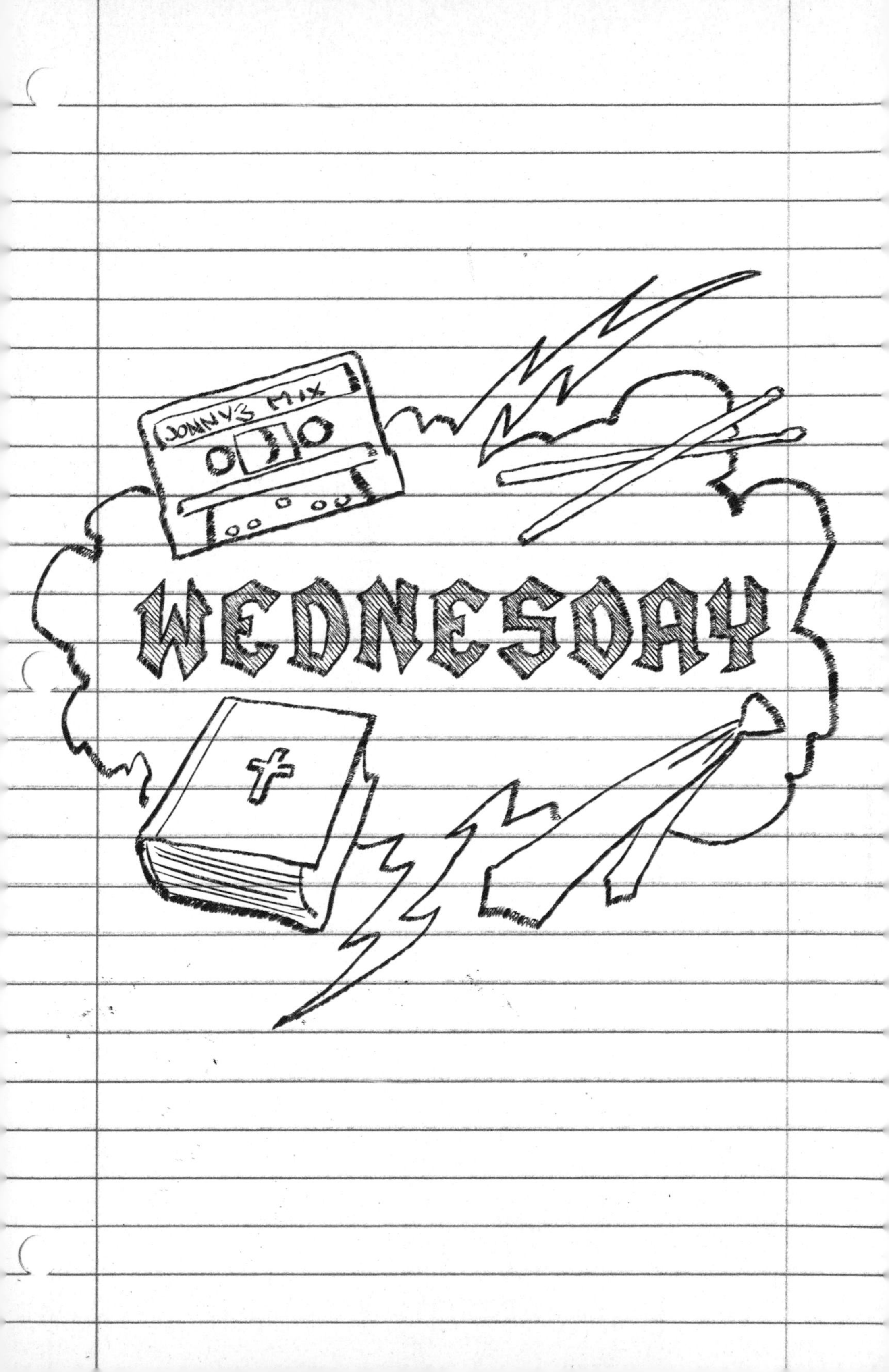
JONNY'S MIX
WEDNESDAY

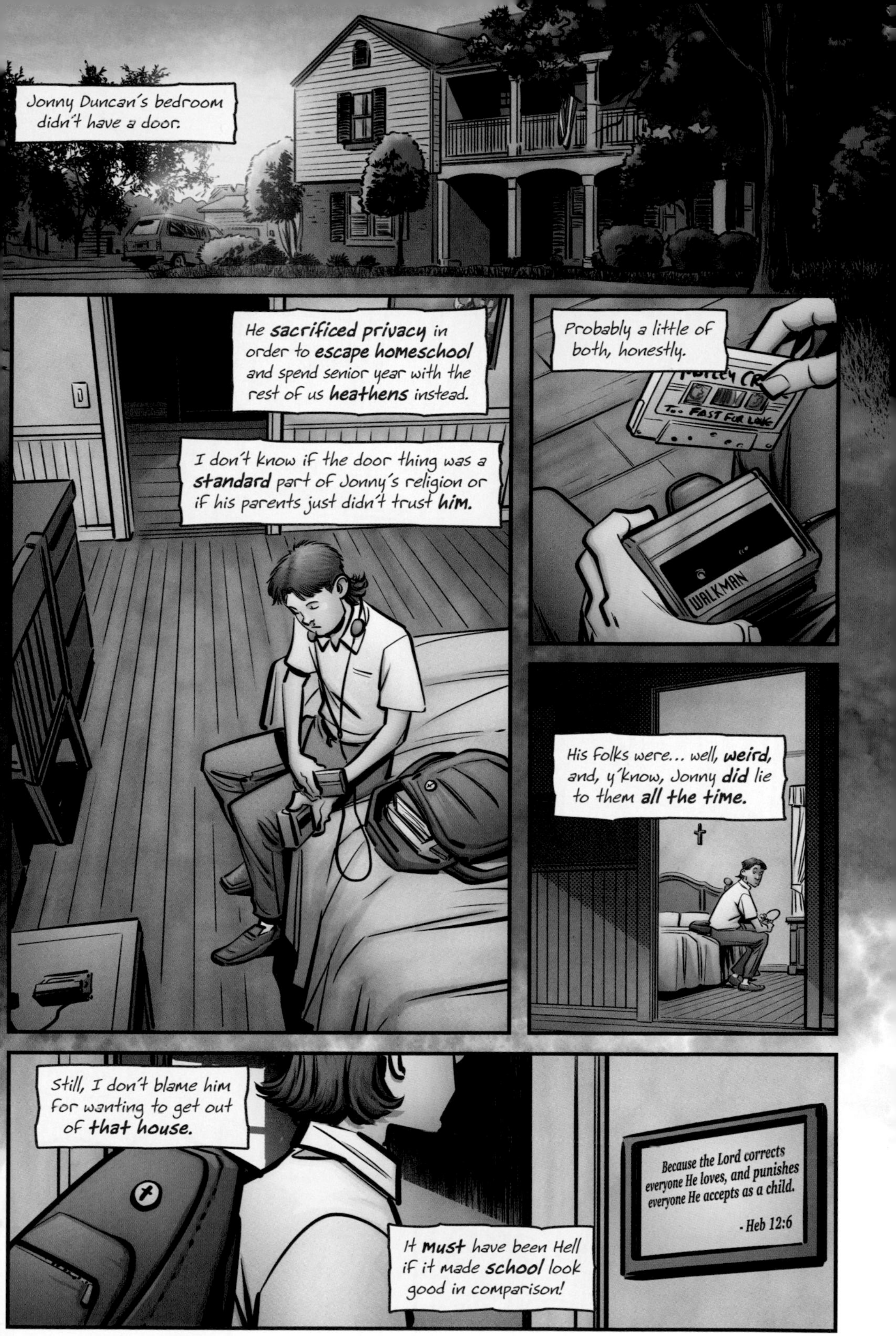
Jonny Duncan's bedroom didn't have a door.
He **sacrificed privacy** in order to **escape homeschool** and spend senior year with the rest of us **heathens** instead.
I don't know if the door thing was a **standard** part of Jonny's religion or if his parents just didn't trust **him.**
Probably a little of both, honestly.
FAST FOR LOVE
WALKMAN
His folks were... well, **weird,** and, y'know, Jonny **did** lie to them **all the time.**
Still, I don't blame him for wanting to get out of **that house.**
It **must** have been Hell if it made **school** look good in comparison!
Because the Lord corrects everyone He loves, and punishes everyone He accepts as a child.
- Heb 12:6

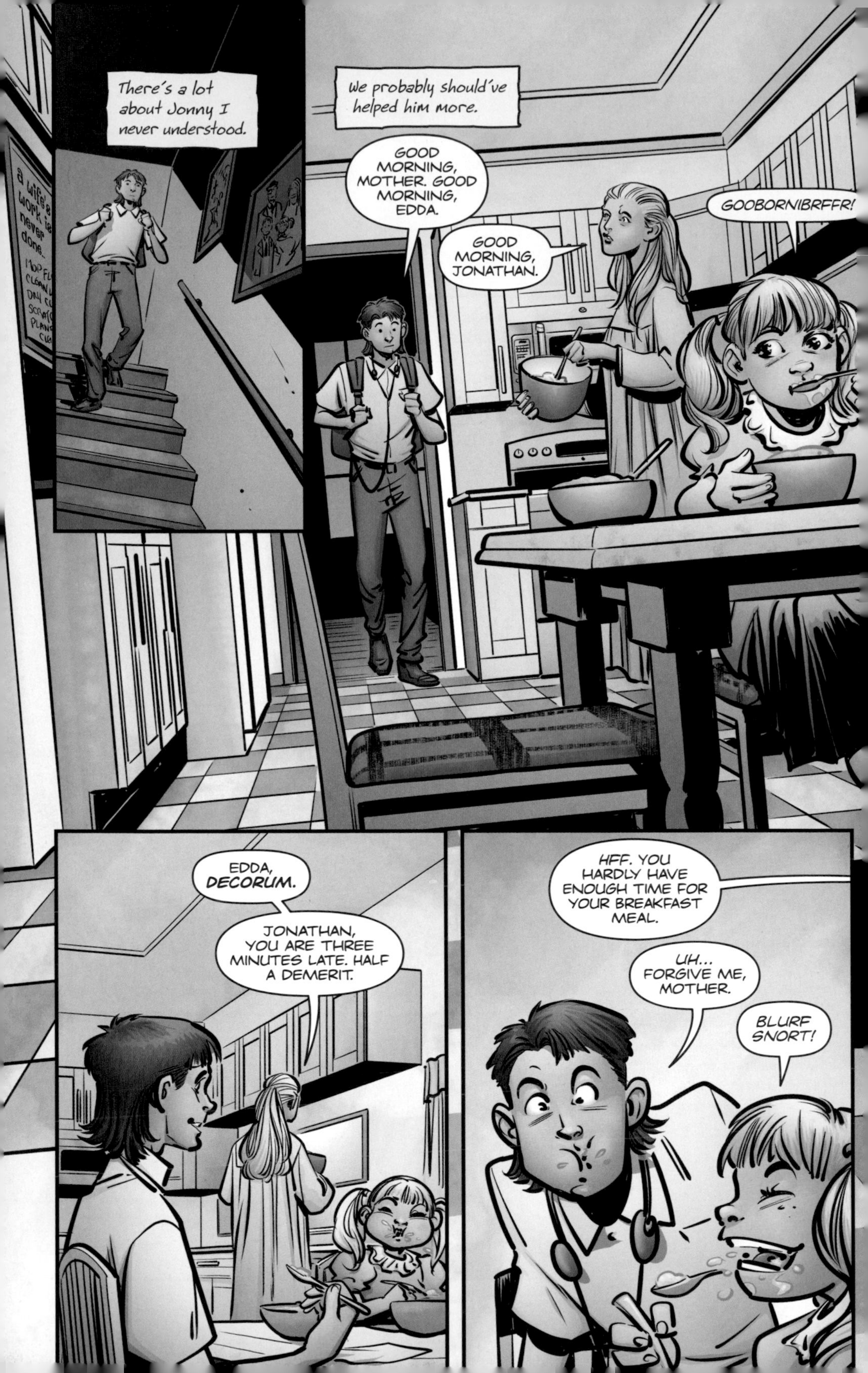
There's a lot about Jonny I never understood.
a wife's work is never done..
MOP FL
CLEAN
DRY CL
SCRAP
PLANT
We probably should've helped him more.
GOOD MORNING, MOTHER. GOOD MORNING, EDDA.
GOOD MORNING, JONATHAN.
GOOBORNIBRFFR!
EDDA, **DECORUM.**
JONATHAN, YOU ARE THREE MINUTES LATE. HALF A DEMERIT.
HFF. YOU HARDLY HAVE ENOUGH TIME FOR YOUR BREAKFAST MEAL.
UH... FORGIVE ME, MOTHER.
BLURF SNORT!

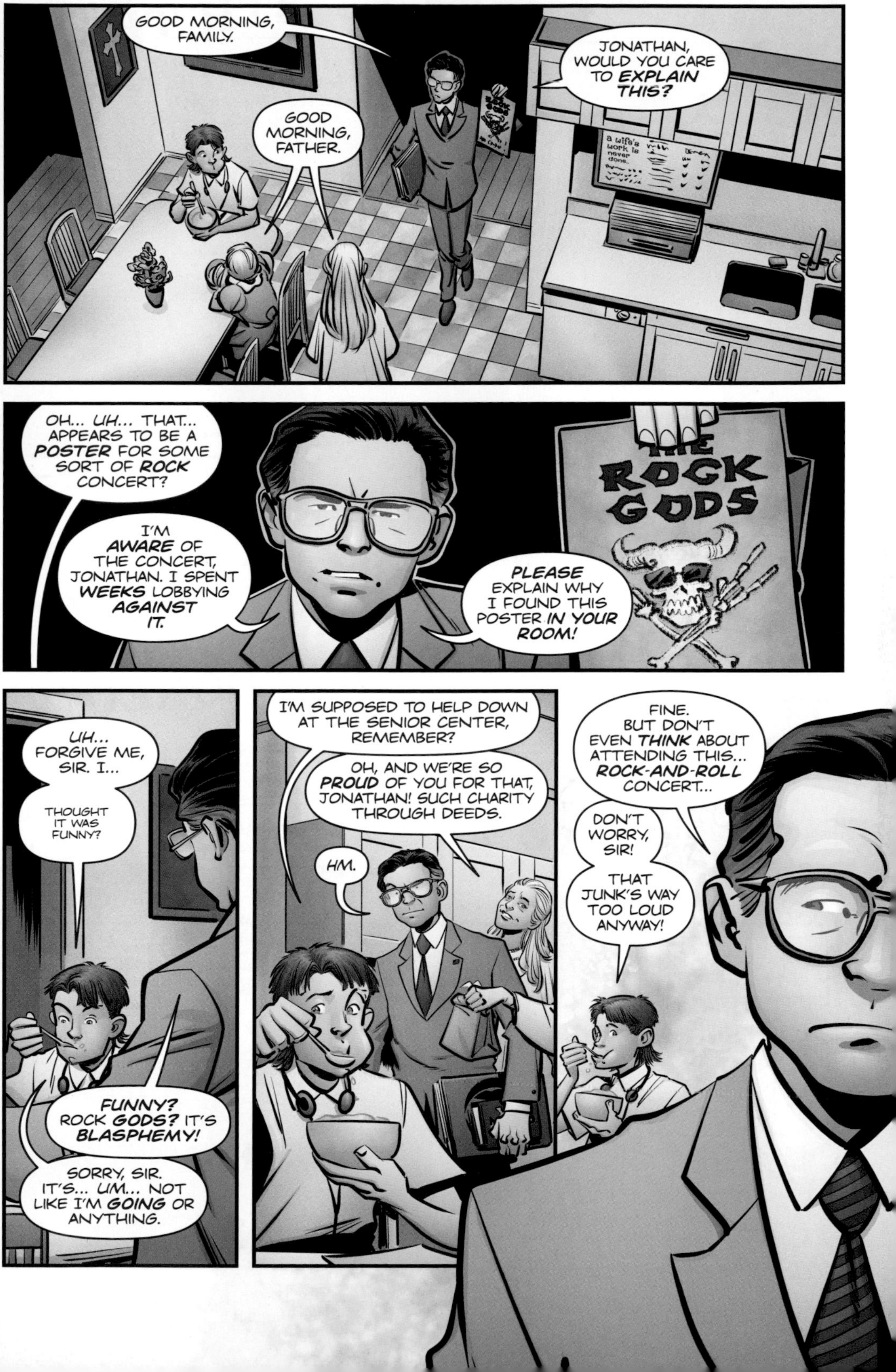

GOOD MORNING, FAMILY.
GOOD MORNING, FATHER.
JONATHAN, WOULD YOU CARE TO **EXPLAIN THIS?**
a wife's work is never done..
OH... UH... THAT... APPEARS TO BE A **POSTER** FOR SOME SORT OF **ROCK** CONCERT?
THE ROCK GODS
I'M **AWARE** OF THE CONCERT, JONATHAN. I SPENT **WEEKS** LOBBYING **AGAINST** IT.
PLEASE EXPLAIN WHY I FOUND THIS POSTER **IN YOUR ROOM!**
UH... FORGIVE ME, SIR. I...
THOUGHT IT WAS FUNNY?
FUNNY? ROCK **GODS?** IT'S **BLASPHEMY!**
SORRY, SIR. IT'S... *UM*... NOT LIKE I'M **GOING** OR ANYTHING.
I'M SUPPOSED TO HELP DOWN AT THE SENIOR CENTER, REMEMBER?
OH, AND WE'RE SO **PROUD** OF YOU FOR THAT, JONATHAN! SUCH CHARITY THROUGH DEEDS.
HM.
FINE. BUT DON'T EVEN **THINK** ABOUT ATTENDING THIS... **ROCK-AND-ROLL** CONCERT...
DON'T WORRY, SIR!
THAT JUNK'S WAY TOO LOUD ANYWAY!

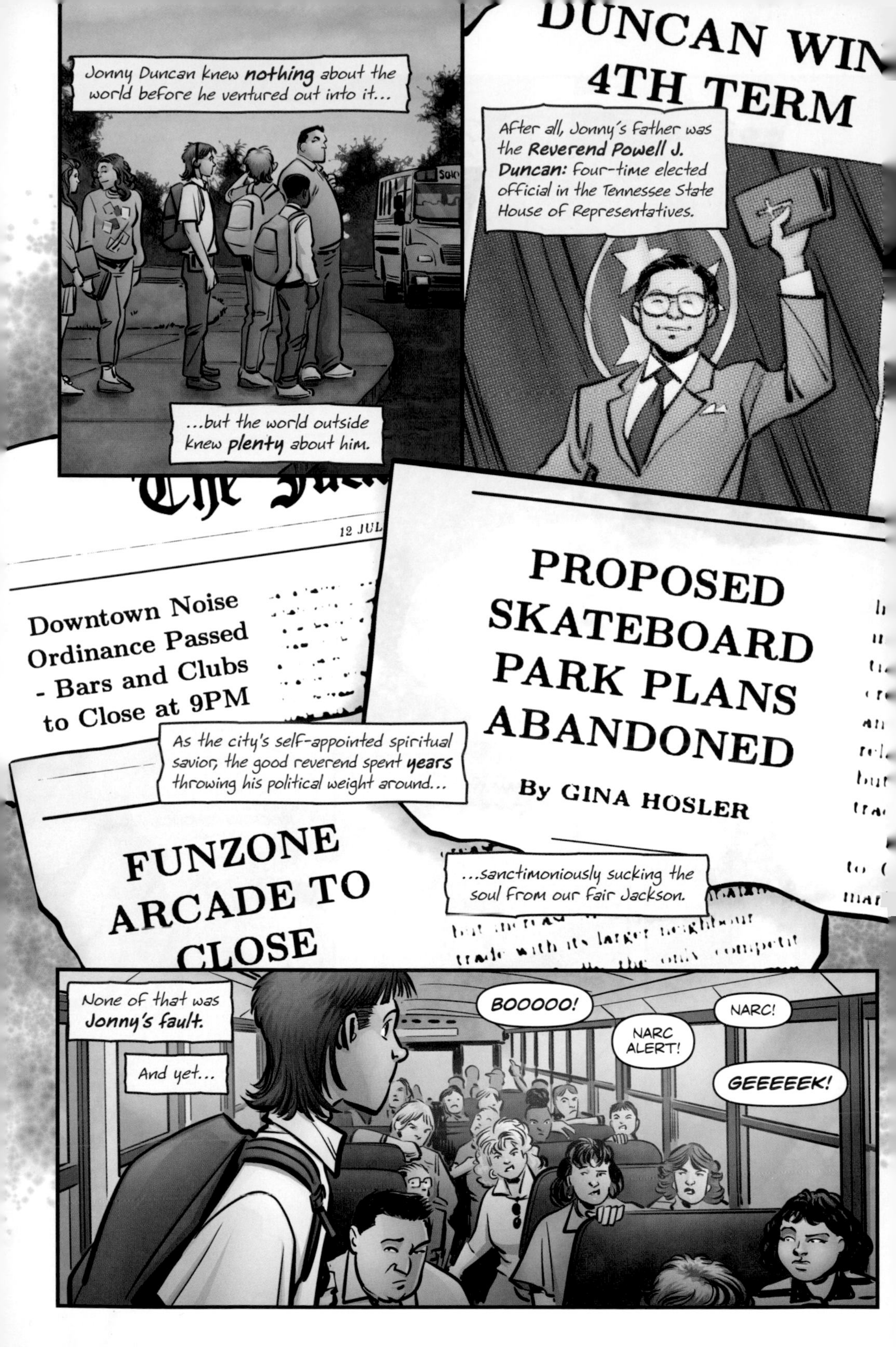

Jonny Duncan knew nothing about the world before he ventured out into it...
...but the world outside knew plenty about him.
DUNCAN WIN
4TH TERM
After all, Jonny's father was the Reverend Powell J. Duncan: four-time elected official in the Tennessee State House of Representatives.
12 JUL
Downtown Noise Ordinance Passed - Bars and Clubs to Close at 9PM
As the city's self-appointed spiritual savior, the good reverend spent years throwing his political weight around...
PROPOSED SKATEBOARD PARK PLANS ABANDONED
By GINA HOSLER
FUNZONE ARCADE TO CLOSE
...sanctimoniously sucking the soul from our fair Jackson.
None of that was Jonny's fault.
And yet...
BOOOOO!
NARC ALERT!
NARC!
GEEEEEK!

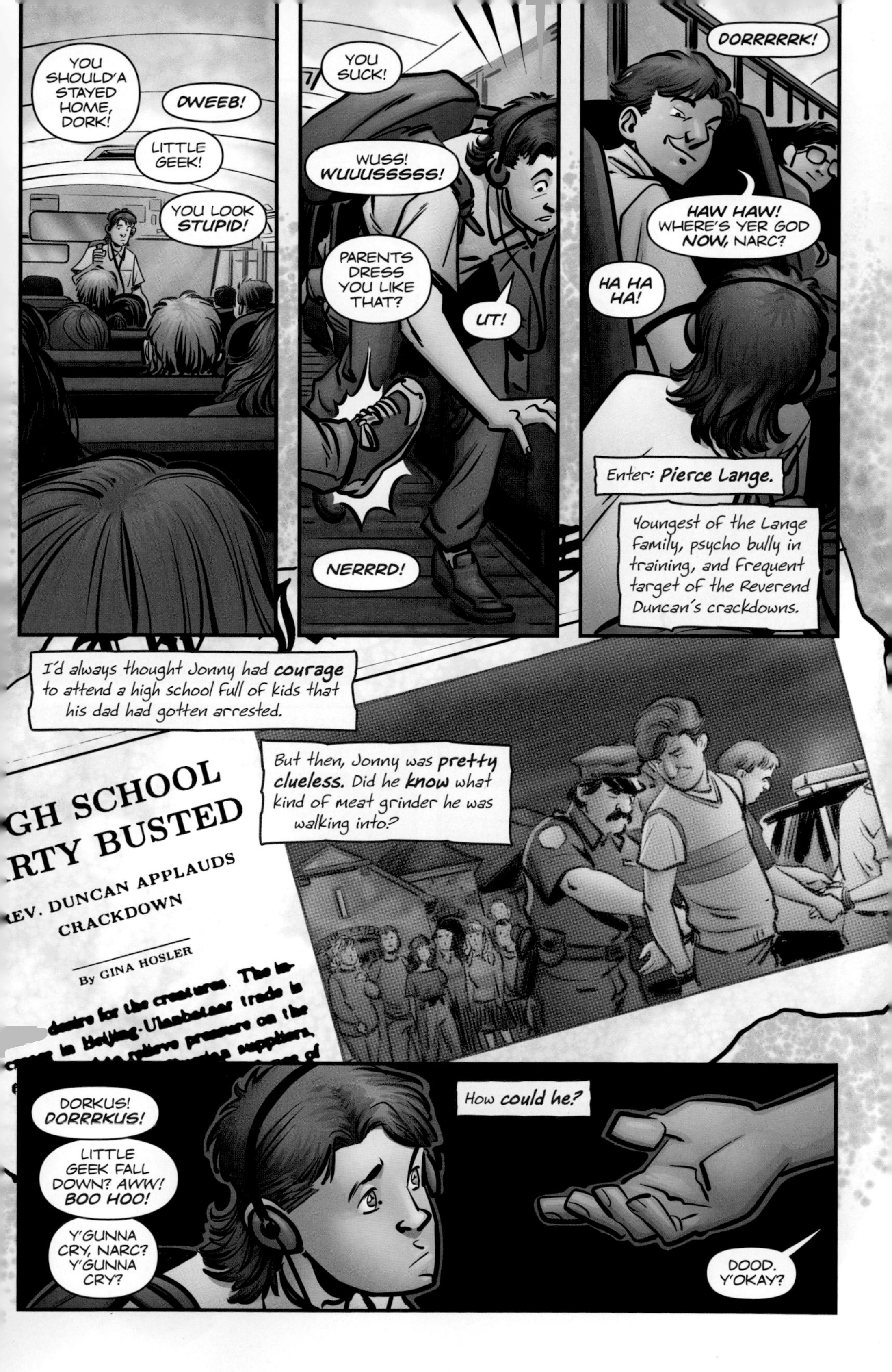
YOU SHOULD'A STAYED HOME, DORK!
DWEEB!
LITTLE GEEK!
YOU LOOK STUPID!
YOU SUCK!
WUSS! WUUUSSSSS!
PARENTS DRESS YOU LIKE THAT?
UT!
NERRRD!
DORRRRRK!
HAW HAW! WHERE'S YER GOD NOW, NARC?
HA HA HA!
Enter: Pierce Lange.
Youngest of the Lange family, psycho bully in training, and frequent target of the Reverend Duncan's crackdowns.
I'd always thought Jonny had courage to attend a high school full of kids that his dad had gotten arrested.
GH SCHOOL
RTY BUSTED
REV. DUNCAN APPLAUDS CRACKDOWN
By GINA HOSLER
But then, Jonny was pretty clueless. Did he know what kind of meat grinder he was walking into?
DORKUS! DORRRKUS!
LITTLE GEEK FALL DOWN? AWW! BOO HOO!
Y'GUNNA CRY, NARC? Y'GUNNA CRY?
How could he?
DOOD. Y'OKAY?

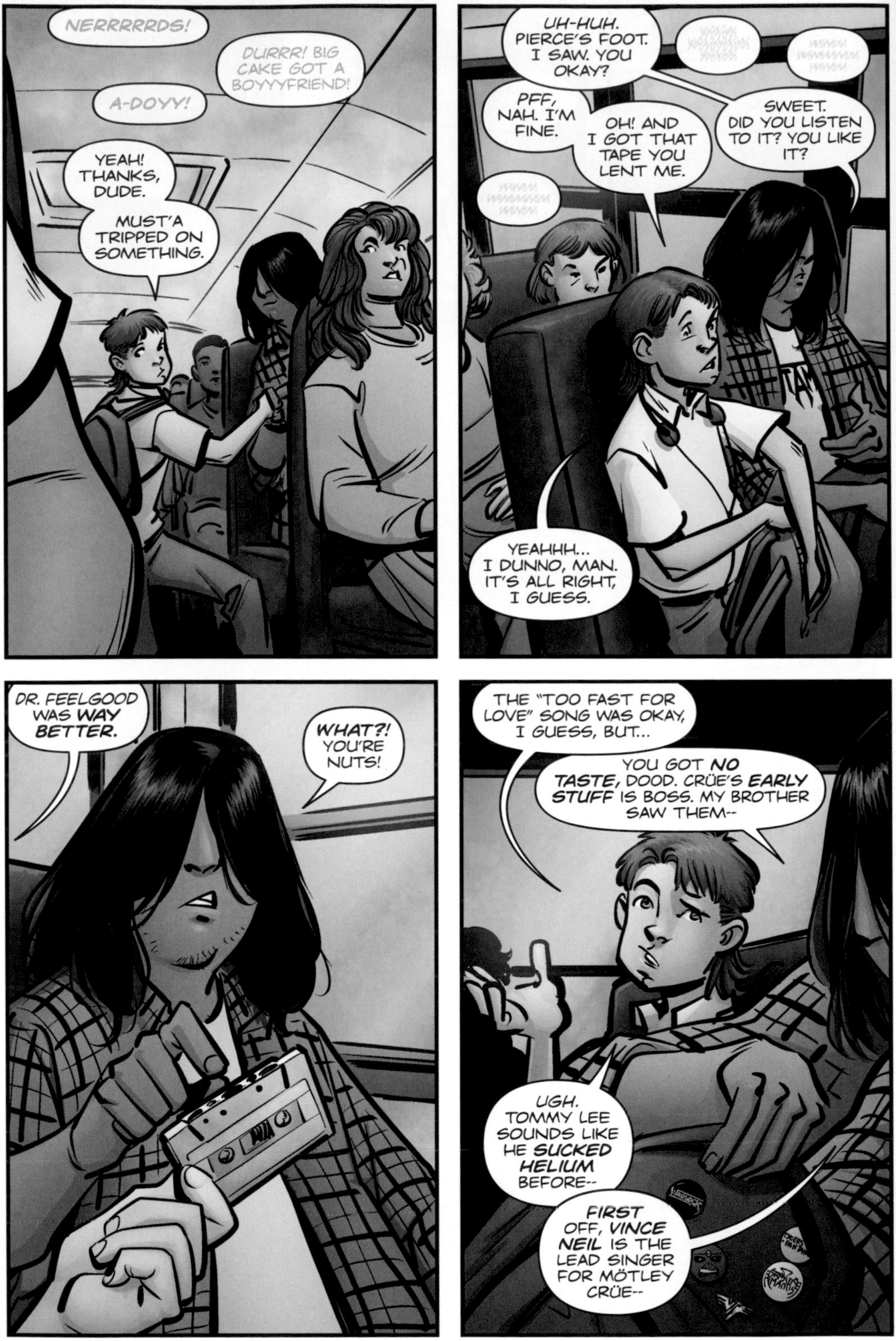
NERRRRRDS!
DURRR! BIG CAKE GOT A BOYYYFRIEND!
A-DOYY!
YEAH! THANKS, DUDE.
MUST'A TRIPPED ON SOMETHING.
UH-HUH. PIERCE'S FOOT. I SAW. YOU OKAY?
PFF, NAH. I'M FINE.
OH! AND I GOT THAT TAPE YOU LENT ME.
SWEET. DID YOU LISTEN TO IT? YOU LIKE IT?
YEAHHH... I DUNNO, MAN. IT'S ALL RIGHT, I GUESS.
DR. FEELGOOD WAS **WAY BETTER.**
WHAT?! YOU'RE NUTS!
THE "TOO FAST FOR LOVE" SONG WAS OKAY, I GUESS, BUT...
YOU GOT **NO TASTE,** DOOD. CRÜE'S **EARLY STUFF** IS BOSS. MY BROTHER SAW THEM--
UGH. TOMMY LEE SOUNDS LIKE HE ***SUCKED HELIUM*** BEFORE--
FIRST OFF, ***VINCE NEIL*** IS THE LEAD SINGER FOR MÖTLEY CRÜE--

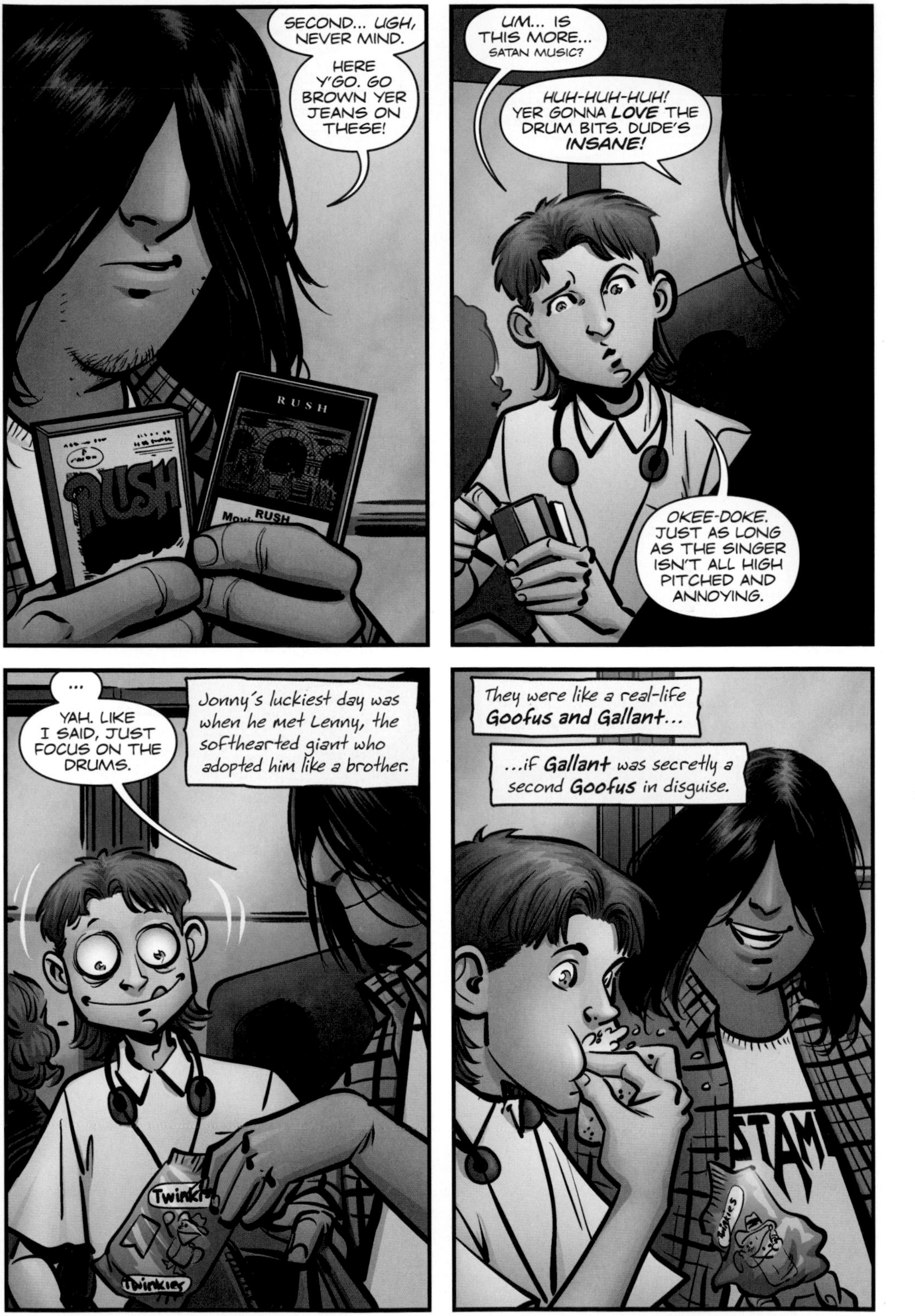

SECOND... UGH, NEVER MIND.
HERE Y'GO. GO BROWN YER JEANS ON THESE!
RUSH
RUSH
RUSH
UM... IS THIS MORE... SATAN MUSIC?
HUH-HUH-HUH! YER GONNA LOVE THE DRUM BITS. DUDE'S INSANE!
OKEE-DOKE. JUST AS LONG AS THE SINGER ISN'T ALL HIGH PITCHED AND ANNOYING.
...
YAH. LIKE I SAID, JUST FOCUS ON THE DRUMS.
Jonny's luckiest day was when he met Lenny, the softhearted giant who adopted him like a brother.
Twinkies
They were like a real-life Goofus and Gallant...
...if Gallant was secretly a second Goofus in disguise.

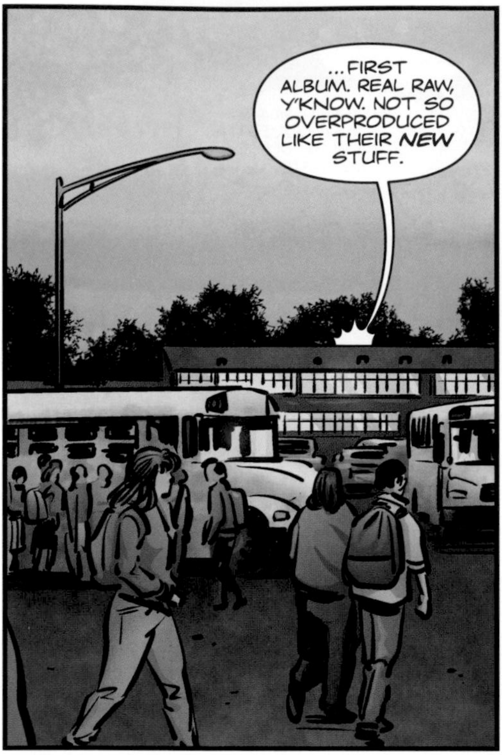
...FIRST ALBUM. REAL RAW, Y'KNOW. NOT SO OVERPRODUCED LIKE THEIR NEW STUFF.

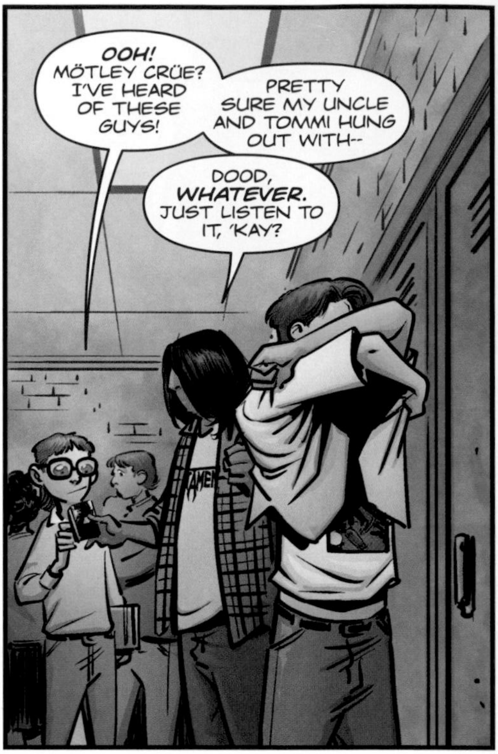
OOH! MÖTLEY CRÜE? I'VE HEARD OF THESE GUYS!
PRETTY SURE MY UNCLE AND TOMMI HUNG OUT WITH--
DOOD, WHATEVER. JUST LISTEN TO IT, 'KAY?

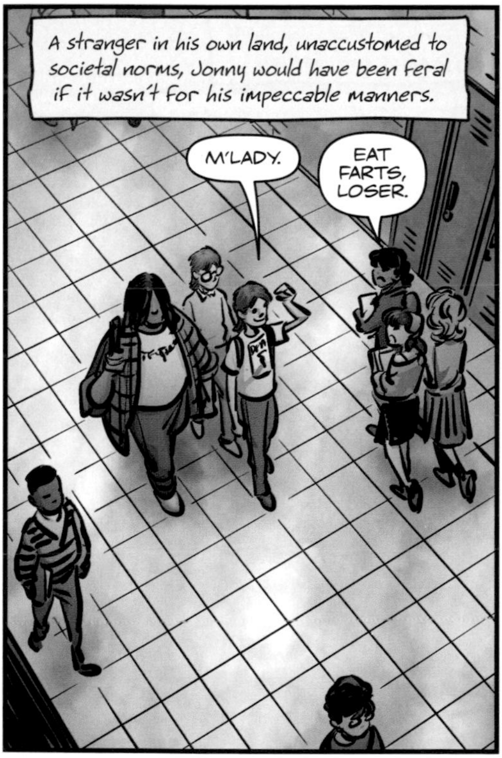
A stranger in his own land, unaccustomed to societal norms, Jonny would have been feral if it wasn't for his impeccable manners.
M'LADY.
EAT FARTS, LOSER.

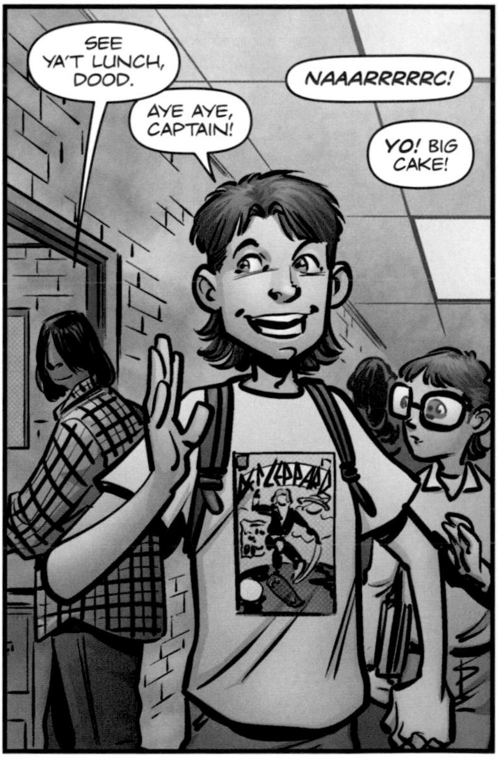
SEE YA'T LUNCH, DOOD.
AYE AYE, CAPTAIN!
NAAARRRRRC!
YO! BIG CAKE!

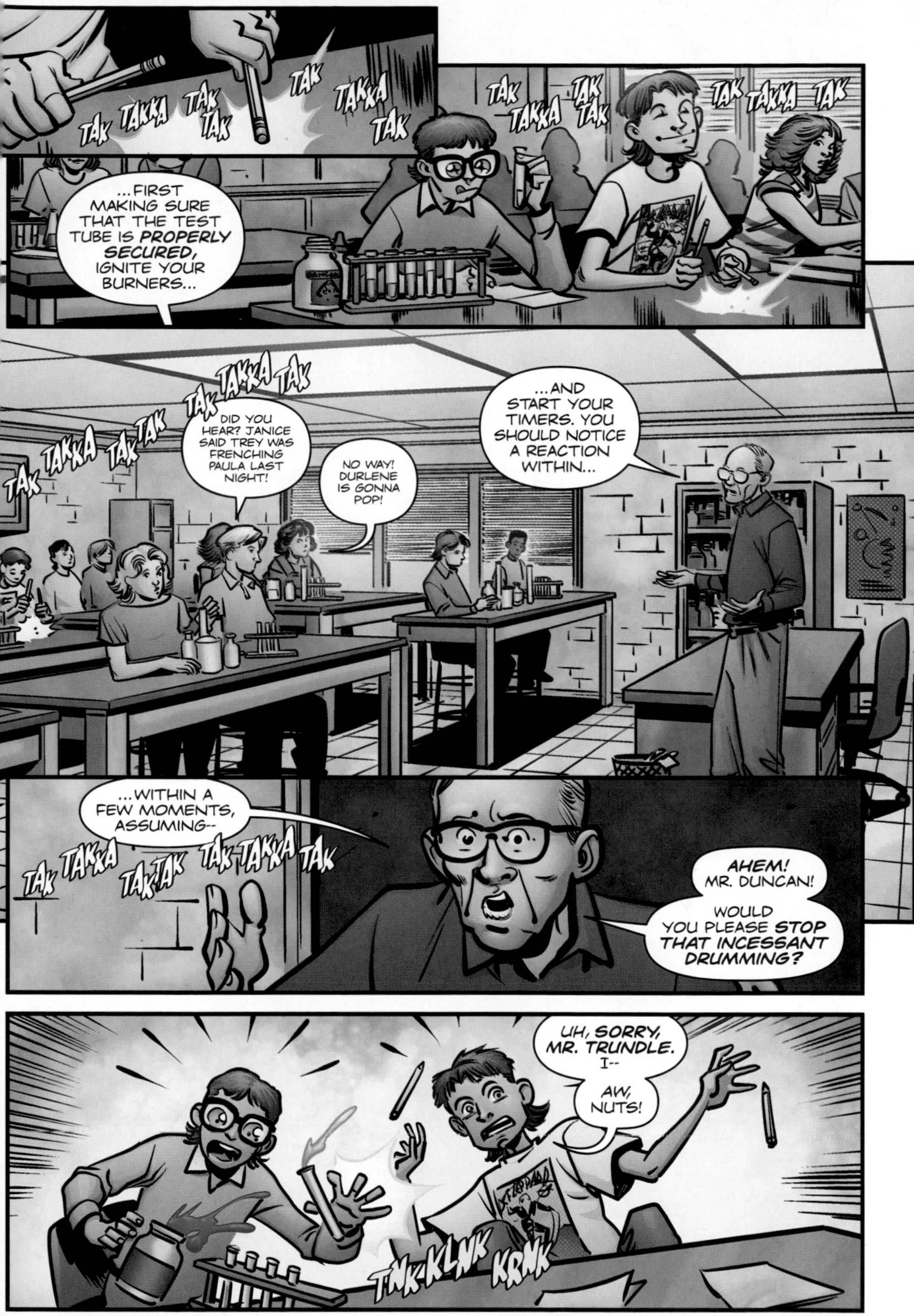
TAK TAKKA TAK TAK TAK TAKKA TAK
...FIRST MAKING SURE THAT THE TEST TUBE IS PROPERLY SECURED, IGNITE YOUR BURNERS...
TAK TAKKA TAK TAK
TAK TAKKA TAK
TAK TAKKA TAK TAK TAK TAKKA TAK
DID YOU HEAR? JANICE SAID TREY WAS FRENCHING PAULA LAST NIGHT!
NO WAY! DURLENE IS GONNA POP!
...AND START YOUR TIMERS. YOU SHOULD NOTICE A REACTION WITHIN...
...WITHIN A FEW MOMENTS, ASSUMING--
TAK TAKKA TAK TAK TAK TAKKA TAK
AHEM! MR. DUNCAN!
WOULD YOU PLEASE STOP THAT INCESSANT DRUMMING?
UH, SORRY, MR. TRUNDLE. I--
AW, NUTS!
TINK KLNK KRNK

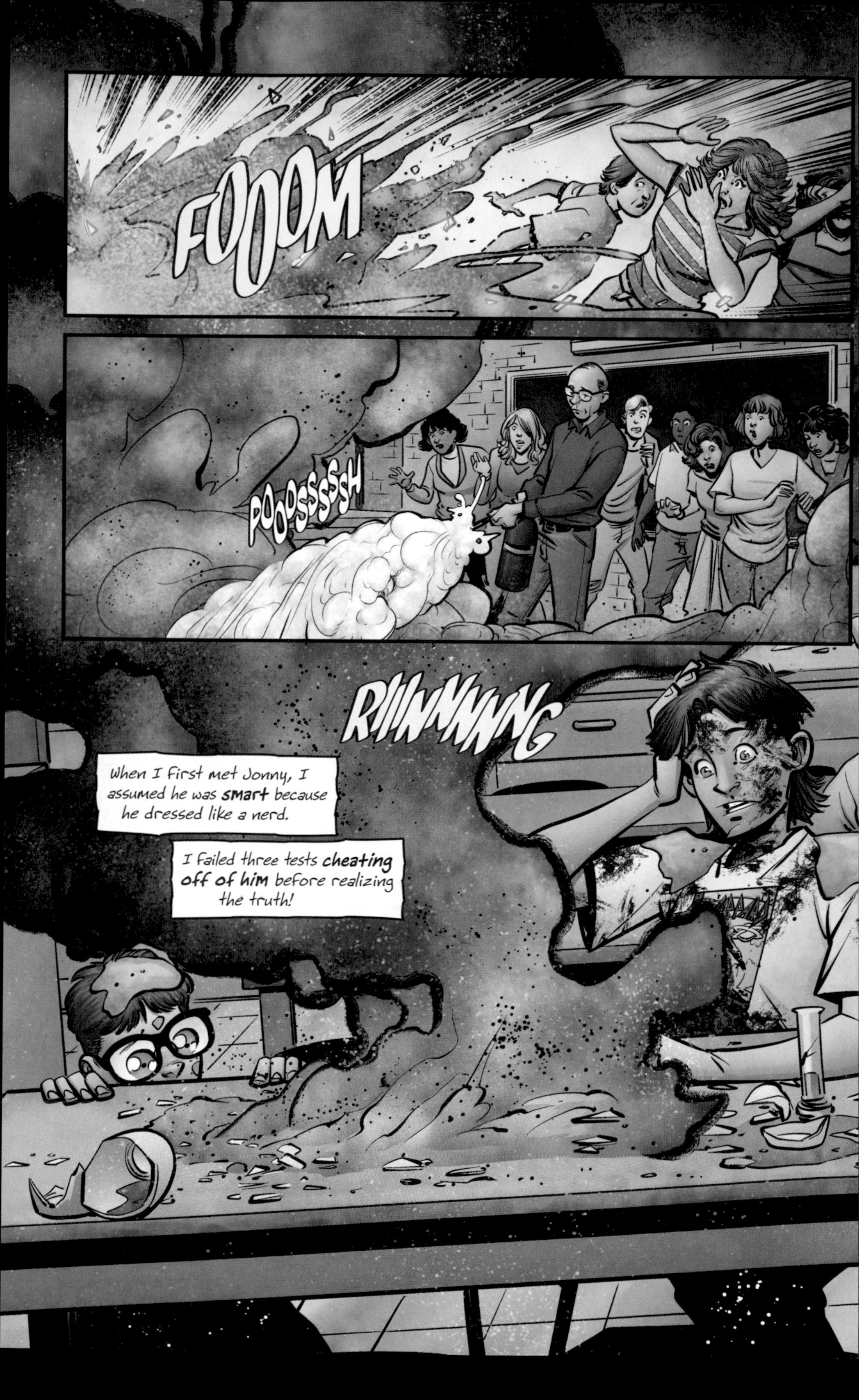
FOOOM
POOOSSSSSH
RIIINNNNNG
When I first met Jonny, I assumed he was **smart** because he dressed like a nerd.
I failed three tests **cheating off of him** before realizing the truth!

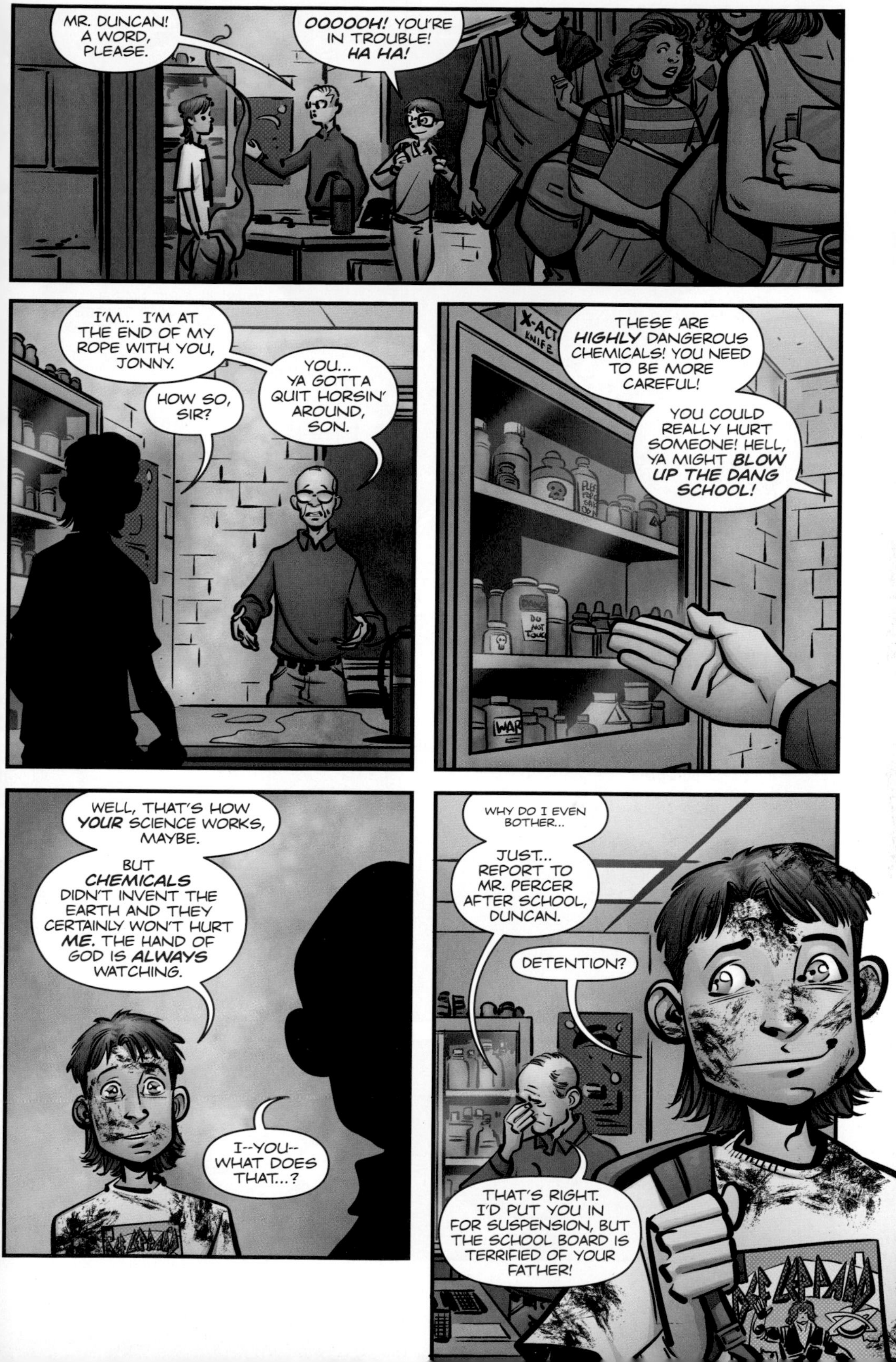

MR. DUNCAN! A WORD, PLEASE.
OOOOOH! YOU'RE IN TROUBLE! HA HA!
I'M... I'M AT THE END OF MY ROPE WITH YOU, JONNY.
HOW SO, SIR?
YOU... YA GOTTA QUIT HORSIN' AROUND, SON.
X-ACTO KNIFE
THESE ARE HIGHLY DANGEROUS CHEMICALS! YOU NEED TO BE MORE CAREFUL!
YOU COULD REALLY HURT SOMEONE! HELL, YA MIGHT BLOW UP THE DANG SCHOOL!
DO NOT TOUCH
WELL, THAT'S HOW YOUR SCIENCE WORKS, MAYBE.
BUT CHEMICALS DIDN'T INVENT THE EARTH AND THEY CERTAINLY WON'T HURT ME. THE HAND OF GOD IS ALWAYS WATCHING.
I--YOU-- WHAT DOES THAT...?
WHY DO I EVEN BOTHER...
JUST... REPORT TO MR. PERCER AFTER SCHOOL, DUNCAN.
DETENTION?
THAT'S RIGHT. I'D PUT YOU IN FOR SUSPENSION, BUT THE SCHOOL BOARD IS TERRIFIED OF YOUR FATHER!

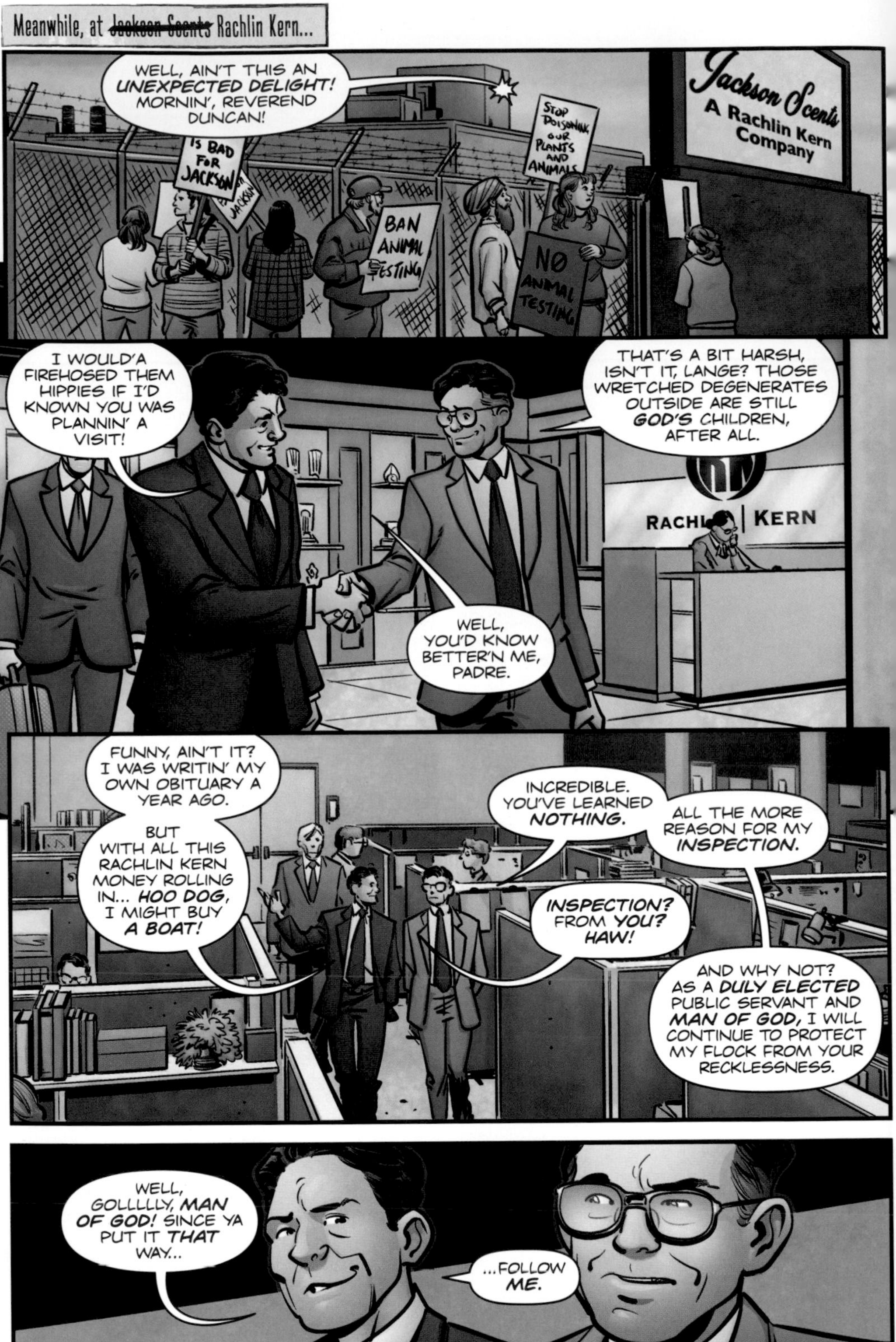
Meanwhile, at Jackson Scents Rachlin Kern...
WELL, AIN'T THIS AN UNEXPECTED DELIGHT! MORNIN', REVEREND DUNCAN!
Jackson Scents A Rachlin Kern Company
IS BAD FOR JACKSON
STOP POISONING OUR PLANTS AND ANIMALS
BAN ANIMAL TESTING
NO ANIMAL TESTING
I WOULD'A FIREHOSED THEM HIPPIES IF I'D KNOWN YOU WAS PLANNIN' A VISIT!
THAT'S A BIT HARSH, ISN'T IT, LANGE? THOSE WRETCHED DEGENERATES OUTSIDE ARE STILL GOD'S CHILDREN, AFTER ALL.
WELL, YOU'D KNOW BETTER'N ME, PADRE.
FUNNY, AIN'T IT? I WAS WRITIN' MY OWN OBITUARY A YEAR AGO.
BUT WITH ALL THIS RACHLIN KERN MONEY ROLLING IN... HOO DOG, I MIGHT BUY A BOAT!
INCREDIBLE. YOU'VE LEARNED NOTHING.
ALL THE MORE REASON FOR MY INSPECTION.
INSPECTION? FROM YOU? HAW!
AND WHY NOT? AS A DULY ELECTED PUBLIC SERVANT AND MAN OF GOD, I WILL CONTINUE TO PROTECT MY FLOCK FROM YOUR RECKLESSNESS.
WELL, GOLLLLLY, MAN OF GOD! SINCE YA PUT IT THAT WAY...
...FOLLOW ME.

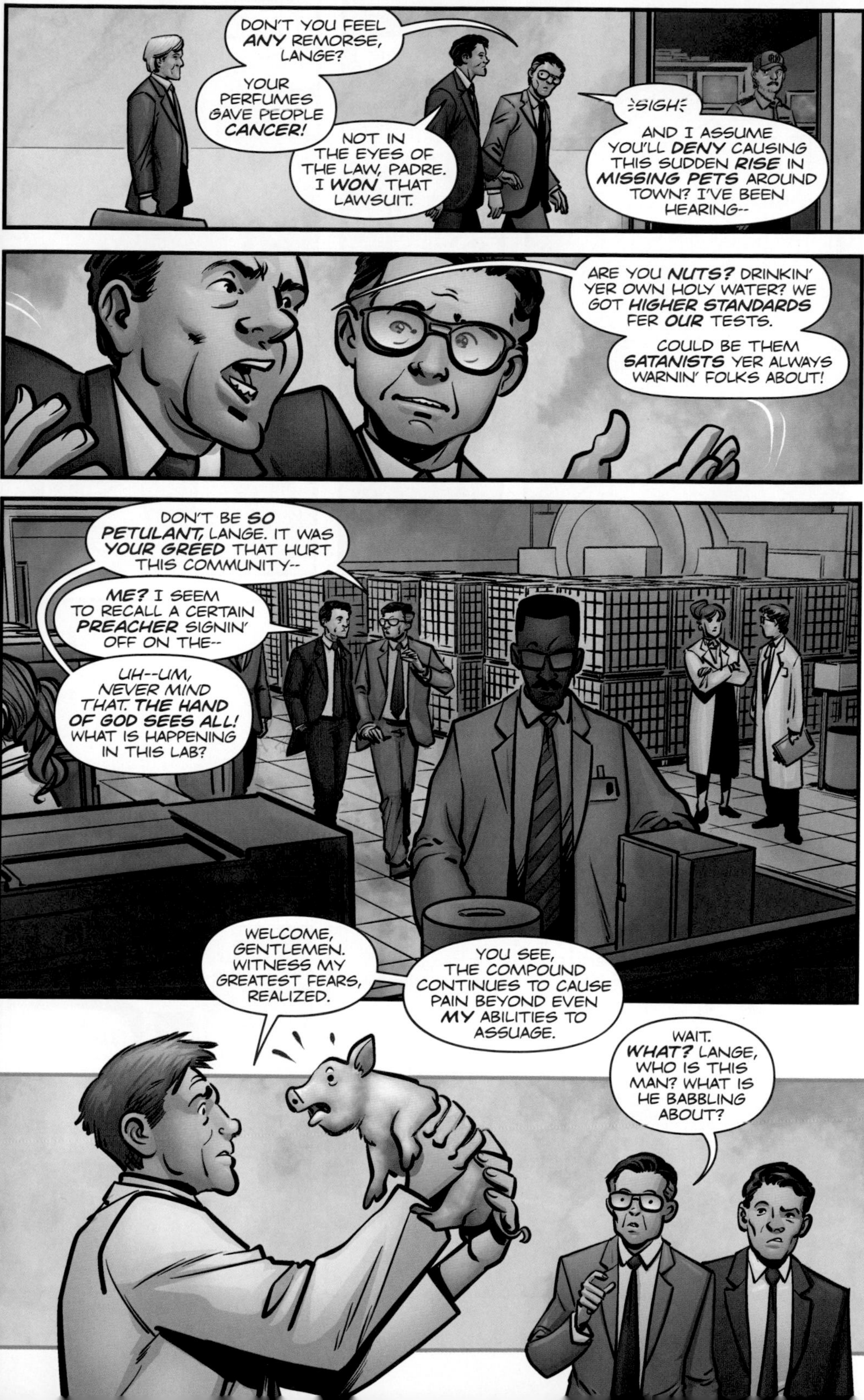
DON'T YOU FEEL ANY REMORSE, LANGE?
YOUR PERFUMES GAVE PEOPLE CANCER!
NOT IN THE EYES OF THE LAW, PADRE. I WON THAT LAWSUIT.
SIGH
AND I ASSUME YOU'LL DENY CAUSING THIS SUDDEN RISE IN MISSING PETS AROUND TOWN? I'VE BEEN HEARING--
ARE YOU NUTS? DRINKIN' YER OWN HOLY WATER? WE GOT HIGHER STANDARDS FER OUR TESTS.
COULD BE THEM SATANISTS YER ALWAYS WARNIN' FOLKS ABOUT!
DON'T BE SO PETULANT, LANGE. IT WAS YOUR GREED THAT HURT THIS COMMUNITY--
ME? I SEEM TO RECALL A CERTAIN PREACHER SIGNIN' OFF ON THE--
UH--UM, NEVER MIND THAT. THE HAND OF GOD SEES ALL! WHAT IS HAPPENING IN THIS LAB?
WELCOME, GENTLEMEN. WITNESS MY GREATEST FEARS, REALIZED.
YOU SEE, THE COMPOUND CONTINUES TO CAUSE PAIN BEYOND EVEN MY ABILITIES TO ASSUAGE.
WAIT. WHAT? LANGE, WHO IS THIS MAN? WHAT IS HE BABBLING ABOUT?

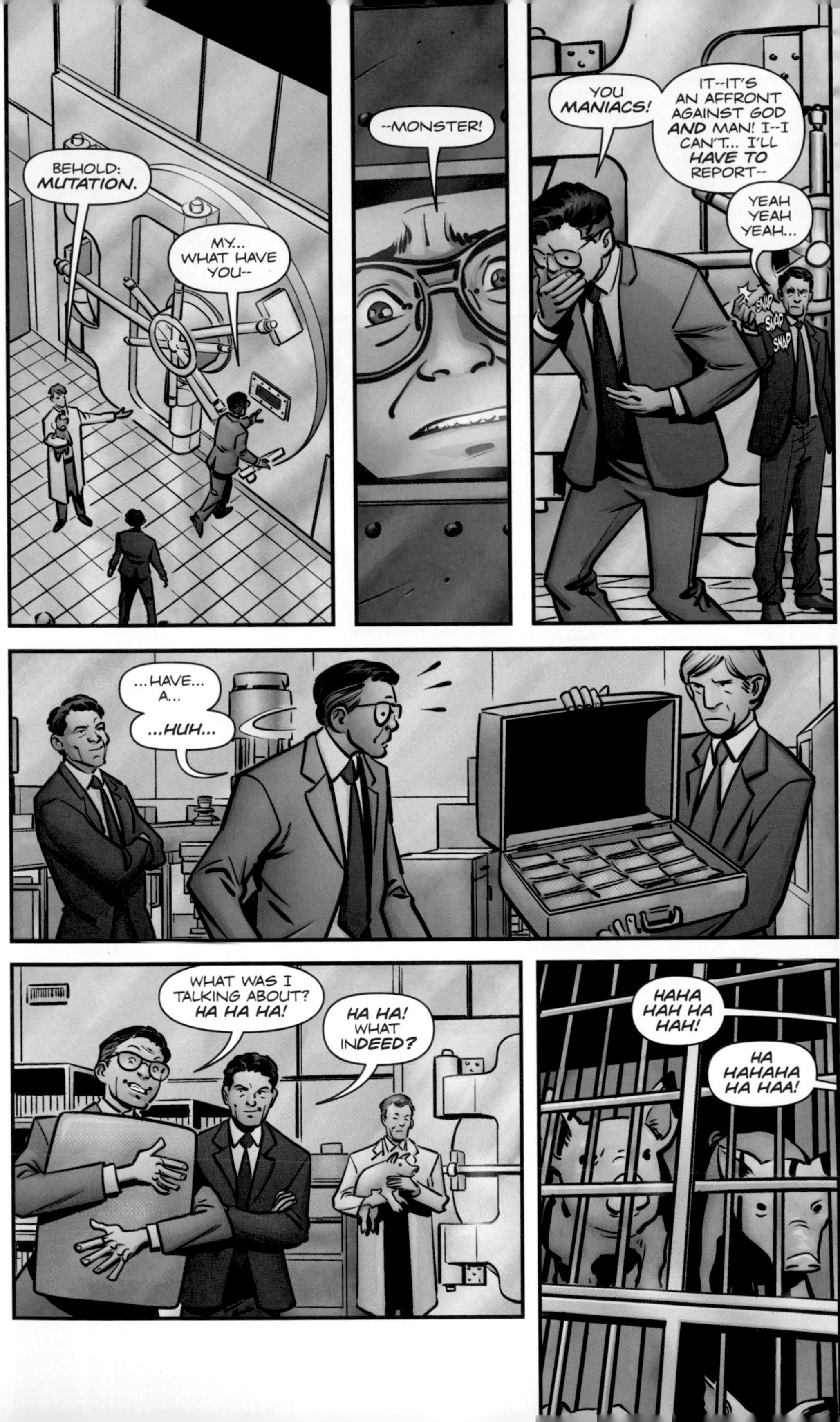
BEHOLD: MUTATION.
MY... WHAT HAVE YOU--
--MONSTER!
YOU MANIACS!
IT--IT'S AN AFFRONT AGAINST GOD AND MAN! I--I CAN'T... I'LL HAVE TO REPORT--
YEAH YEAH YEAH...
SNAP SNAP SNAP
...HAVE... A... ...HUH...
WHAT WAS I TALKING ABOUT? HA HA HA!
HA HA! WHAT INDEED?
HAHA HAH HA HAH!
HA HAHAHA HA HAA!

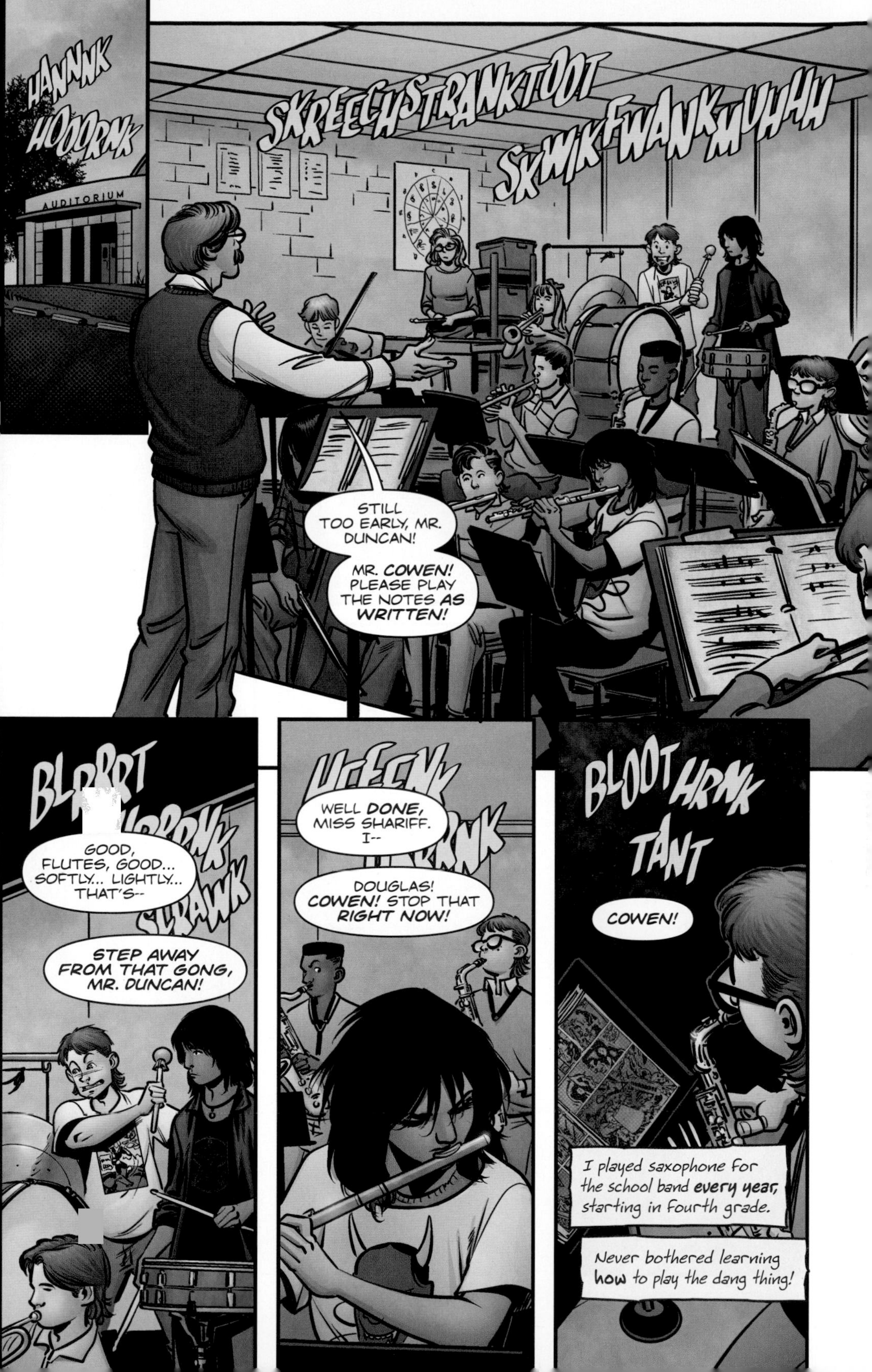
HANNNK
HOOORNK
AUDITORIUM
SKREECHSTRANKTOOT
SKWIKFWANKMUHHH
STILL TOO EARLY, MR. DUNCAN!
MR. COWEN! PLEASE PLAY THE NOTES AS WRITTEN!
BLRRRT
GOOD, FLUTES, GOOD... SOFTLY... LIGHTLY... THAT'S--
STEP AWAY FROM THAT GONG, MR. DUNCAN!
WELL DONE, MISS SHARIFF. I--
DOUGLAS! COWEN! STOP THAT RIGHT NOW!
BLOOT HRNK
TANT
COWEN!
I played saxophone for the school band every year, starting in fourth grade.
Never bothered learning how to play the dang thing!

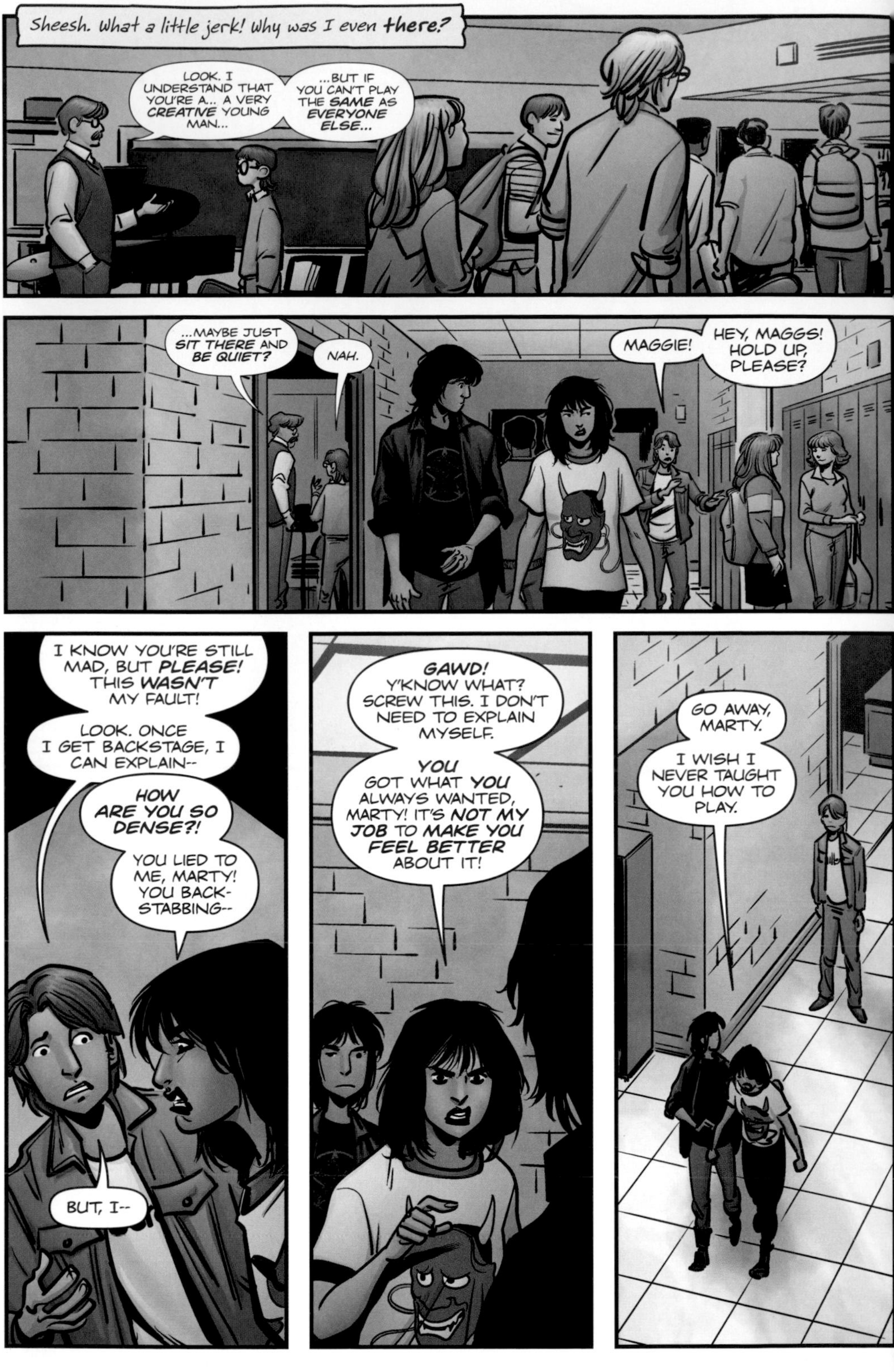
Sheesh. What a little jerk! Why was I even there?
LOOK. I UNDERSTAND THAT YOU'RE A... A VERY CREATIVE YOUNG MAN...
...BUT IF YOU CAN'T PLAY THE SAME AS EVERYONE ELSE...
...MAYBE JUST SIT THERE AND BE QUIET?
NAH.
MAGGIE!
HEY, MAGGS! HOLD UP, PLEASE?
I KNOW YOU'RE STILL MAD, BUT PLEASE! THIS WASN'T MY FAULT!
LOOK. ONCE I GET BACKSTAGE, I CAN EXPLAIN--
HOW ARE YOU SO DENSE?!
YOU LIED TO ME, MARTY! YOU BACK-STABBING--
BUT, I--
GAWD! Y'KNOW WHAT? SCREW THIS. I DON'T NEED TO EXPLAIN MYSELF.
YOU GOT WHAT YOU ALWAYS WANTED, MARTY! IT'S NOT MY JOB TO MAKE YOU FEEL BETTER ABOUT IT!
GO AWAY, MARTY.
I WISH I NEVER TAUGHT YOU HOW TO PLAY.

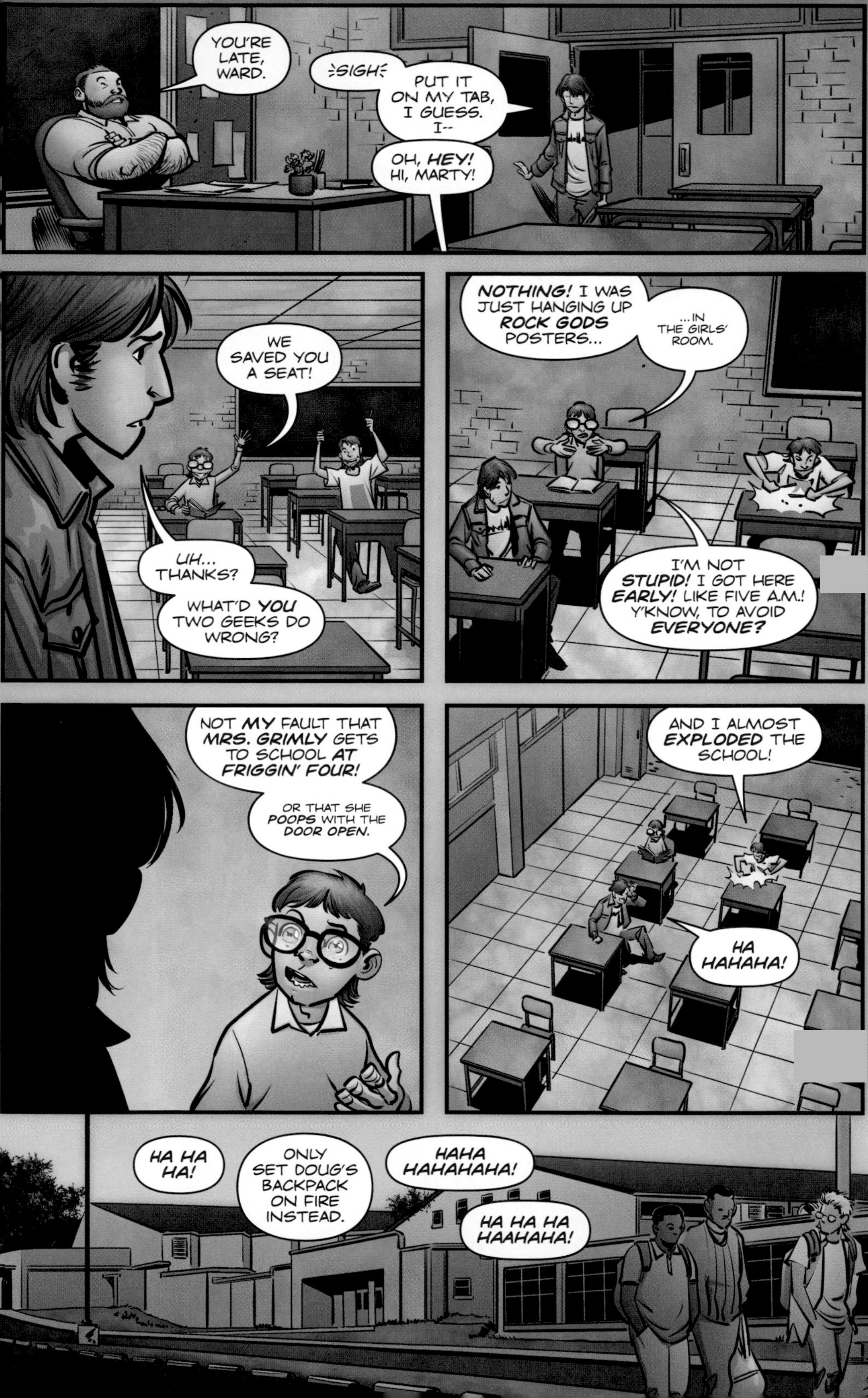

YOU'RE LATE, WARD.
SIGH
PUT IT ON MY TAB, I GUESS. I--
OH, HEY! HI, MARTY!
WE SAVED YOU A SEAT!
UH... THANKS?
WHAT'D YOU TWO GEEKS DO WRONG?
NOTHING! I WAS JUST HANGING UP ROCK GODS POSTERS...
...IN THE GIRLS' ROOM.
I'M NOT STUPID! I GOT HERE EARLY! LIKE FIVE A.M.! Y'KNOW, TO AVOID EVERYONE?
NOT MY FAULT THAT MRS. GRIMLY GETS TO SCHOOL AT FRIGGIN' FOUR!
OR THAT SHE POOPS WITH THE DOOR OPEN.
AND I ALMOST EXPLODED THE SCHOOL!
HA HAHAHA!
HA HA HA!
ONLY SET DOUG'S BACKPACK ON FIRE INSTEAD.
HAHA HAHAHAHA!
HA HA HA HAAHAHA!

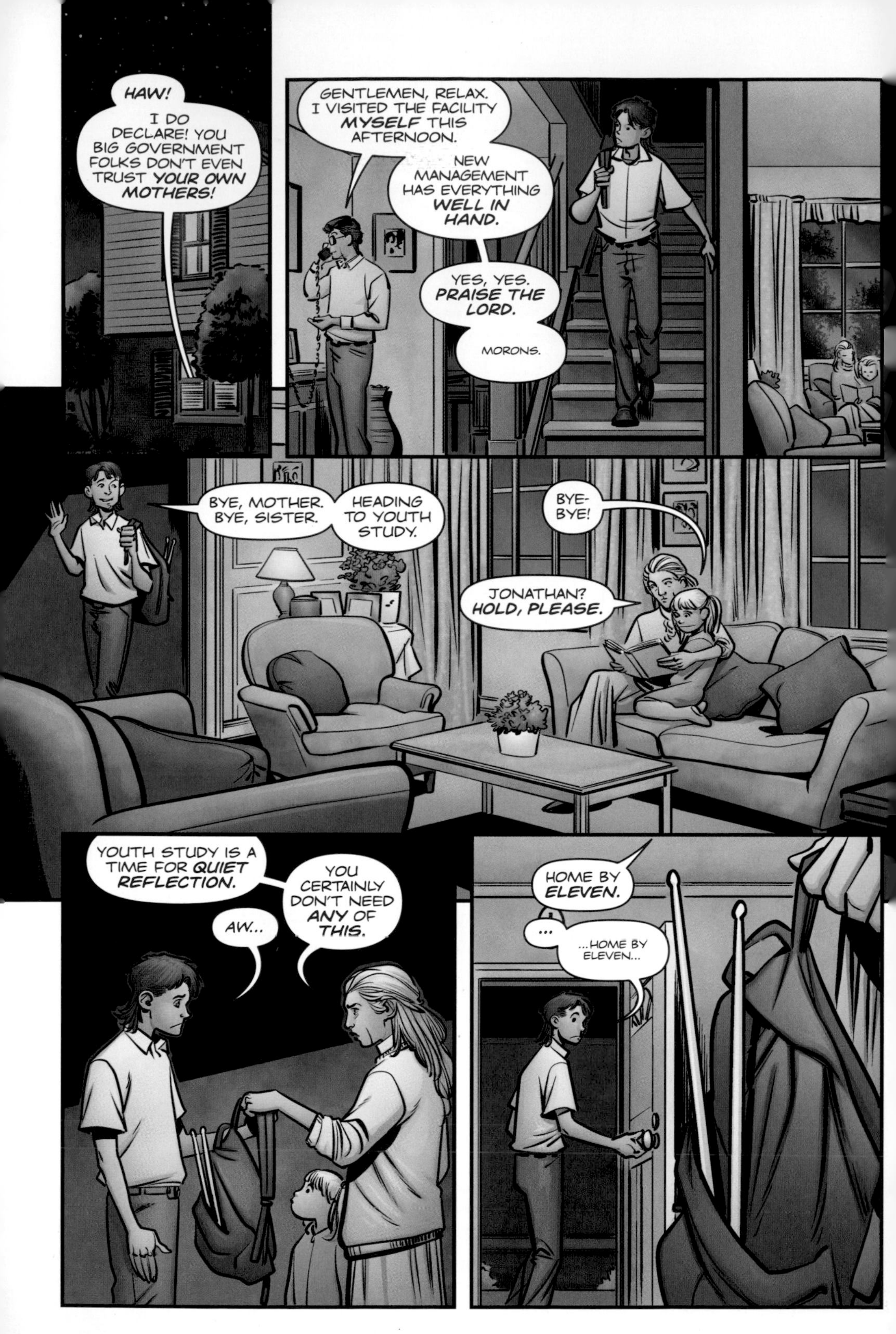
HAW!
I DO DECLARE! YOU BIG GOVERNMENT FOLKS DON'T EVEN TRUST YOUR OWN MOTHERS!
GENTLEMEN, RELAX. I VISITED THE FACILITY MYSELF THIS AFTERNOON.
NEW MANAGEMENT HAS EVERYTHING WELL IN HAND.
YES, YES. PRAISE THE LORD.
MORONS.
BYE, MOTHER. BYE, SISTER.
HEADING TO YOUTH STUDY.
BYE-BYE!
JONATHAN? HOLD, PLEASE.
YOUTH STUDY IS A TIME FOR QUIET REFLECTION.
YOU CERTAINLY DON'T NEED ANY OF THIS.
AW...
HOME BY ELEVEN.
...
...HOME BY ELEVEN...

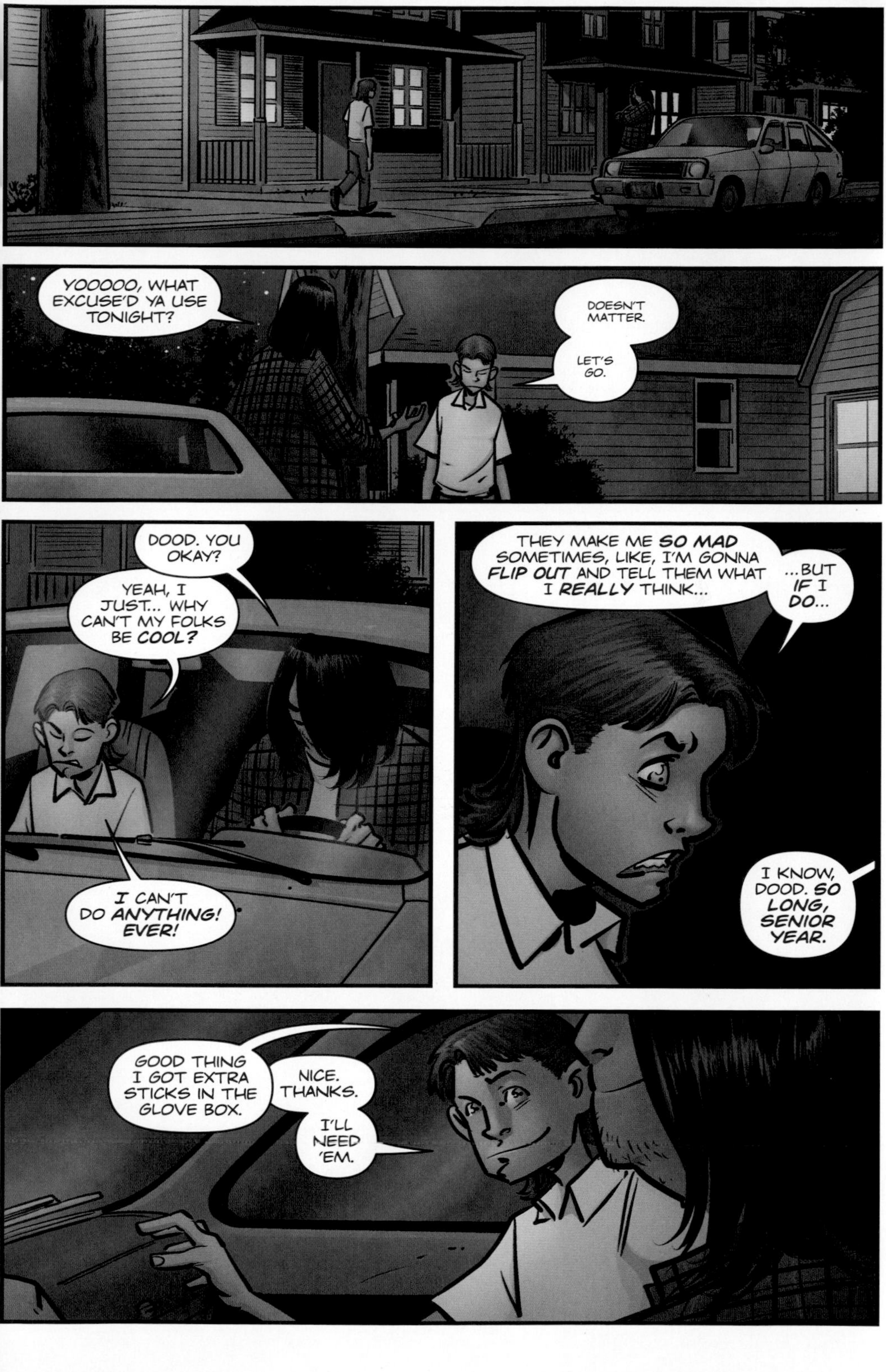
YOOOOO, WHAT EXCUSE'D YA USE TONIGHT?
DOESN'T MATTER.
LET'S GO.
DOOD. YOU OKAY?
YEAH, I JUST... WHY CAN'T MY FOLKS BE COOL?
I CAN'T DO ANYTHING! EVER!
THEY MAKE ME SO MAD SOMETIMES, LIKE, I'M GONNA FLIP OUT AND TELL THEM WHAT I REALLY THINK...
...BUT IF I DO...
I KNOW, DOOD. SO LONG, SENIOR YEAR.
GOOD THING I GOT EXTRA STICKS IN THE GLOVE BOX.
NICE. THANKS.
I'LL NEED 'EM.

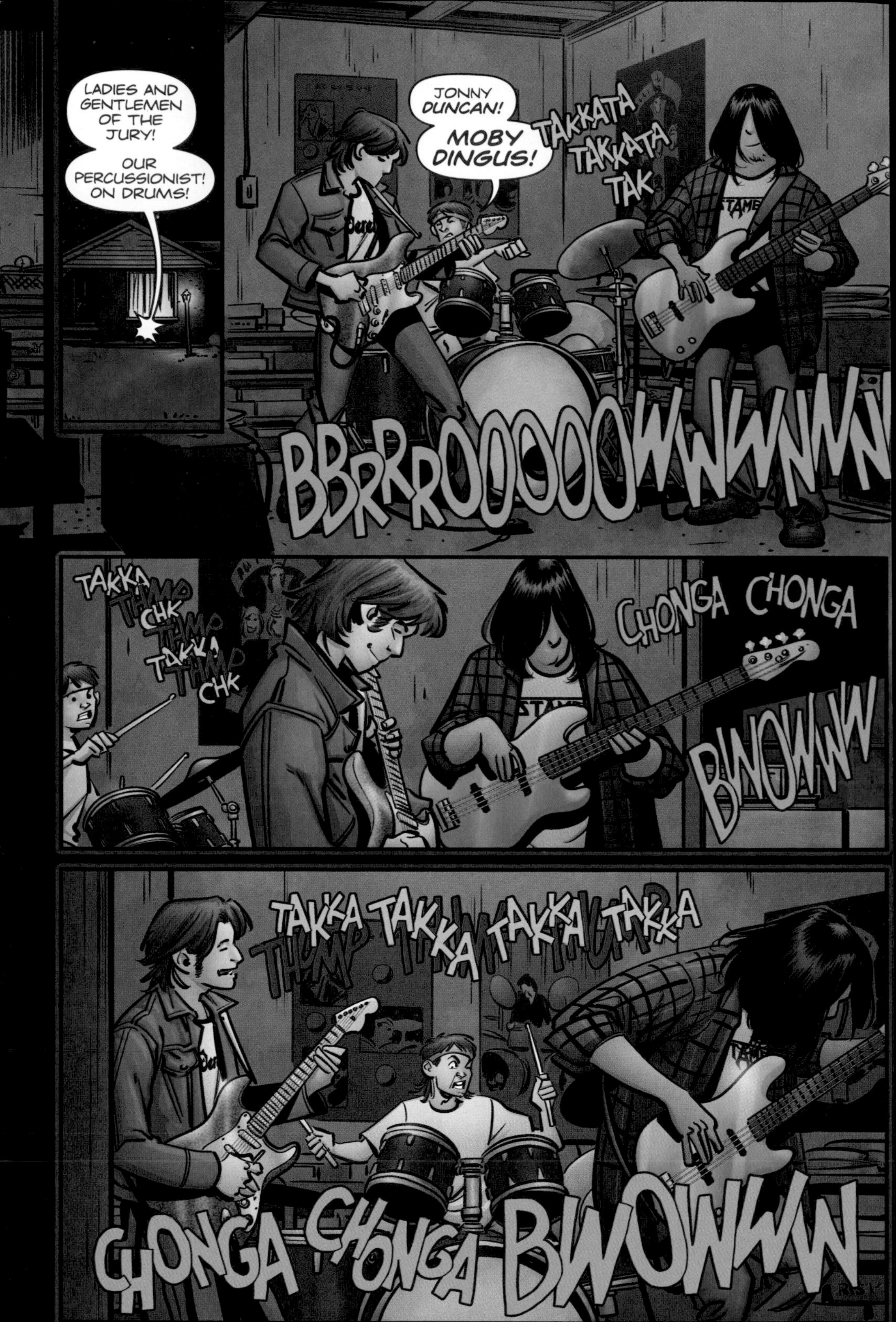

LADIES AND GENTLEMEN OF THE JURY!
OUR PERCUSSIONIST! ON DRUMS!
JONNY DUNCAN!
MOBY DINGUS!
TAKKATA TAKKATA TAK
BBRRROOOOOOWWWNNN
TAKKA THMP CHK THMP TAKKA THMP CHK
CHONGA CHONGA
BWOWWW
TAKKA TAKKA TAKKA TAKKA
THMP
CHONGA CHONGA BWOWWN

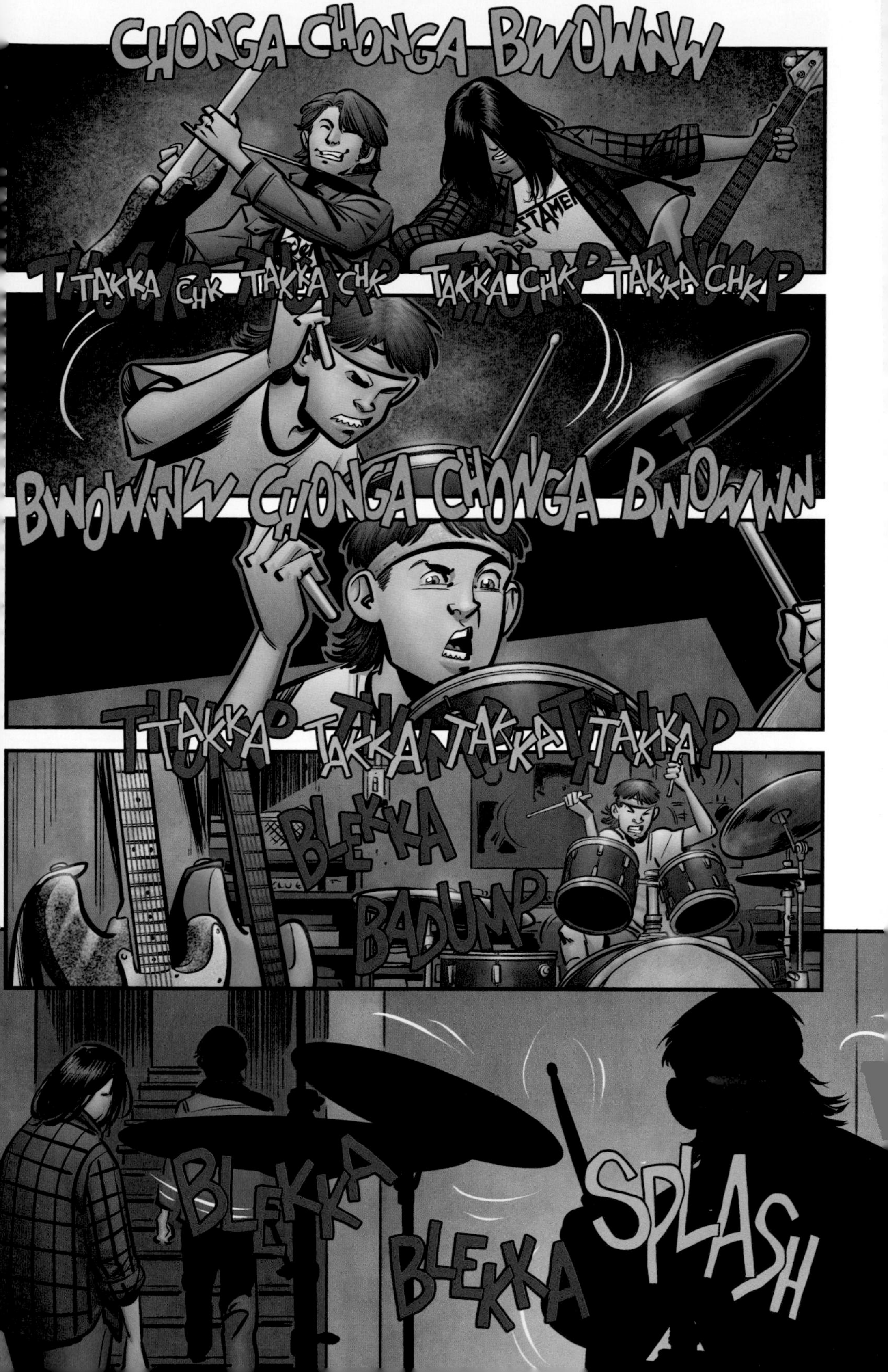
CHONGA CHONGA BWOWWW
TAKKA CHK TAKKA CHK TAKKA CHK TAKKA CHK
BWOWWW CHONGA CHONGA BWOWWW
TAKKA TAKKA TAKKA TAKKA
BLEKKA
BADUMP
BLEKKA
BLEKKA
SPLASH

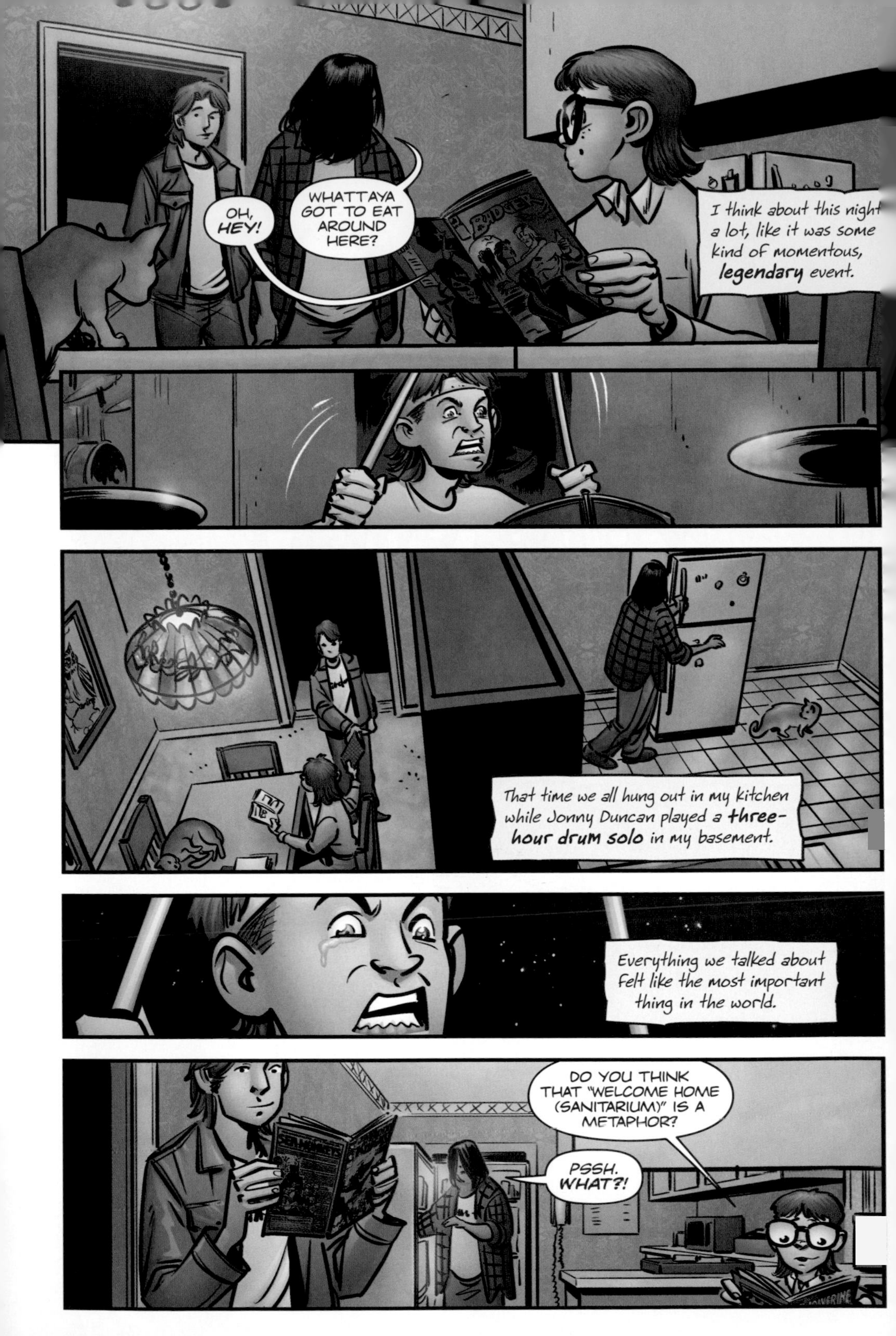
WHATTAYA GOT TO EAT AROUND HERE?
OH, HEY!
I think about this night a lot, like it was some kind of momentous, legendary event.
That time we all hung out in my kitchen while Jonny Duncan played a three-hour drum solo in my basement.
Everything we talked about felt like the most important thing in the world.
DO YOU THINK THAT "WELCOME HOME (SANITARIUM)" IS A METAPHOR?
PSSH. WHAT?!

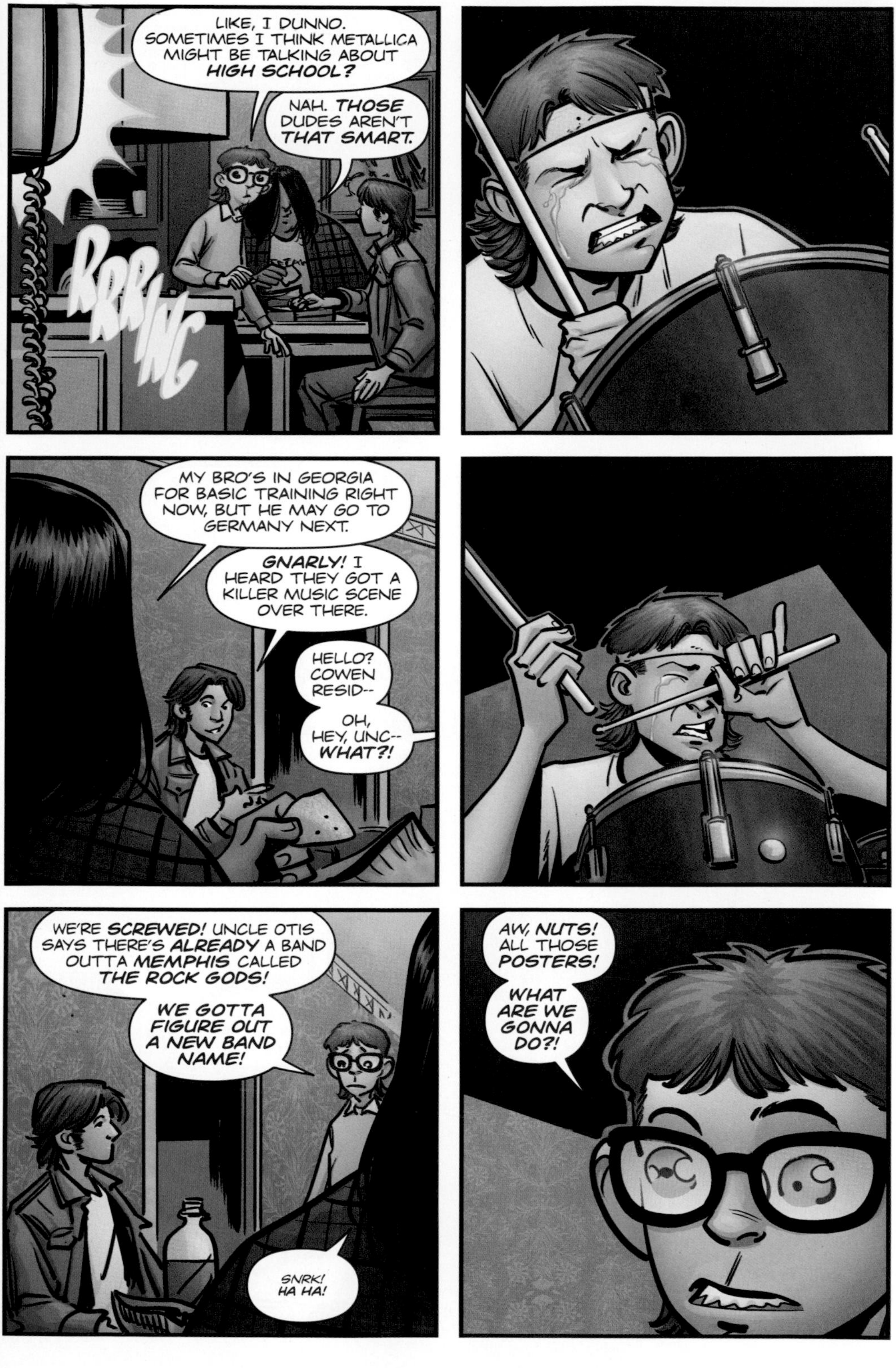
LIKE, I DUNNO. SOMETIMES I THINK METALLICA MIGHT BE TALKING ABOUT HIGH SCHOOL?
NAH. THOSE DUDES AREN'T THAT SMART.
RRRING
MY BRO'S IN GEORGIA FOR BASIC TRAINING RIGHT NOW, BUT HE MAY GO TO GERMANY NEXT.
GNARLY! I HEARD THEY GOT A KILLER MUSIC SCENE OVER THERE.
HELLO? COWEN RESID--
OH, HEY, UNC-- WHAT?!
WE'RE SCREWED! UNCLE OTIS SAYS THERE'S ALREADY A BAND OUTTA MEMPHIS CALLED THE ROCK GODS!
WE GOTTA FIGURE OUT A NEW BAND NAME!
SNRK! HA HA!
AW, NUTS! ALL THOSE POSTERS!
WHAT ARE WE GONNA DO?!

YEAH, I GUESS MAGGIE'S GOT A POINT BUT I DUNNO...

DOOD, YA GOTTA QUIT OBSESSING.

UH... TOMBSTONE? PANCREAS IN REMISSION? *UGH,* NO. CHERNOBYLMEN? NO, THAT'S STUPID...

SASQUATCH ARMY?

DREAM RIVER EXPLOSION?

DEATH STINK? STINK DEATH?

BARTHOLOMEW! JAY! *PETTIBONE!*

CHÜBÄKKÄ? WE COULD SPELL IT ALL METAL...

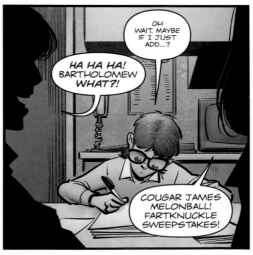

OH WAIT. MAYBE IF I JUST ADD...?

HA HA HA! BARTHOLOMEW *WHAT?!*

COUGAR JAMES MELONBALL! FARTKNUCKLE SWEEPSTAKES!

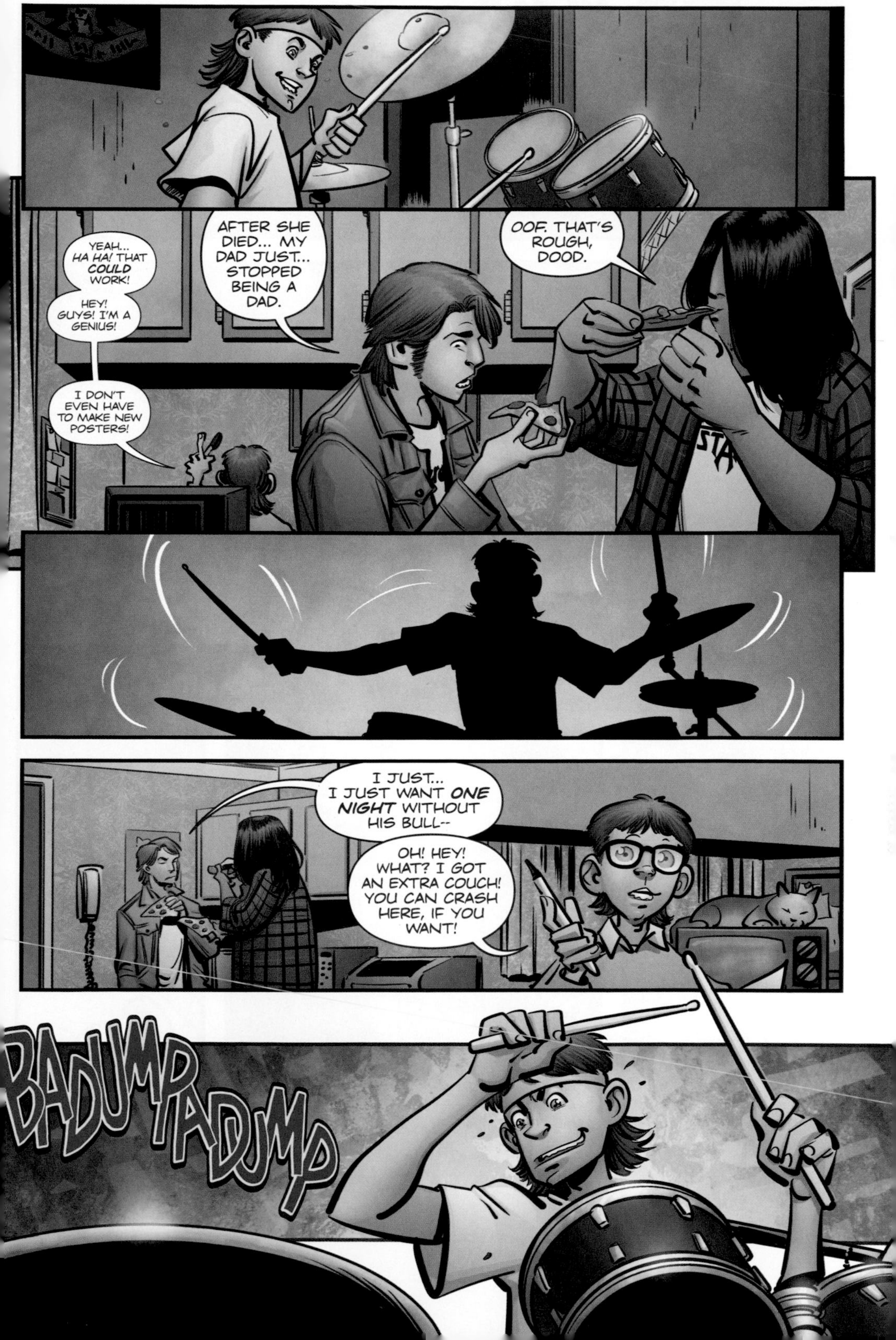
YEAH... HA HA! THAT COULD WORK!
HEY! GUYS! I'M A GENIUS!
I DON'T EVEN HAVE TO MAKE NEW POSTERS!
AFTER SHE DIED... MY DAD JUST... STOPPED BEING A DAD.
OOF. THAT'S ROUGH, DOOD.
I JUST... I JUST WANT ONE NIGHT WITHOUT HIS BULL--
OH! HEY! WHAT? I GOT AN EXTRA COUCH! YOU CAN CRASH HERE, IF YOU WANT!
BADUMPADUMP

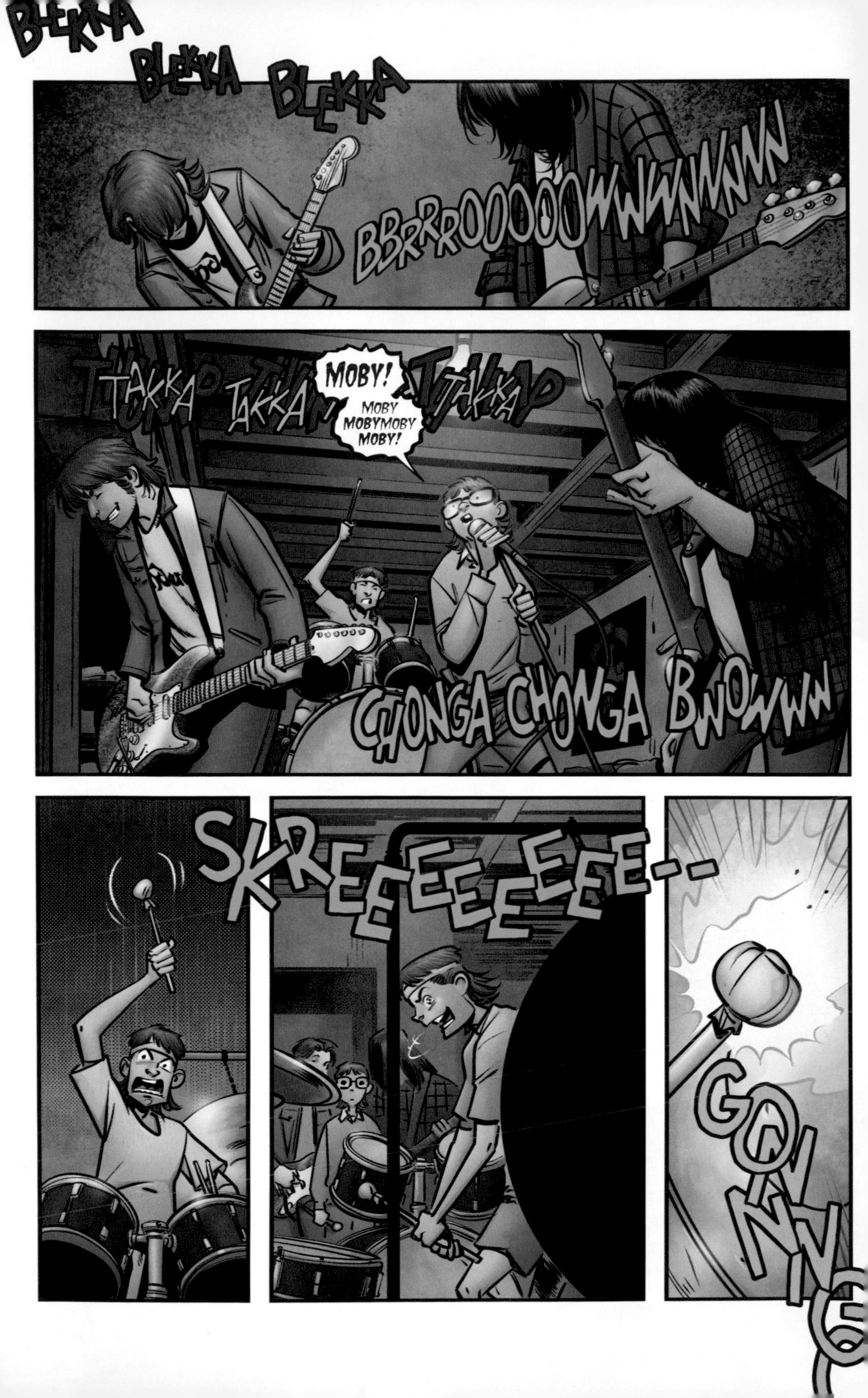
BLEKKA
BLEKKA
BLEKKA
BBRRROOOOOOWWWNNNNN
TTAKKAP
TAKKA
TTAKKAP
MOBY!
MOBY MOBYMOBY MOBY!
CHONGA CHONGA BNOWWW
SKREEEEEEEEEE--
GONNNNG

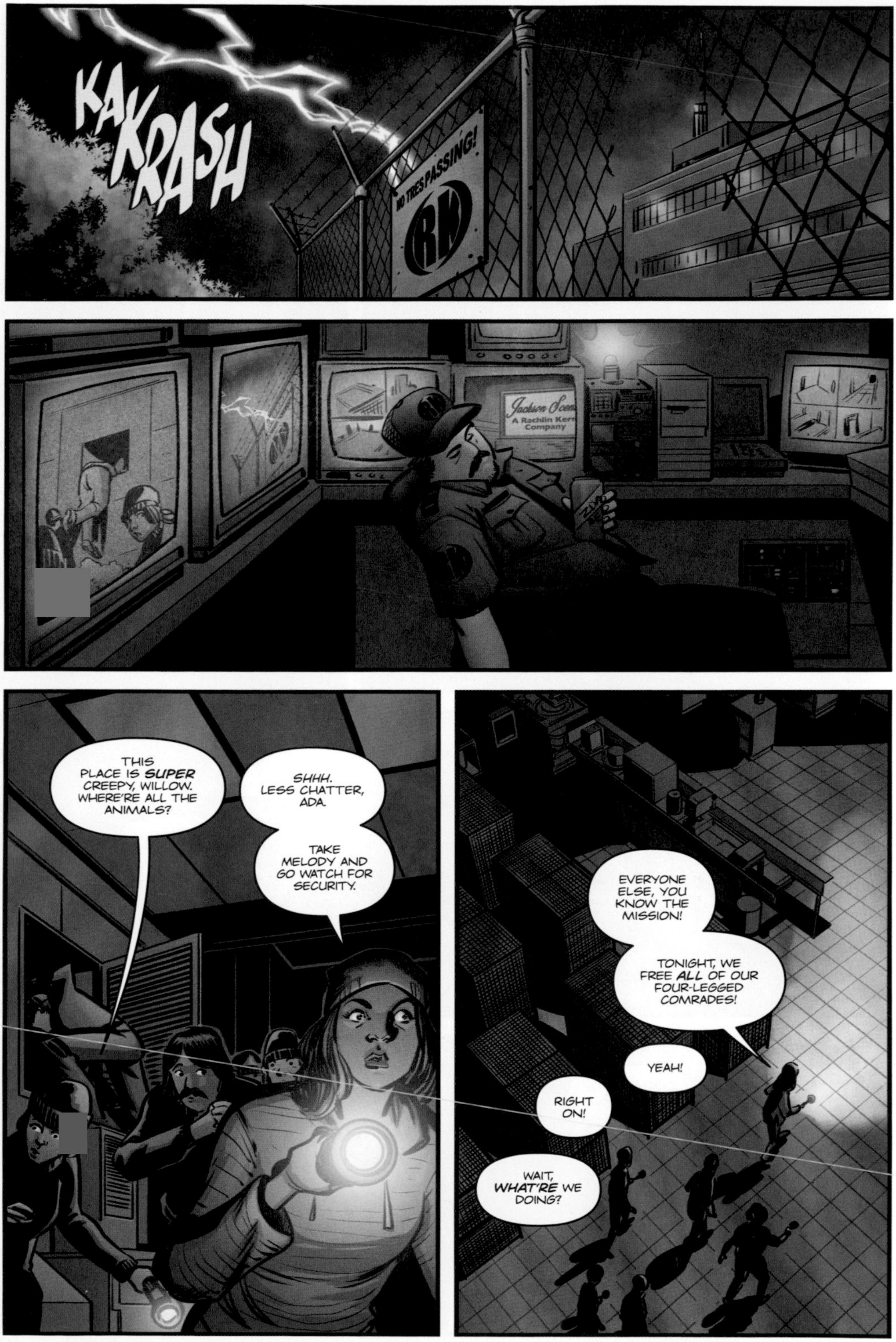
KAKRASH
NO TRESPASSING!
RK
THIS PLACE IS SUPER CREEPY, WILLOW. WHERE'RE ALL THE ANIMALS?
SHHH. LESS CHATTER, ADA.
TAKE MELODY AND GO WATCH FOR SECURITY.
EVERYONE ELSE, YOU KNOW THE MISSION!
TONIGHT, WE FREE ALL OF OUR FOUR-LEGGED COMRADES!
YEAH!
RIGHT ON!
WAIT, WHAT'RE WE DOING?

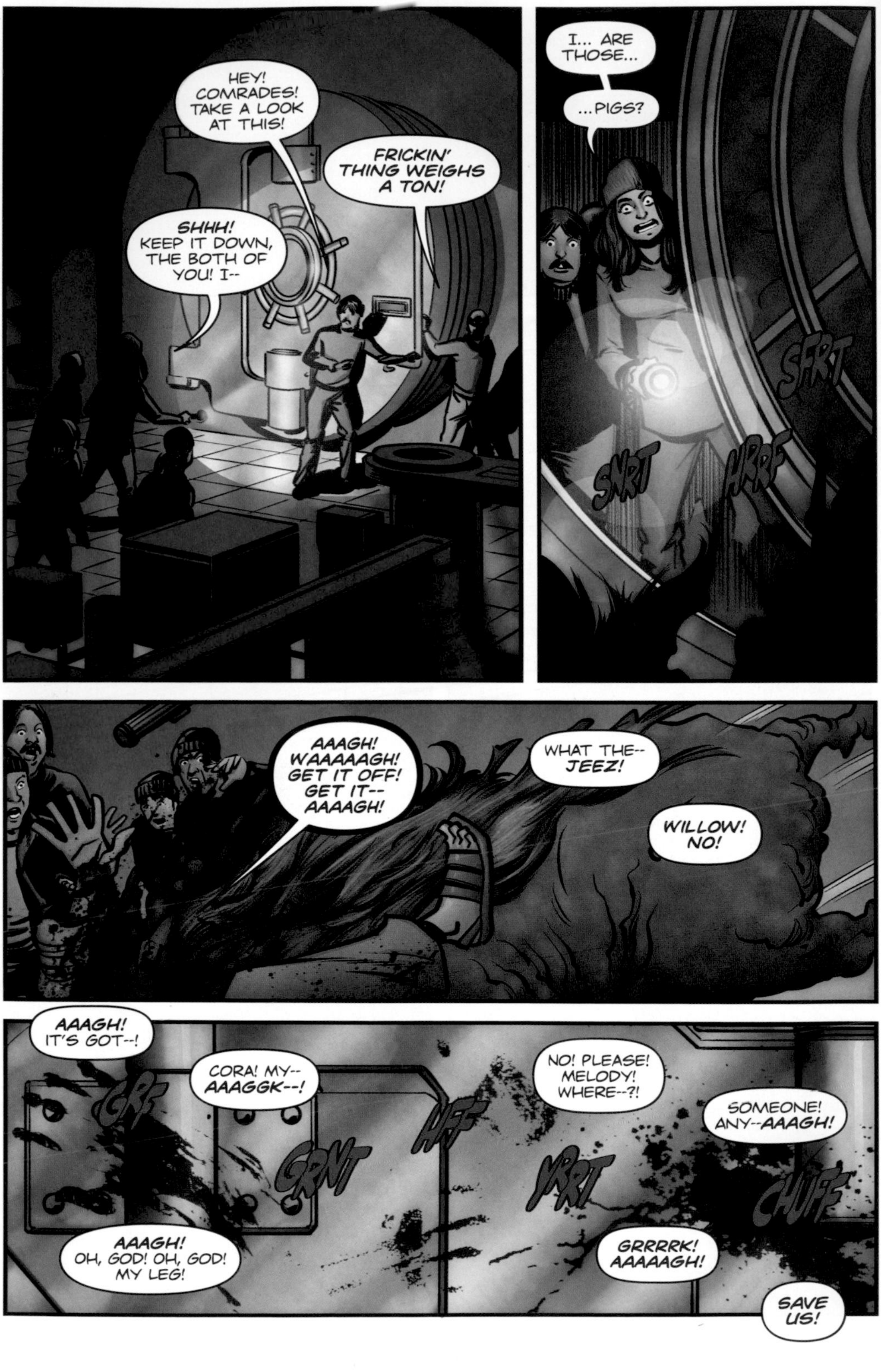
HEY! COMRADES! TAKE A LOOK AT THIS!
FRICKIN' THING WEIGHS A TON!
SHHH! KEEP IT DOWN, THE BOTH OF YOU! I--
I... ARE THOSE...
...PIGS?
SFRT
SNRT
HRRF
AAAGH! WAAAAAGH! GET IT OFF! GET IT-- AAAAGH!
WHAT THE-- JEEZ!
WILLOW! NO!
AAAGH! IT'S GOT--!
CORA! MY-- AAAGGK--!
NO! PLEASE! MELODY! WHERE--?!
SOMEONE! ANY--AAAGH!
GRF
GRNT
HFF
YRRT
CHUFF
AAAGH! OH, GOD! OH, GOD! MY LEG!
GRRRRK! AAAAAGH!
SAVE US!

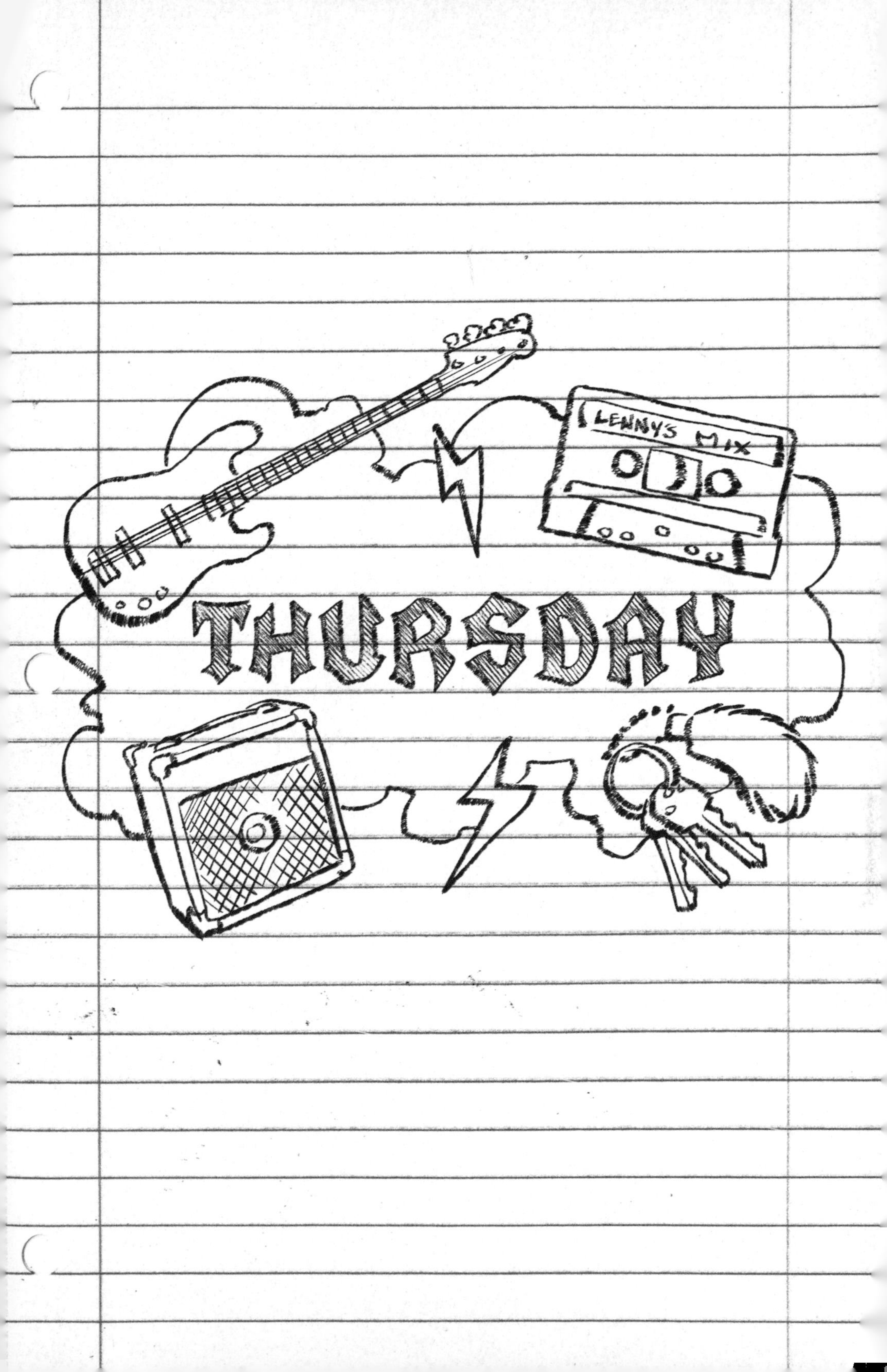
LENNY'S MIX
THURSDAY

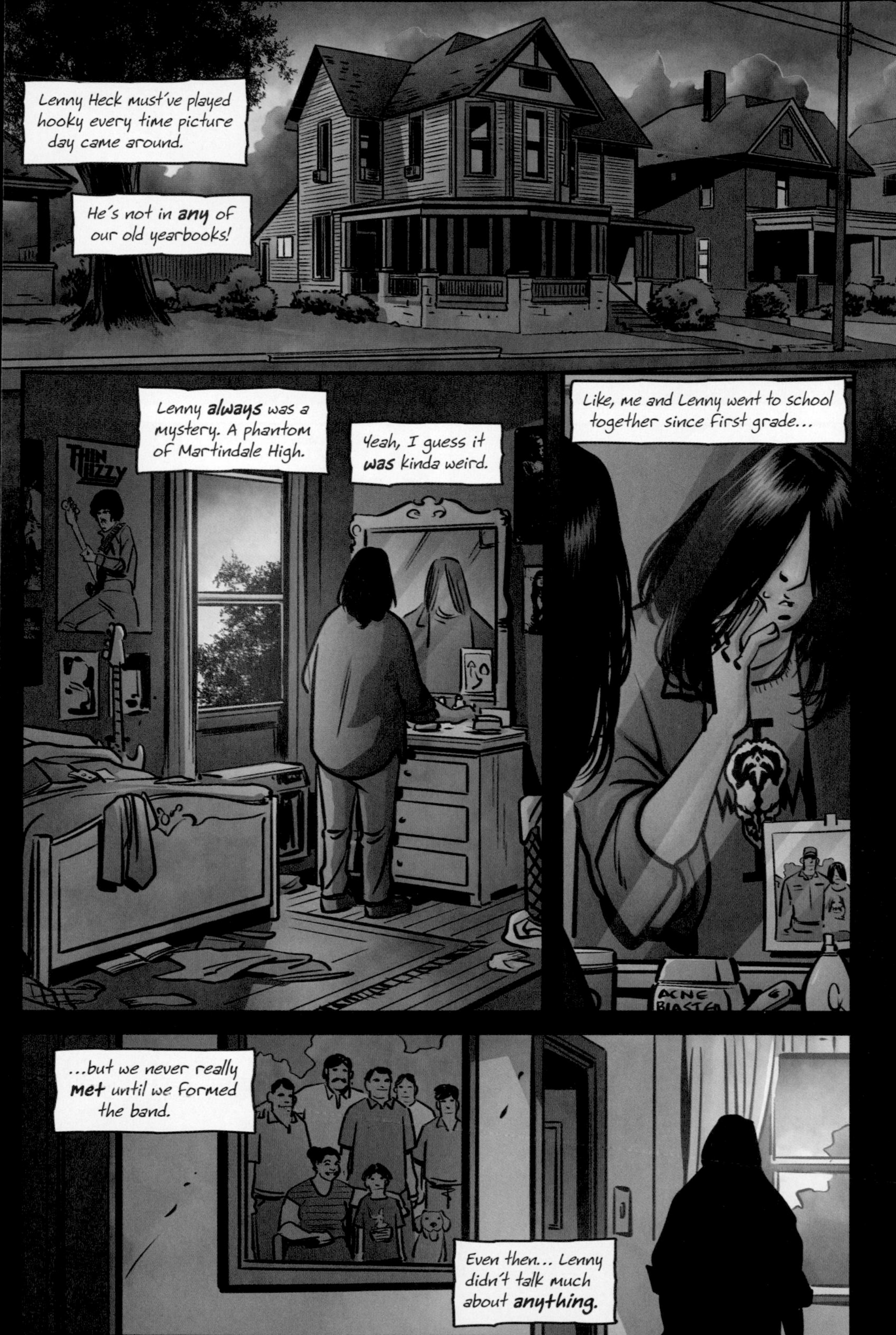

Lenny Heck must've played hooky every time picture day came around.
He's not in **any** of our old yearbooks!
Lenny **always** was a mystery. A phantom of Martindale High.
Yeah, I guess it **was** kinda weird.
THIN LIZZY
Like, me and Lenny went to school together since first grade...
ACNE BLASTER
...but we never really **met** until we formed the band.
Even then... Lenny didn't talk much about **anything**.

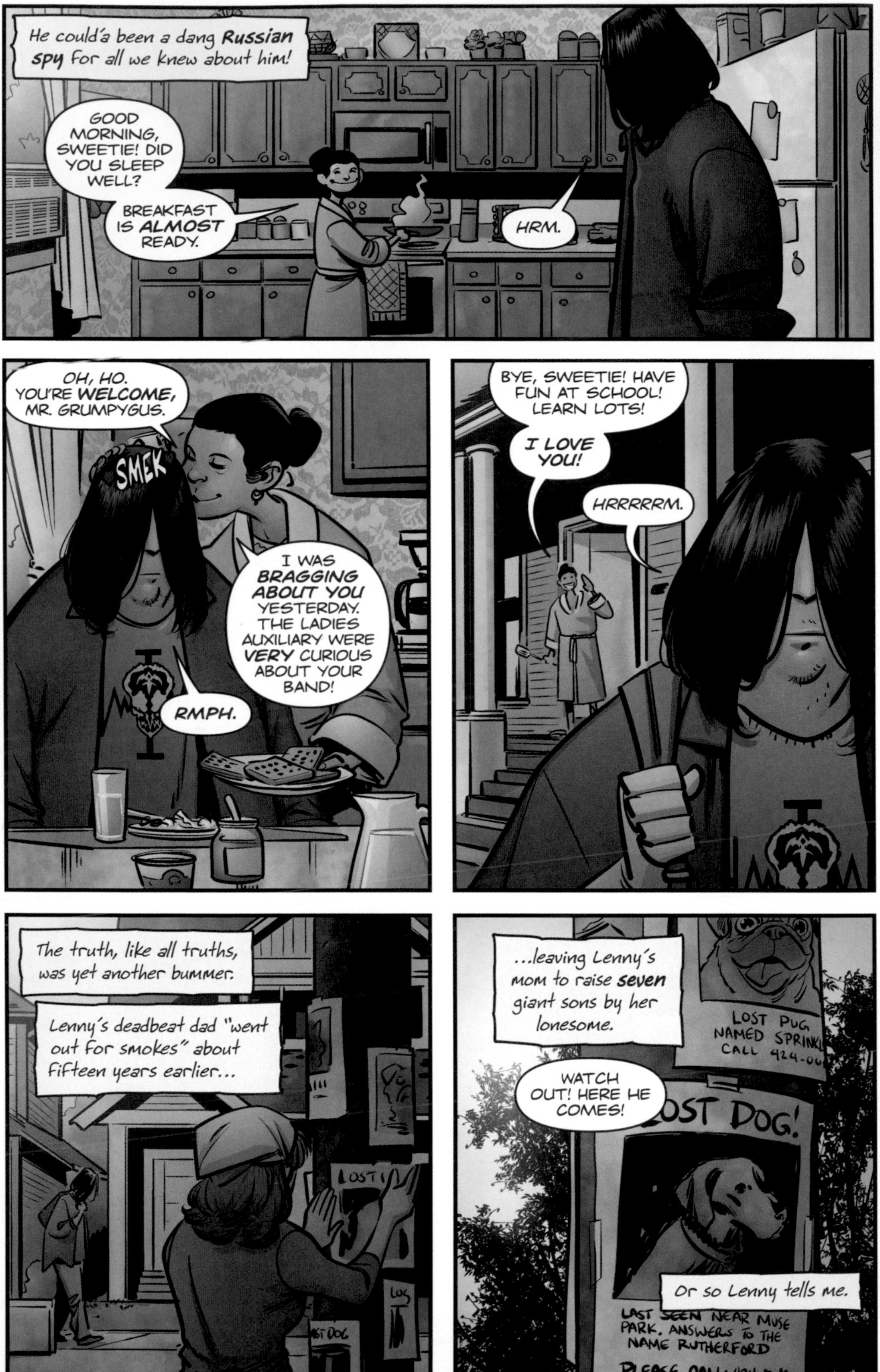
He could'a been a dang **Russian spy** for all we knew about him!
GOOD MORNING, SWEETIE! DID YOU SLEEP WELL?
BREAKFAST IS **ALMOST** READY.
HRM.
OH, HO. YOU'RE **WELCOME,** MR. GRUMPYGUS.
SMEK
I WAS **BRAGGING ABOUT YOU** YESTERDAY. THE LADIES AUXILIARY WERE **VERY** CURIOUS ABOUT YOUR BAND!
RMPH.
BYE, SWEETIE! HAVE FUN AT SCHOOL! LEARN LOTS!
I LOVE YOU!
HRRRRRM.
The truth, like all truths, was yet another bummer.
Lenny's deadbeat dad "went out for smokes" about fifteen years earlier...
...leaving Lenny's mom to raise **seven** giant sons by her lonesome.
LOST PUG
WATCH OUT! HERE HE COMES!
Or so Lenny tells me.
LAST SEEN NEAR MUSE PARK. ANSWERS TO THE NAME RUTHERFORD

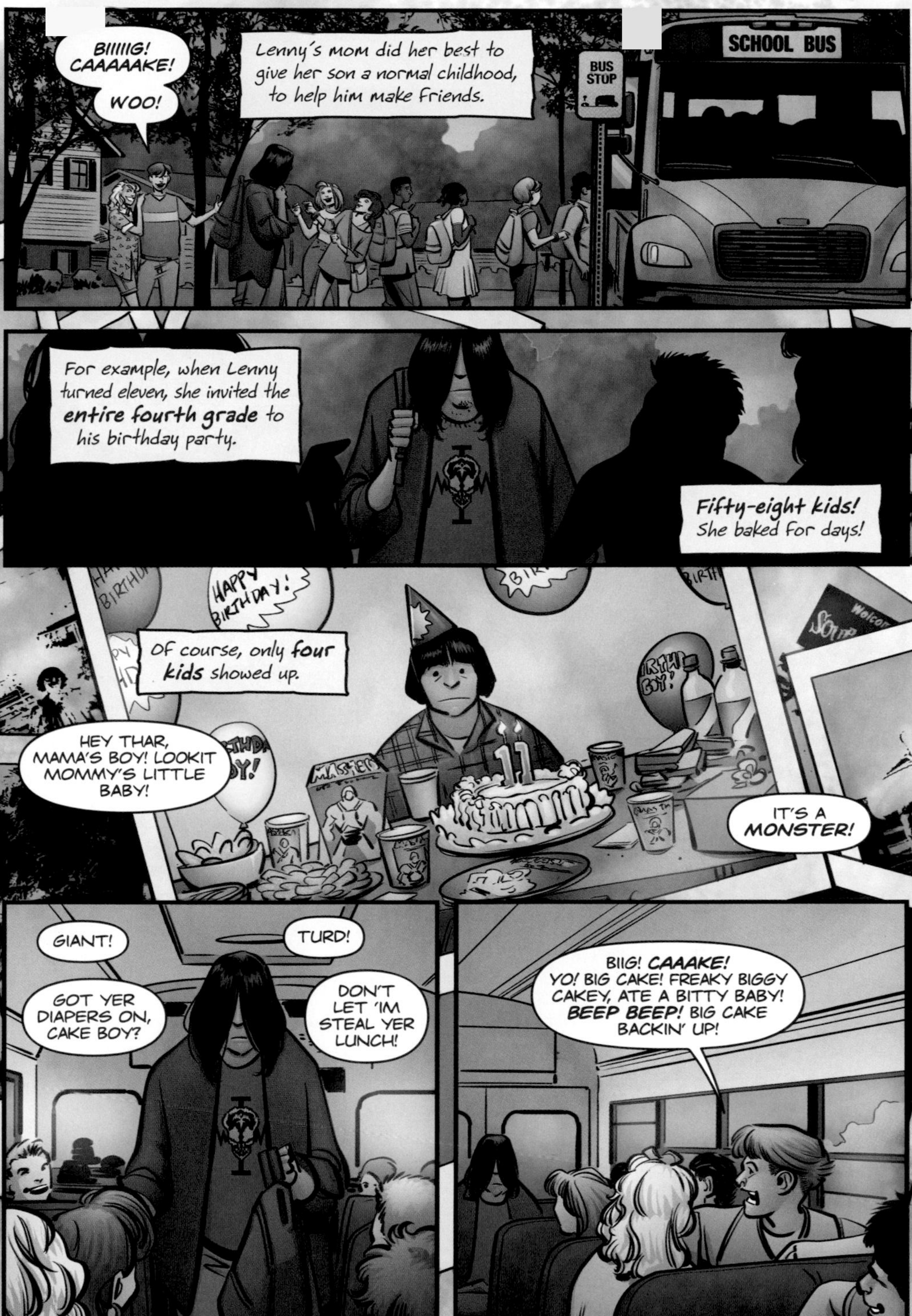
BIIIIIG! CAAAAAKE!
WOO!
Lenny's mom did her best to give her son a normal childhood, to help him make friends.
SCHOOL BUS
BUS STOP
For example, when Lenny turned eleven, she invited the **entire fourth grade** to his birthday party.
Fifty-eight kids! She baked for days!
HAPPY BIRTHDAY!
Of course, only **four kids** showed up.
HEY THAR, MAMA'S BOY! LOOKIT MOMMY'S LITTLE BABY!
IT'S A **MONSTER!**
GIANT!
TURD!
GOT YER DIAPERS ON, CAKE BOY?
DON'T LET 'IM STEAL YER LUNCH!
BIIG! ***CAAAKE!*** YO! BIG CAKE! FREAKY BIGGY CAKEY, ATE A BITTY BABY! ***BEEP BEEP!*** BIG CAKE BACKIN' UP!

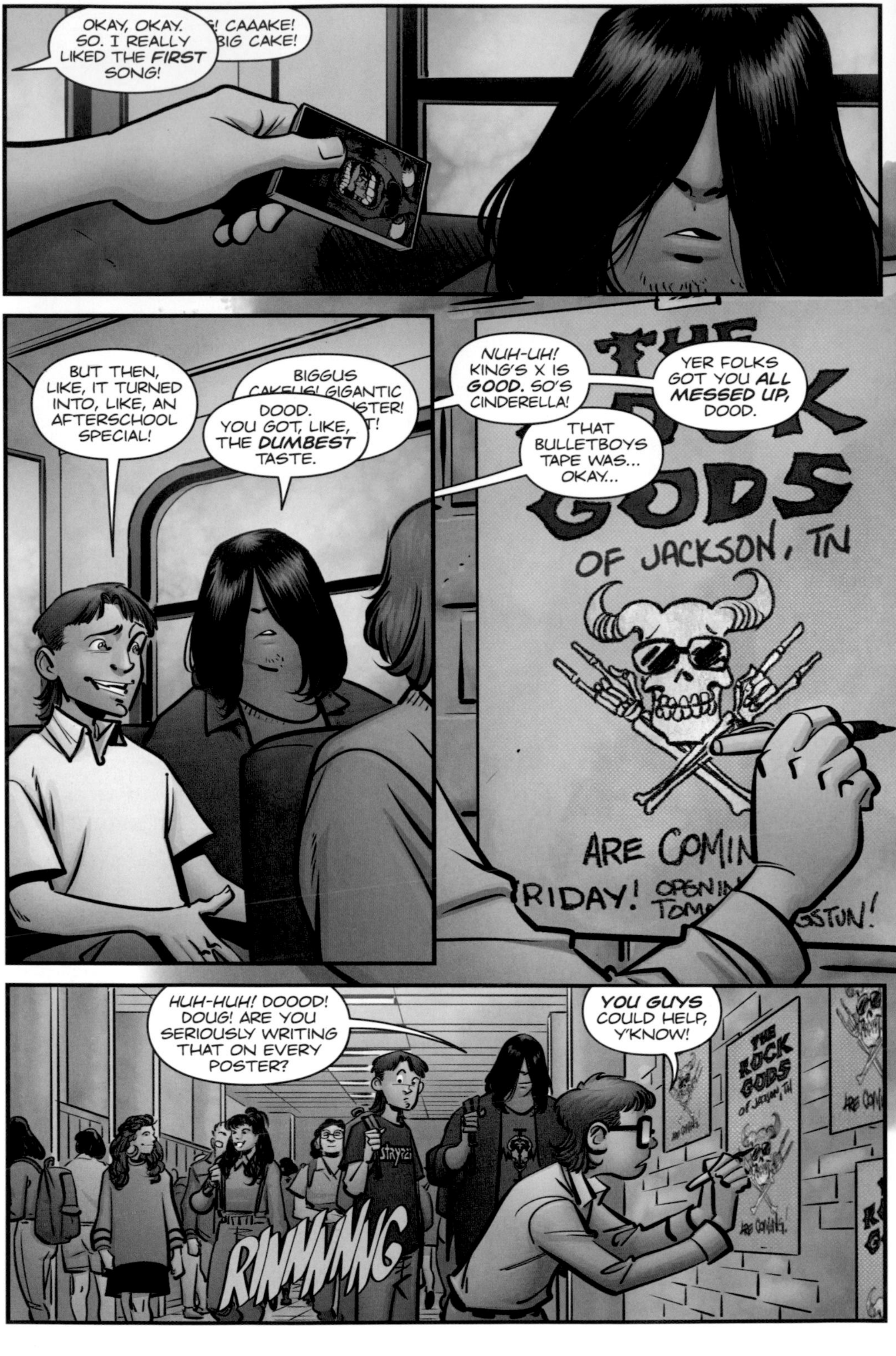
OKAY, OKAY. SO. I REALLY LIKED THE ***FIRST*** SONG!
CAAAKE! BIG CAKE!
BUT THEN, LIKE, IT TURNED INTO, LIKE, AN AFTERSCHOOL SPECIAL!
BIGGUS
DOOD. YOU GOT, LIKE, THE ***DUMBEST*** TASTE.
NUH-UH! KING'S X IS ***GOOD.*** SO'S CINDERELLA!
YER FOLKS GOT YOU ***ALL MESSED UP,*** DOOD.
THAT BULLETBOYS TAPE WAS... OKAY...
GODS
OF JACKSON, TN
ARE COMIN
RIDAY!
HUH-HUH! DOOOD! DOUG! ARE YOU SERIOUSLY WRITING THAT ON EVERY POSTER?
YOU GUYS COULD HELP, Y'KNOW!
RINNNNNG

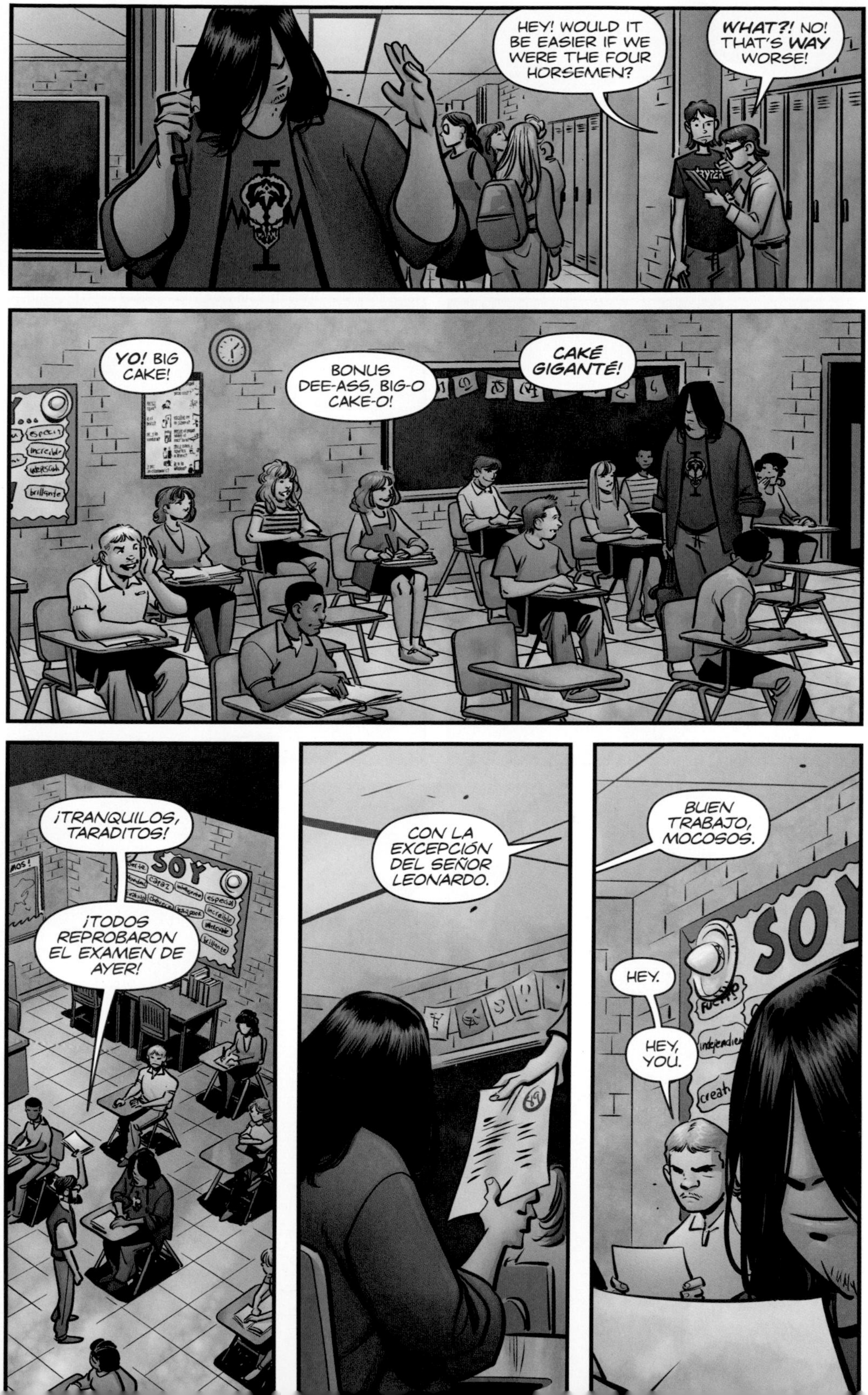
HEY! WOULD IT BE EASIER IF WE WERE THE FOUR HORSEMEN?
WHAT?! NO! THAT'S WAY WORSE!
YO! BIG CAKE!
BONUS DEE-ASS, BIG-O CAKE-O!
CAKÉ GIGANTÉ!
¡TRANQUILOS, TARADITOS!
SOY
¡TODOS REPROBARON EL EXAMEN DE AYER!
CON LA EXCEPCIÓN DEL SEÑOR LEONARDO.
BUEN TRABAJO, MOCOSOS.
SOY
HEY.
HEY, YOU.

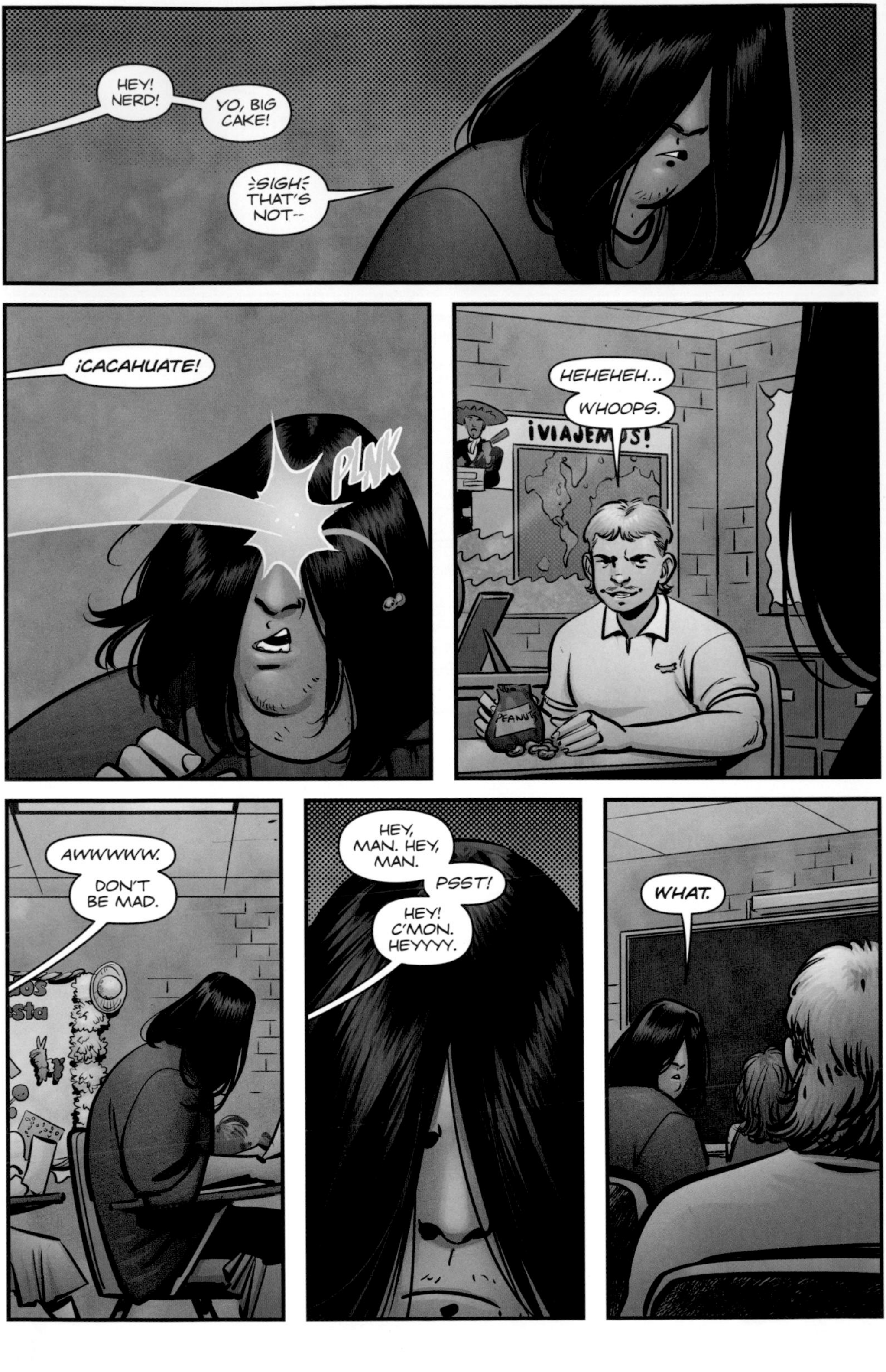
HEY! NERD!
YO, BIG CAKE!
SIGH THAT'S NOT--
¡CACAHUATE!
PLNK
HEHEHEH... WHOOPS.
¡VIAJEMOS!
PEANUTS
AWWWWW. DON'T BE MAD.
HEY, MAN. HEY, MAN.
PSST!
HEY! C'MON. HEYYYY.
WHAT.

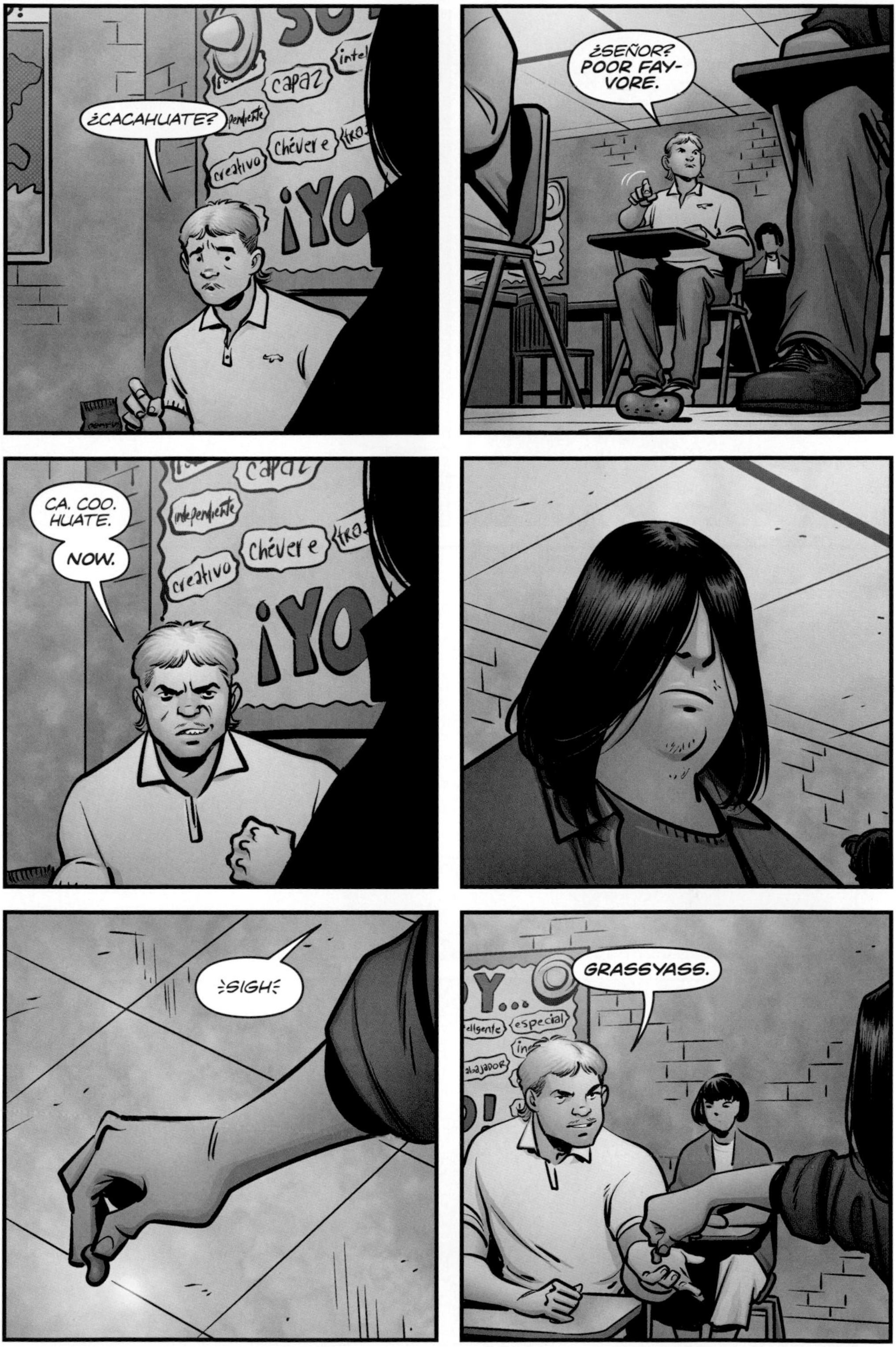
¿CACAHUATE?
¿SEÑOR? POOR FAY-VORE.
CA. COO. HUATE.
NOW.
⁝SIGH⁝
GRASSYASS.

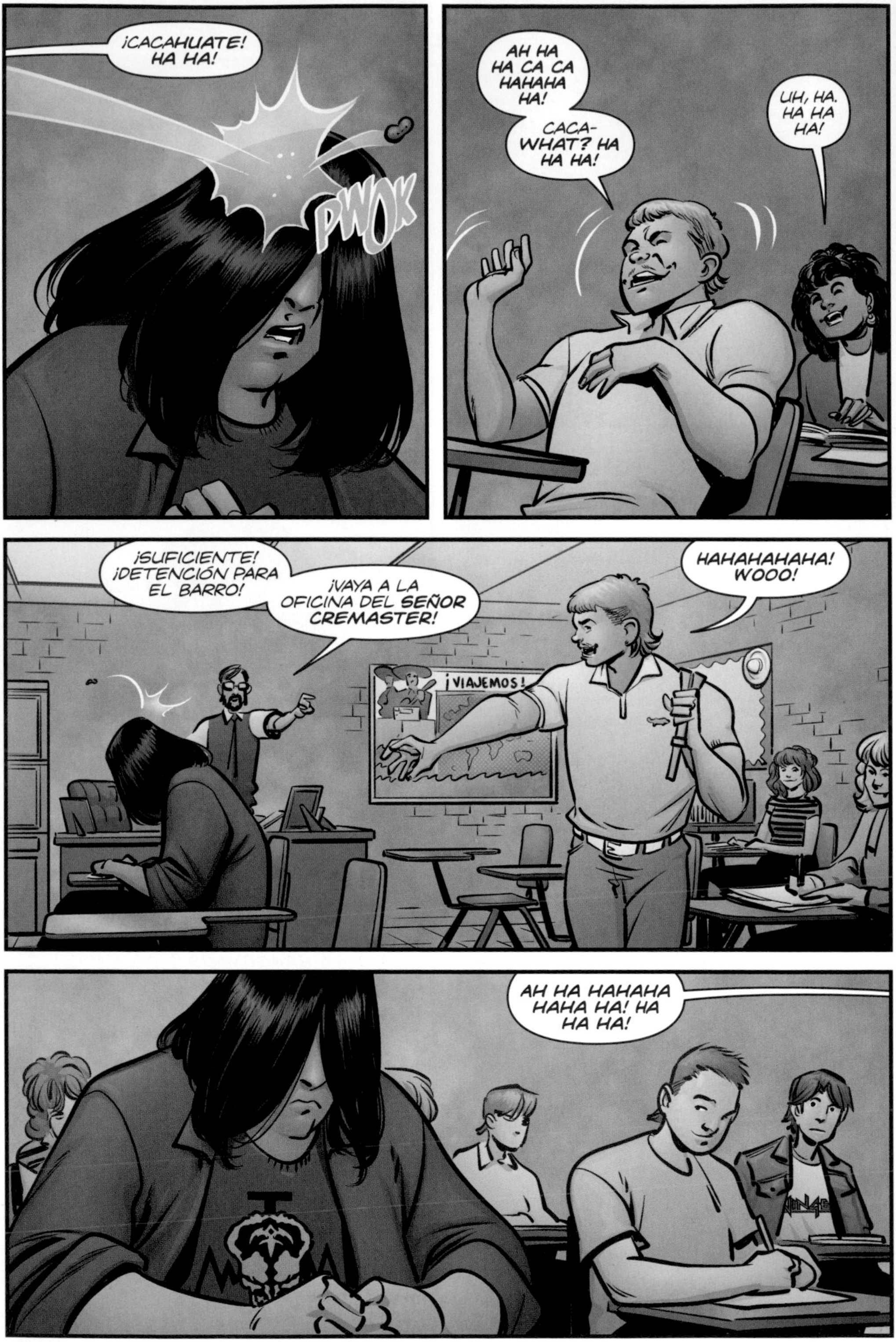
¡CACAHUATE! HA HA!
PWOK
AH HA HA CA CA HAHAHA HA!
CACA-WHAT? HA HA HA!
UH, HA. HA HA HA!
¡SUFICIENTE! ¡DETENCIÓN PARA EL BARRO!
¡VAYA A LA OFICINA DEL SEÑOR CREMASTER!
HAHAHAHAHA! WOOO!
¡VIAJEMOS!
AH HA HAHAHA HAHA HA! HA HA HA!

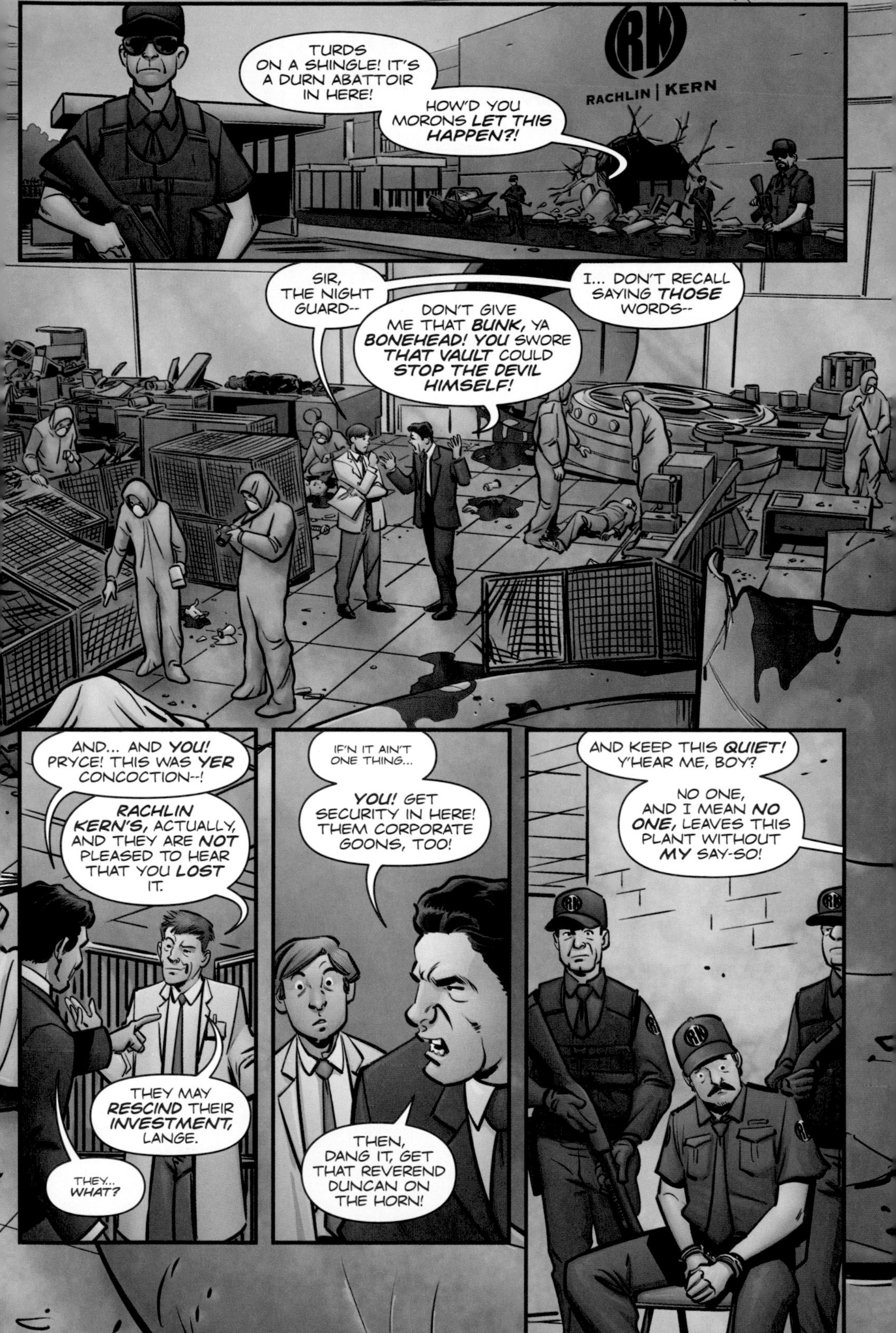
RACHLIN | KERN
TURDS ON A SHINGLE! IT'S A DURN ABATTOIR IN HERE!
HOW'D YOU MORONS LET THIS HAPPEN?!
SIR, THE NIGHT GUARD--
DON'T GIVE ME THAT BUNK, YA BONEHEAD! YOU SWORE THAT VAULT COULD STOP THE DEVIL HIMSELF!
I... DON'T RECALL SAYING THOSE WORDS--
AND... AND YOU! PRYCE! THIS WAS YER CONCOCTION--!
RACHLIN KERN'S, ACTUALLY, AND THEY ARE NOT PLEASED TO HEAR THAT YOU LOST IT.
THEY MAY RESCIND THEIR INVESTMENT, LANGE.
THEY... WHAT?
IF'N IT AIN'T ONE THING...
YOU! GET SECURITY IN HERE! THEM CORPORATE GOONS, TOO!
THEN, DANG IT, GET THAT REVEREND DUNCAN ON THE HORN!
AND KEEP THIS QUIET! Y'HEAR ME, BOY?
NO ONE, AND I MEAN NO ONE, LEAVES THIS PLANT WITHOUT MY SAY-SO!

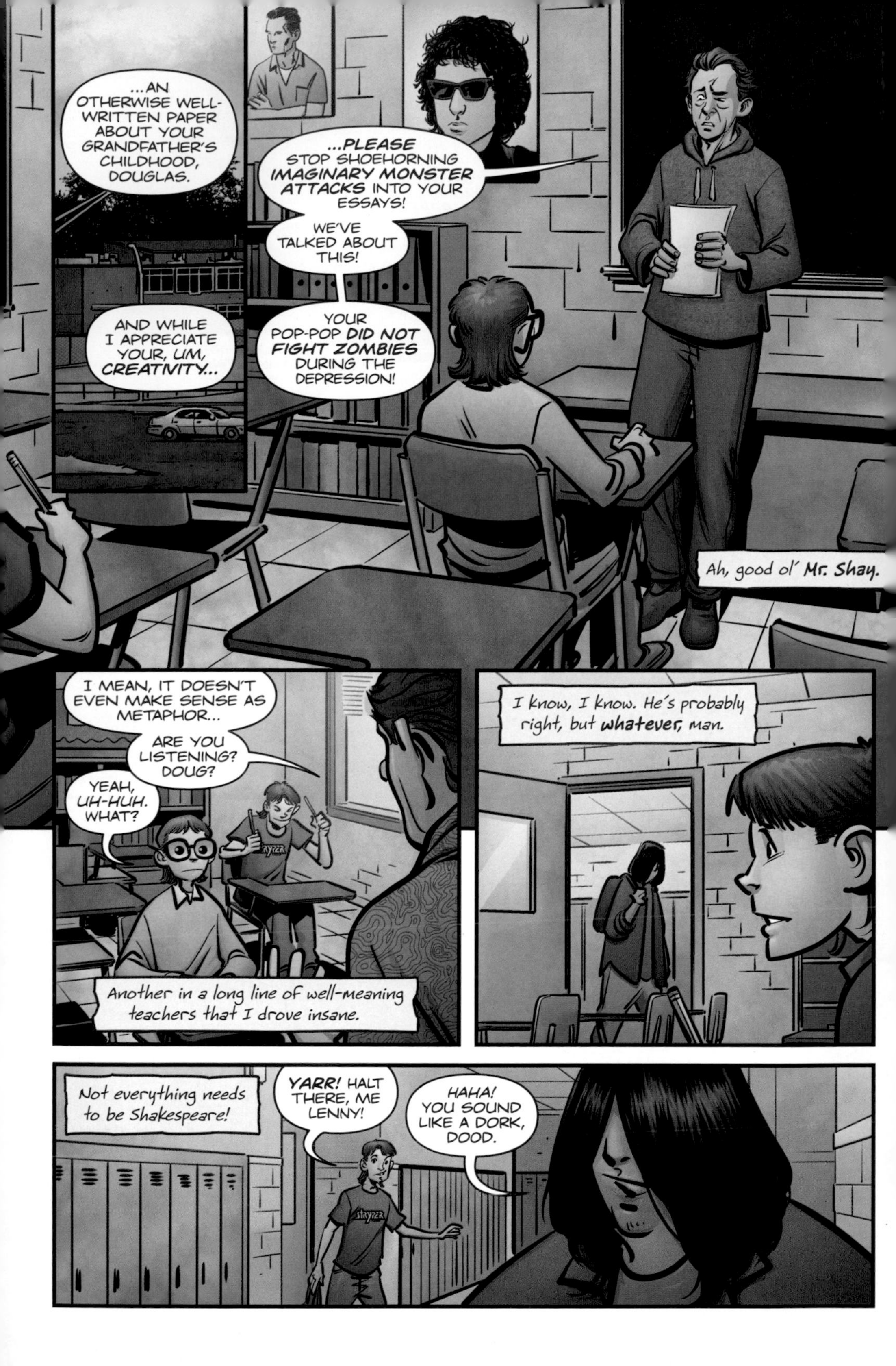
...AN OTHERWISE WELL-WRITTEN PAPER ABOUT YOUR GRANDFATHER'S CHILDHOOD, DOUGLAS.
AND WHILE I APPRECIATE YOUR, UM, CREATIVITY...
...PLEASE STOP SHOEHORNING IMAGINARY MONSTER ATTACKS INTO YOUR ESSAYS!
WE'VE TALKED ABOUT THIS!
YOUR POP-POP DID NOT FIGHT ZOMBIES DURING THE DEPRESSION!
Ah, good ol' Mr. Shay.
I MEAN, IT DOESN'T EVEN MAKE SENSE AS METAPHOR...
ARE YOU LISTENING? DOUG?
YEAH, UH-HUH. WHAT?
Another in a long line of well-meaning teachers that I drove insane.
I know, I know. He's probably right, but whatever, man.
Not everything needs to be Shakespeare!
YARR! HALT THERE, ME LENNY!
HAHA! YOU SOUND LIKE A DORK, DOOD.

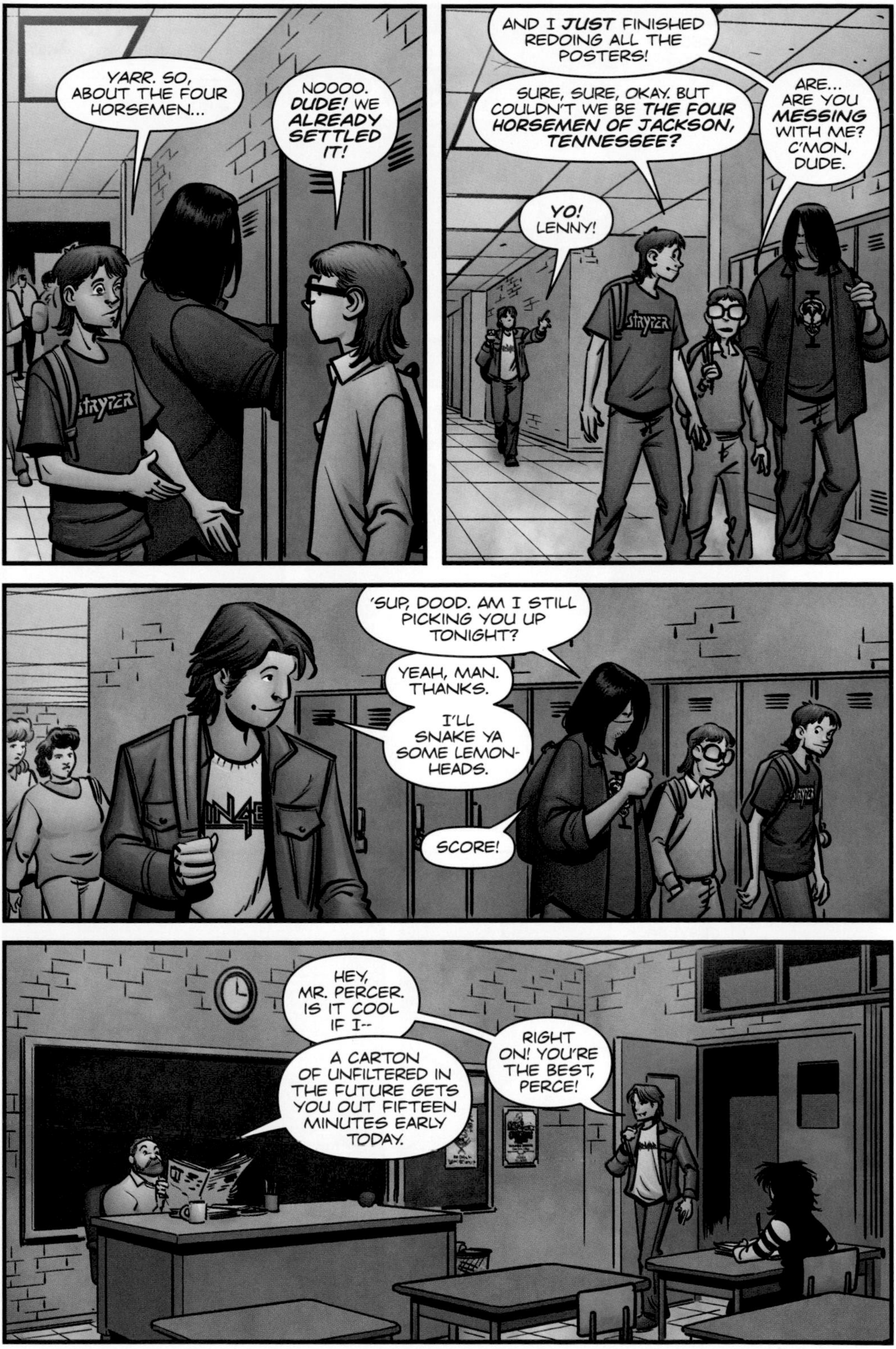
YARR. SO, ABOUT THE FOUR HORSEMEN...
NOOOO. **DUDE!** WE **ALREADY SETTLED** IT!
AND I **JUST** FINISHED REDOING ALL THE POSTERS!
SURE, SURE, OKAY. BUT COULDN'T WE BE **THE FOUR HORSEMEN OF JACKSON, TENNESSEE?**
ARE... ARE YOU **MESSING** WITH ME? C'MON, DUDE.
YO! LENNY!
'SUP, DOOD. AM I STILL PICKING YOU UP TONIGHT?
YEAH, MAN. THANKS.
I'LL SNAKE YA SOME LEMON-HEADS.
SCORE!
HEY, MR. PERCER. IS IT COOL IF I--
A CARTON OF UNFILTERED IN THE FUTURE GETS YOU OUT FIFTEEN MINUTES EARLY TODAY.
RIGHT ON! YOU'RE THE BEST, PERCE!

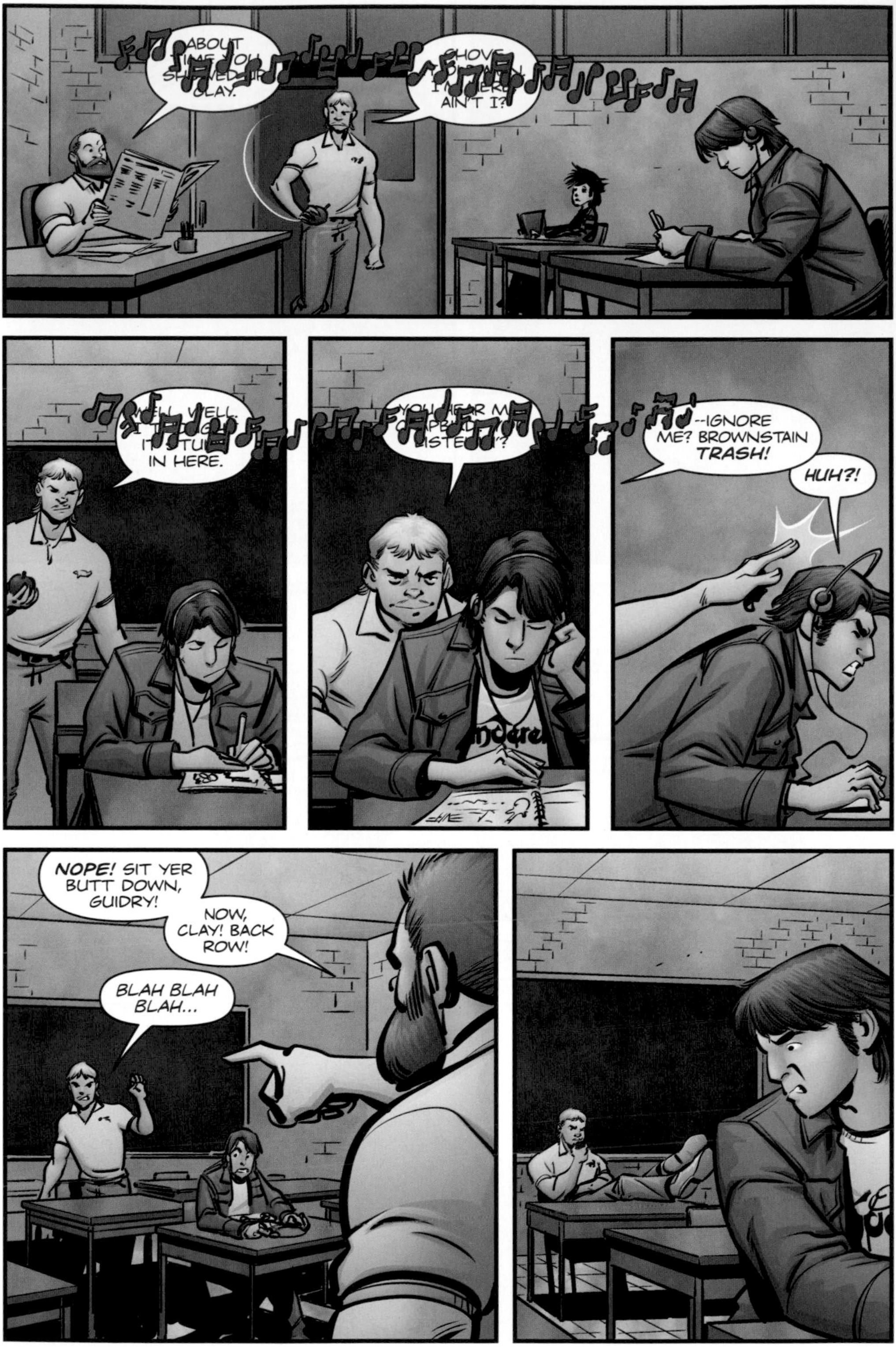
--IGNORE ME? BROWNSTAIN TRASH!
HUH?!
NOPE! SIT YER BUTT DOWN, GUIDRY!
NOW, CLAY! BACK ROW!
BLAH BLAH BLAH...

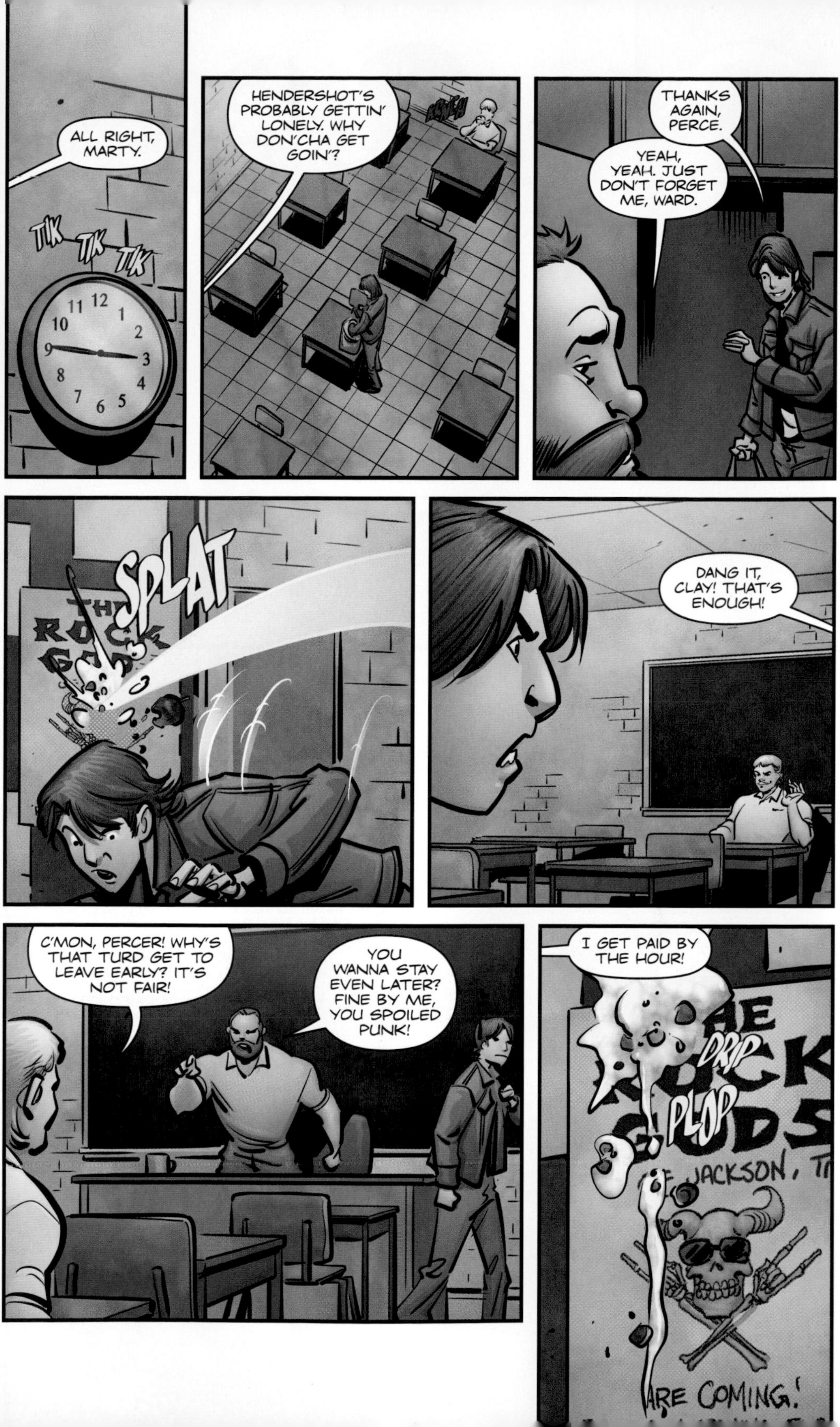
ALL RIGHT, MARTY.
TIK TIK TIK
HENDERSHOT'S PROBABLY GETTIN' LONELY. WHY DON'CHA GET GOIN'?
THANKS AGAIN, PERCE.
YEAH, YEAH. JUST DON'T FORGET ME, WARD.
SPLAT
DANG IT, CLAY! THAT'S ENOUGH!
C'MON, PERCER! WHY'S THAT TURD GET TO LEAVE EARLY? IT'S NOT FAIR!
YOU WANNA STAY EVEN LATER? FINE BY ME, YOU SPOILED PUNK!
I GET PAID BY THE HOUR!
DRIP
PLOP
ARE COMING!

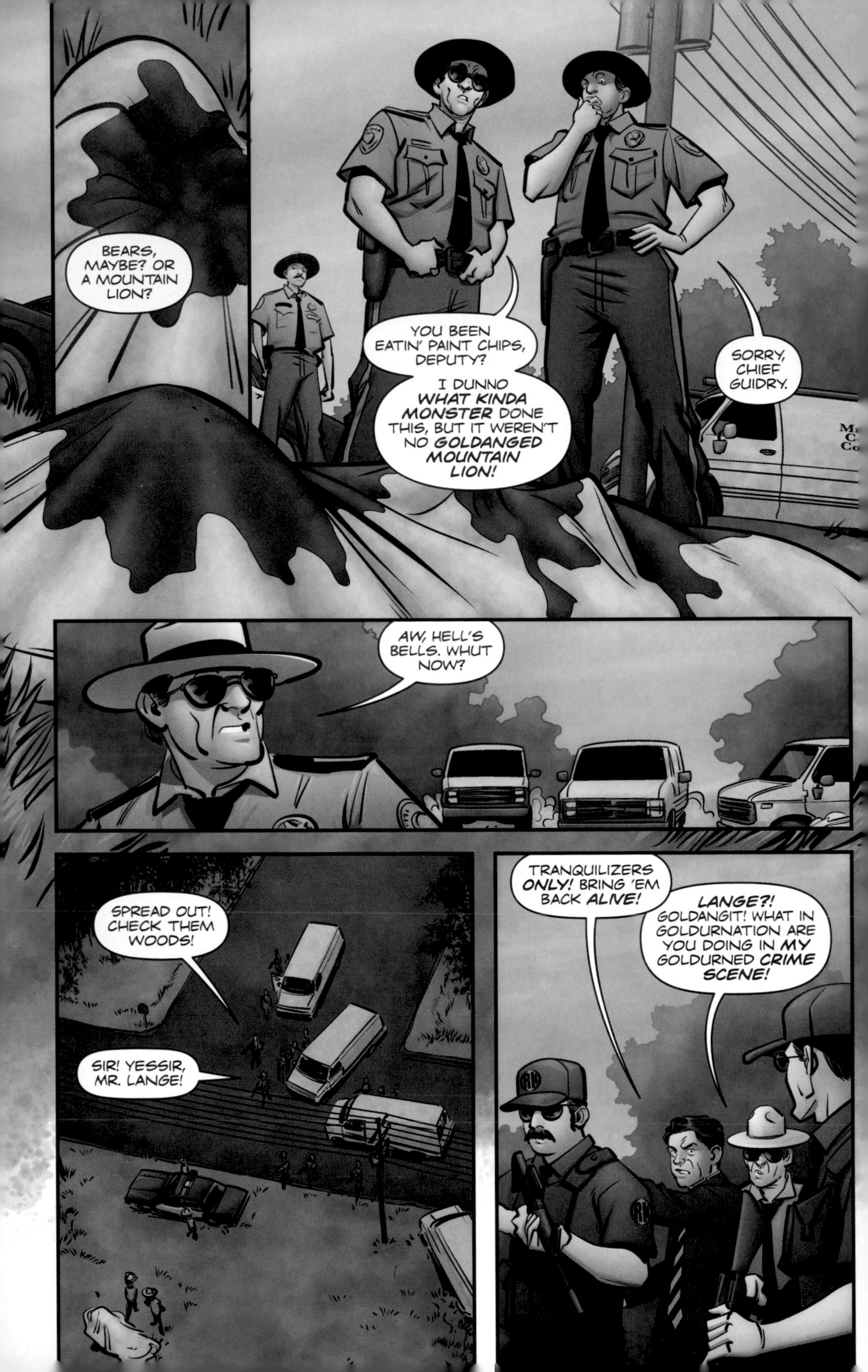
BEARS, MAYBE? OR A MOUNTAIN LION?
YOU BEEN EATIN' PAINT CHIPS, DEPUTY?
I DUNNO **WHAT KINDA MONSTER** DONE THIS, BUT IT WEREN'T NO **GOLDANGED MOUNTAIN LION!**
SORRY, CHIEF GUIDRY.
AW, HELL'S BELLS. WHUT NOW?
SPREAD OUT! CHECK THEM WOODS!
SIR! YESSIR, MR. LANGE!
TRANQUILIZERS **ONLY!** BRING 'EM BACK **ALIVE!**
LANGE?! GOLDANGIT! WHAT IN GOLDURNATION ARE YOU DOING IN **MY** GOLDURNED **CRIME SCENE!**

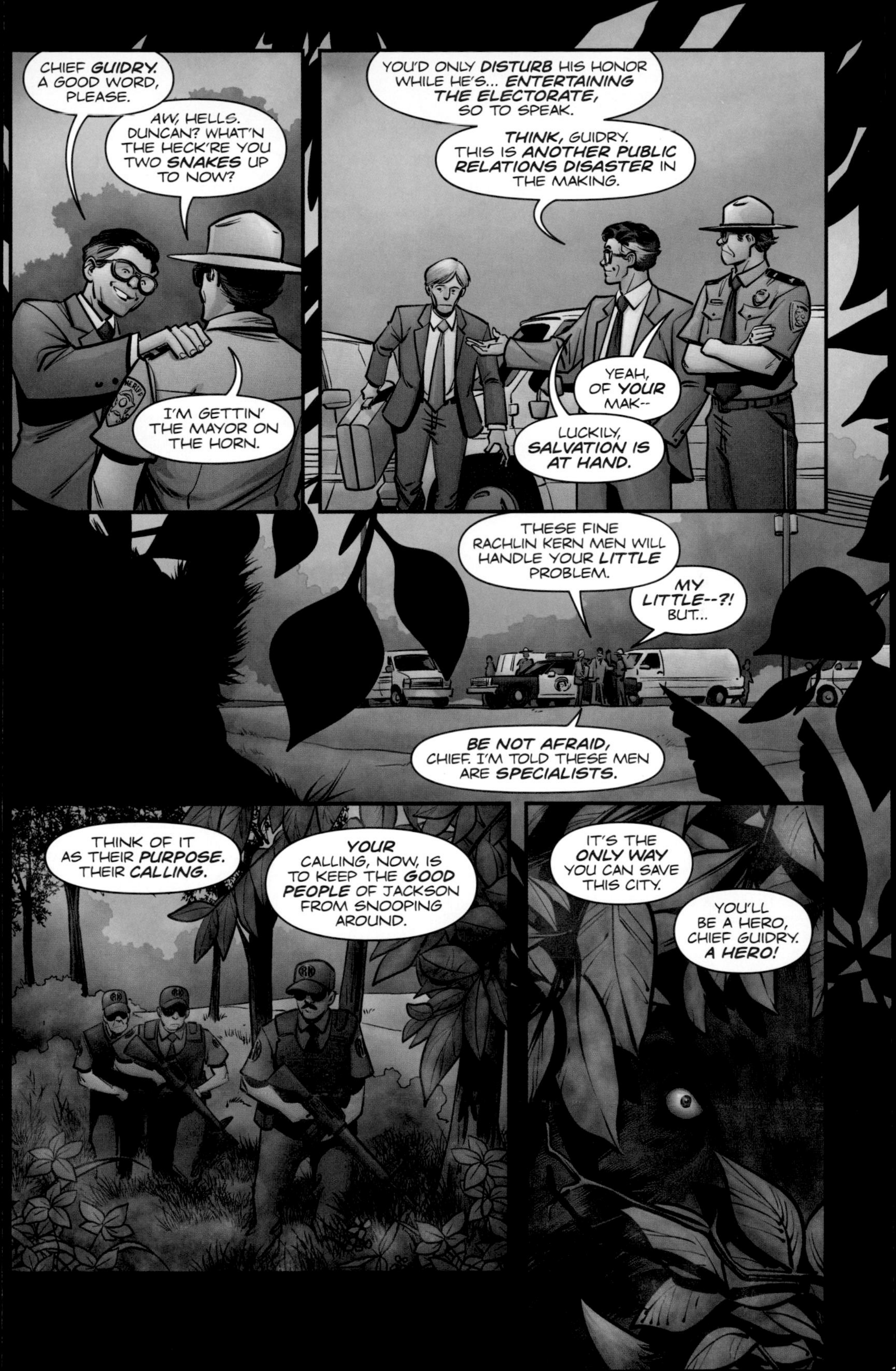
CHIEF GUIDRY. A GOOD WORD, PLEASE.
AW, HELLS. DUNCAN? WHAT'N THE HECK'RE YOU TWO SNAKES UP TO NOW?
I'M GETTIN' THE MAYOR ON THE HORN.
SHERIFF
YOU'D ONLY DISTURB HIS HONOR WHILE HE'S... ENTERTAINING THE ELECTORATE, SO TO SPEAK.
THINK, GUIDRY. THIS IS ANOTHER PUBLIC RELATIONS DISASTER IN THE MAKING.
YEAH, OF YOUR MAK--
LUCKILY, SALVATION IS AT HAND.
THESE FINE RACHLIN KERN MEN WILL HANDLE YOUR LITTLE PROBLEM.
MY LITTLE--?! BUT...
BE NOT AFRAID, CHIEF. I'M TOLD THESE MEN ARE SPECIALISTS.
THINK OF IT AS THEIR PURPOSE. THEIR CALLING.
YOUR CALLING, NOW, IS TO KEEP THE GOOD PEOPLE OF JACKSON FROM SNOOPING AROUND.
IT'S THE ONLY WAY YOU CAN SAVE THIS CITY.
YOU'LL BE A HERO, CHIEF GUIDRY. A HERO!

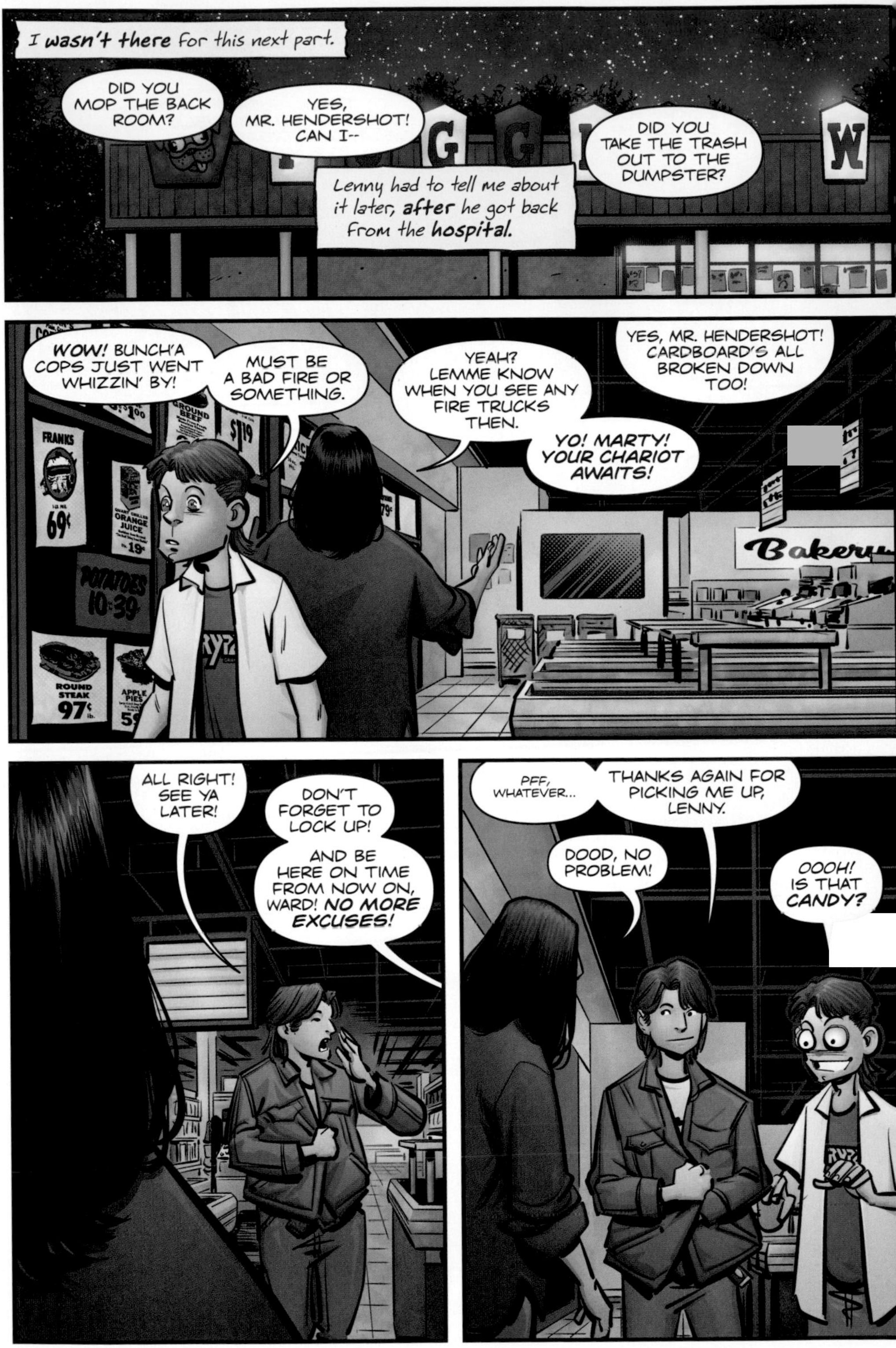
I **wasn't there** for this next part.
DID YOU MOP THE BACK ROOM?
YES, MR. HENDERSHOT! CAN I--
Lenny had to tell me about it later, **after** he got back from the **hospital.**
DID YOU TAKE THE TRASH OUT TO THE DUMPSTER?
WOW! BUNCH'A COPS JUST WENT WHIZZIN' BY!
MUST BE A BAD FIRE OR SOMETHING.
YEAH? LEMME KNOW WHEN YOU SEE ANY FIRE TRUCKS THEN.
YES, MR. HENDERSHOT! CARDBOARD'S ALL BROKEN DOWN TOO!
YO! MARTY! YOUR CHARIOT AWAITS!
FRANKS
69¢
ORANGE JUICE
POTATOES 10 39
ROUND STEAK 97¢
APPLE PIES
GROUND BEEF
Bakery
ALL RIGHT! SEE YA LATER!
DON'T FORGET TO LOCK UP!
AND BE HERE ON TIME FROM NOW ON, WARD! ***NO MORE EXCUSES!***
PFF, WHATEVER...
THANKS AGAIN FOR PICKING ME UP, LENNY.
DOOD, NO PROBLEM!
OOOH! IS THAT ***CANDY?***

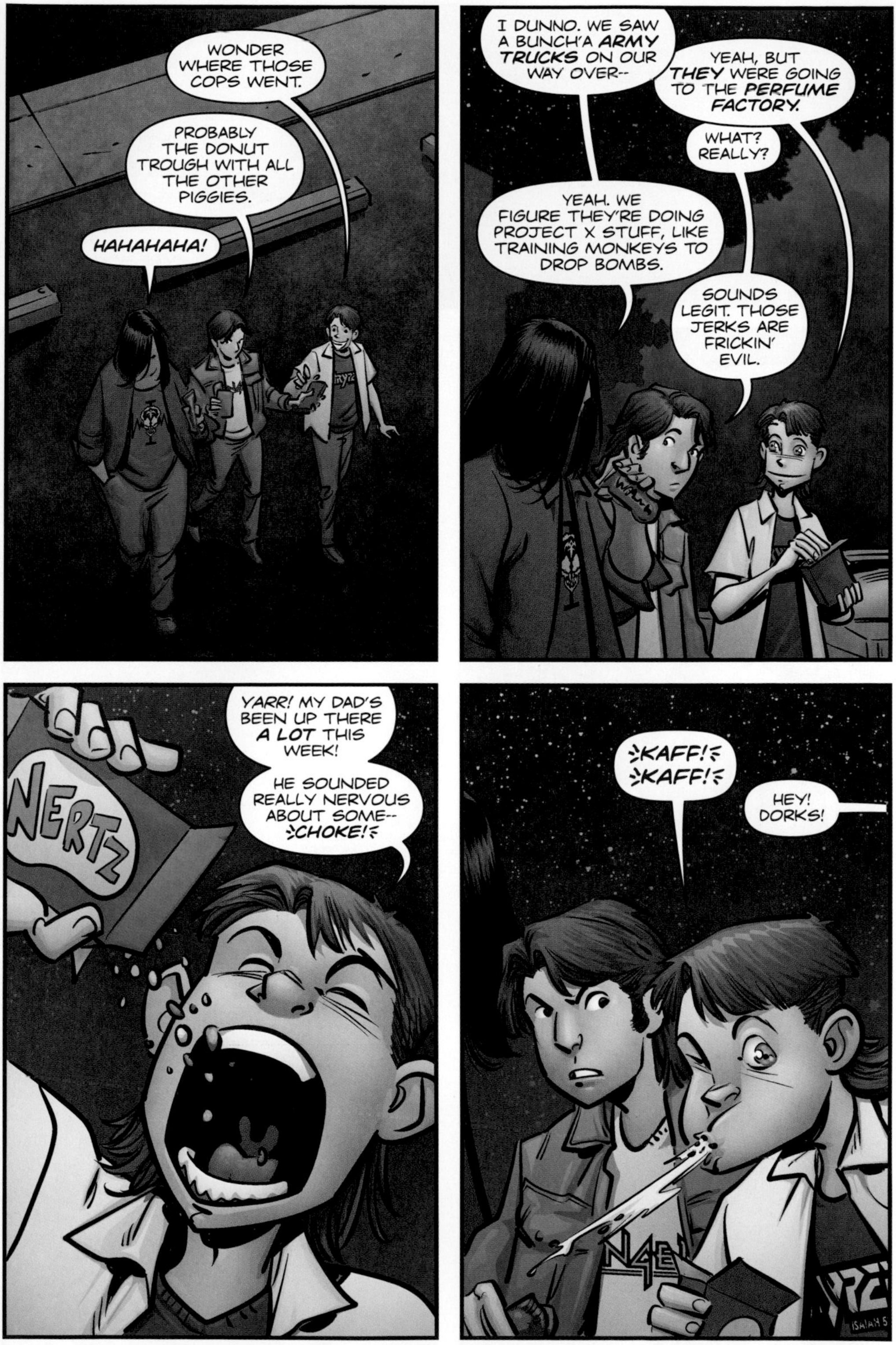
WONDER WHERE THOSE COPS WENT.
PROBABLY THE DONUT TROUGH WITH ALL THE OTHER PIGGIES.
HAHAHAHA!
I DUNNO. WE SAW A BUNCH'A ARMY TRUCKS ON OUR WAY OVER--
YEAH, BUT THEY WERE GOING TO THE PERFUME FACTORY.
WHAT? REALLY?
YEAH. WE FIGURE THEY'RE DOING PROJECT X STUFF, LIKE TRAINING MONKEYS TO DROP BOMBS.
SOUNDS LEGIT. THOSE JERKS ARE FRICKIN' EVIL.
NERTZ
YARR! MY DAD'S BEEN UP THERE A LOT THIS WEEK!
HE SOUNDED REALLY NERVOUS ABOUT SOME-- CHOKE!
KAFF! KAFF!
HEY! DORKS!

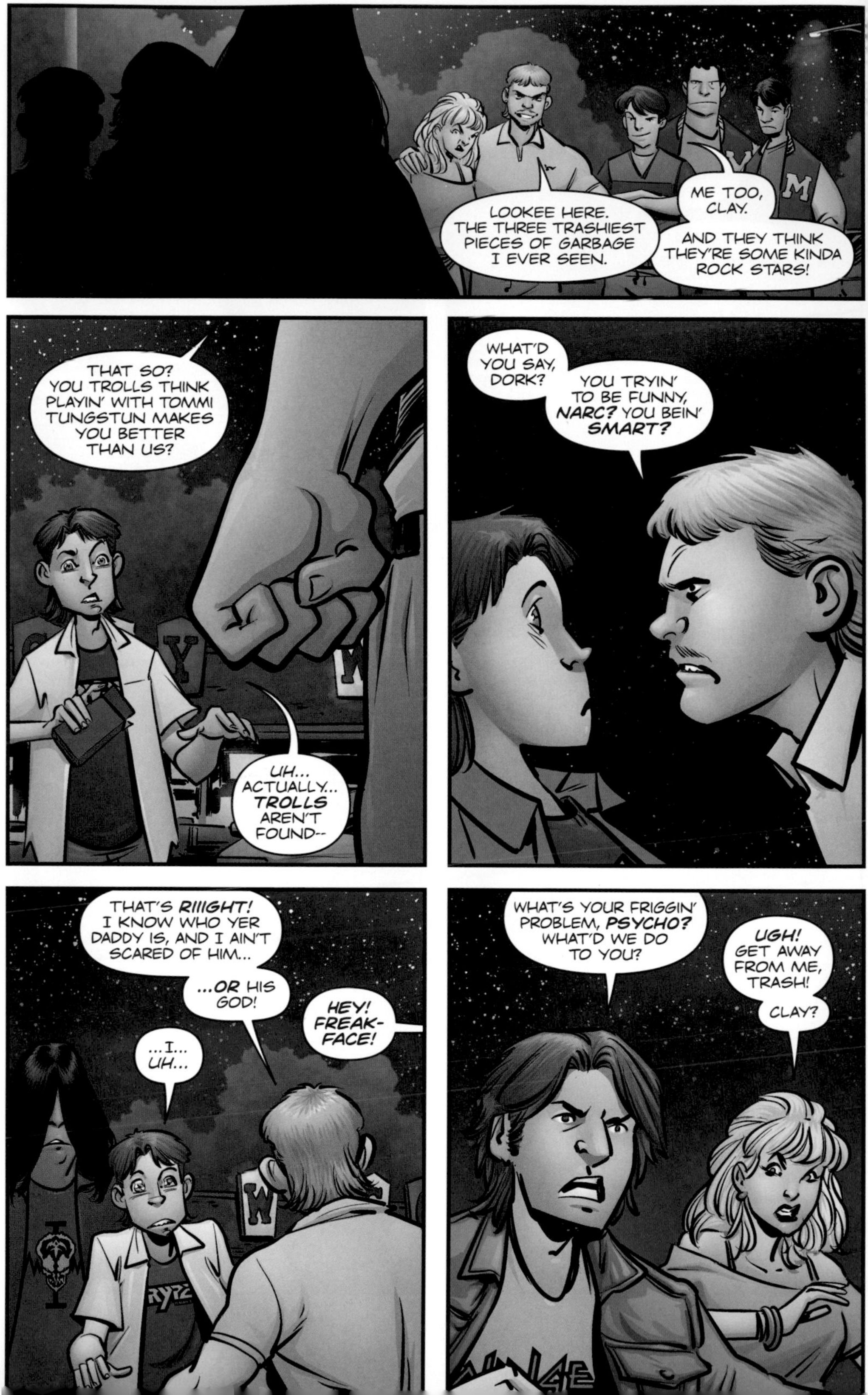
LOOKEE HERE. THE THREE TRASHIEST PIECES OF GARBAGE I EVER SEEN.
ME TOO, CLAY.
AND THEY THINK THEY'RE SOME KINDA ROCK STARS!
THAT SO? YOU TROLLS THINK PLAYIN' WITH TOMMI TUNGSTUN MAKES YOU BETTER THAN US?
UH... ACTUALLY... TROLLS AREN'T FOUND--
WHAT'D YOU SAY, DORK?
YOU TRYIN' TO BE FUNNY, NARC? YOU BEIN' SMART?
THAT'S RIIIGHT! I KNOW WHO YER DADDY IS, AND I AIN'T SCARED OF HIM...
...OR HIS GOD!
...I... UH...
HEY! FREAK-FACE!
WHAT'S YOUR FRIGGIN' PROBLEM, PSYCHO? WHAT'D WE DO TO YOU?
UGH! GET AWAY FROM ME, TRASH!
CLAY?

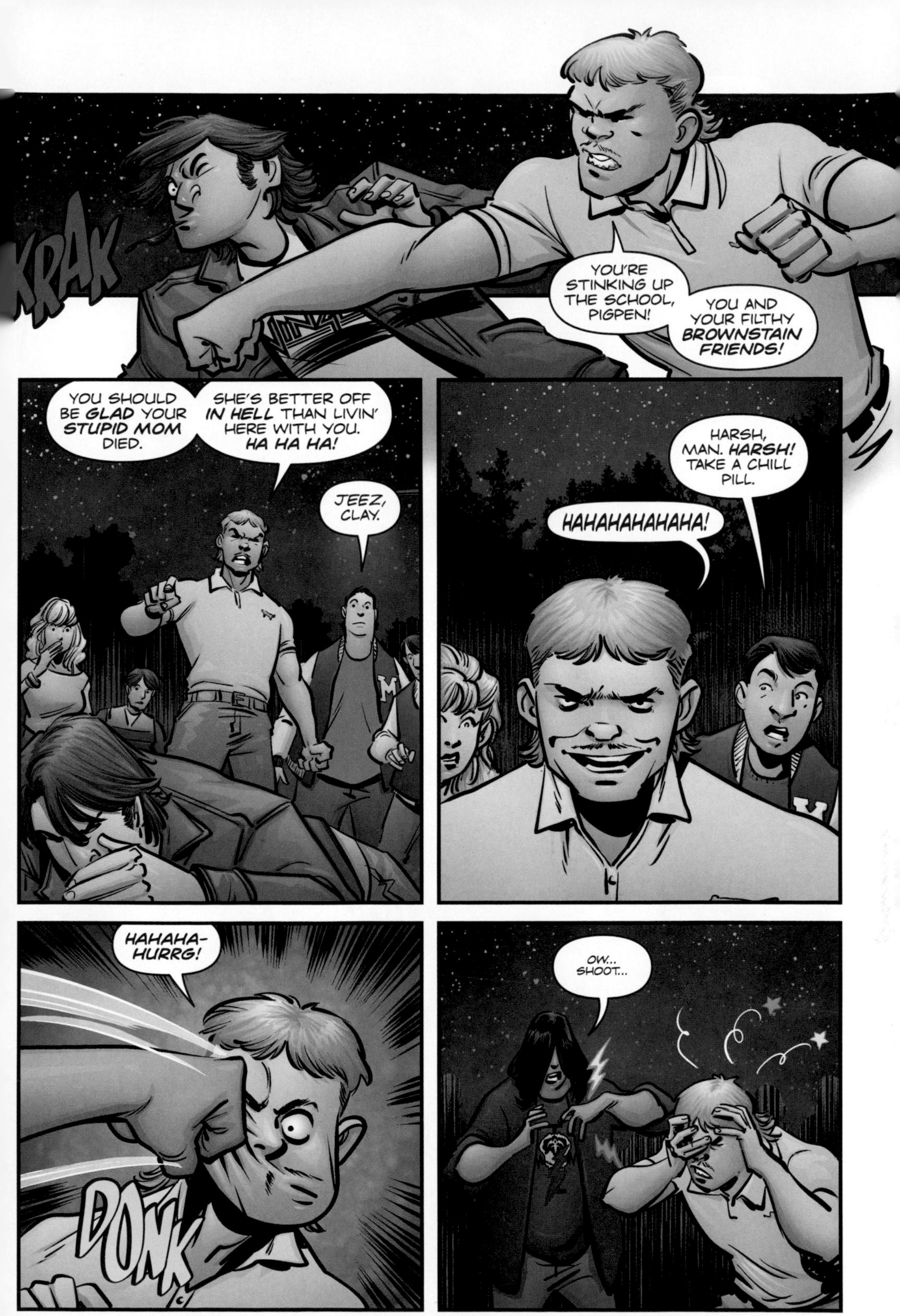
KRAK
YOU'RE STINKING UP THE SCHOOL, PIGPEN!
YOU AND YOUR FILTHY BROWNSTAIN FRIENDS!
YOU SHOULD BE GLAD YOUR STUPID MOM DIED.
SHE'S BETTER OFF IN HELL THAN LIVIN' HERE WITH YOU. HA HA HA!
JEEZ, CLAY.
HARSH, MAN. HARSH! TAKE A CHILL PILL.
HAHAHAHAHAHA!
HAHAHA-HURRG!
DONK
OW... SHOOT...

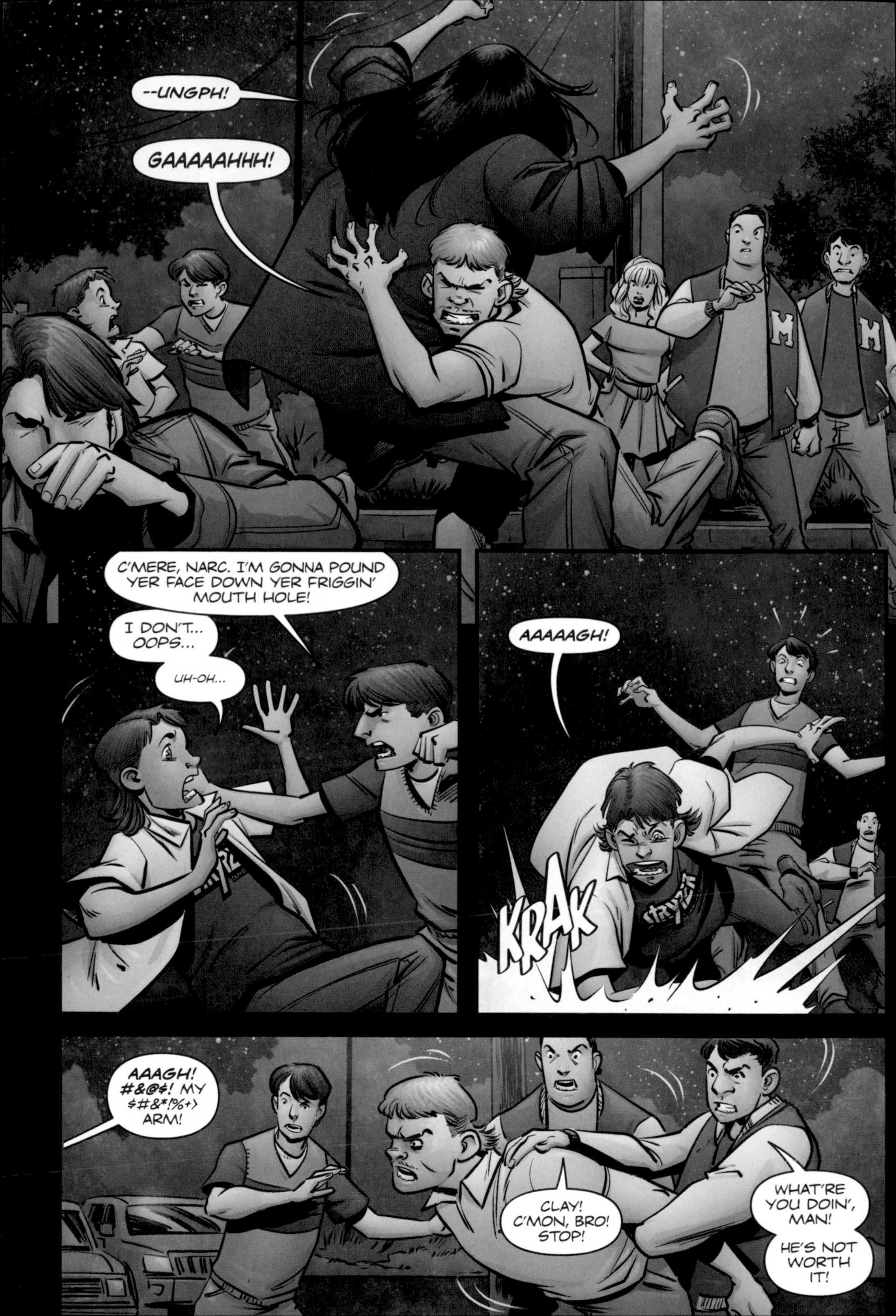
--UNGPH!
GAAAAAHHH!
C'MERE, NARC. I'M GONNA POUND YER FACE DOWN YER FRIGGIN' MOUTH HOLE!
I DON'T... OOPS...
UH-OH...
AAAAAGH!
KRAK
AAAGH! #&@$! MY $#&*!%+> ARM!
CLAY! C'MON, BRO! STOP!
WHAT'RE YOU DOIN', MAN!
HE'S NOT WORTH IT!

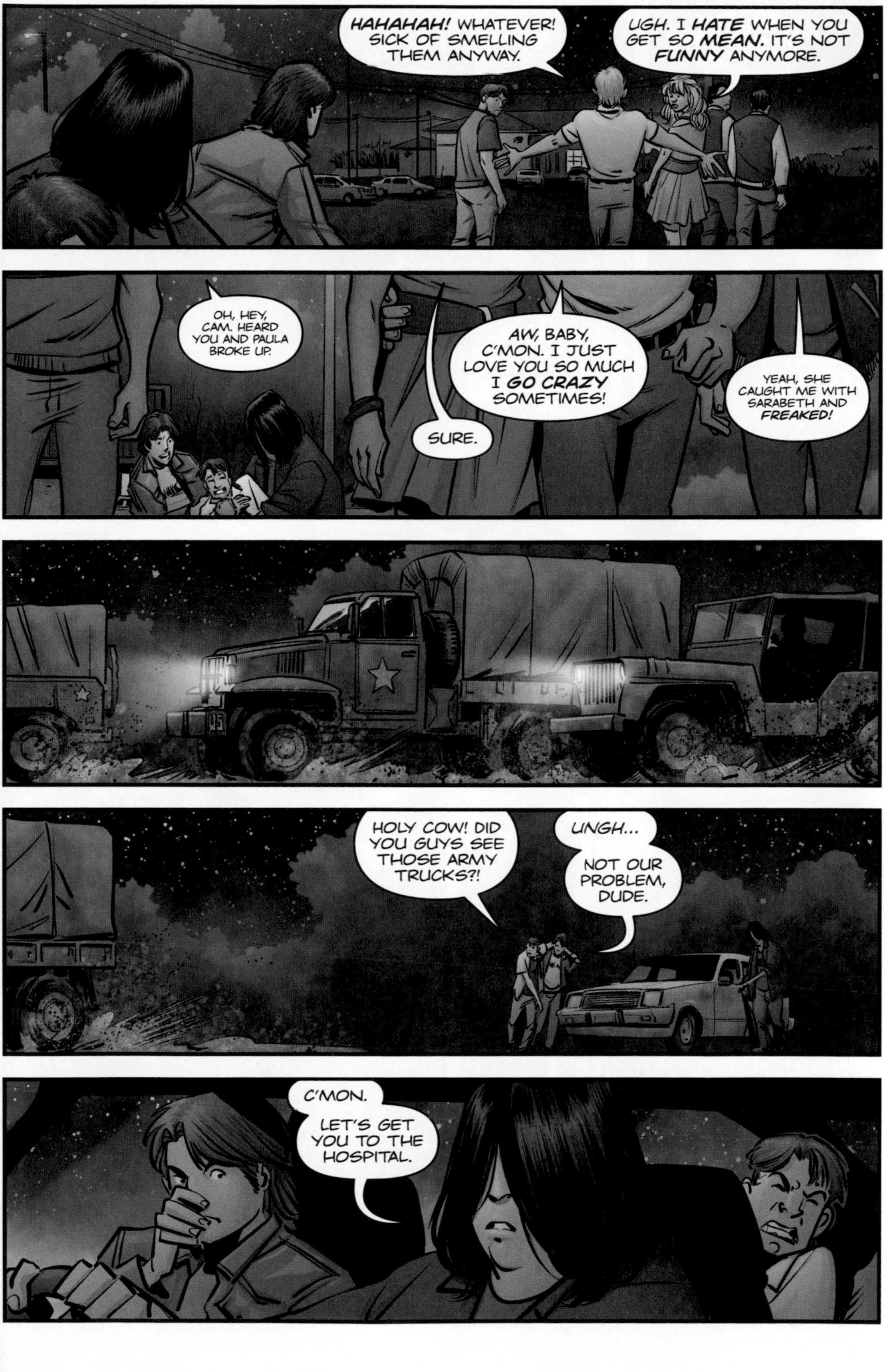
HAHAHAH! WHATEVER! SICK OF SMELLING THEM ANYWAY.
UGH. I HATE WHEN YOU GET SO MEAN. IT'S NOT FUNNY ANYMORE.
OH, HEY, CAM. HEARD YOU AND PAULA BROKE UP.
SURE.
AW, BABY, C'MON. I JUST LOVE YOU SO MUCH I GO CRAZY SOMETIMES!
YEAH, SHE CAUGHT ME WITH SARABETH AND FREAKED!
US
HOLY COW! DID YOU GUYS SEE THOSE ARMY TRUCKS?!
UNGH...
NOT OUR PROBLEM, DUDE.
C'MON.
LET'S GET YOU TO THE HOSPITAL.

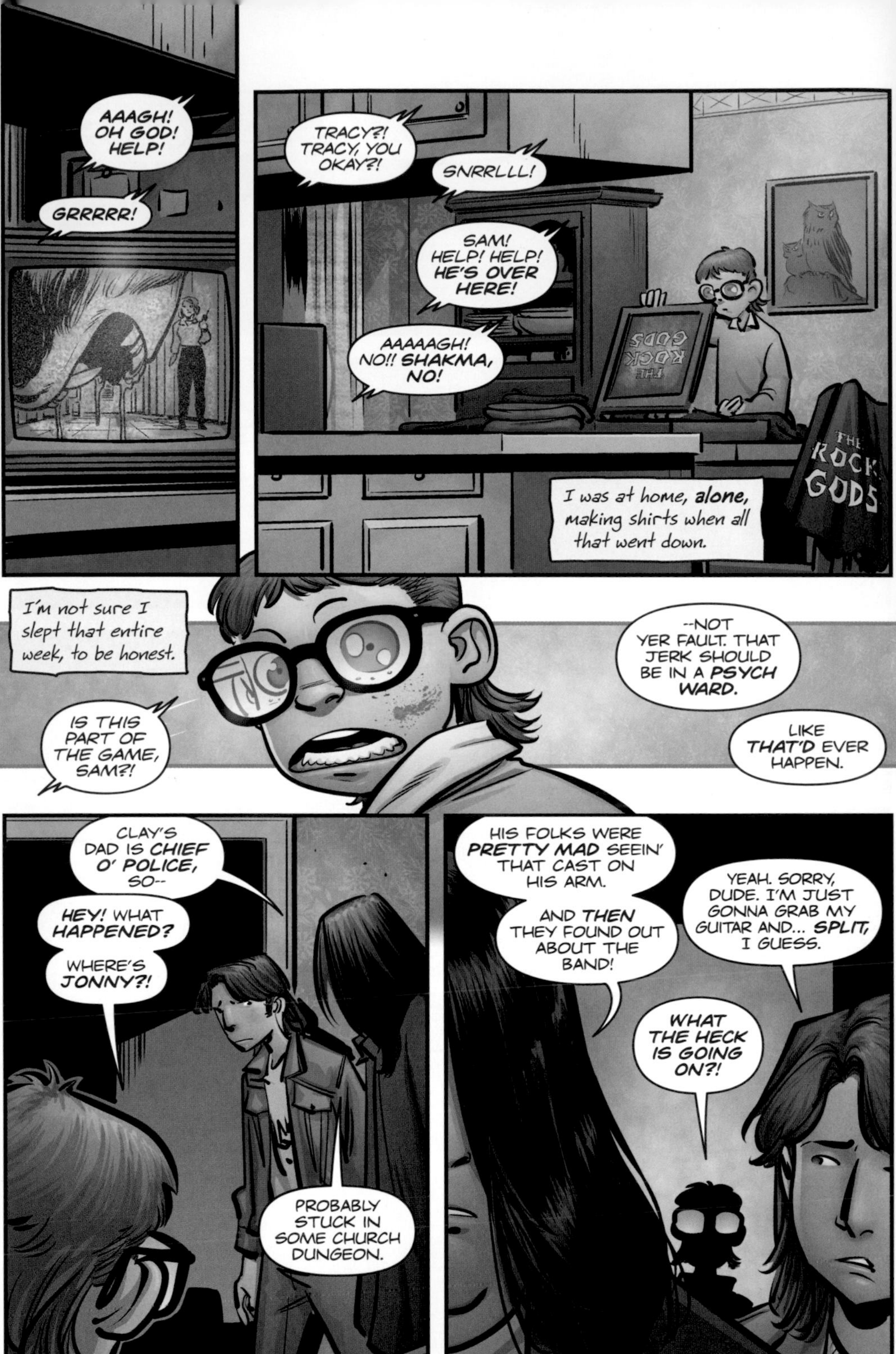
AAAGH! OH GOD! HELP!
GRRRRR!
TRACY?! TRACY, YOU OKAY?!
SNRRLLL!
SAM! HELP! HELP! HE'S OVER HERE!
AAAAAGH! NO!! SHAKMA, NO!
THE ROCK GODS
I was at home, alone, making shirts when all that went down.
I'm not sure I slept that entire week, to be honest.
IS THIS PART OF THE GAME, SAM?!
--NOT YER FAULT. THAT JERK SHOULD BE IN A PSYCH WARD.
LIKE THAT'D EVER HAPPEN.
CLAY'S DAD IS CHIEF O' POLICE, SO--
HEY! WHAT HAPPENED?
WHERE'S JONNY?!
PROBABLY STUCK IN SOME CHURCH DUNGEON.
HIS FOLKS WERE PRETTY MAD SEEIN' THAT CAST ON HIS ARM.
AND THEN THEY FOUND OUT ABOUT THE BAND!
YEAH. SORRY, DUDE. I'M JUST GONNA GRAB MY GUITAR AND... SPLIT, I GUESS.
WHAT THE HECK IS GOING ON?!

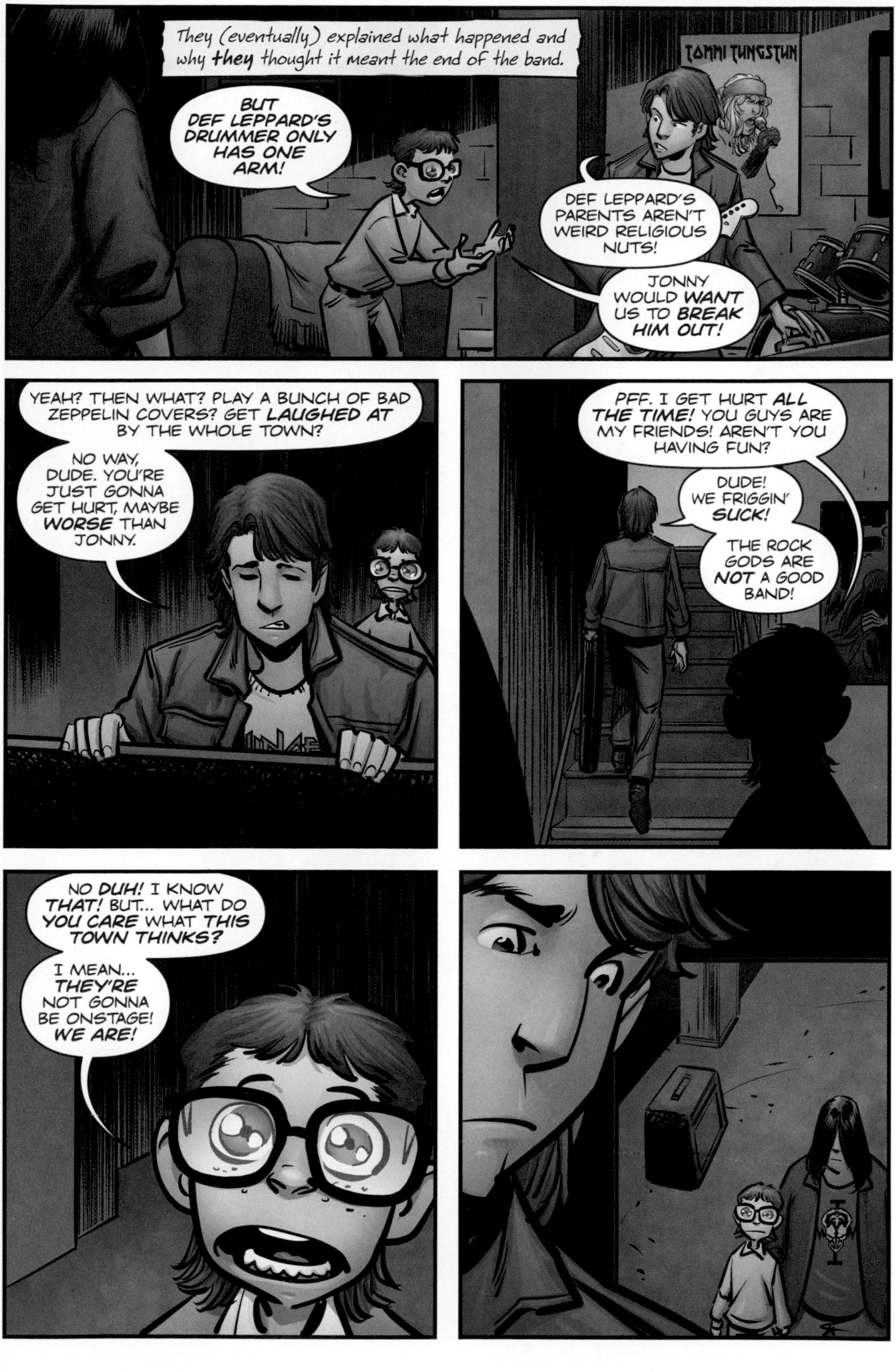
They (eventually) explained what happened and why **they** thought it meant the end of the band.
TOMMI TUNGSTUN
BUT DEF LEPPARD'S DRUMMER ONLY HAS ONE ARM!
DEF LEPPARD'S PARENTS AREN'T WEIRD RELIGIOUS NUTS!
JONNY WOULD **WANT** US TO **BREAK HIM OUT!**
YEAH? THEN WHAT? PLAY A BUNCH OF BAD ZEPPELIN COVERS? GET **LAUGHED AT** BY THE WHOLE TOWN?
NO WAY, DUDE. YOU'RE JUST GONNA GET HURT, MAYBE **WORSE** THAN JONNY.
PFF. I GET HURT **ALL THE TIME!** YOU GUYS ARE MY FRIENDS! AREN'T YOU HAVING FUN?
DUDE! WE FRIGGIN' **SUCK!**
THE ROCK GODS ARE **NOT** A GOOD BAND!
NO **DUH!** I KNOW **THAT!** BUT... WHAT DO **YOU CARE** WHAT **THIS TOWN THINKS?**
I MEAN... **THEY'RE** NOT GONNA BE ONSTAGE! **WE ARE!**

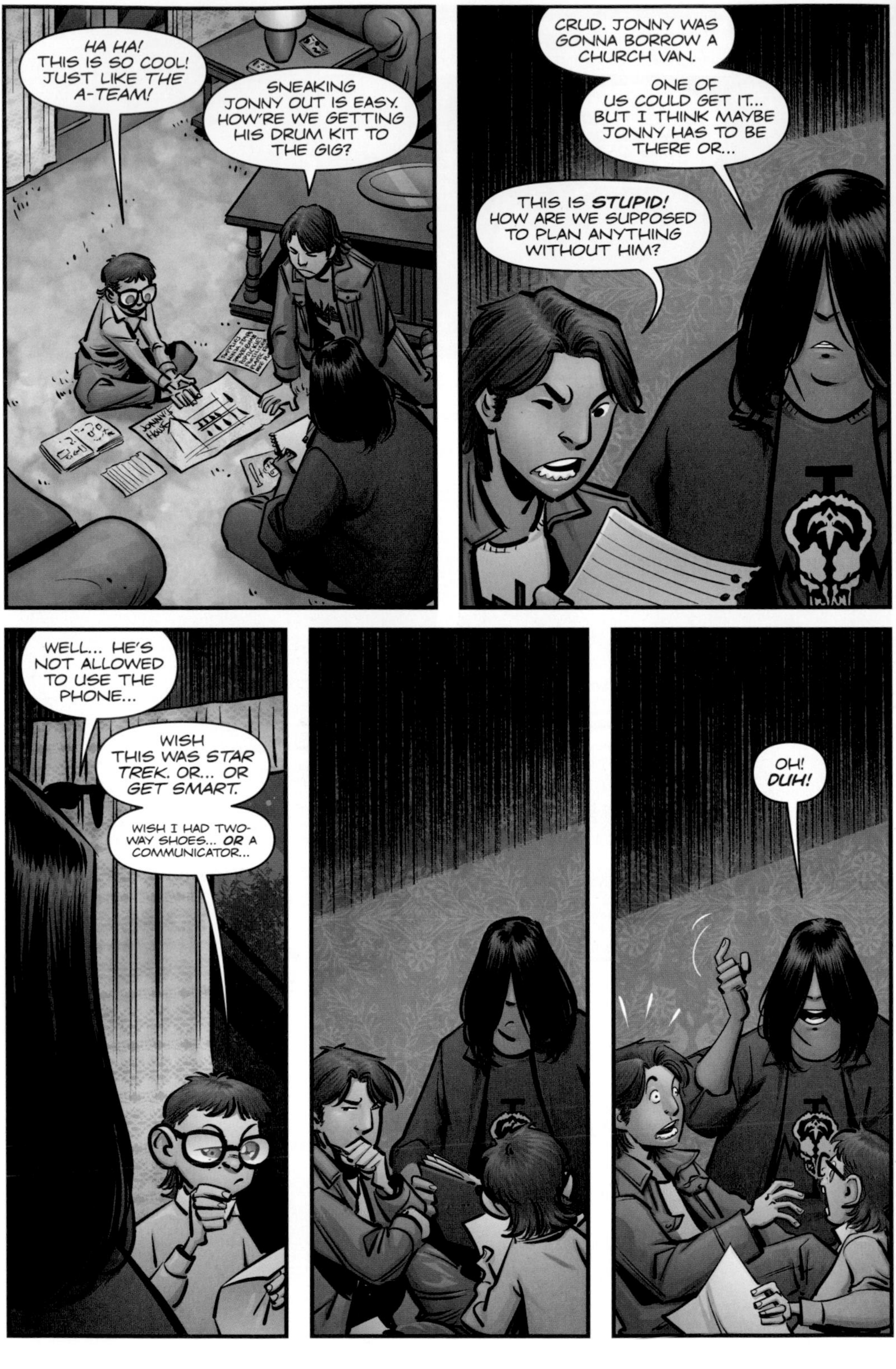
HA HA! THIS IS SO COOL! JUST LIKE THE A-TEAM!
SNEAKING JONNY OUT IS EASY. HOW'RE WE GETTING HIS DRUM KIT TO THE GIG?
CRUD. JONNY WAS GONNA BORROW A CHURCH VAN.
ONE OF US COULD GET IT... BUT I THINK MAYBE JONNY HAS TO BE THERE OR...
THIS IS STUPID! HOW ARE WE SUPPOSED TO PLAN ANYTHING WITHOUT HIM?
WELL... HE'S NOT ALLOWED TO USE THE PHONE...
WISH THIS WAS STAR TREK. OR... OR GET SMART.
WISH I HAD TWO-WAY SHOES... OR A COMMUNICATOR...
OH! DUH!

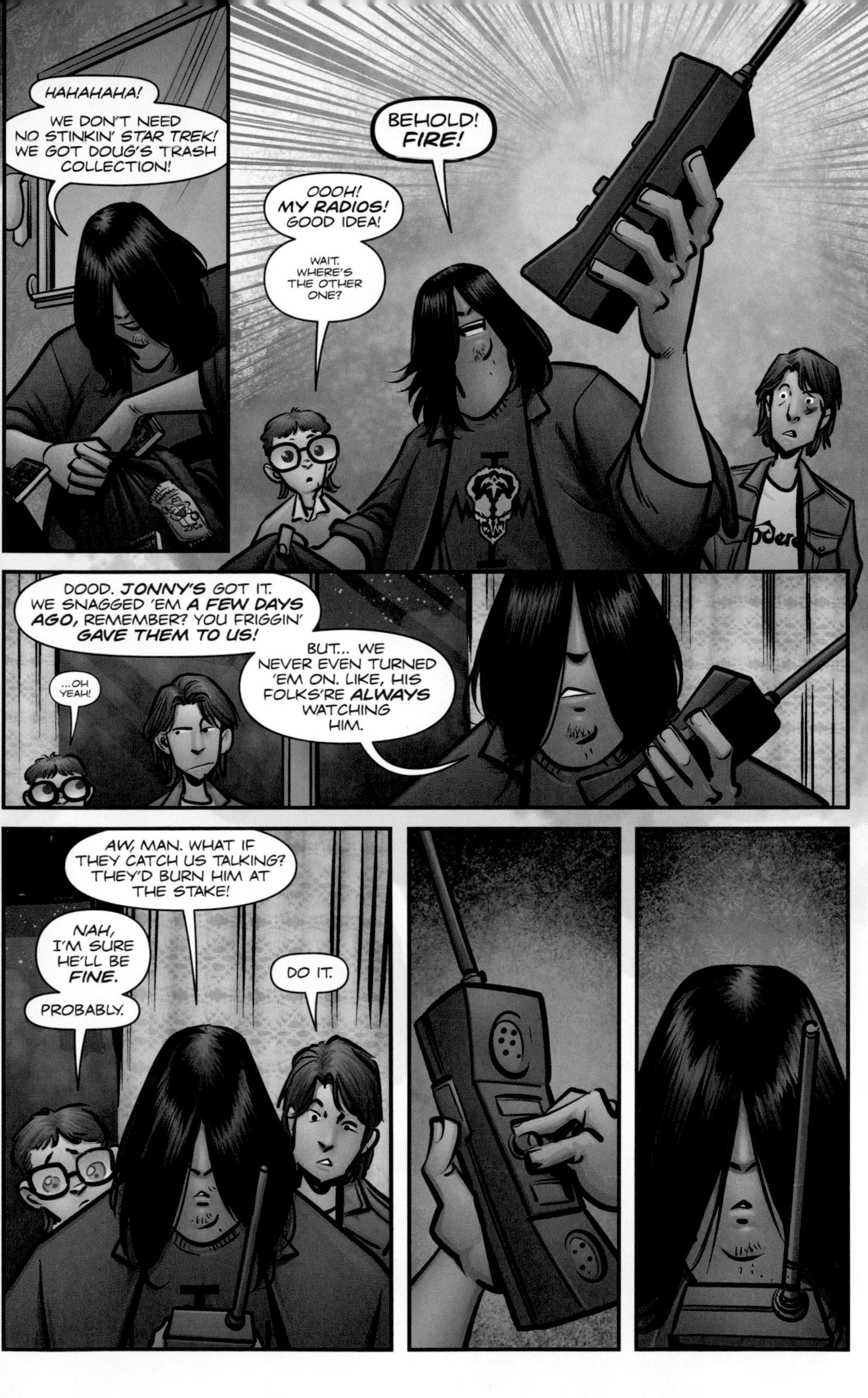

HAHAHAHA!
WE DON'T NEED NO STINKIN' STAR TREK! WE GOT DOUG'S TRASH COLLECTION!
OOOH! MY RADIOS! GOOD IDEA!
WAIT. WHERE'S THE OTHER ONE?
BEHOLD! FIRE!
DOOD. JONNY'S GOT IT. WE SNAGGED 'EM A FEW DAYS AGO, REMEMBER? YOU FRIGGIN' GAVE THEM TO US!
...OH YEAH!
BUT... WE NEVER EVEN TURNED 'EM ON. LIKE, HIS FOLKS'RE ALWAYS WATCHING HIM.
AW, MAN. WHAT IF THEY CATCH US TALKING? THEY'D BURN HIM AT THE STAKE!
NAH, I'M SURE HE'LL BE FINE.
PROBABLY.
DO IT.

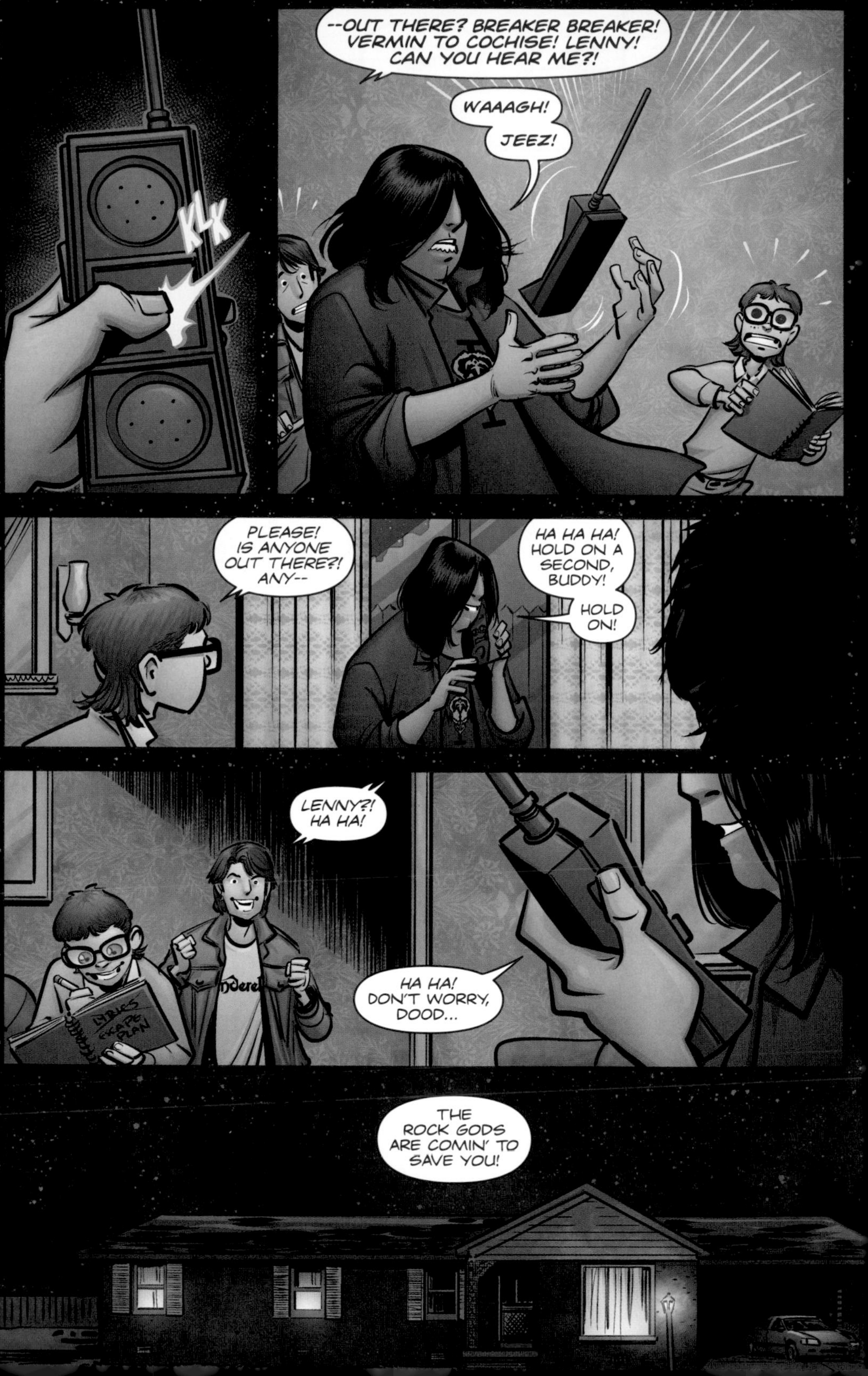

KLK
--OUT THERE? BREAKER BREAKER! VERMIN TO COCHISE! LENNY! CAN YOU HEAR ME?!
WAAAGH!
JEEZ!
PLEASE! IS ANYONE OUT THERE?! ANY--
HA HA HA! HOLD ON A SECOND, BUDDY!
HOLD ON!
LENNY?! HA HA!
LYRICS
ESCAPE PLAN
HA HA! DON'T WORRY, DOOD...
THE ROCK GODS ARE COMIN' TO SAVE YOU!

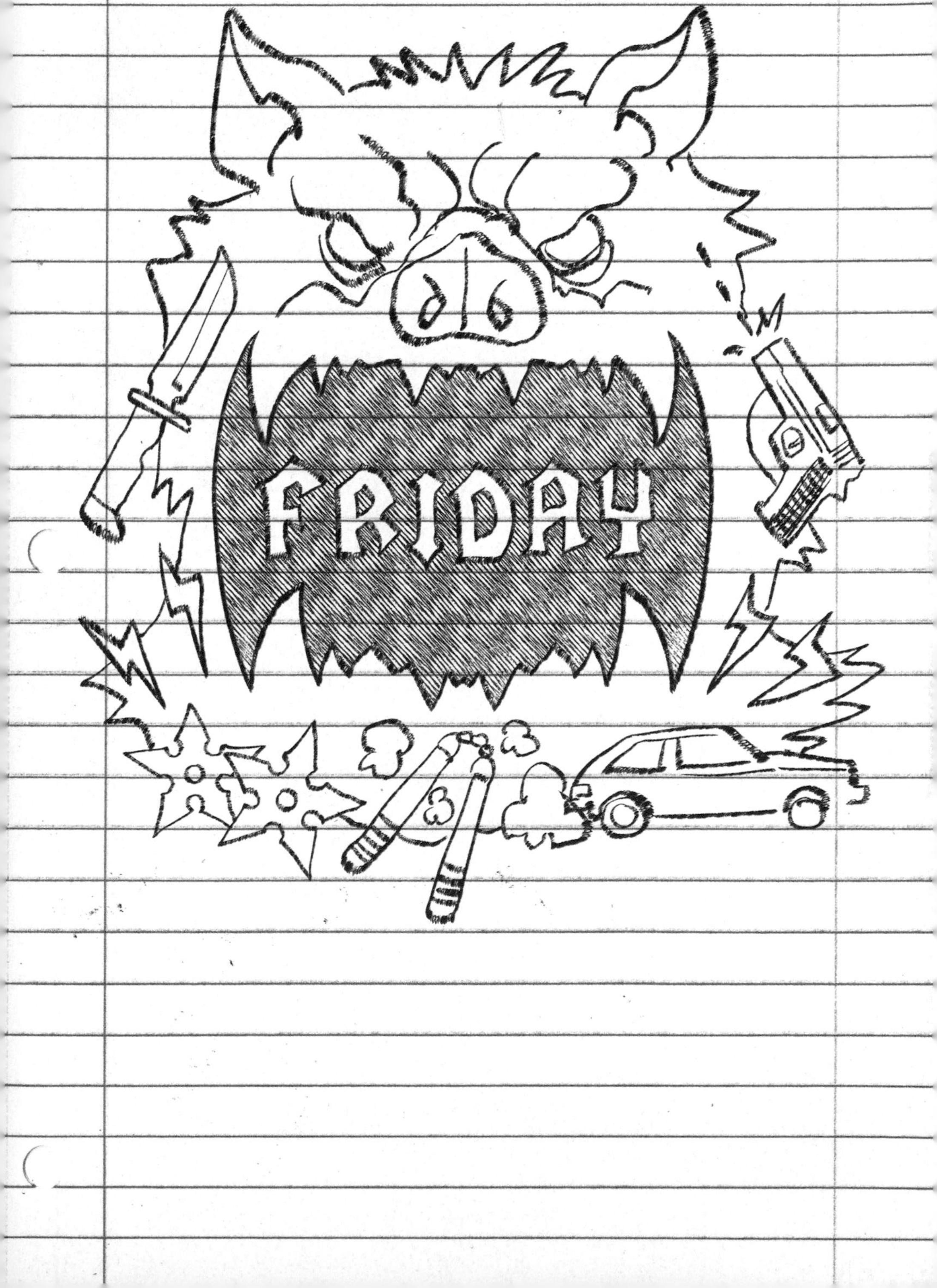
FRIDAY

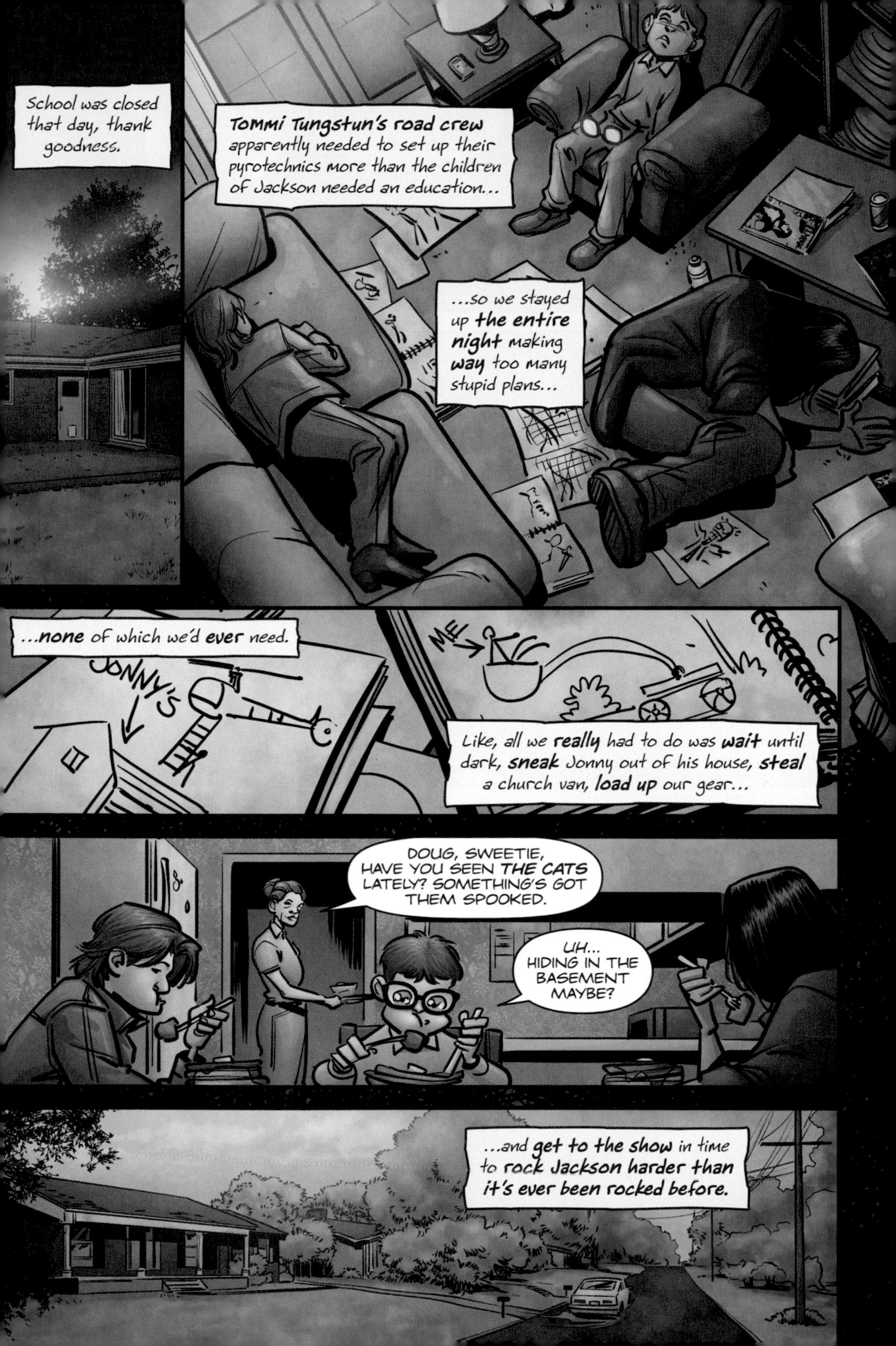

School was closed that day, thank goodness.
Tommi Tungstun's road crew apparently needed to set up their pyrotechnics more than the children of Jackson needed an education...
...so we stayed up the entire night making way too many stupid plans...
...none of which we'd ever need.
JONNY'S
ME
Like, all we really had to do was wait until dark, sneak Jonny out of his house, steal a church van, load up our gear...
DOUG, SWEETIE, HAVE YOU SEEN THE CATS LATELY? SOMETHING'S GOT THEM SPOOKED.
UH... HIDING IN THE BASEMENT MAYBE?
...and get to the show in time to rock Jackson harder than it's ever been rocked before.

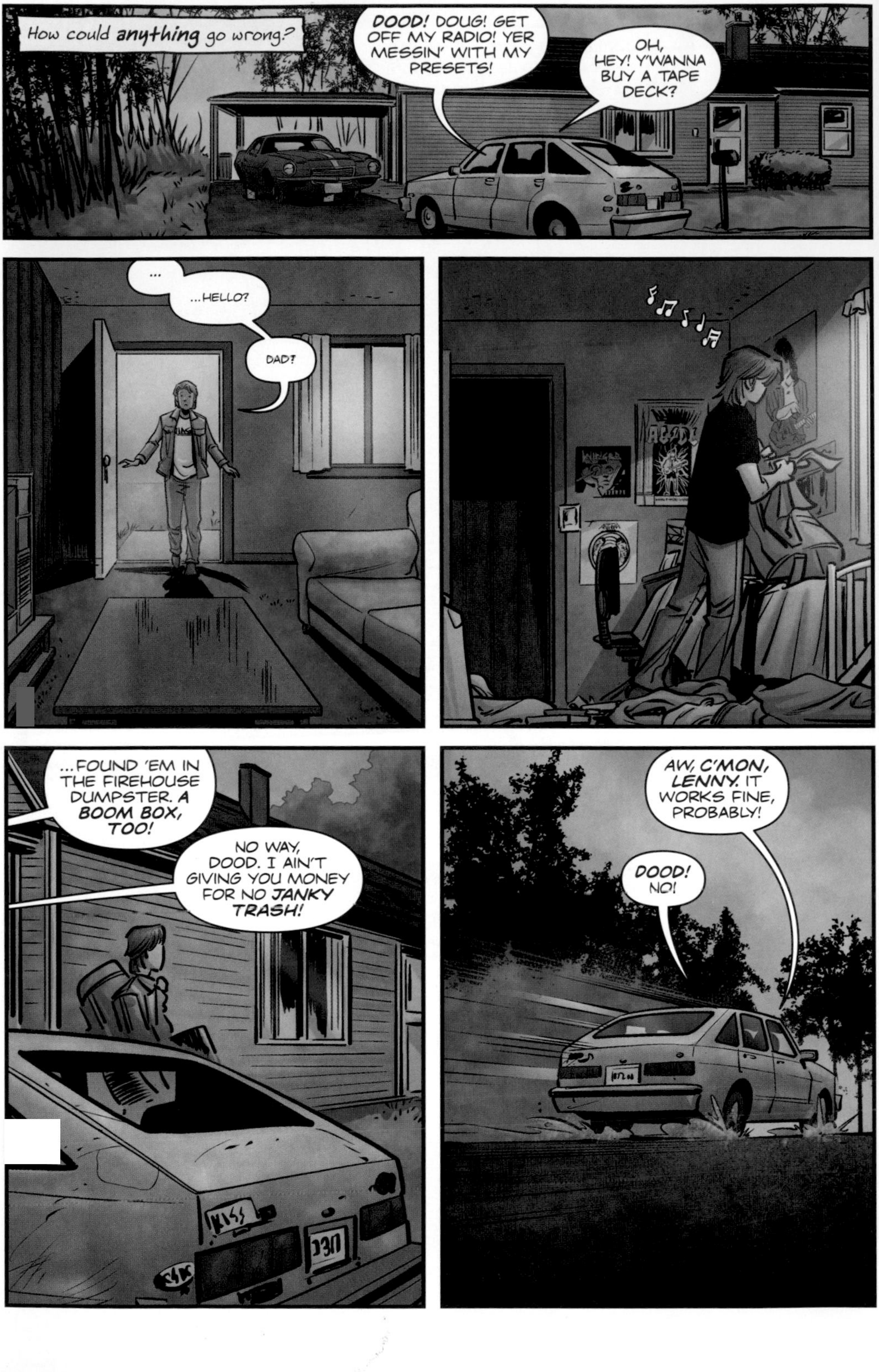
How could **anything** go wrong?
DOOD! DOUG! GET OFF MY RADIO! YER MESSIN' WITH MY PRESETS!
OH, HEY! Y'WANNA BUY A TAPE DECK?
...
...HELLO?
DAD?
...FOUND 'EM IN THE FIREHOUSE DUMPSTER. **A BOOM BOX, TOO!**
NO WAY, DOOD. I AIN'T GIVING YOU MONEY FOR NO **JANKY TRASH!**
AW, **C'MON, LENNY.** IT WORKS FINE, PROBABLY!
DOOD! NO!

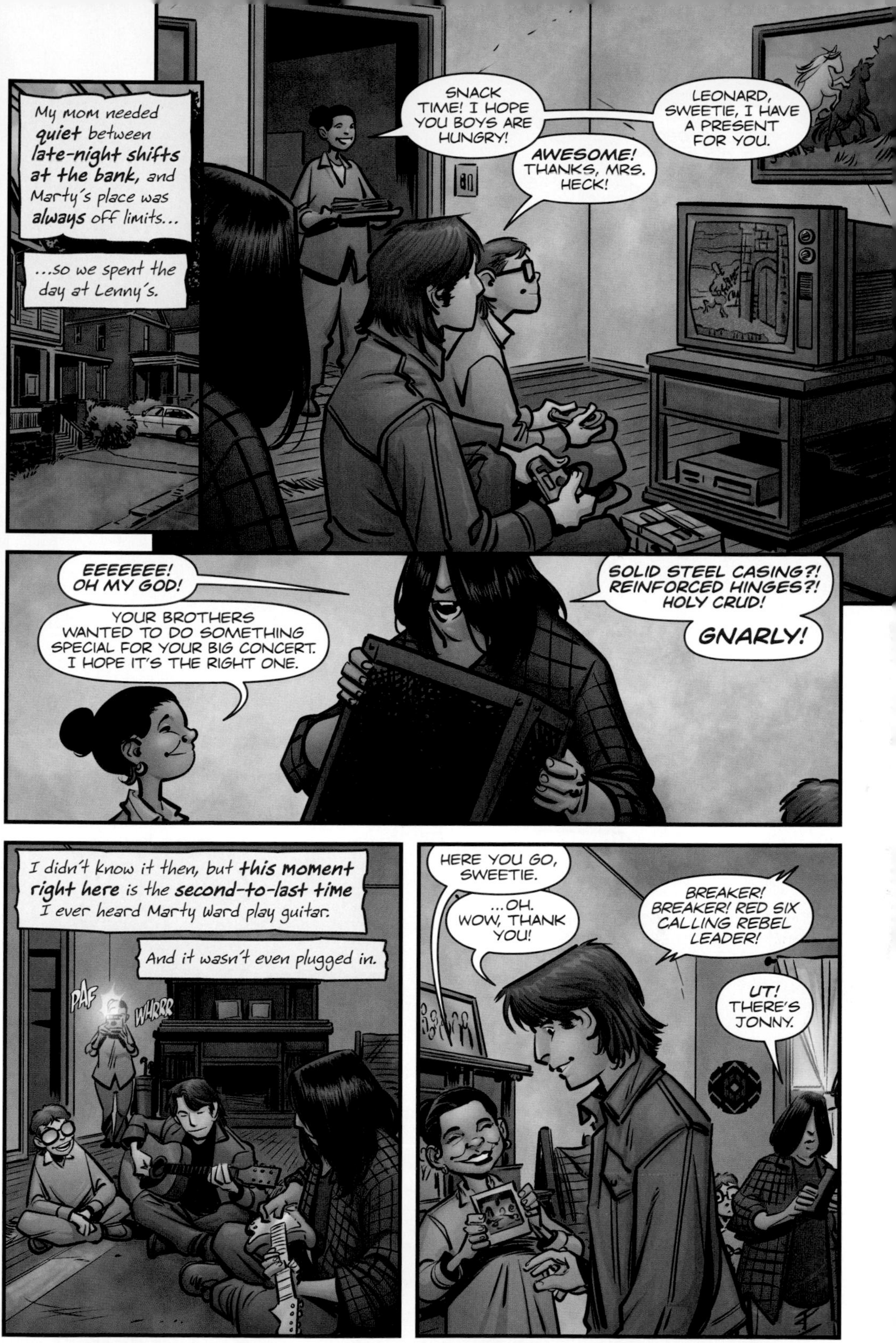
My mom needed quiet between late-night shifts at the bank, and Marty's place was always off limits...
...so we spent the day at Lenny's.
SNACK TIME! I HOPE YOU BOYS ARE HUNGRY!
AWESOME! THANKS, MRS. HECK!
LEONARD, SWEETIE, I HAVE A PRESENT FOR YOU.
EEEEEEE! OH MY GOD!
YOUR BROTHERS WANTED TO DO SOMETHING SPECIAL FOR YOUR BIG CONCERT. I HOPE IT'S THE RIGHT ONE.
SOLID STEEL CASING?! REINFORCED HINGES?! HOLY CRUD!
GNARLY!
I didn't know it then, but this moment right here is the second-to-last time I ever heard Marty Ward play guitar.
And it wasn't even plugged in.
PAF
WHRRR
HERE YOU GO, SWEETIE.
...OH. WOW, THANK YOU!
BREAKER! BREAKER! RED SIX CALLING REBEL LEADER!
UT! THERE'S JONNY.

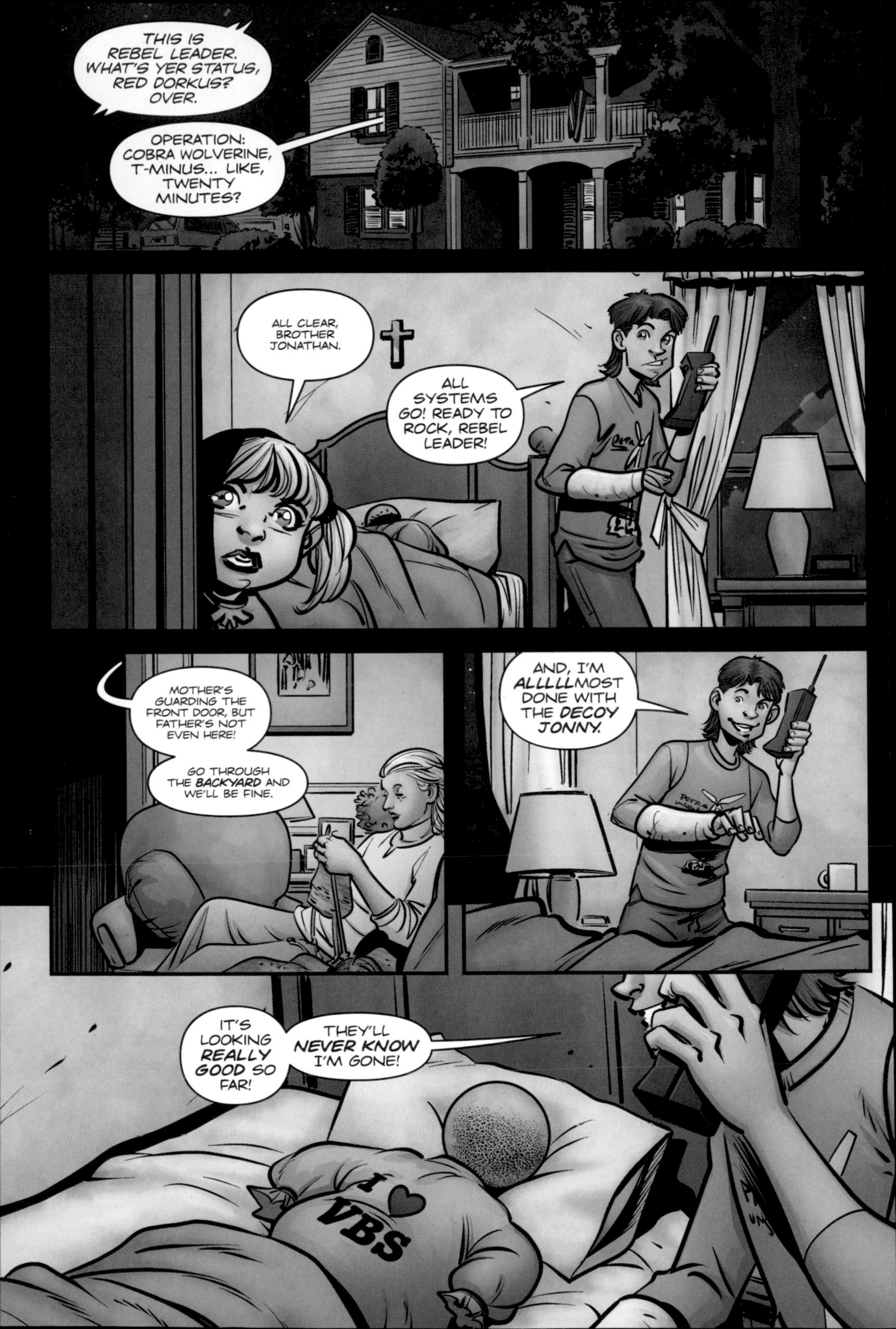
THIS IS REBEL LEADER. WHAT'S YER STATUS, RED DORKUS? OVER.
OPERATION: COBRA WOLVERINE, T-MINUS... LIKE, TWENTY MINUTES?
ALL CLEAR, BROTHER JONATHAN.
ALL SYSTEMS GO! READY TO ROCK, REBEL LEADER!
MOTHER'S GUARDING THE FRONT DOOR, BUT FATHER'S NOT EVEN HERE!
GO THROUGH THE BACKYARD AND WE'LL BE FINE.
AND, I'M ALLLLLMOST DONE WITH THE DECOY JONNY.
IT'S LOOKING REALLY GOOD SO FAR!
THEY'LL NEVER KNOW I'M GONE!
I ♥ VBS

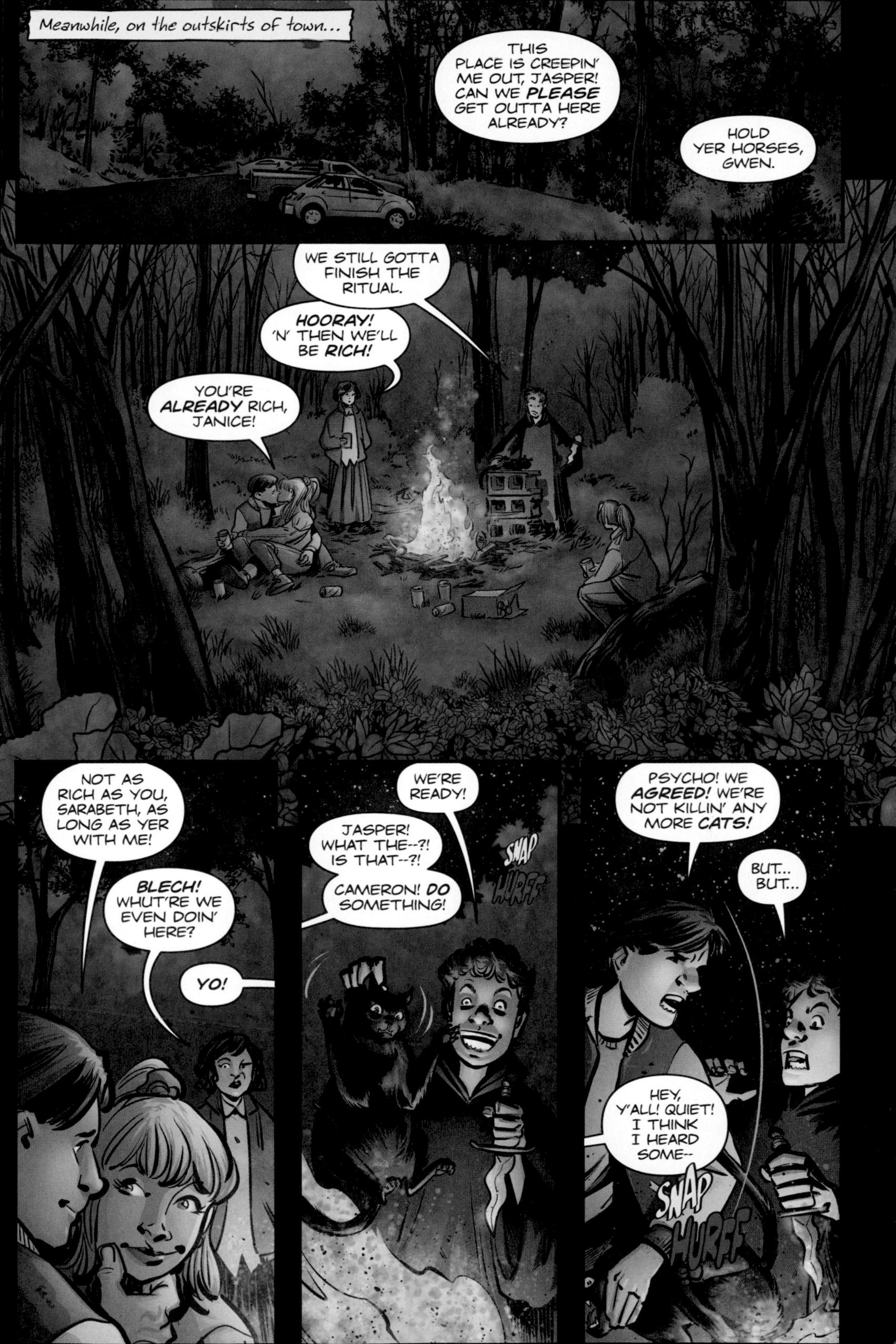
Meanwhile, on the outskirts of town...
THIS PLACE IS CREEPIN' ME OUT, JASPER! CAN WE PLEASE GET OUTTA HERE ALREADY?
HOLD YER HORSES, GWEN.
WE STILL GOTTA FINISH THE RITUAL.
HOORAY! 'N' THEN WE'LL BE RICH!
YOU'RE ALREADY RICH, JANICE!
NOT AS RICH AS YOU, SARABETH, AS LONG AS YER WITH ME!
BLECH! WHUT'RE WE EVEN DOIN' HERE?
YO!
WE'RE READY!
JASPER! WHAT THE--?! IS THAT--?!
CAMERON! DO SOMETHING!
SNAP
HURFF
PSYCHO! WE AGREED! WE'RE NOT KILLIN' ANY MORE CATS!
BUT... BUT...
HEY, Y'ALL! QUIET! I THINK I HEARD SOME--
SNAP
HURFF

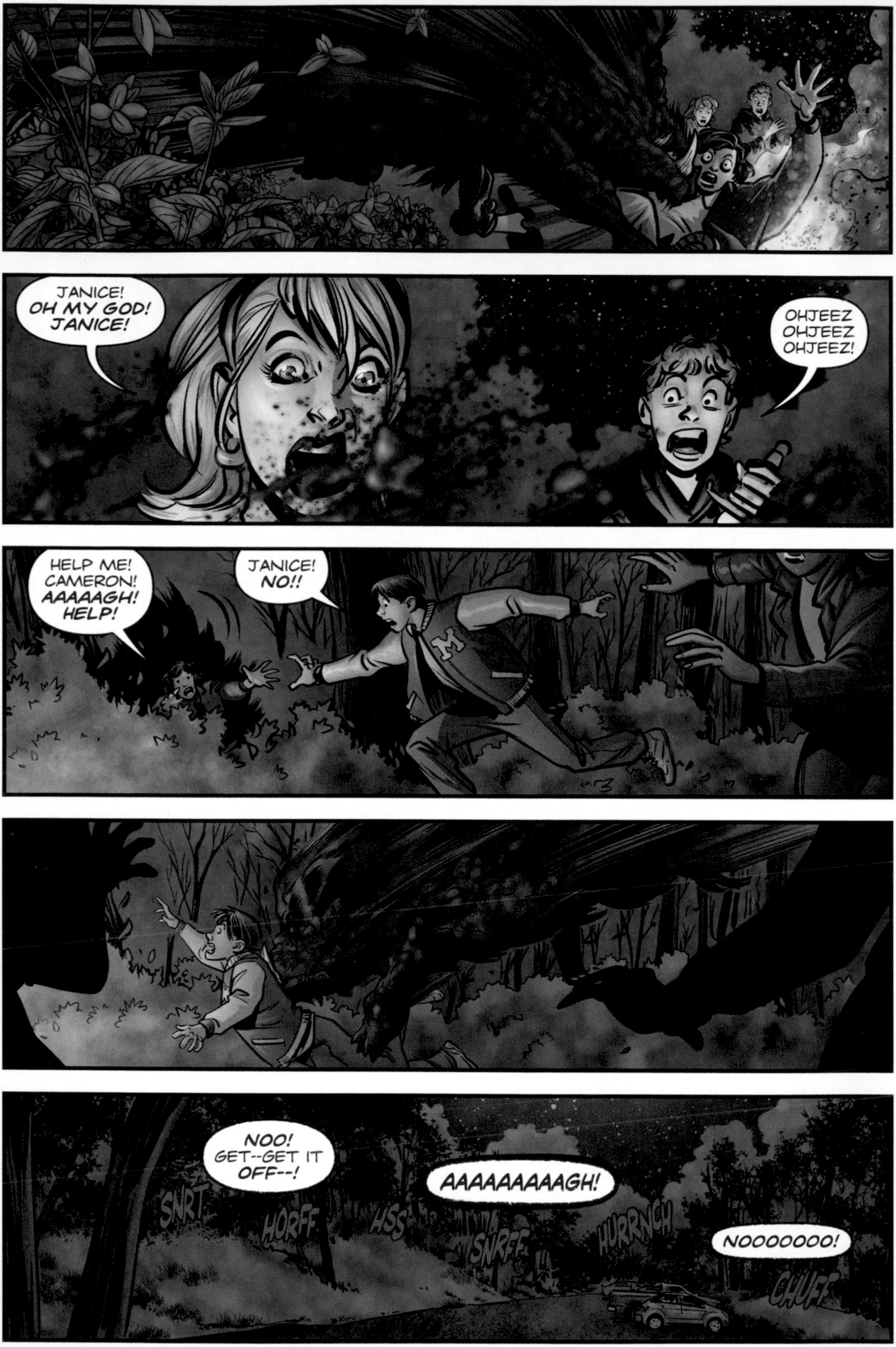
JANICE! OH MY GOD! JANICE!
OHJEEZ OHJEEZ OHJEEZ!
HELP ME! CAMERON! AAAAAGH! HELP!
JANICE! NO!!
NOO! GET--GET IT OFF--!
AAAAAAAAAGH!
SNRT
HORFF
HSS
SNRFF
HURRNCH
NOOOOOOO!
CHUFF

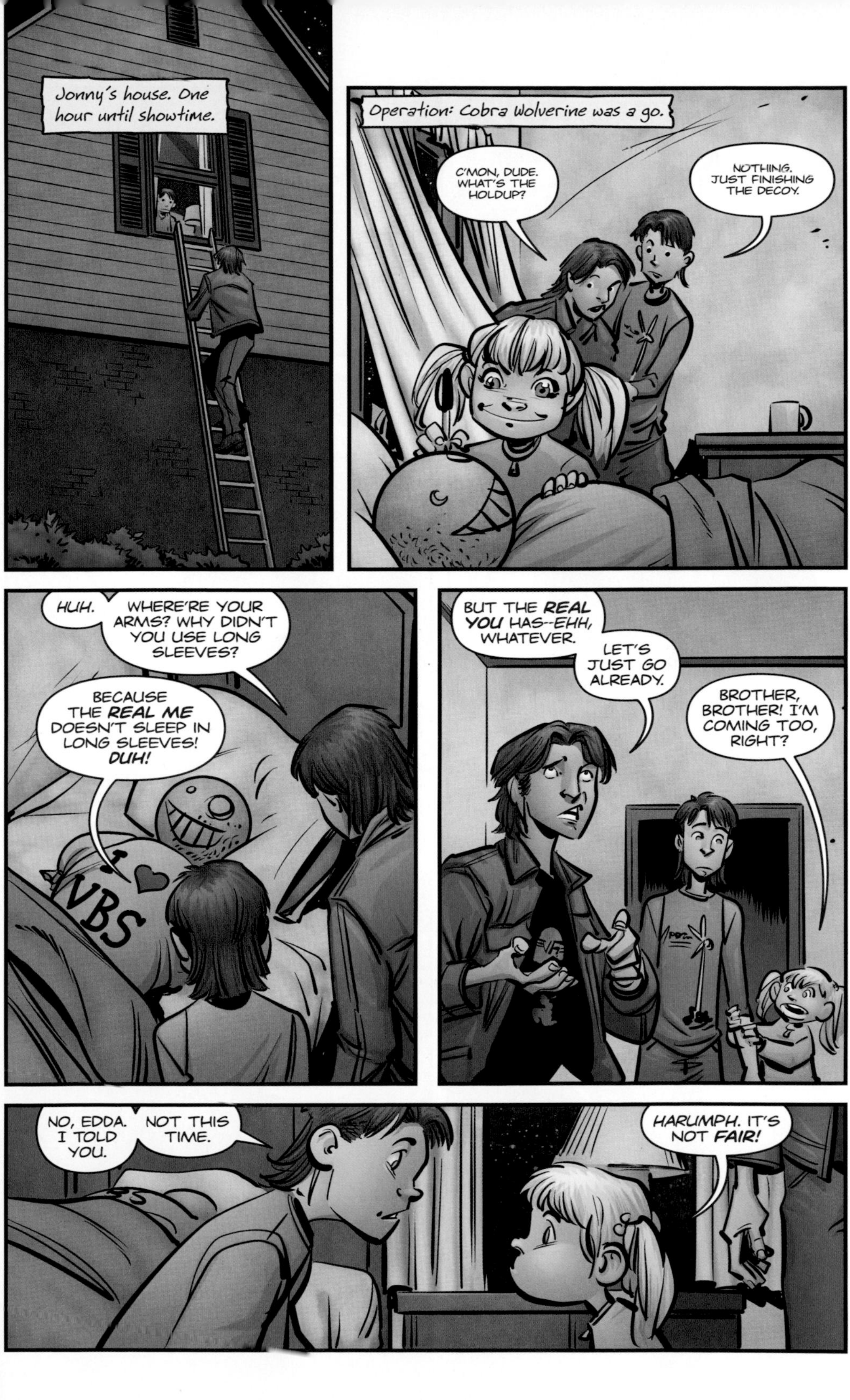
Jonny's house. One hour until showtime.
Operation: Cobra Wolverine was a go.
C'MON, DUDE. WHAT'S THE HOLDUP?
NOTHING. JUST FINISHING THE DECOY.
HUH.
WHERE'RE YOUR ARMS? WHY DIDN'T YOU USE LONG SLEEVES?
BECAUSE THE REAL ME DOESN'T SLEEP IN LONG SLEEVES! DUH!
I ♥ VBS
BUT THE REAL YOU HAS--EHH, WHATEVER.
LET'S JUST GO ALREADY.
BROTHER, BROTHER! I'M COMING TOO, RIGHT?
NO, EDDA. I TOLD YOU.
NOT THIS TIME.
HARUMPH. IT'S NOT FAIR!

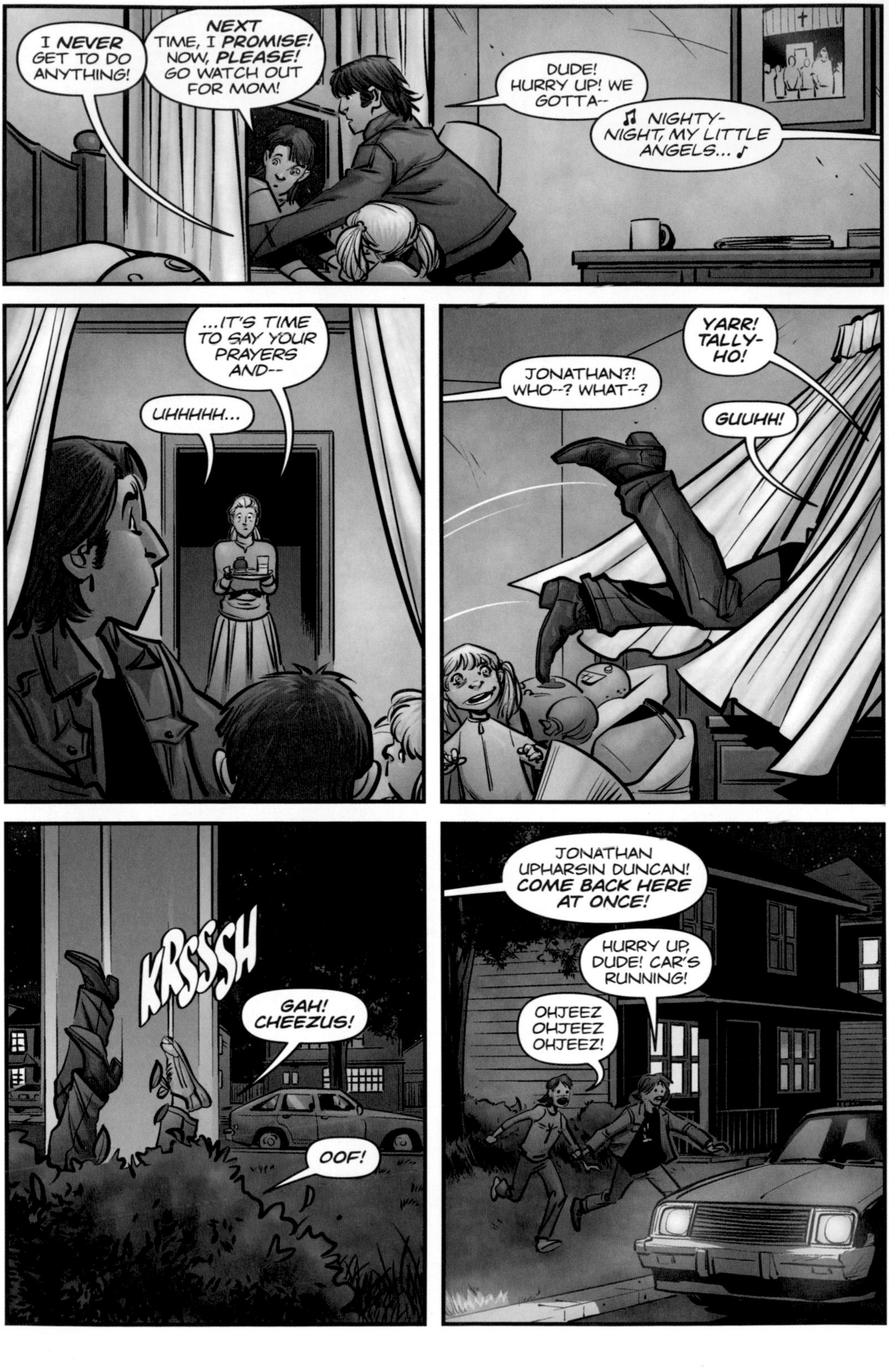
I NEVER GET TO DO ANYTHING!
NEXT TIME, I PROMISE! NOW, PLEASE! GO WATCH OUT FOR MOM!
DUDE! HURRY UP! WE GOTTA--
♫ NIGHTY-NIGHT, MY LITTLE ANGELS... ♪
...IT'S TIME TO SAY YOUR PRAYERS AND--
UHHHHH...
YARR! TALLY-HO!
JONATHAN?! WHO--? WHAT--?
GUUHH!
KRSSSH
GAH! CHEEZUS!
OOF!
JONATHAN UPHARSIN DUNCAN! COME BACK HERE AT ONCE!
HURRY UP, DUDE! CAR'S RUNNING!
OHJEEZ OHJEEZ OHJEEZ!

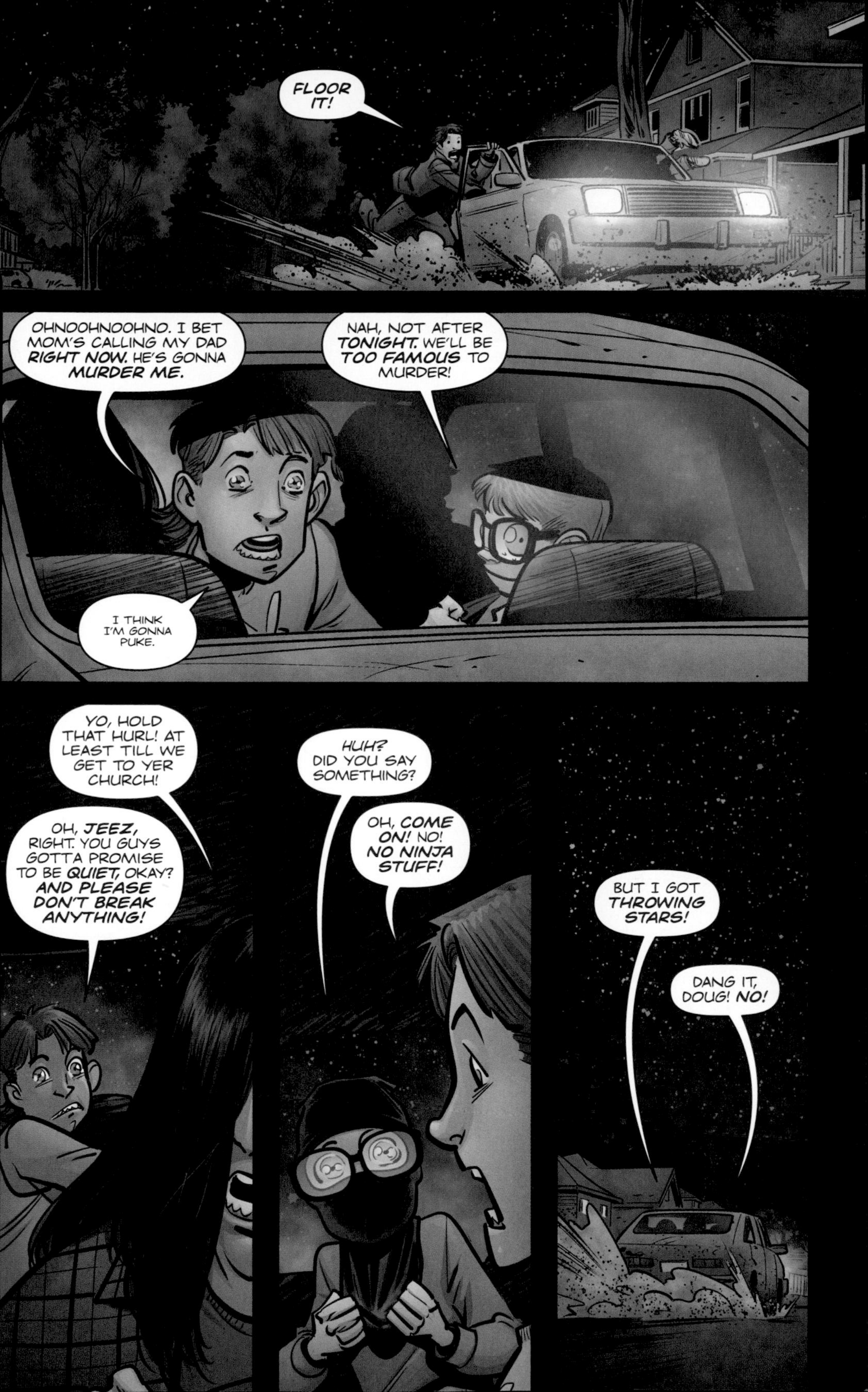
FLOOR IT!
OHNOOHNOOHNO. I BET MOM'S CALLING MY DAD RIGHT NOW. HE'S GONNA MURDER ME.
NAH, NOT AFTER TONIGHT. WE'LL BE TOO FAMOUS TO MURDER!
I THINK I'M GONNA PUKE.
YO, HOLD THAT HURL! AT LEAST TILL WE GET TO YER CHURCH!
OH, JEEZ, RIGHT. YOU GUYS GOTTA PROMISE TO BE QUIET, OKAY? AND PLEASE DON'T BREAK ANYTHING!
HUH? DID YOU SAY SOMETHING?
OH, COME ON! NO! NO NINJA STUFF!
BUT I GOT THROWING STARS!
DANG IT, DOUG! NO!

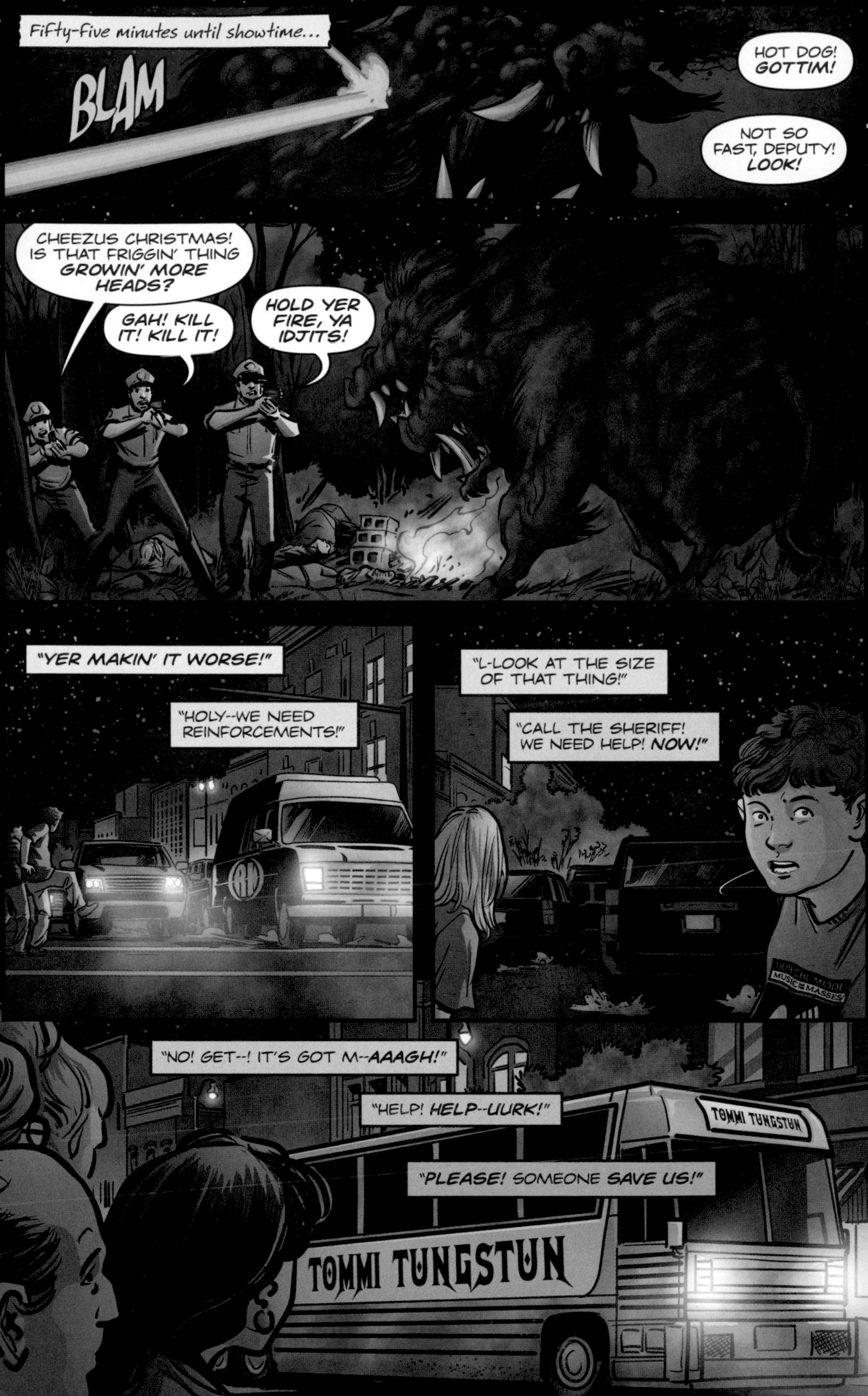
Fifty-five minutes until showtime...
BLAM
HOT DOG! GOTTIM!
NOT SO FAST, DEPUTY! LOOK!
CHEEZUS CHRISTMAS! IS THAT FRIGGIN' THING GROWIN' MORE HEADS?
GAH! KILL IT! KILL IT!
HOLD YER FIRE, YA IDJITS!
"YER MAKIN' IT WORSE!"
"HOLY--WE NEED REINFORCEMENTS!"
"L-LOOK AT THE SIZE OF THAT THING!"
"CALL THE SHERIFF! WE NEED HELP! NOW!"
DEPECHE MODE
MUSIC FOR THE MASSES
"NO! GET--! IT'S GOT M--AAAGH!"
"HELP! HELP--UURK!"
TOMMI TUNGSTUN
"PLEASE! SOMEONE SAVE US!"
TOMMI TUNGSTUN

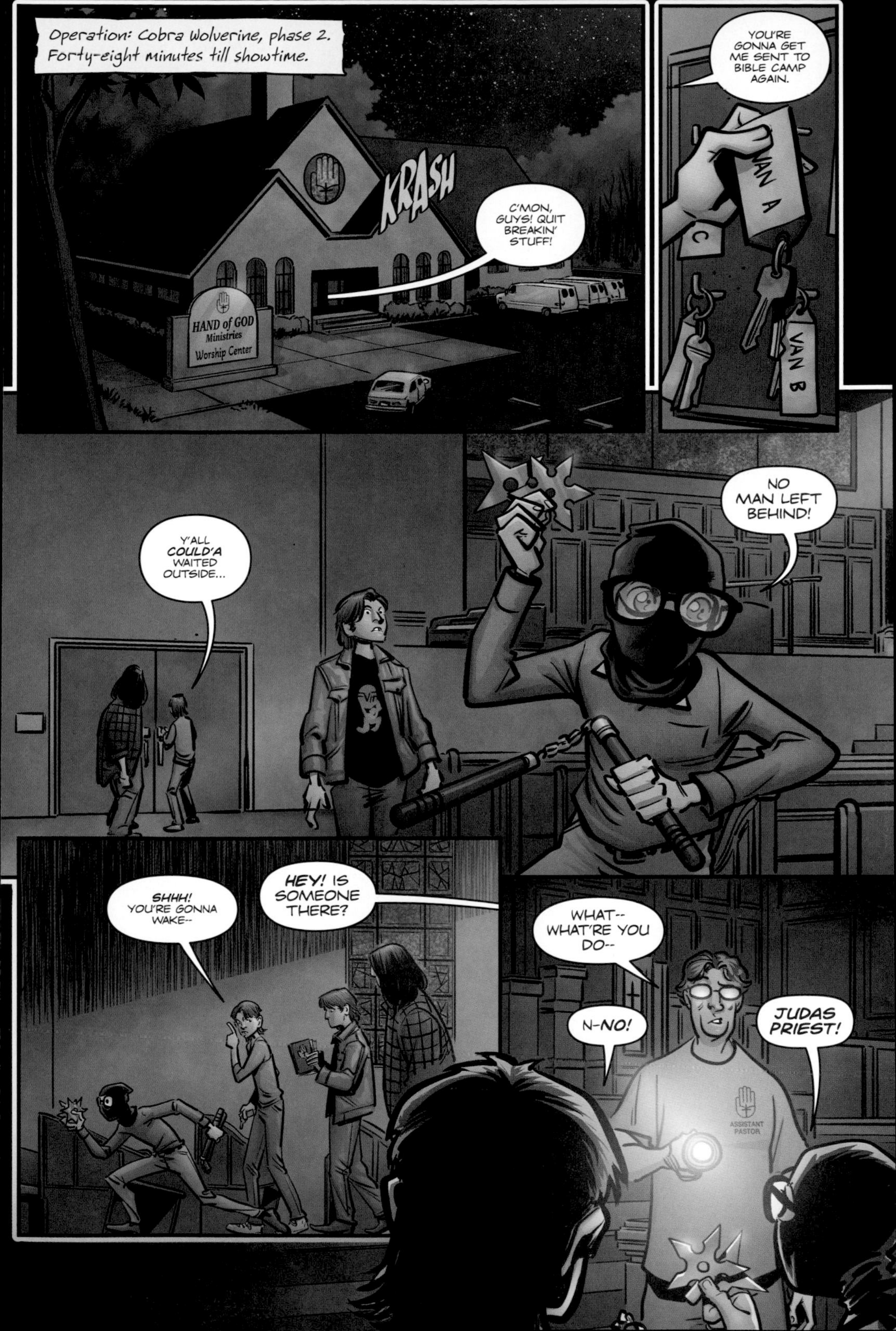
Operation: Cobra Wolverine, phase 2. Forty-eight minutes till showtime.
KRASH
HAND of GOD Ministries Worship Center
C'MON, GUYS! QUIT BREAKIN' STUFF!
YOU'RE GONNA GET ME SENT TO BIBLE CAMP AGAIN.
VAN A
C
VAN B
Y'ALL COULD'A WAITED OUTSIDE...
NO MAN LEFT BEHIND!
SHHH! YOU'RE GONNA WAKE--
HEY! IS SOMEONE THERE?
WHAT-- WHAT'RE YOU DO--
N-NO!
JUDAS PRIEST!
ASSISTANT PASTOR

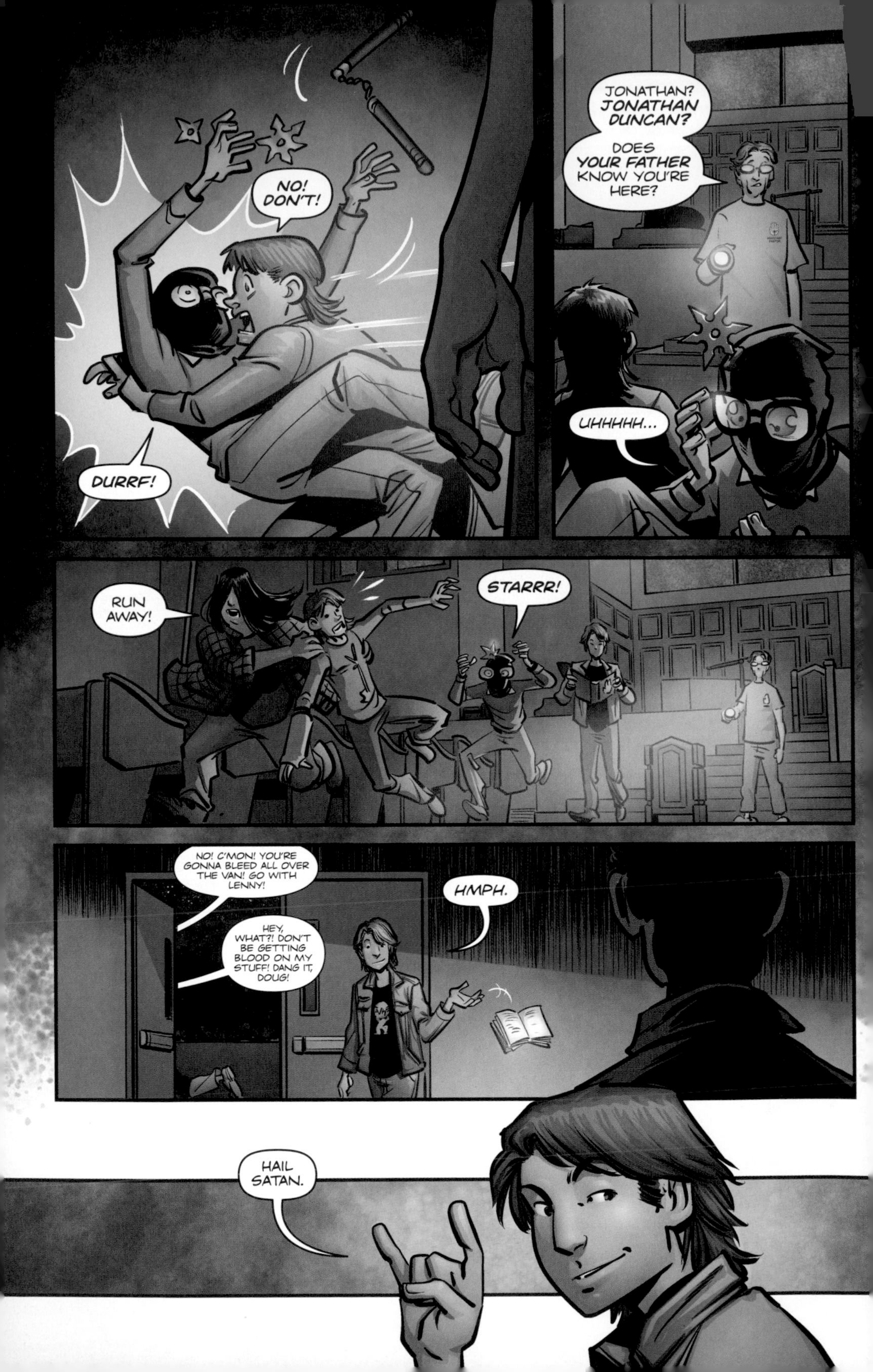
NO! DON'T!
DURRF!
JONATHAN? JONATHAN DUNCAN?
DOES YOUR FATHER KNOW YOU'RE HERE?
UHHHHH...
RUN AWAY!
STARRR!
NO! C'MON! YOU'RE GONNA BLEED ALL OVER THE VAN! GO WITH LENNY!
HEY, WHAT?! DON'T BE GETTING BLOOD ON MY STUFF! DANG IT, DOUG!
HMPH.
HAIL SATAN.

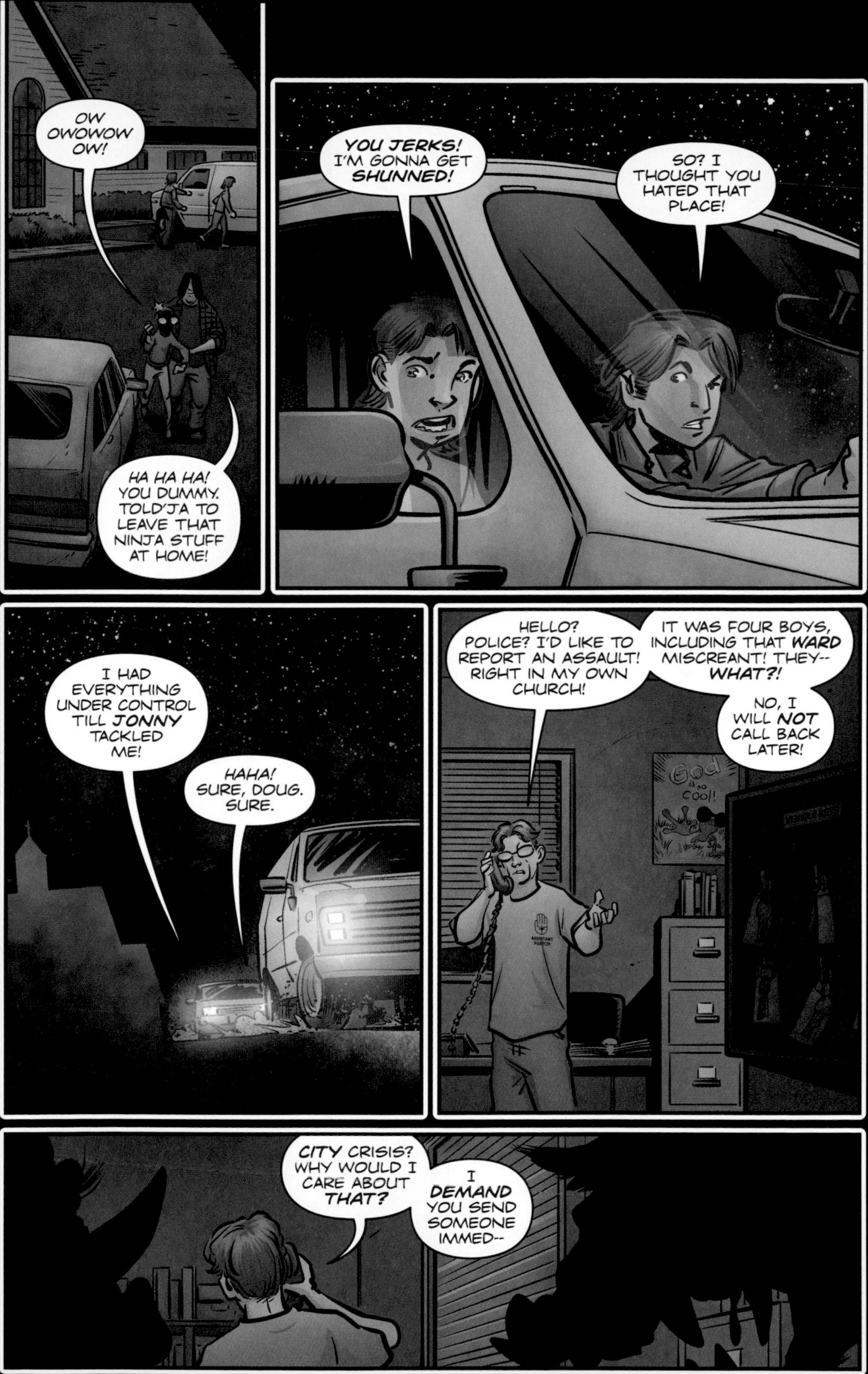
OW OWOWOW OW!
HA HA HA! YOU DUMMY. TOLD'JA TO LEAVE THAT NINJA STUFF AT HOME!
YOU JERKS! I'M GONNA GET SHUNNED!
SO? I THOUGHT YOU HATED THAT PLACE!
I HAD EVERYTHING UNDER CONTROL TILL JONNY TACKLED ME!
HAHA! SURE, DOUG. SURE.
HELLO? POLICE? I'D LIKE TO REPORT AN ASSAULT! RIGHT IN MY OWN CHURCH!
IT WAS FOUR BOYS, INCLUDING THAT WARD MISCREANT! THEY-- WHAT?!
NO, I WILL NOT CALL BACK LATER!
God is so cool!
ASSISTANT PASTOR
CITY CRISIS? WHY WOULD I CARE ABOUT THAT?
I DEMAND YOU SEND SOMEONE IMMED--

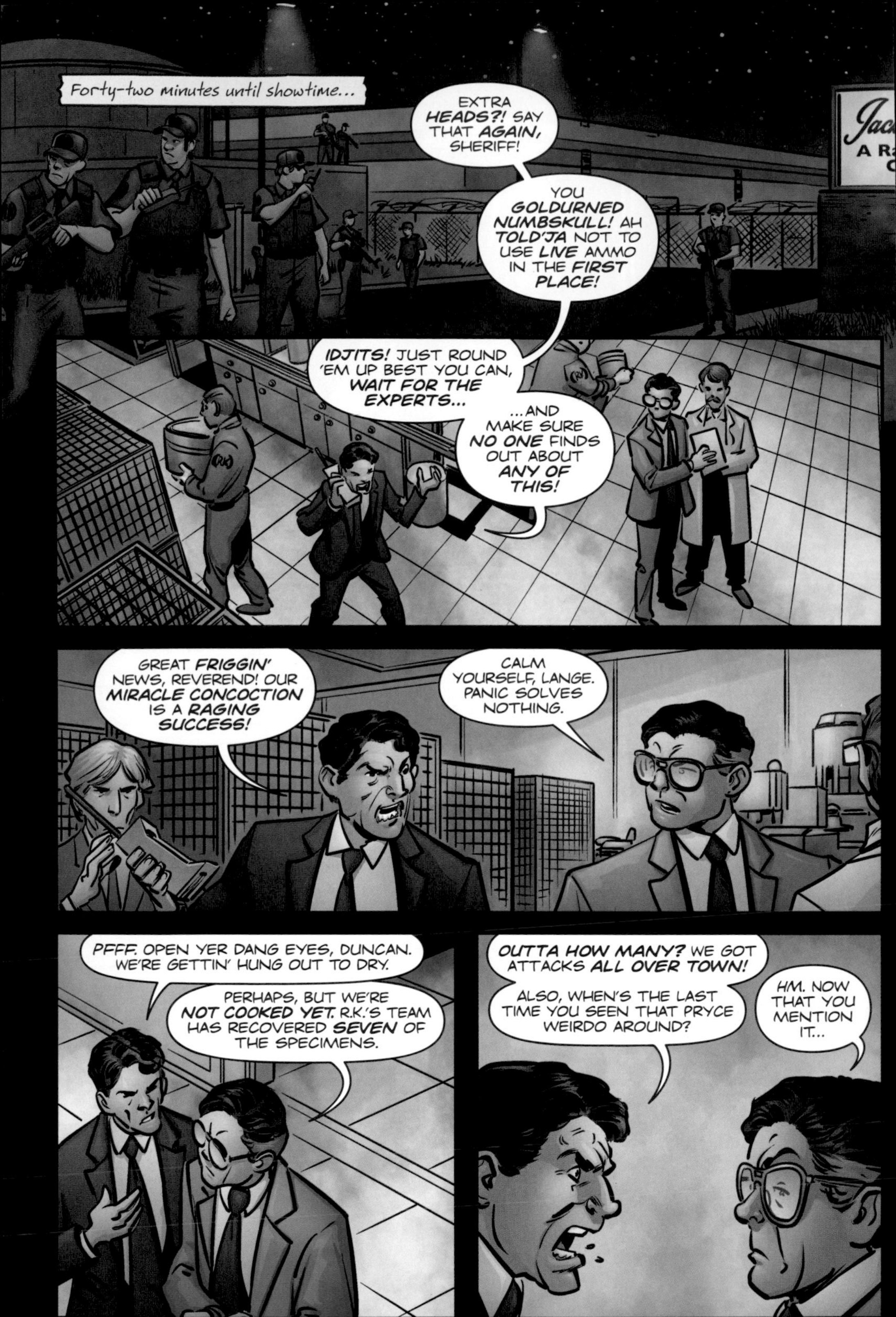
Forty-two minutes until showtime...
EXTRA HEADS?! SAY THAT AGAIN, SHERIFF!
YOU GOLDURNED NUMBSKULL! AH TOLD'JA NOT TO USE LIVE AMMO IN THE FIRST PLACE!
IDJITS! JUST ROUND 'EM UP BEST YOU CAN, WAIT FOR THE EXPERTS...
...AND MAKE SURE NO ONE FINDS OUT ABOUT ANY OF THIS!
GREAT FRIGGIN' NEWS, REVEREND! OUR MIRACLE CONCOCTION IS A RAGING SUCCESS!
CALM YOURSELF, LANGE. PANIC SOLVES NOTHING.
PFFF. OPEN YER DANG EYES, DUNCAN. WE'RE GETTIN' HUNG OUT TO DRY.
PERHAPS, BUT WE'RE NOT COOKED YET. R.K.'S TEAM HAS RECOVERED SEVEN OF THE SPECIMENS.
OUTTA HOW MANY? WE GOT ATTACKS ALL OVER TOWN!
ALSO, WHEN'S THE LAST TIME YOU SEEN THAT PRYCE WEIRDO AROUND?
HM. NOW THAT YOU MENTION IT...

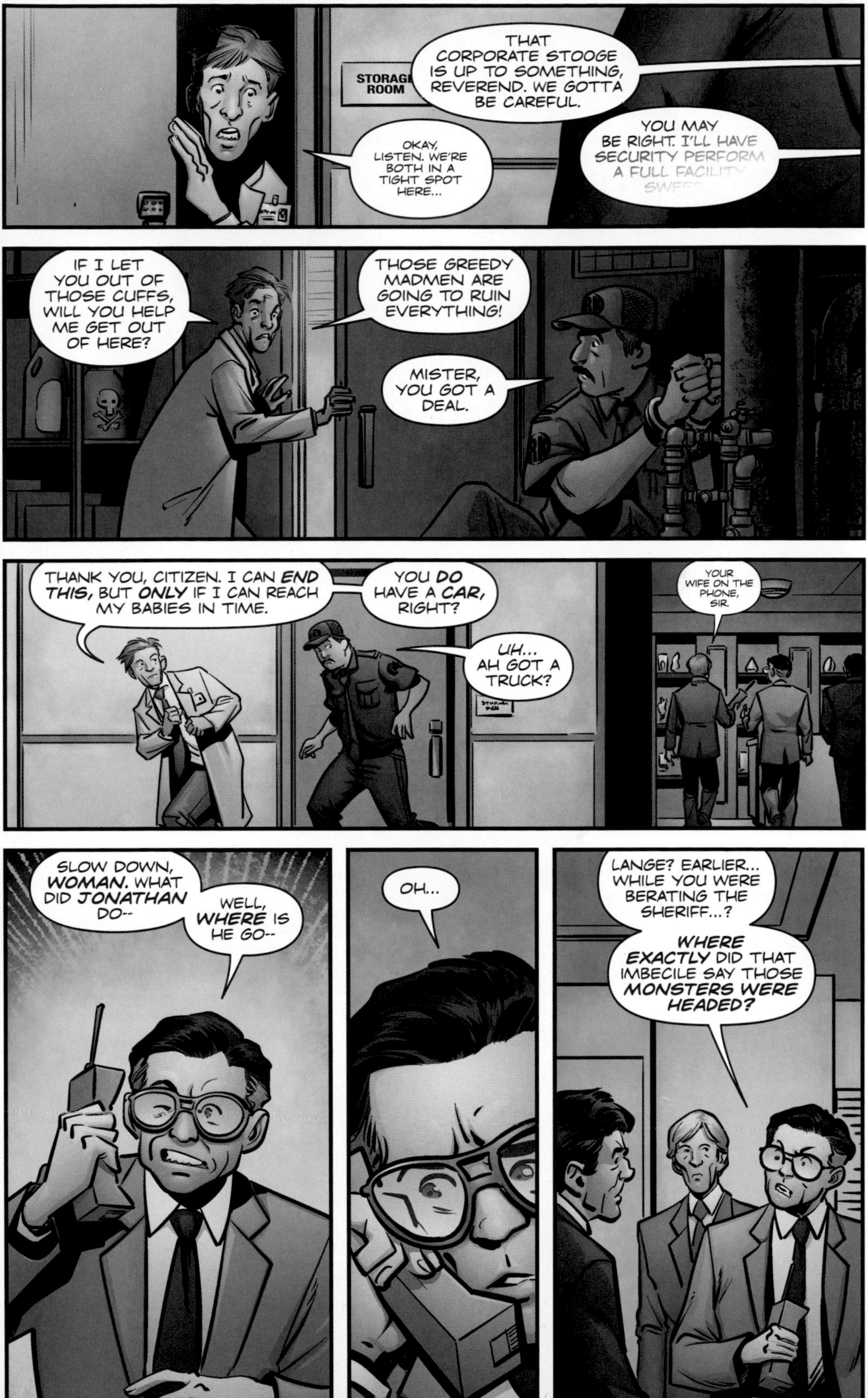
STORAGE ROOM
THAT CORPORATE STOOGE IS UP TO SOMETHING, REVEREND. WE GOTTA BE CAREFUL.
OKAY, LISTEN. WE'RE BOTH IN A TIGHT SPOT HERE...
YOU MAY BE RIGHT. I'LL HAVE SECURITY PERFORM A FULL FACILITY
IF I LET YOU OUT OF THOSE CUFFS, WILL YOU HELP ME GET OUT OF HERE?
THOSE GREEDY MADMEN ARE GOING TO RUIN EVERYTHING!
MISTER, YOU GOT A DEAL.
THANK YOU, CITIZEN. I CAN END THIS, BUT ONLY IF I CAN REACH MY BABIES IN TIME.
YOU DO HAVE A CAR, RIGHT?
UH... AH GOT A TRUCK?
YOUR WIFE ON THE PHONE, SIR.
SLOW DOWN, WOMAN. WHAT DID JONATHAN DO--
WELL, WHERE IS HE GO--
OH...
LANGE? EARLIER... WHILE YOU WERE BERATING THE SHERIFF...?
WHERE EXACTLY DID THAT IMBECILE SAY THOSE MONSTERS WERE HEADED?

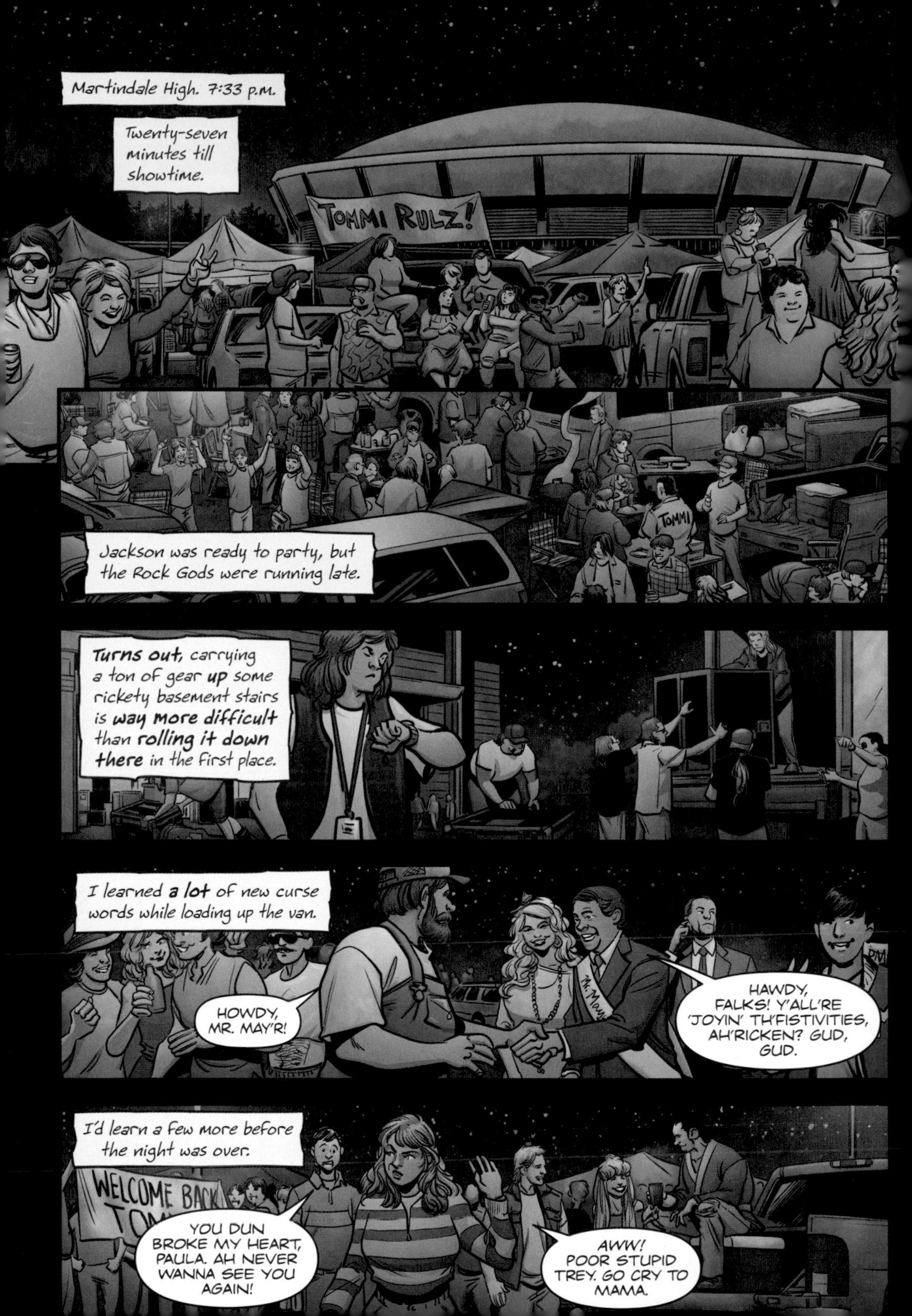

Martindale High. 7:33 p.m.
Twenty-seven minutes till showtime.
TOMMI RULZ!
Jackson was ready to party, but the Rock Gods were running late.
TOMMI
Turns out, carrying a ton of gear up some rickety basement stairs is way more difficult than rolling it down there in the first place.
I learned a lot of new curse words while loading up the van.
HOWDY, MR. MAY'R!
HAWDY, FALKS! Y'ALL'RE 'JOYIN' TH'FISTIVITIES, AH'RICKEN? GUD, GUD.
I'd learn a few more before the night was over.
WELCOME BACK
YOU DUN BROKE MY HEART, PAULA. AH NEVER WANNA SEE YOU AGAIN!
AWW! POOR STUPID TREY. GO CRY TO MAMA.

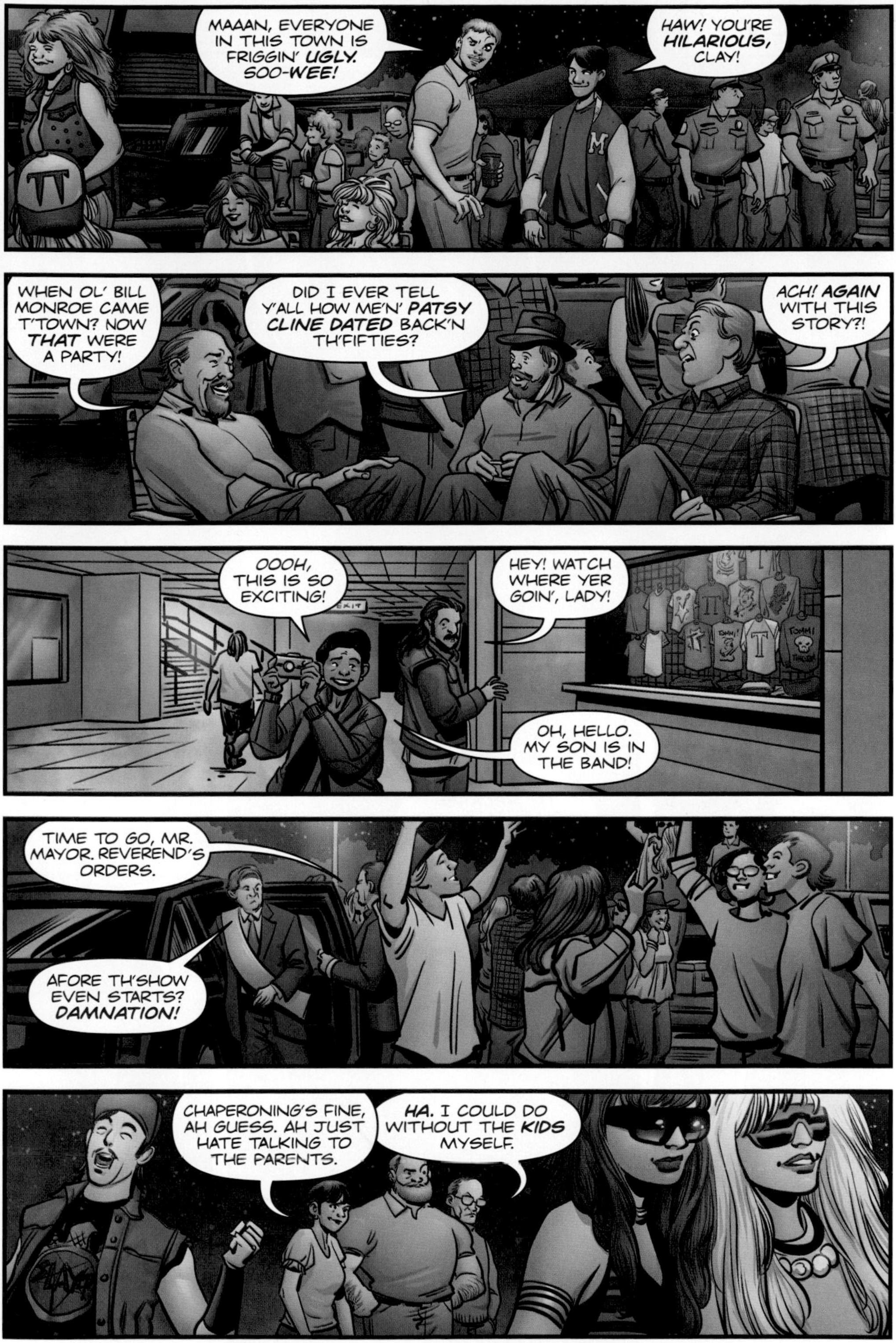
MAAAN, EVERYONE IN THIS TOWN IS FRIGGIN' UGLY. SOO-WEE!
HAW! YOU'RE HILARIOUS, CLAY!
WHEN OL' BILL MONROE CAME T'TOWN? NOW THAT WERE A PARTY!
DID I EVER TELL Y'ALL HOW ME'N' PATSY CLINE DATED BACK'N TH'FIFTIES?
ACH! AGAIN WITH THIS STORY?!
OOOH, THIS IS SO EXCITING!
HEY! WATCH WHERE YER GOIN', LADY!
OH, HELLO. MY SON IS IN THE BAND!
TIME TO GO, MR. MAYOR. REVEREND'S ORDERS.
AFORE TH'SHOW EVEN STARTS? DAMNATION!
CHAPERONING'S FINE, AH GUESS. AH JUST HATE TALKING TO THE PARENTS.
HA. I COULD DO WITHOUT THE KIDS MYSELF.

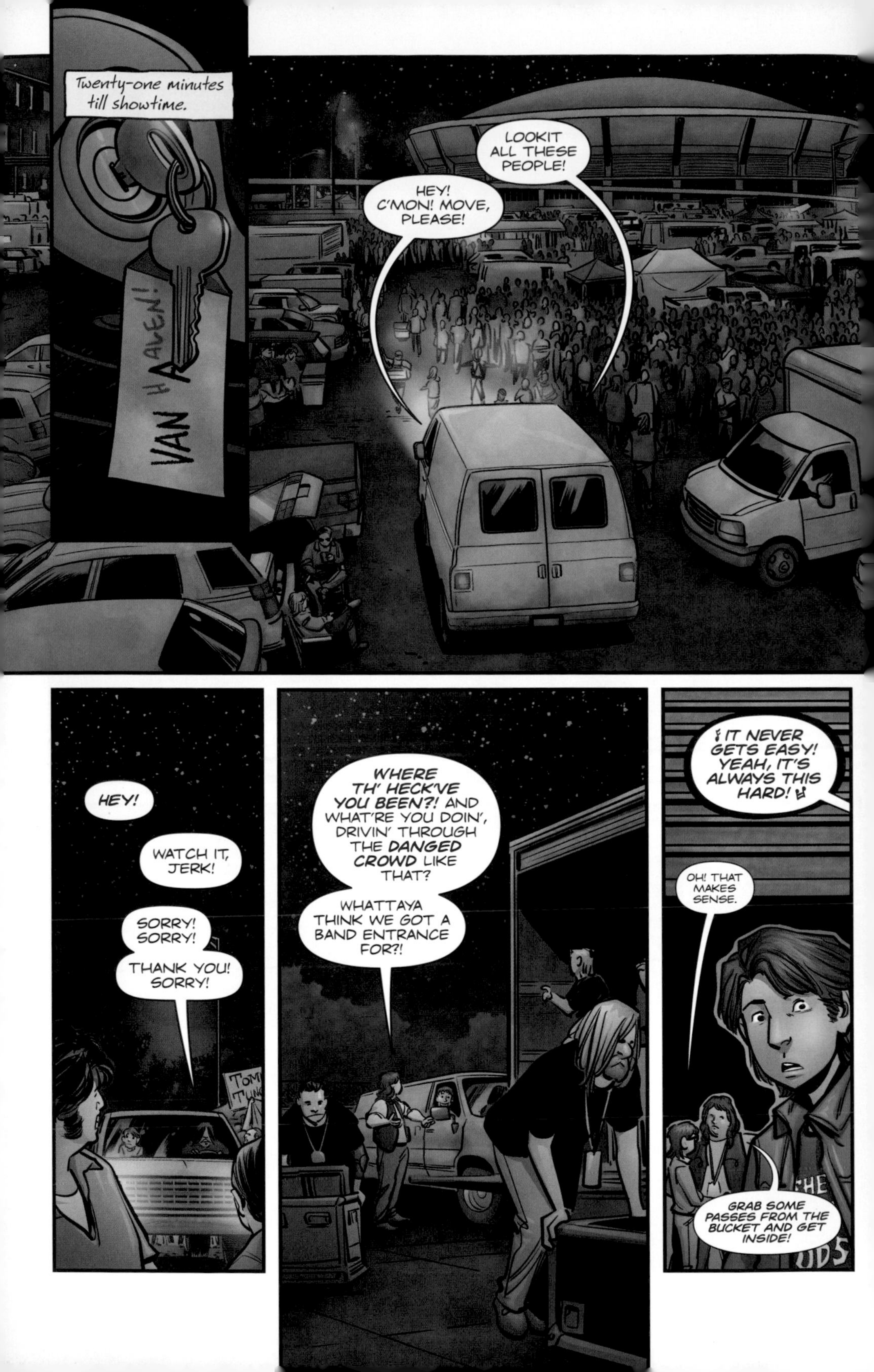
Twenty-one minutes till showtime.
VAN HALEN!
LOOKIT ALL THESE PEOPLE!
HEY! C'MON! MOVE, PLEASE!
HEY!
WATCH IT, JERK!
SORRY! SORRY!
THANK YOU! SORRY!
WHERE TH' HECK'VE YOU BEEN?! AND WHAT'RE YOU DOIN', DRIVIN' THROUGH THE DANGED CROWD LIKE THAT?
WHATTAYA THINK WE GOT A BAND ENTRANCE FOR?!
IT NEVER GETS EASY! YEAH, IT'S ALWAYS THIS HARD!
OH! THAT MAKES SENSE.
GRAB SOME PASSES FROM THE BUCKET AND GET INSIDE!

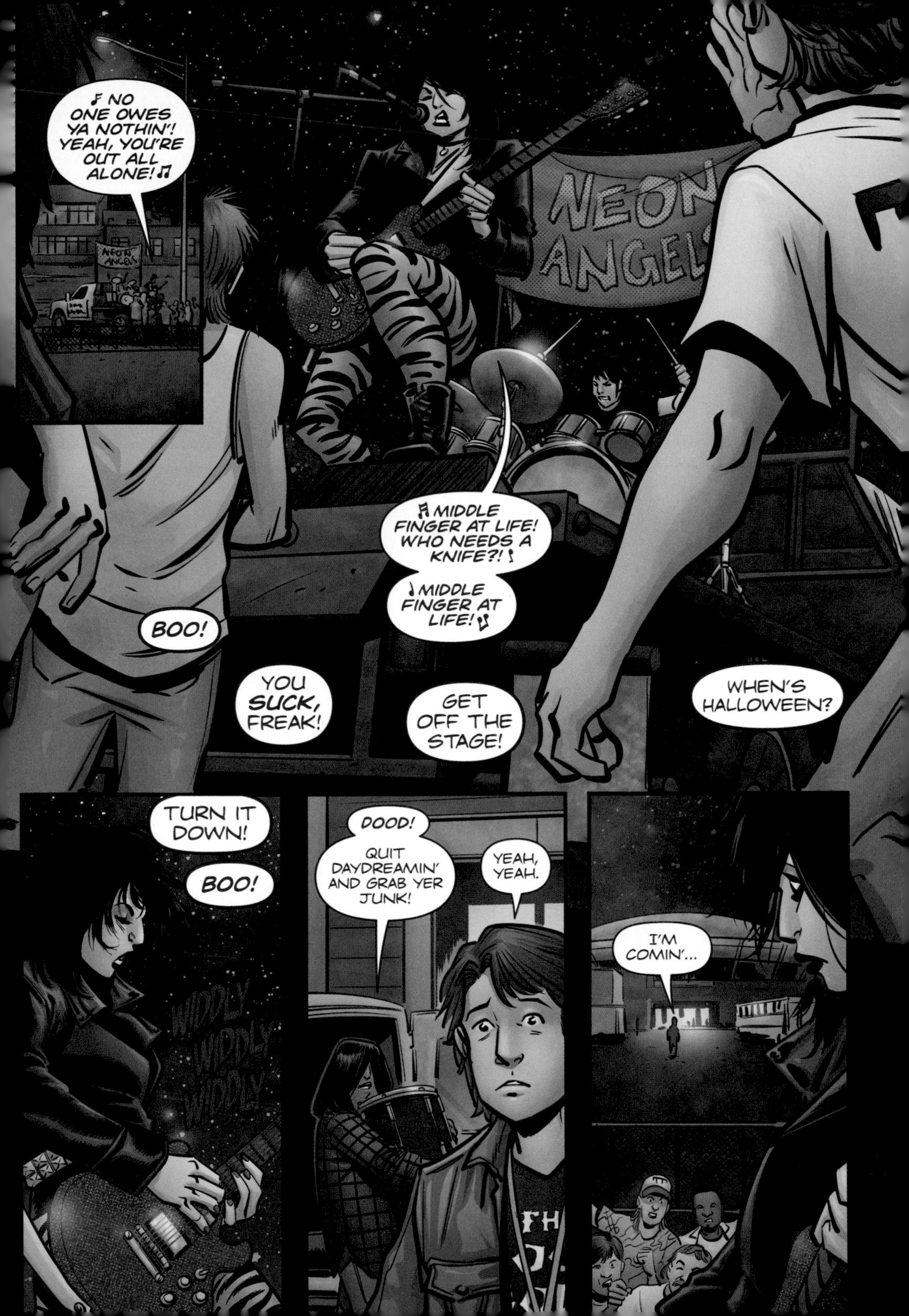
♪ NO ONE OWES YA NOTHIN'! YEAH, YOU'RE OUT ALL ALONE! ♫
NEON ANGELS
♫ MIDDLE FINGER AT LIFE! WHO NEEDS A KNIFE?! ♪
♪ MIDDLE FINGER AT LIFE! ♫
BOO!
YOU SUCK, FREAK!
GET OFF THE STAGE!
WHEN'S HALLOWEEN?
TURN IT DOWN!
BOO!
WIDDLY WIDDLY WIDDLY
DOOD!
QUIT DAYDREAMIN' AND GRAB YER JUNK!
YEAH, YEAH.
I'M COMIN'...

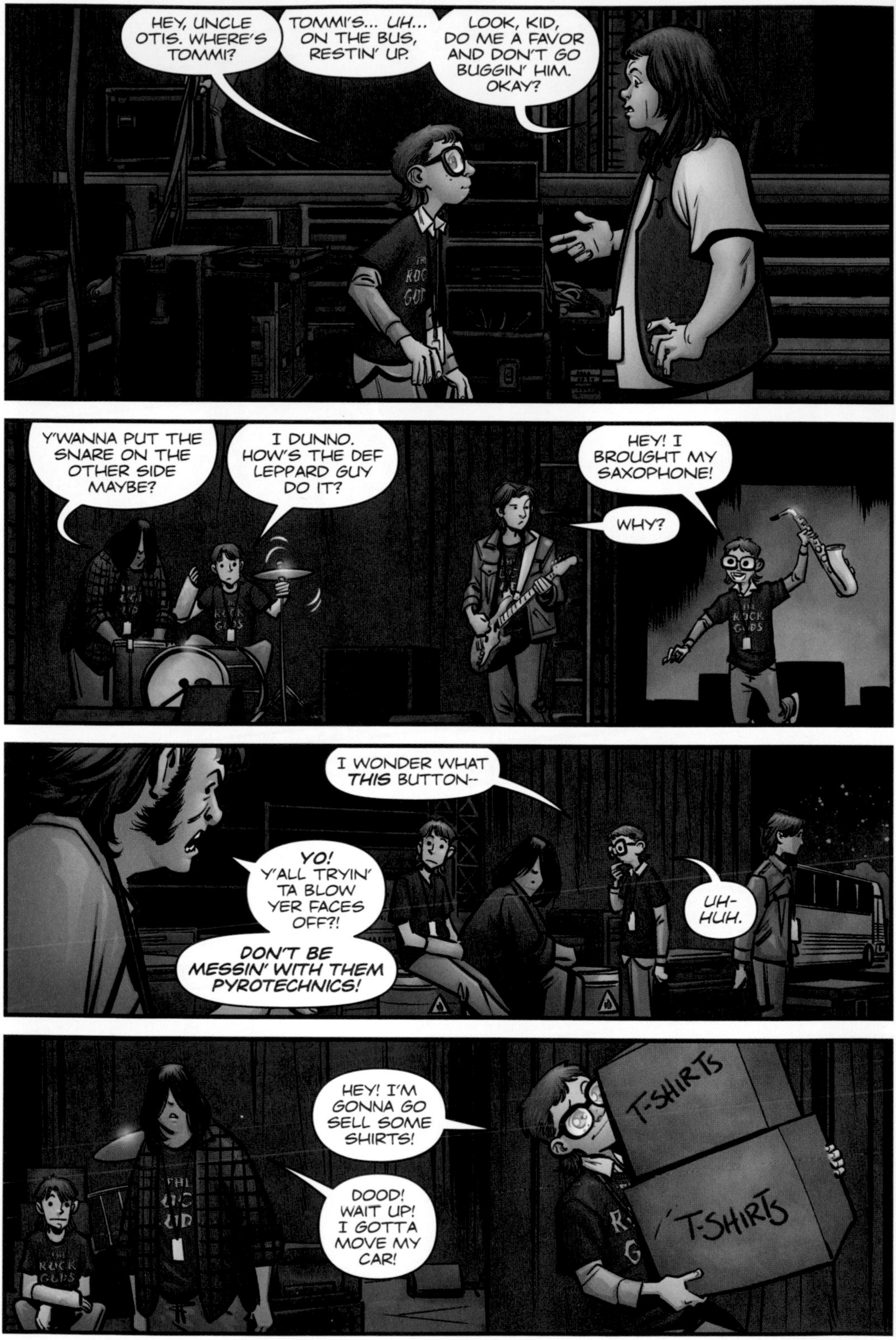
HEY, UNCLE OTIS. WHERE'S TOMMI?
TOMMI'S... *UH*... ON THE BUS, RESTIN' UP.
LOOK, KID, DO ME A FAVOR AND DON'T GO BUGGIN' HIM. OKAY?
Y'WANNA PUT THE SNARE ON THE OTHER SIDE MAYBE?
I DUNNO. HOW'S THE DEF LEPPARD GUY DO IT?
HEY! I BROUGHT MY SAXOPHONE!
WHY?
I WONDER WHAT *THIS* BUTTON--
YO! Y'ALL TRYIN' TA BLOW YER FACES OFF?!
DON'T BE MESSIN' WITH THEM PYROTECHNICS!
UH-HUH.
HEY! I'M GONNA GO SELL SOME SHIRTS!
T-SHIRTS
T-SHIRTS
DOOD! WAIT UP! I GOTTA MOVE MY CAR!

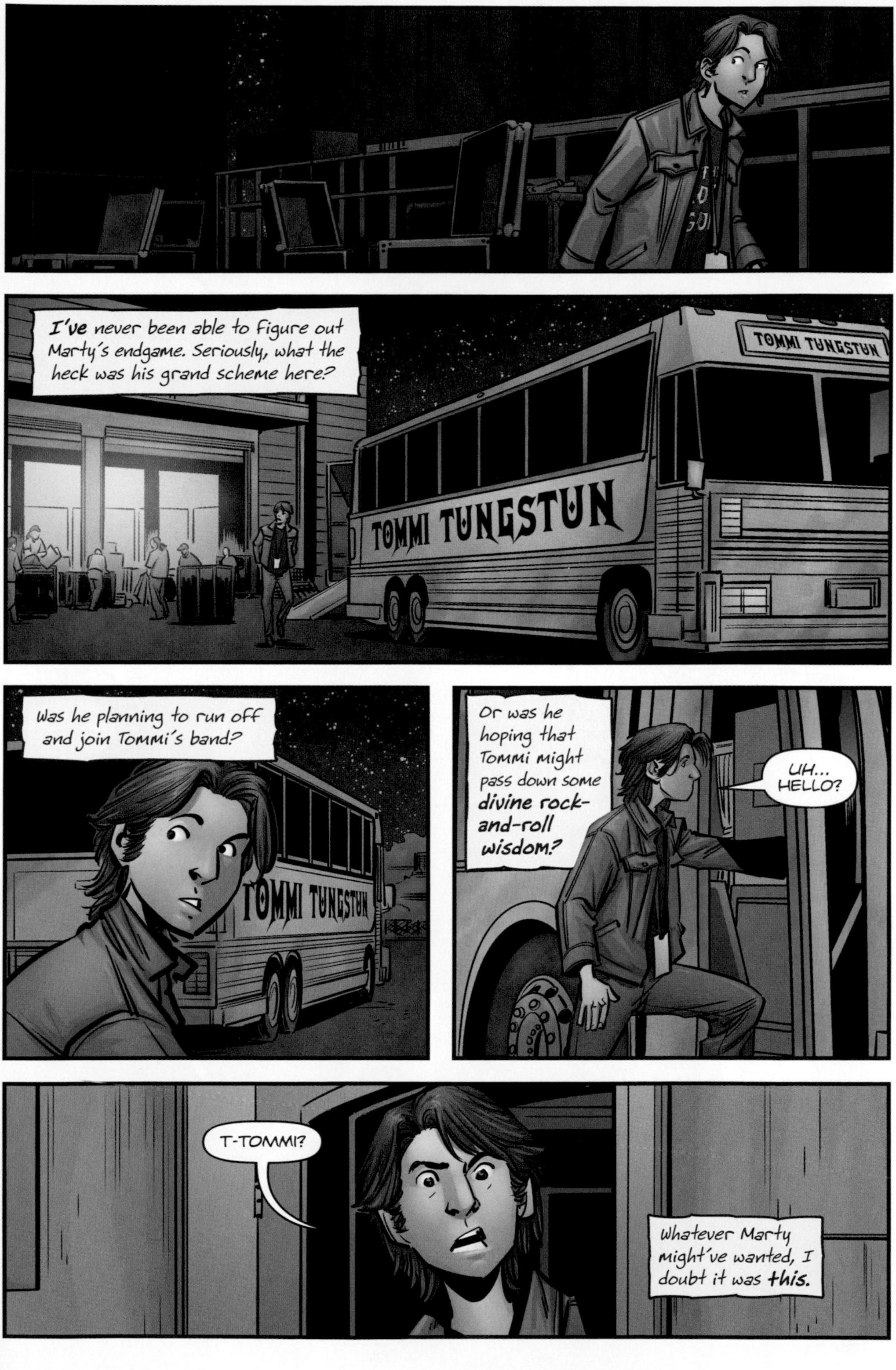

TOMMI TUNGSTUN
I've never been able to figure out Marty's endgame. Seriously, what the heck was his grand scheme here?
TOMMI TUNGSTUN
Was he planning to run off and join Tommi's band?
TOMMI TUNGSTUN
Or was he hoping that Tommi might pass down some divine rock-and-roll wisdom?
UH... HELLO?
T-TOMMI?
Whatever Marty might've wanted, I doubt it was this.

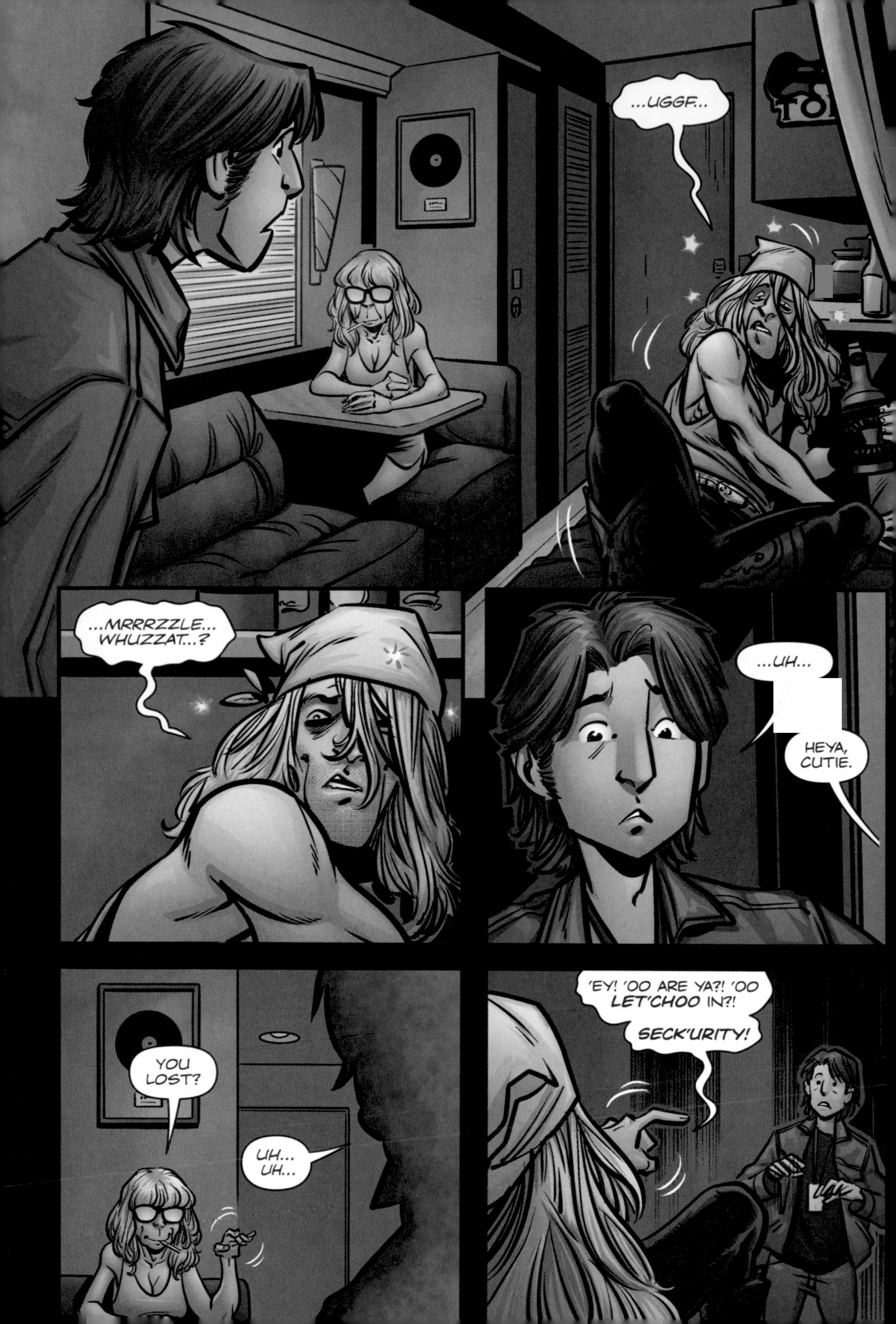
...UGGF...
...MRRRZZLE... WHUZZAT...?
...UH...
HEYA, CUTIE.
YOU LOST?
UH... UH...
'EY! 'OO ARE YA?! 'OO LET'CHOO IN?!
SECK'URITY!

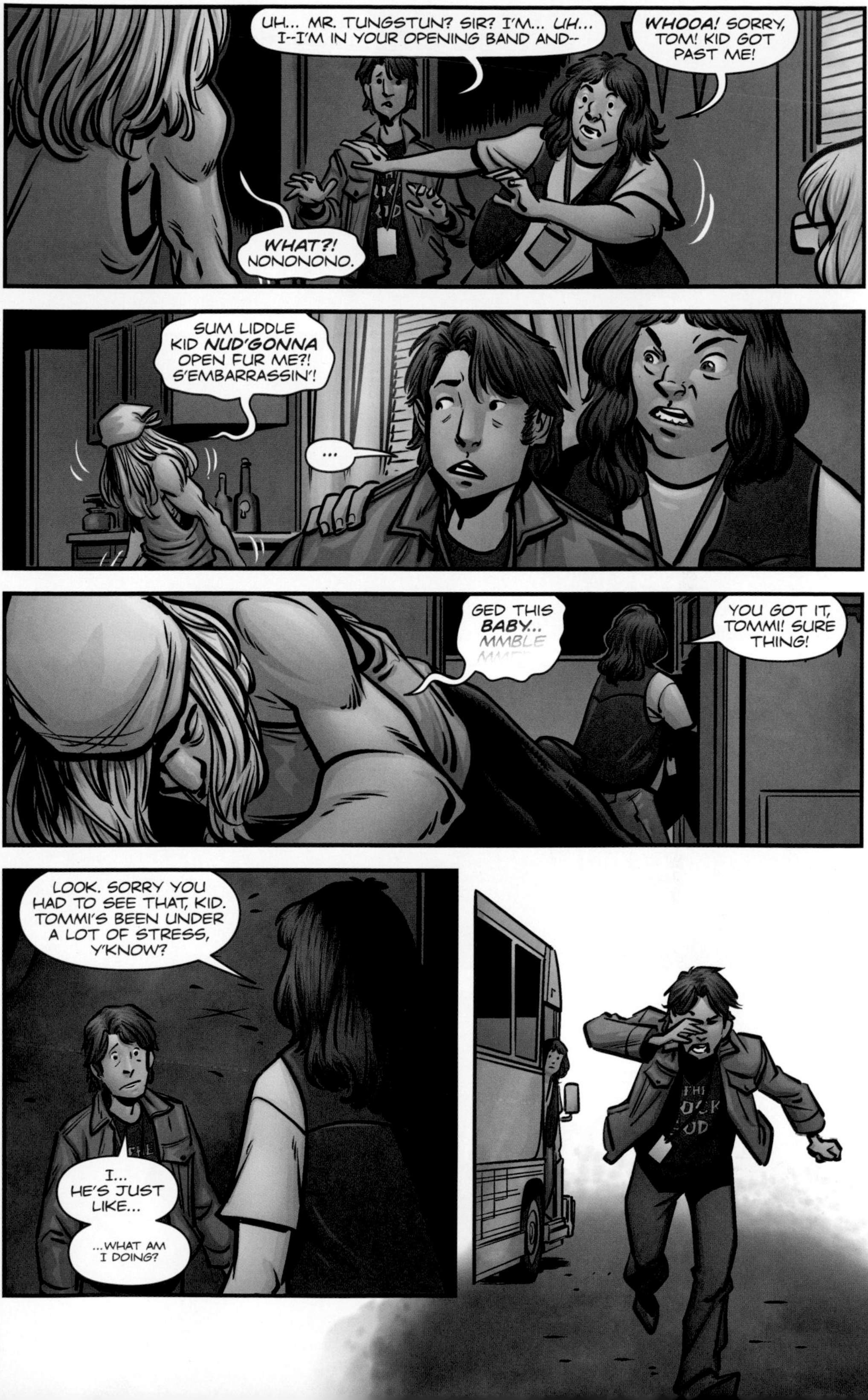
UH... MR. TUNGSTUN? SIR? I'M... UH... I--I'M IN YOUR OPENING BAND AND--
WHOOA! SORRY, TOM! KID GOT PAST ME!
WHAT?! NONONONO.
SUM LIDDLE KID NUD'GONNA OPEN FUR ME?! S'EMBARRASSIN'!
...
GED THIS BABY... MMBLE
YOU GOT IT, TOMMI! SURE THING!
LOOK. SORRY YOU HAD TO SEE THAT, KID. TOMMI'S BEEN UNDER A LOT OF STRESS, Y'KNOW?
I... HE'S JUST LIKE...
...WHAT AM I DOING?

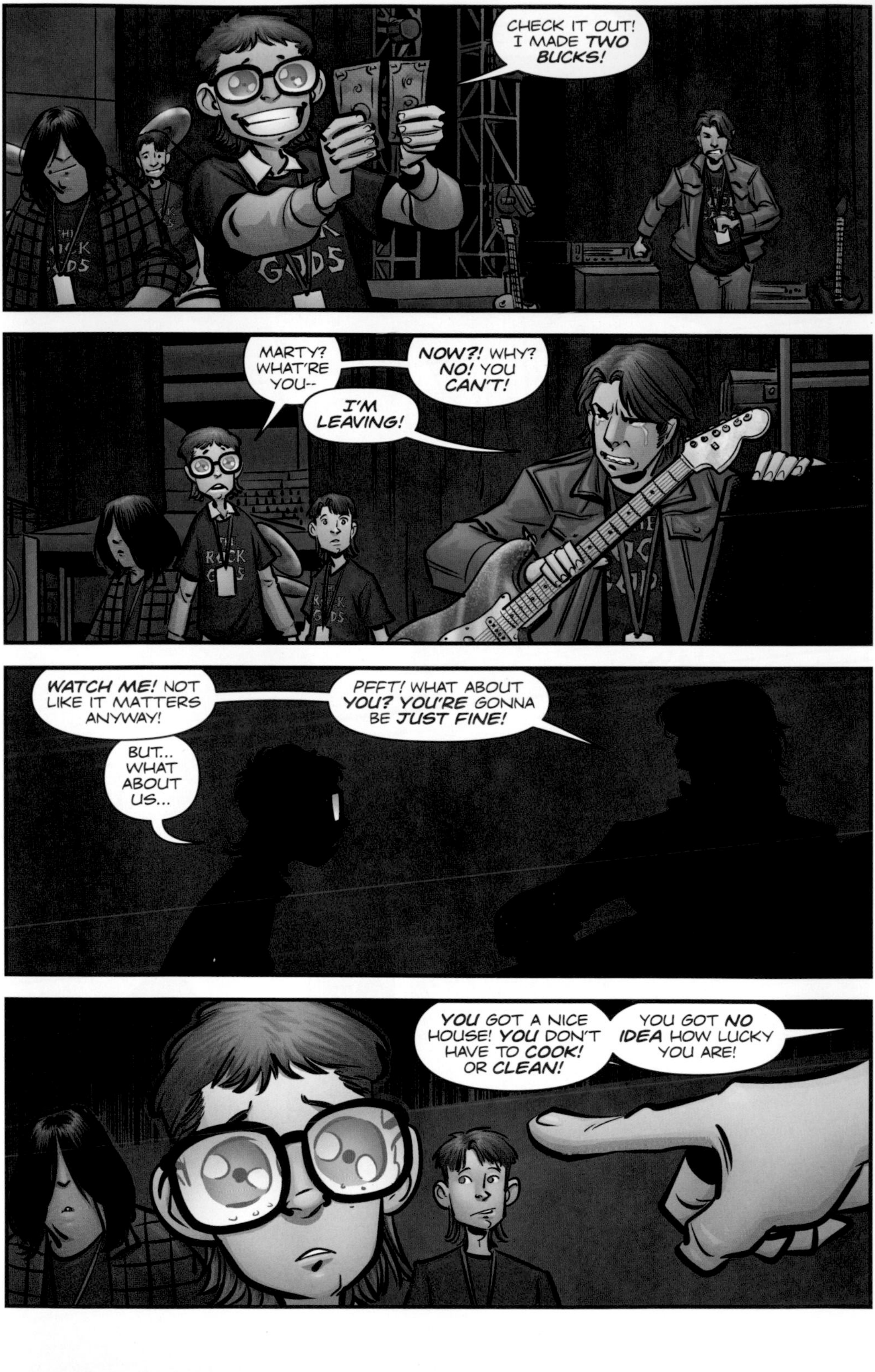
CHECK IT OUT! I MADE **TWO BUCKS!**
MARTY? WHAT'RE YOU--
NOW?! WHY? ***NO!*** YOU ***CAN'T!***
I'M LEAVING!
WATCH ME! NOT LIKE IT MATTERS ANYWAY!
BUT... WHAT ABOUT US...
PFFT! WHAT ABOUT ***YOU? YOU'RE*** GONNA BE ***JUST FINE!***
YOU GOT A NICE HOUSE! ***YOU*** DON'T HAVE TO ***COOK!*** OR ***CLEAN!***
YOU GOT ***NO IDEA*** HOW LUCKY YOU ARE!

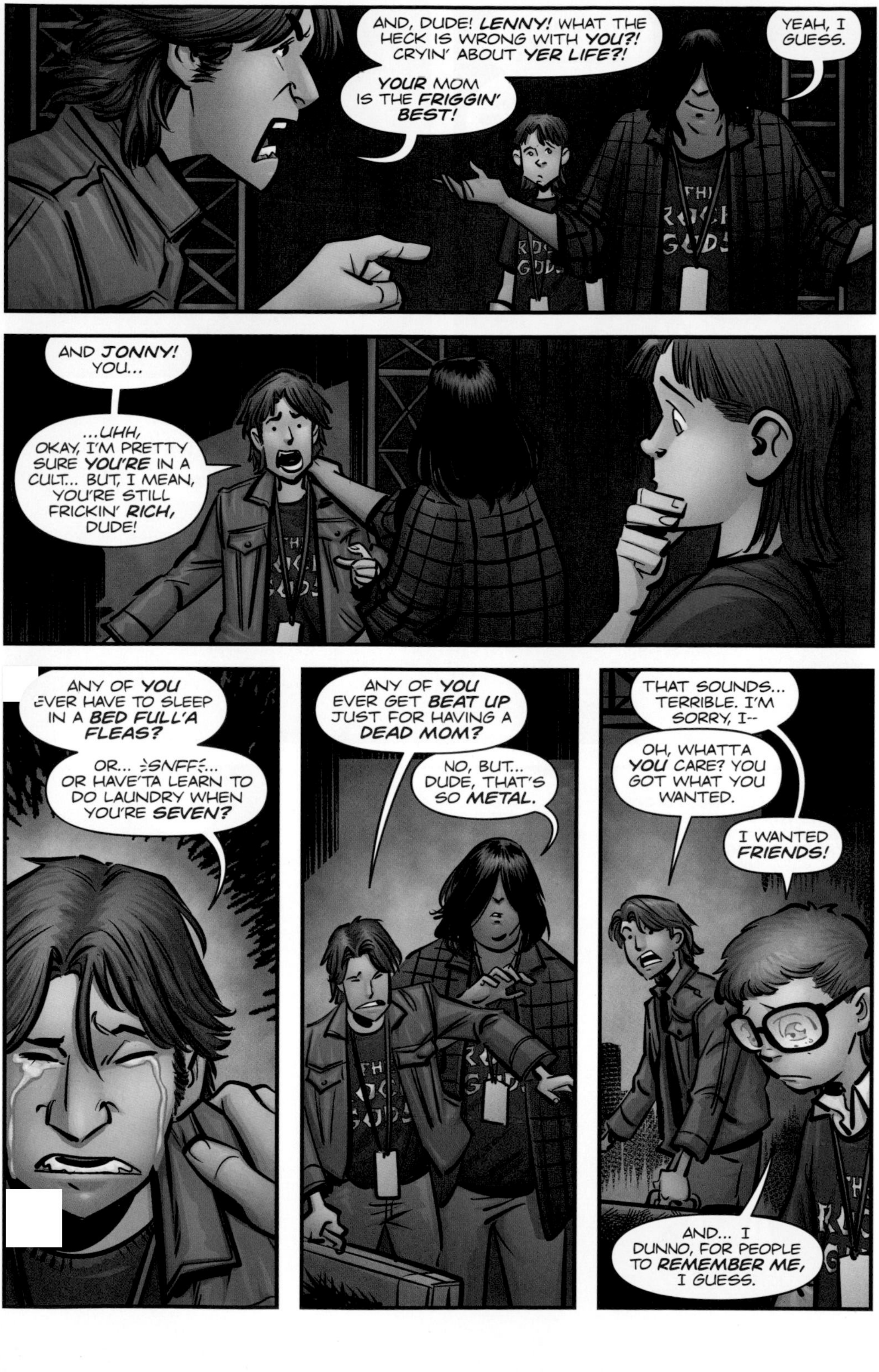
AND, DUDE! LENNY! WHAT THE HECK IS WRONG WITH YOU?! CRYIN' ABOUT YER LIFE?!
YOUR MOM IS THE FRIGGIN' BEST!
YEAH, I GUESS.
AND JONNY! YOU...
...UHH, OKAY, I'M PRETTY SURE YOU'RE IN A CULT... BUT, I MEAN, YOU'RE STILL FRICKIN' RICH, DUDE!
ANY OF YOU EVER HAVE TO SLEEP IN A BED FULL'A FLEAS?
OR... SNFF... OR HAVE'TA LEARN TO DO LAUNDRY WHEN YOU'RE SEVEN?
ANY OF YOU EVER GET BEAT UP JUST FOR HAVING A DEAD MOM?
NO, BUT... DUDE, THAT'S SO METAL.
THAT SOUNDS... TERRIBLE. I'M SORRY, I--
OH, WHATTA YOU CARE? YOU GOT WHAT YOU WANTED.
I WANTED FRIENDS!
AND... I DUNNO, FOR PEOPLE TO REMEMBER ME, I GUESS.

AWESOME WAY FOR YOU TO BE REMEMBERED!

SLIMY LITTLE GEEK WHO *CONS* HIS *FRIENDS* INTO PLAYING ROCK STAR!

YEAH, OKAY, *MAYBE* I SCREWED UP! *I'M SORRY!* BUT *PLEASE* DON'T QUIT!

DUMMY! TOMMI DOESN'T WANT US HERE!

NO ONE WANTS US HERE! SO FRICKIN' *WHAT?* NO ONE EVER WANTS US *ANYWHERE!*

BUT WE'RE THE *ROCK GODS OF JACKSON, TENNESSEE,* AND WE'RE THE ONLY BAND THAT SHOWED UP!

I MEAN, IF YOU *WANNA* QUIT... BUT, *PLEASE,* JONNY'S DRUMS WERE *SUPER HEAVY* AND, Y'KNOW, HIS PARENTS ARE *GONNA MURDER* HIM...

...DON'T YOU WANNA SEE THE *DUMB LOOK* ON EVERYONE'S FACE?

...SPECIALLY THAT JERKUS *CLAY* AND ALL HIS STUPID FRIENDS—

JUST...

SHUT UP.

DANG IT.

DON'T GO ANYWHERE.

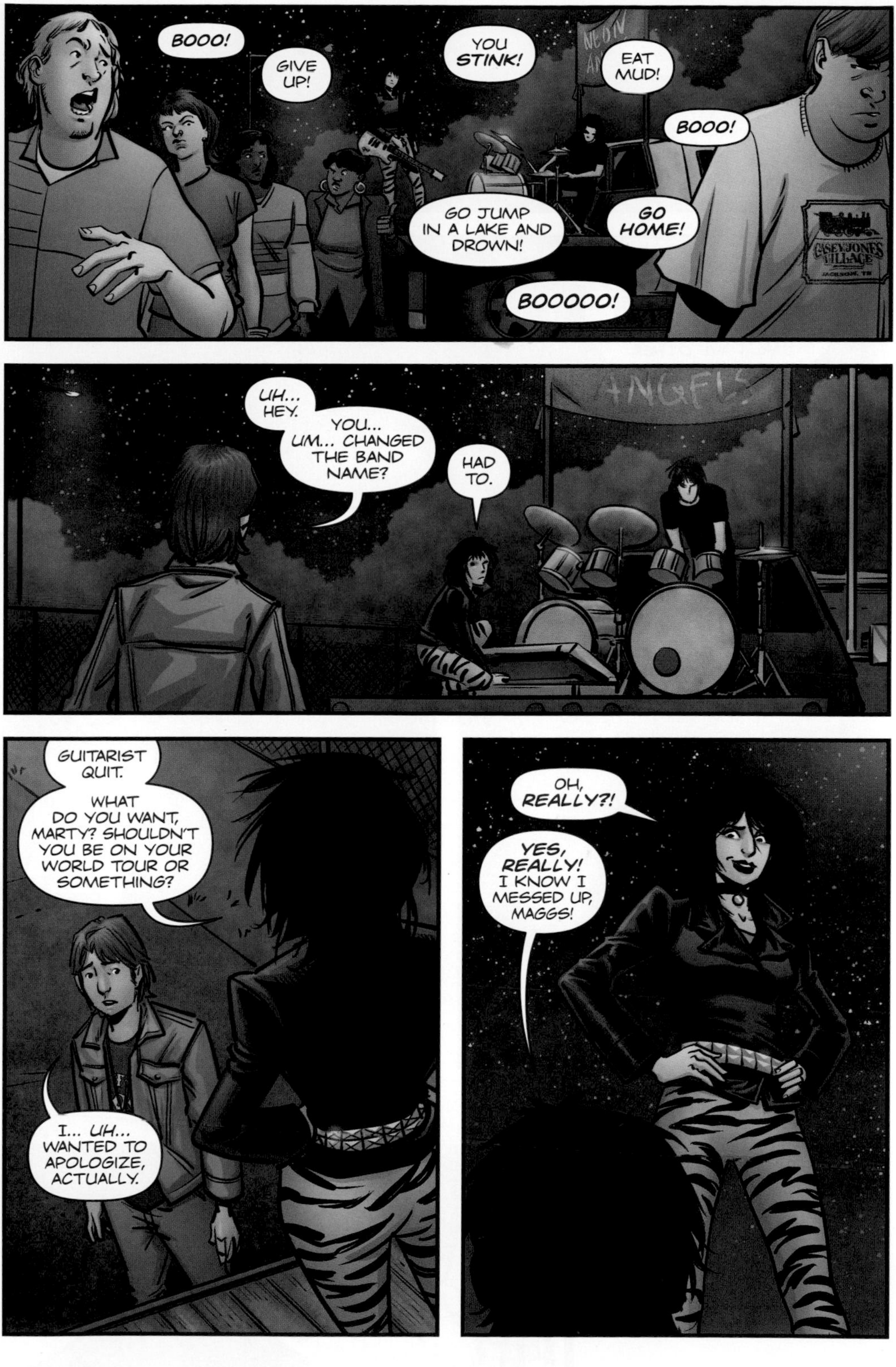
BOOO!
GIVE UP!
YOU STINK!
EAT MUD!
BOOO!
GO JUMP IN A LAKE AND DROWN!
GO HOME!
BOOOOO!
CASEY JONES VILLAGE
JACKSON, TN
ANGELS
UH... HEY.
YOU... UM... CHANGED THE BAND NAME?
HAD TO.
GUITARIST QUIT.
WHAT DO YOU WANT, MARTY? SHOULDN'T YOU BE ON YOUR WORLD TOUR OR SOMETHING?
I... UH... WANTED TO APOLOGIZE, ACTUALLY.
OH, REALLY?!
YES, REALLY! I KNOW I MESSED UP, MAGGS!

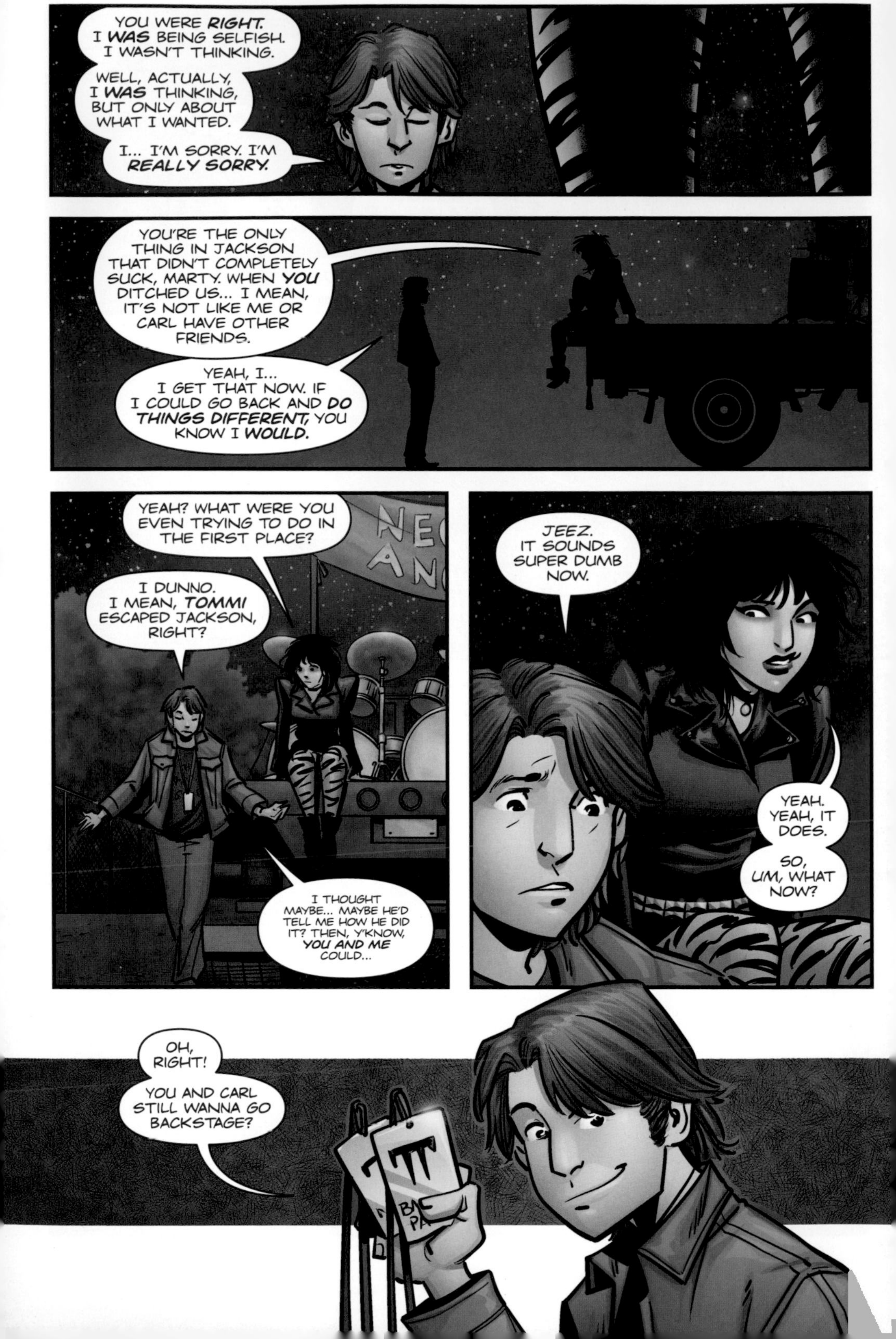

YOU WERE RIGHT. I WAS BEING SELFISH. I WASN'T THINKING.
WELL, ACTUALLY, I WAS THINKING, BUT ONLY ABOUT WHAT I WANTED.
I... I'M SORRY. I'M REALLY SORRY.
YOU'RE THE ONLY THING IN JACKSON THAT DIDN'T COMPLETELY SUCK, MARTY. WHEN YOU DITCHED US... I MEAN, IT'S NOT LIKE ME OR CARL HAVE OTHER FRIENDS.
YEAH, I... I GET THAT NOW. IF I COULD GO BACK AND DO THINGS DIFFERENT, YOU KNOW I WOULD.
YEAH? WHAT WERE YOU EVEN TRYING TO DO IN THE FIRST PLACE?
I DUNNO. I MEAN, TOMMI ESCAPED JACKSON, RIGHT?
I THOUGHT MAYBE... MAYBE HE'D TELL ME HOW HE DID IT? THEN, Y'KNOW, YOU AND ME COULD...
JEEZ. IT SOUNDS SUPER DUMB NOW.
YEAH. YEAH, IT DOES.
SO, UM, WHAT NOW?
OH, RIGHT!
YOU AND CARL STILL WANNA GO BACKSTAGE?

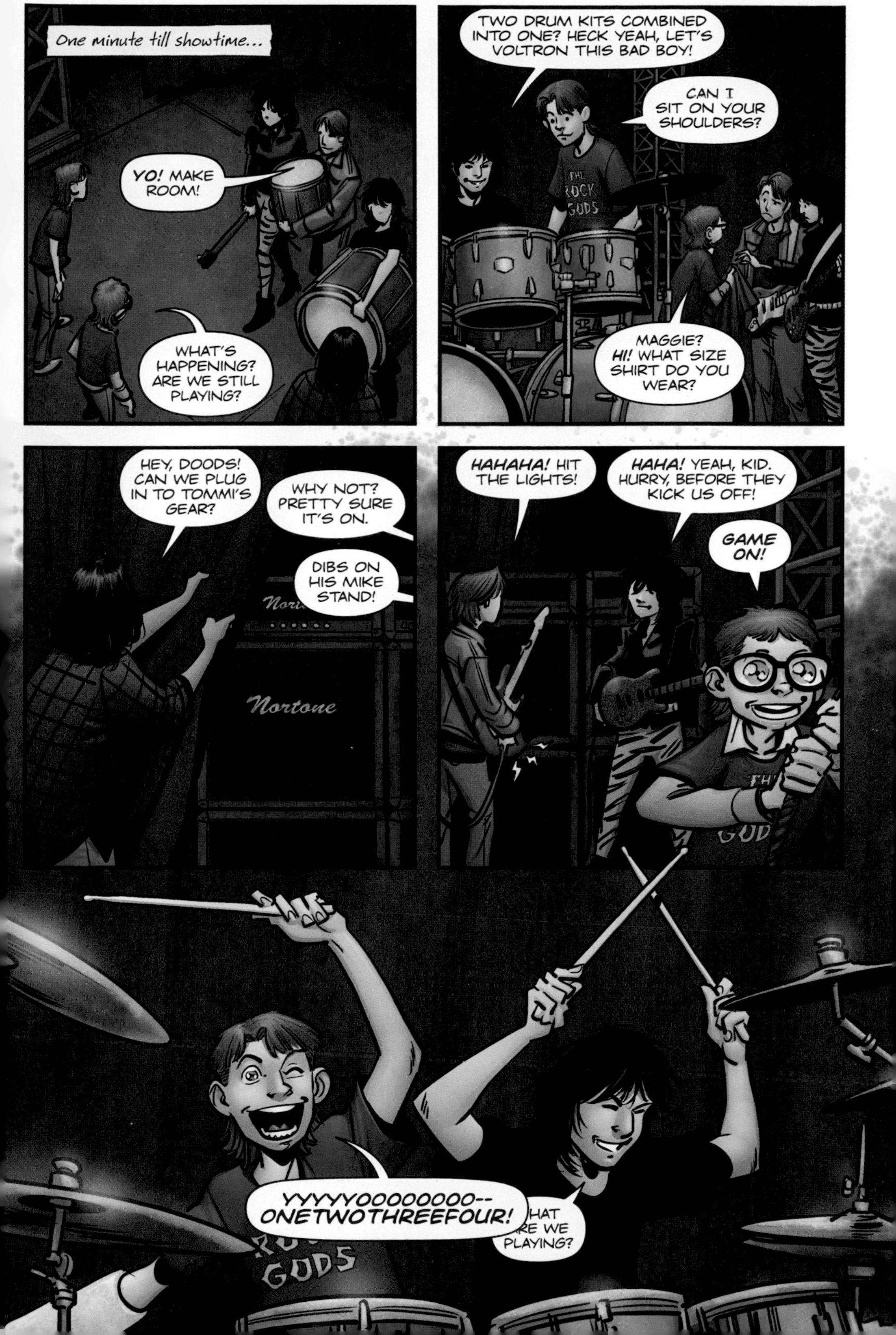
One minute till showtime...
YO! MAKE ROOM!
WHAT'S HAPPENING? ARE WE STILL PLAYING?
TWO DRUM KITS COMBINED INTO ONE? HECK YEAH, LET'S VOLTRON THIS BAD BOY!
CAN I SIT ON YOUR SHOULDERS?
MAGGIE? HI! WHAT SIZE SHIRT DO YOU WEAR?
HEY, DOODS! CAN WE PLUG IN TO TOMMI'S GEAR?
WHY NOT? PRETTY SURE IT'S ON.
DIBS ON HIS MIKE STAND!
Nortone
HAHAHA! HIT THE LIGHTS!
HAHA! YEAH, KID. HURRY, BEFORE THEY KICK US OFF!
GAME ON!
YYYYYOOOOOOOO-- ONETWOTHREEFOUR!
HAT RE WE PLAYING?

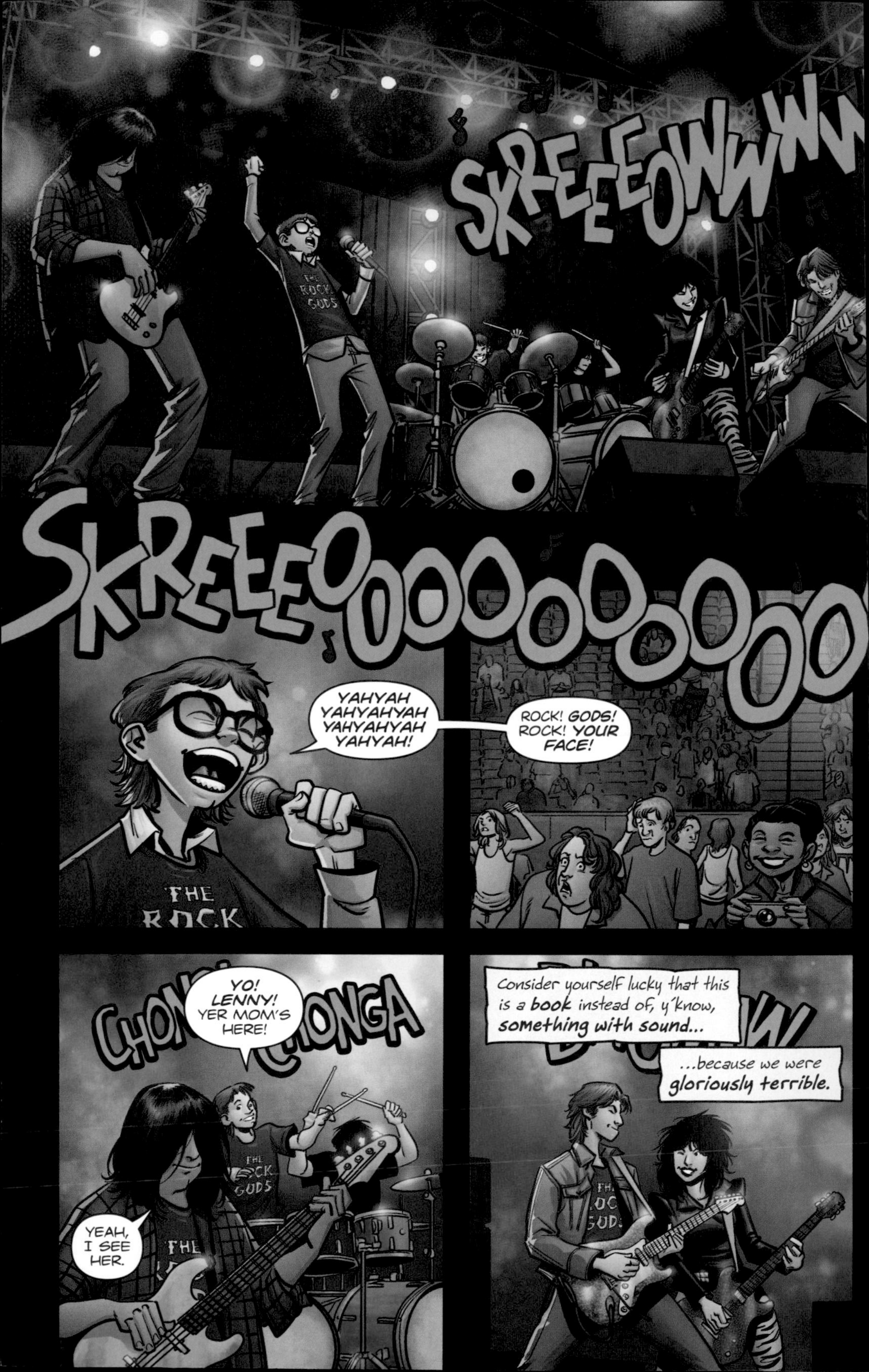
SKREEEOWWW
THE ROCK GODS
SKREEEOOOOOOOOOOO
YAHYAH YAHYAHYAH YAHYAHYAH YAHYAH!
ROCK! GODS! ROCK! YOUR FACE!
THE ROCK
CHONGA
YO! LENNY! YER MOM'S HERE!
YEAH, I SEE HER.
THE ROCK GODS
Consider yourself lucky that this is a **book** instead of, y'know, **something with sound...**
...because we were **gloriously terrible.**

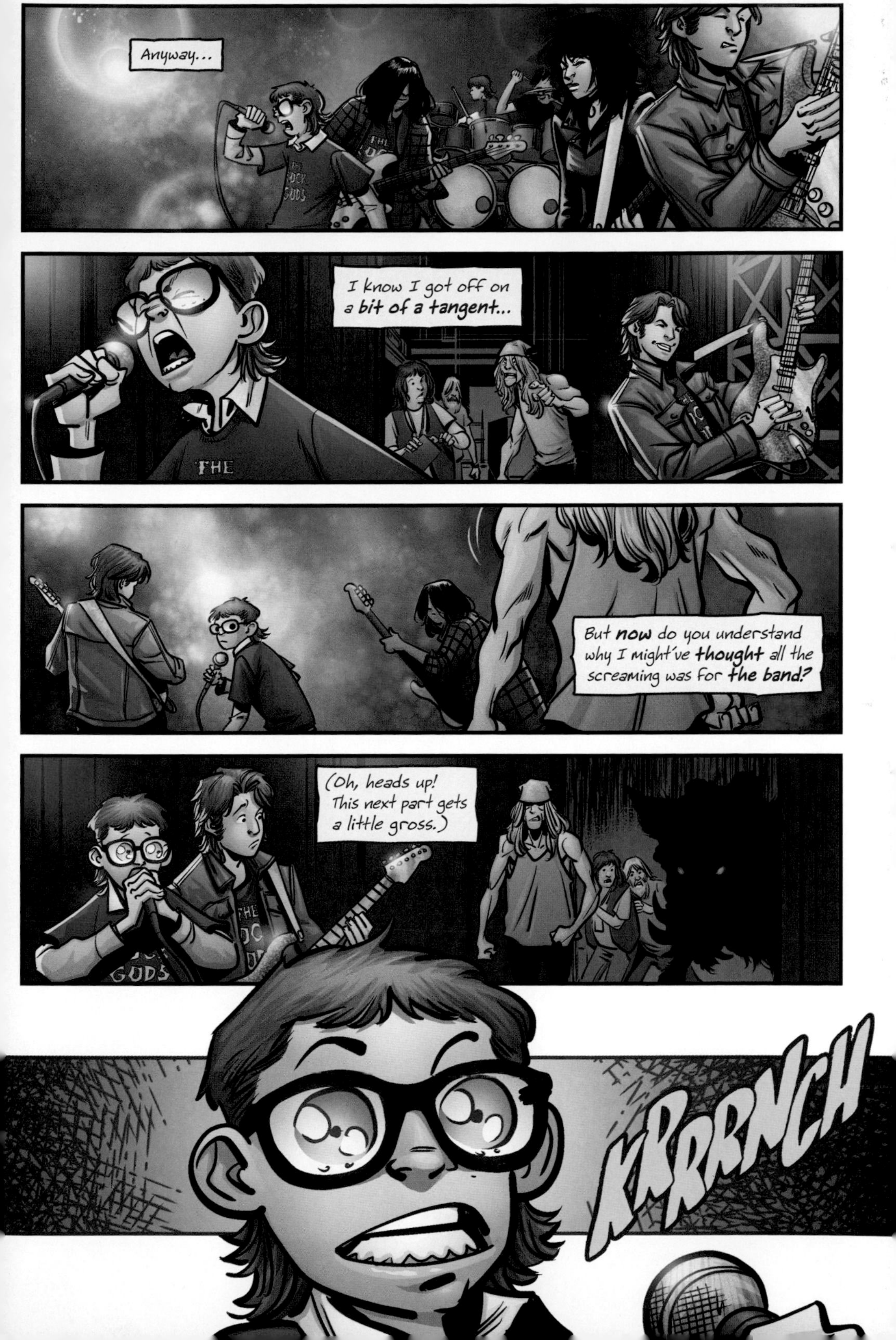
Anyway...
I know I got off on a bit of a tangent...
But now do you understand why I might've thought all the screaming was for the band?
(Oh, heads up! This next part gets a little gross.)
KRRRNCH

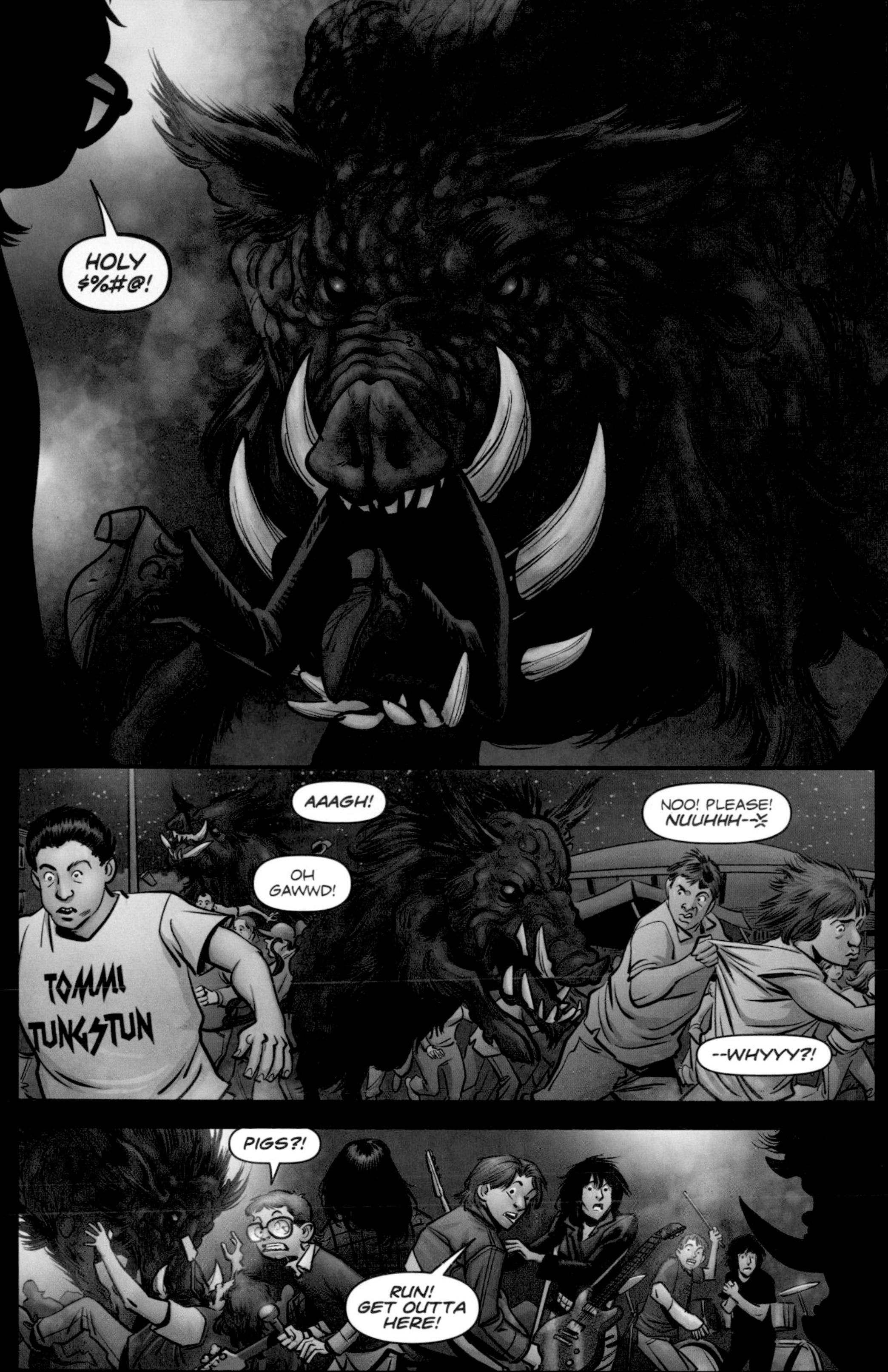
HOLY $%#@!
AAAGH!
OH GAWWD!
NOO! PLEASE! NUUHHH--
--WHYYY?!
TOMMI TUNGSTUN
PIGS?!
RUN! GET OUTTA HERE!

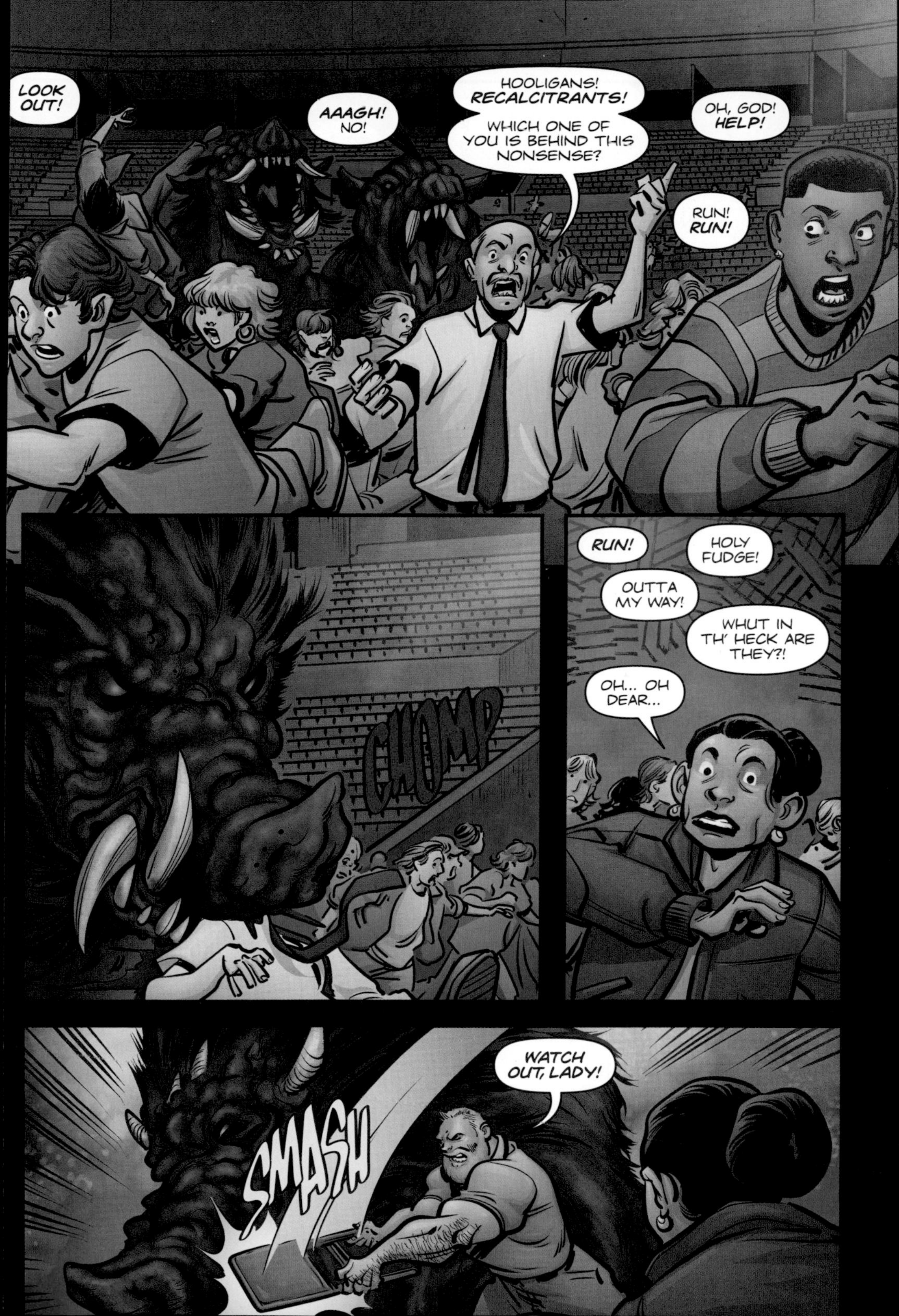
LOOK OUT!
AAAGH! NO!
HOOLIGANS! RECALCITRANTS!
WHICH ONE OF YOU IS BEHIND THIS NONSENSE?
OH, GOD! HELP!
RUN! RUN!
CHOMP
RUN!
HOLY FUDGE!
OUTTA MY WAY!
WHUT IN TH' HECK ARE THEY?!
OH... OH DEAR...
WATCH OUT, LADY!
SMASH

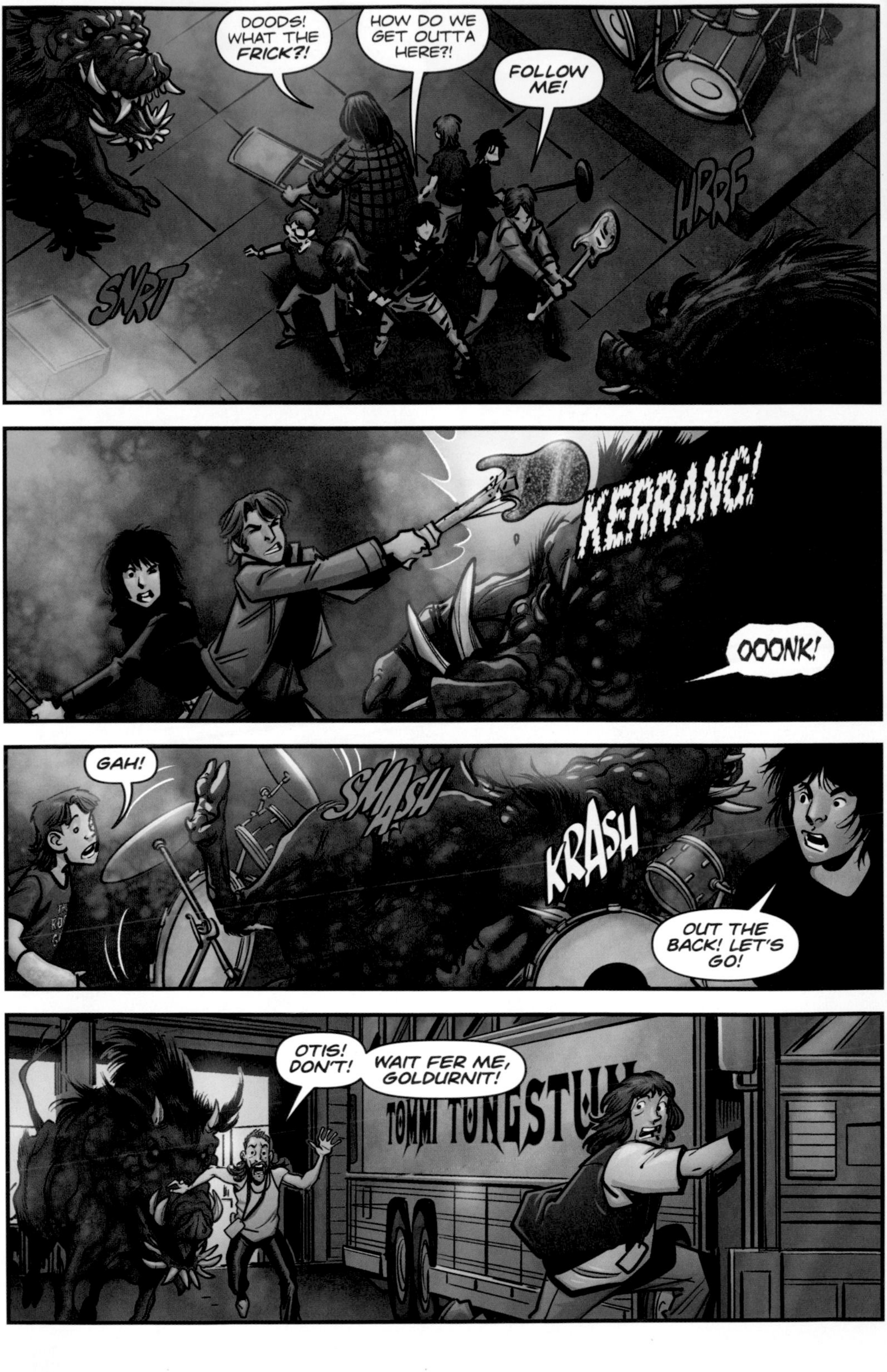
DOODS! WHAT THE FRICK?!
HOW DO WE GET OUTTA HERE?!
FOLLOW ME!
HRRF
SNRT
KERRANG!
OOONK!
GAH!
SMASH
KRASH
OUT THE BACK! LET'S GO!
OTIS! DON'T!
WAIT FER ME, GOLDURNIT!

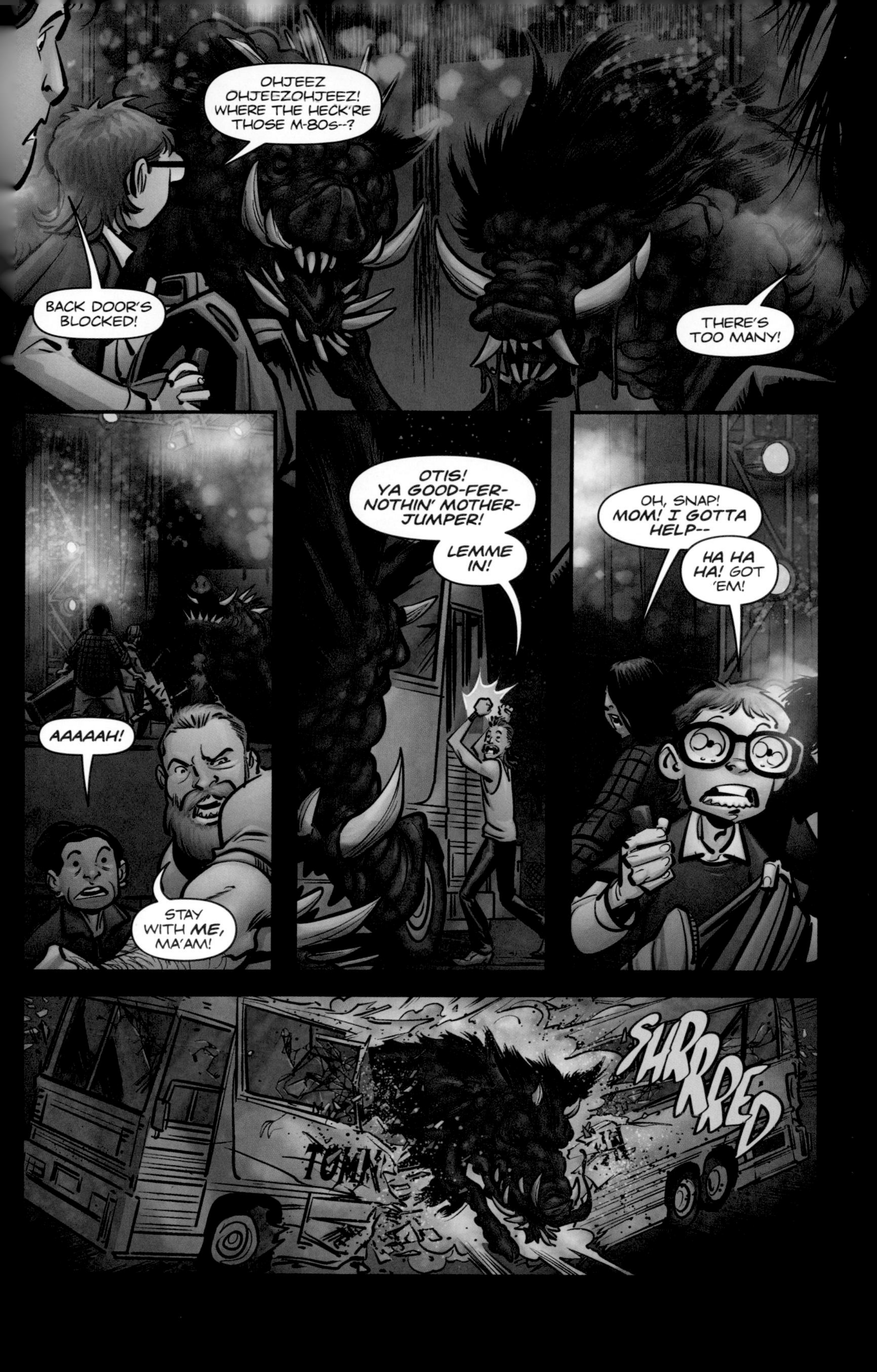
OHJEEZ OHJEEZOHJEEZ! WHERE THE HECK'RE THOSE M-80s--?
BACK DOOR'S BLOCKED!
THERE'S TOO MANY!
AAAAAH!
STAY WITH ME, MA'AM!
OTIS! YA GOOD-FER-NOTHIN' MOTHER-JUMPER!
LEMME IN!
OH, SNAP! MOM! I GOTTA HELP--
HA HA HA! GOT 'EM!
SHRRRED
TOMM

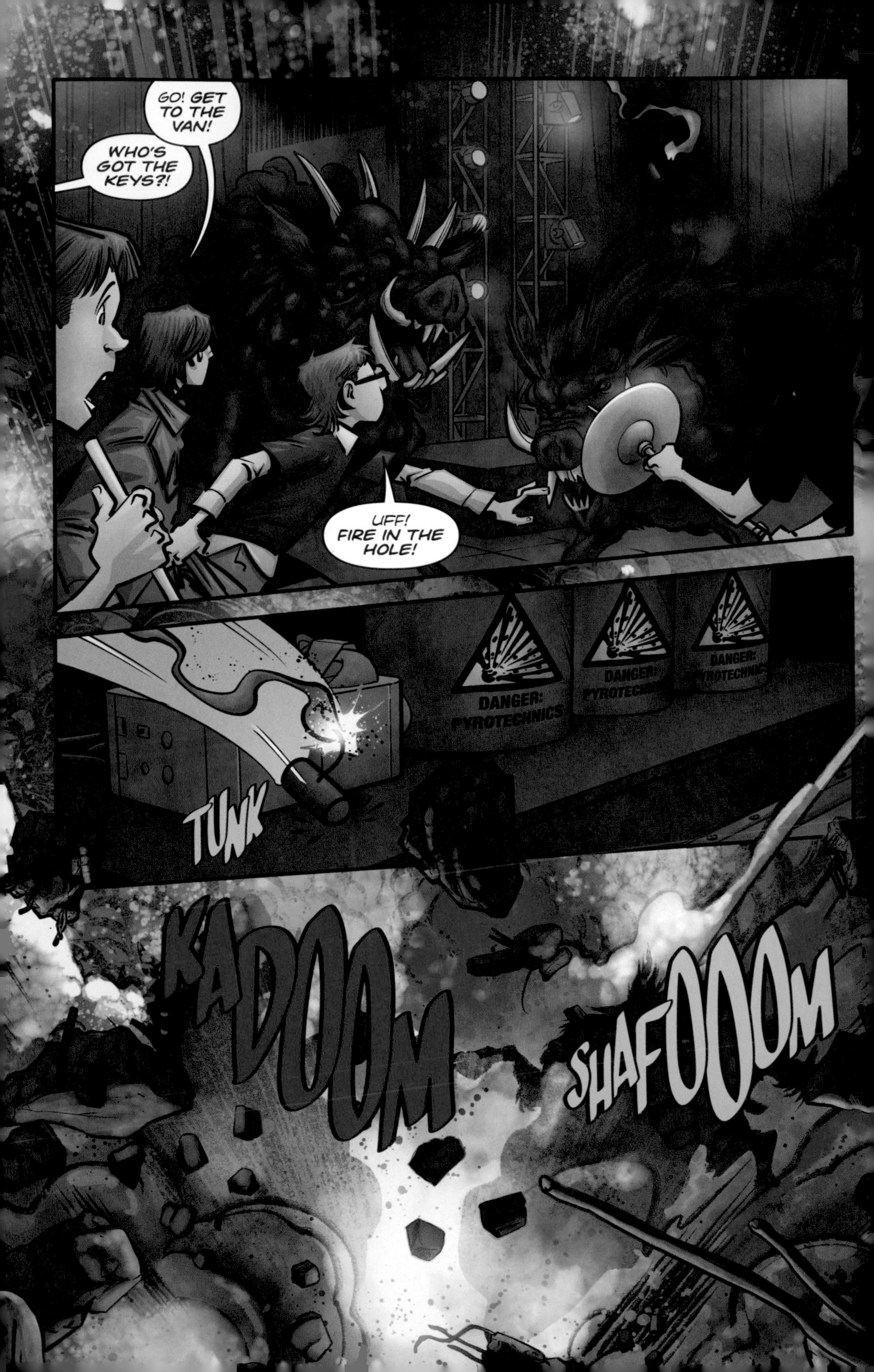

GO! GET TO THE VAN!
WHO'S GOT THE KEYS?!
UFF! FIRE IN THE HOLE!
DANGER: PYROTECHNICS
DANGER: PYROTECHNICS
DANGER: PYROTECHNICS
TUNK
KADOOOM
SHAFOOOM

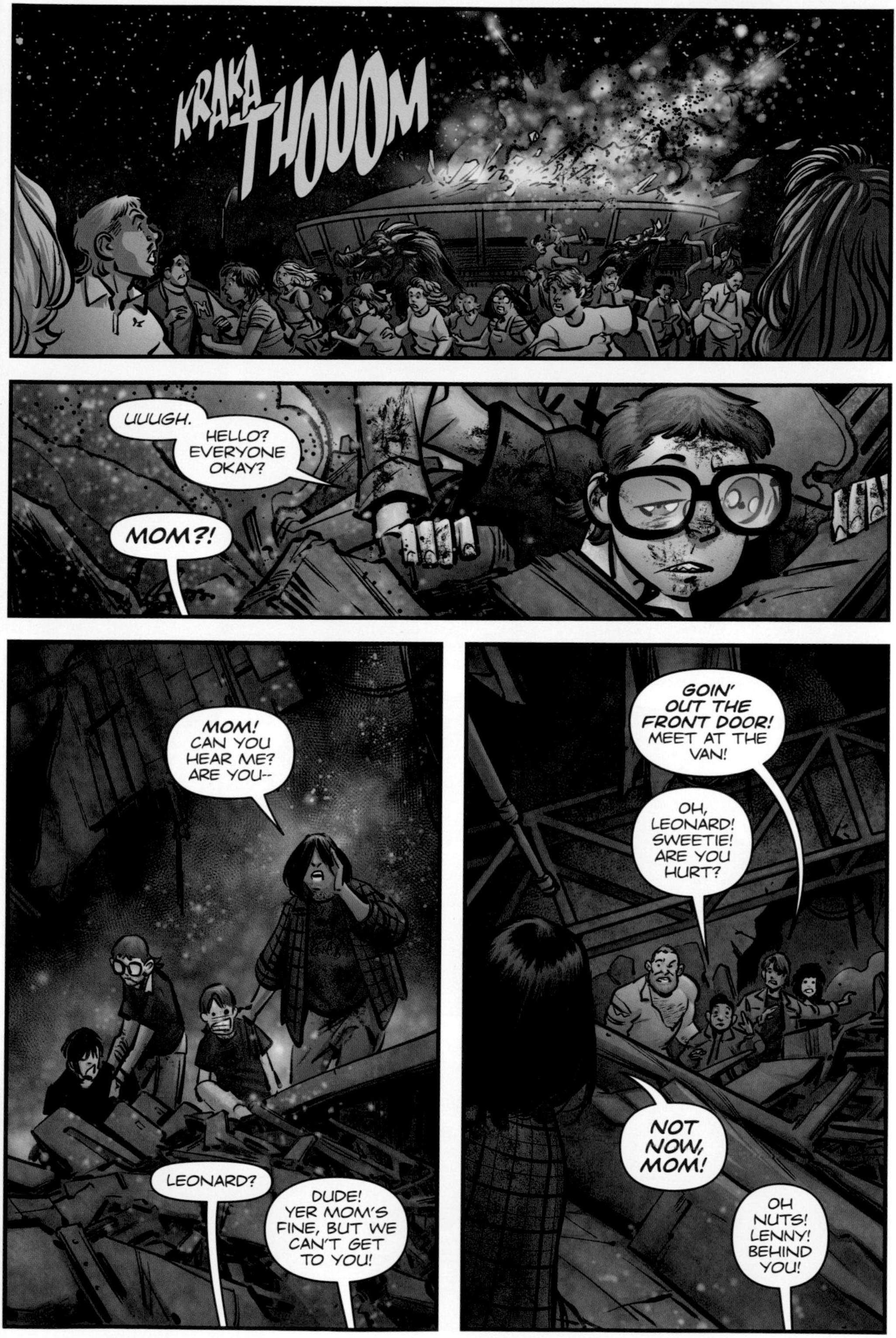
KRAKA THOOOM
UUUGH.
HELLO? EVERYONE OKAY?
MOM?!
MOM! CAN YOU HEAR ME? ARE YOU--
LEONARD?
DUDE! YER MOM'S FINE, BUT WE CAN'T GET TO YOU!
GOIN' OUT THE FRONT DOOR! MEET AT THE VAN!
OH, LEONARD! SWEETIE! ARE YOU HURT?
NOT NOW, MOM!
OH NUTS! LENNY! BEHIND YOU!

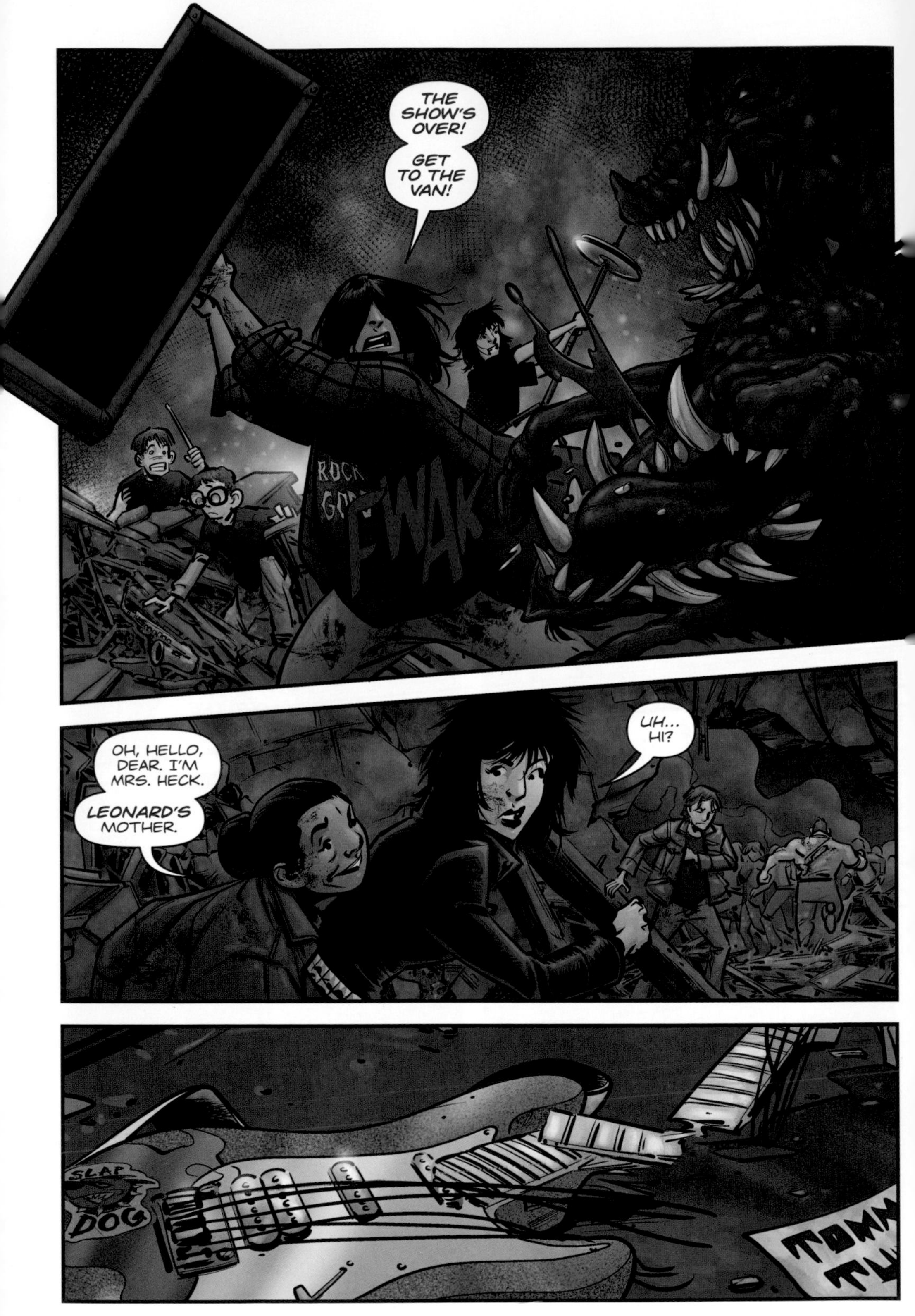
THE SHOW'S OVER!
GET TO THE VAN!
ROCK
FWAK
OH, HELLO, DEAR. I'M MRS. HECK.
LEONARD'S MOTHER.
UH... HI?
SLAP DOG

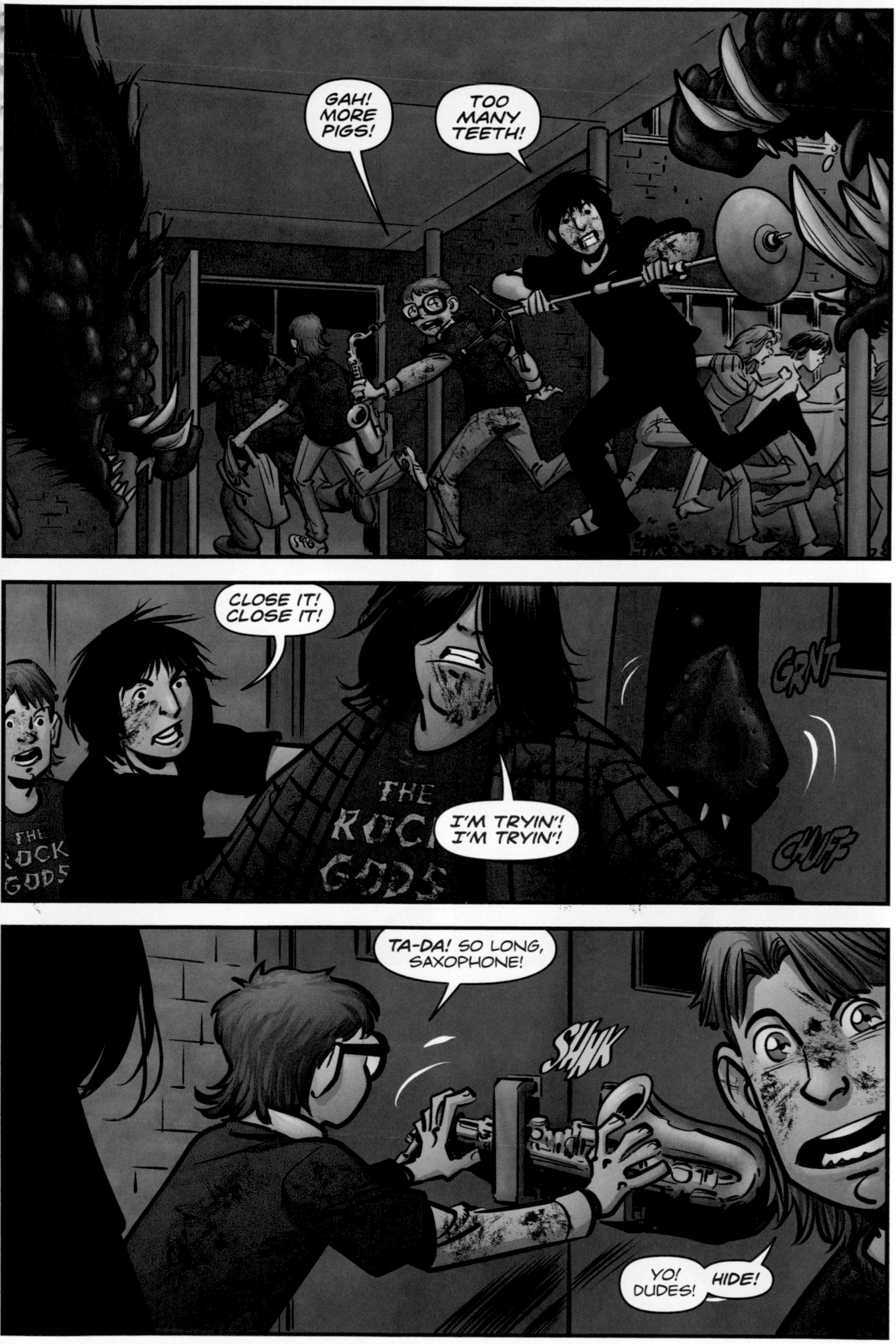
GAH! MORE PIGS!
TOO MANY TEETH!
CLOSE IT! CLOSE IT!
GRNT
I'M TRYIN'! I'M TRYIN'!
CHUFF
TA-DA! SO LONG, SAXOPHONE!
SHNK
YO! DUDES!
HIDE!

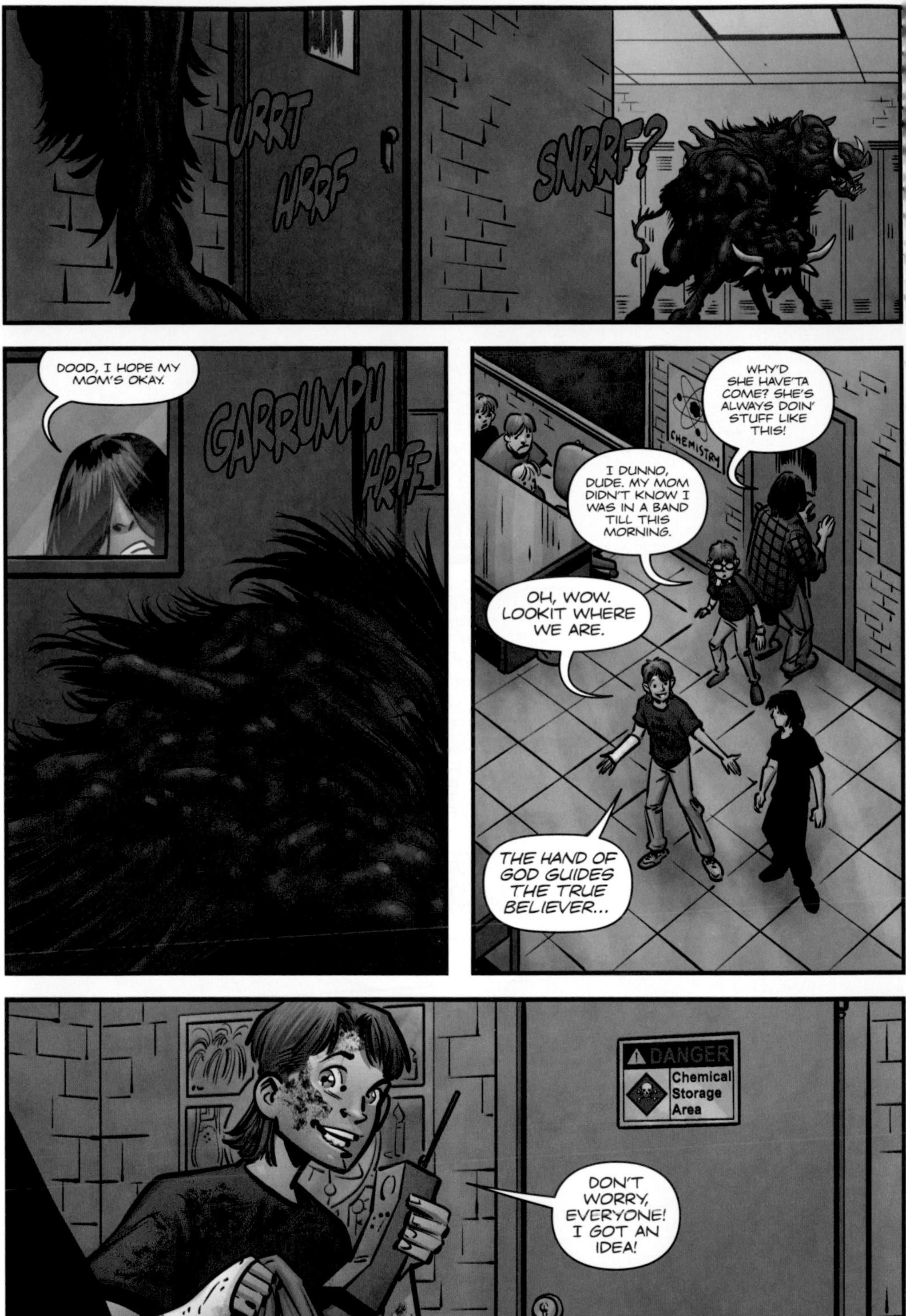
URRT
HRRF
SNRRF?
DOOD, I HOPE MY MOM'S OKAY.
GARRUMPH
HRFF
WHY'D SHE HAVE'TA COME? SHE'S ALWAYS DOIN' STUFF LIKE THIS!
CHEMISTRY
I DUNNO, DUDE. MY MOM DIDN'T KNOW I WAS IN A BAND TILL THIS MORNING.
OH, WOW. LOOKIT WHERE WE ARE.
THE HAND OF GOD GUIDES THE TRUE BELIEVER...
DANGER
Chemical Storage Area
DON'T WORRY, EVERYONE! I GOT AN IDEA!

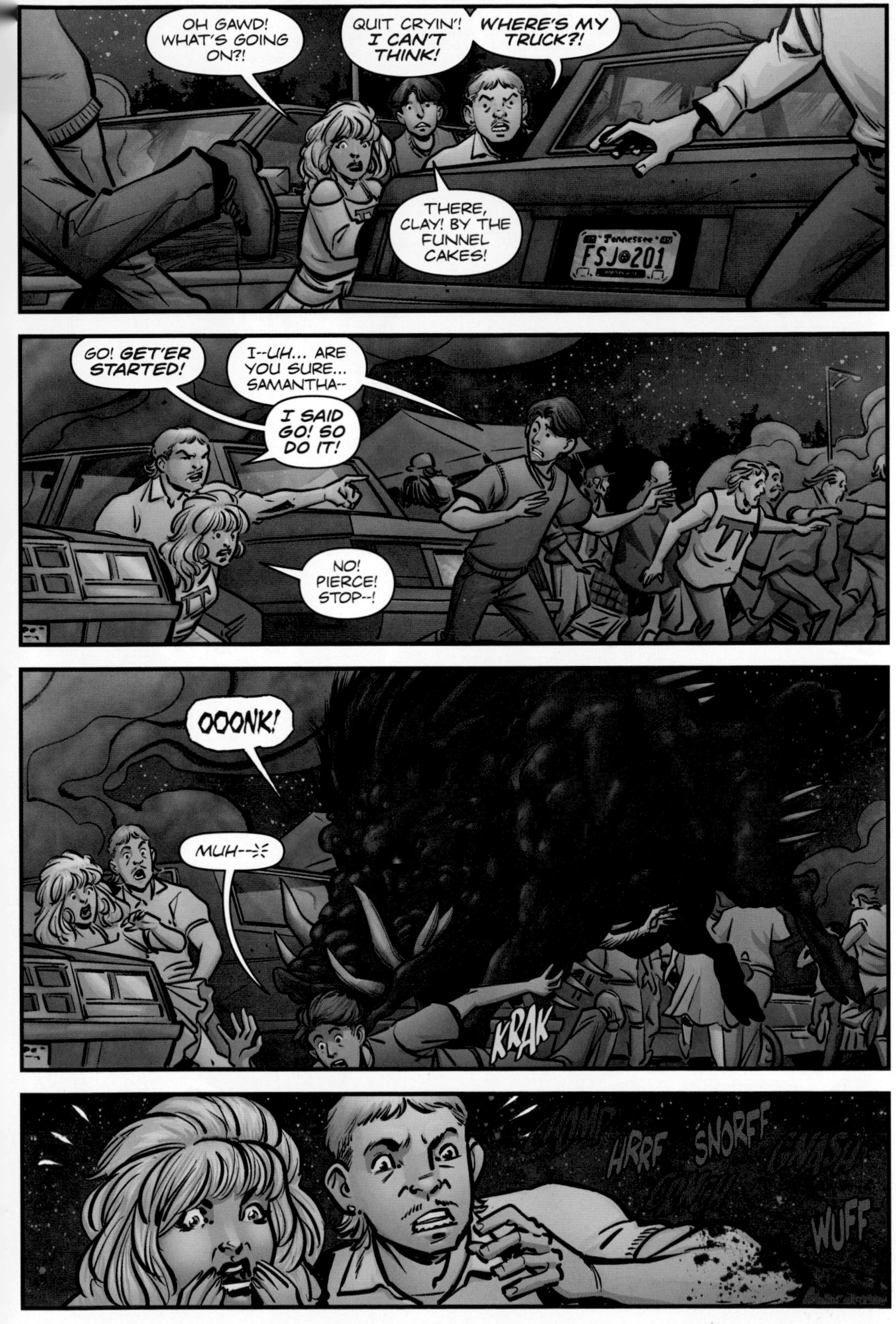
OH GAWD! WHAT'S GOING ON?!
QUIT CRYIN'! I CAN'T THINK!
WHERE'S MY TRUCK?!
THERE, CLAY! BY THE FUNNEL CAKES!
GO! GET'ER STARTED!
I--UH... ARE YOU SURE... SAMANTHA--
I SAID GO! SO DO IT!
NO! PIERCE! STOP--!
OOONK!
MUH--
KRAK
HRRF
SNORFF
WUFF

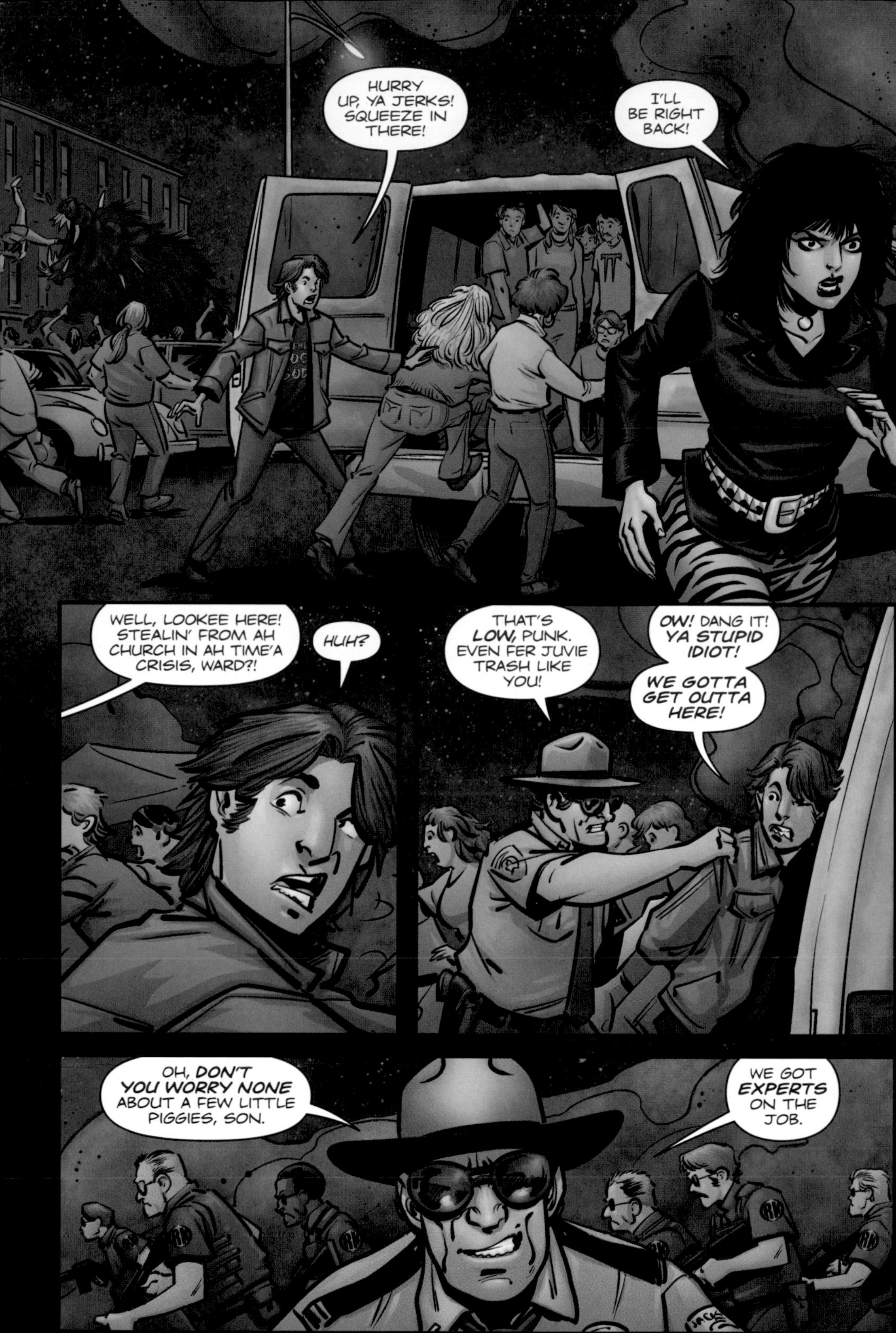
HURRY UP, YA JERKS! SQUEEZE IN THERE!
I'LL BE RIGHT BACK!
WELL, LOOKEE HERE! STEALIN' FROM AH CHURCH IN AH TIME'A CRISIS, WARD?!
HUH?
THAT'S LOW, PUNK. EVEN FER JUVIE TRASH LIKE YOU!
OW! DANG IT! YA STUPID IDIOT!
WE GOTTA GET OUTTA HERE!
OH, DON'T YOU WORRY NONE ABOUT A FEW LITTLE PIGGIES, SON.
WE GOT EXPERTS ON THE JOB.

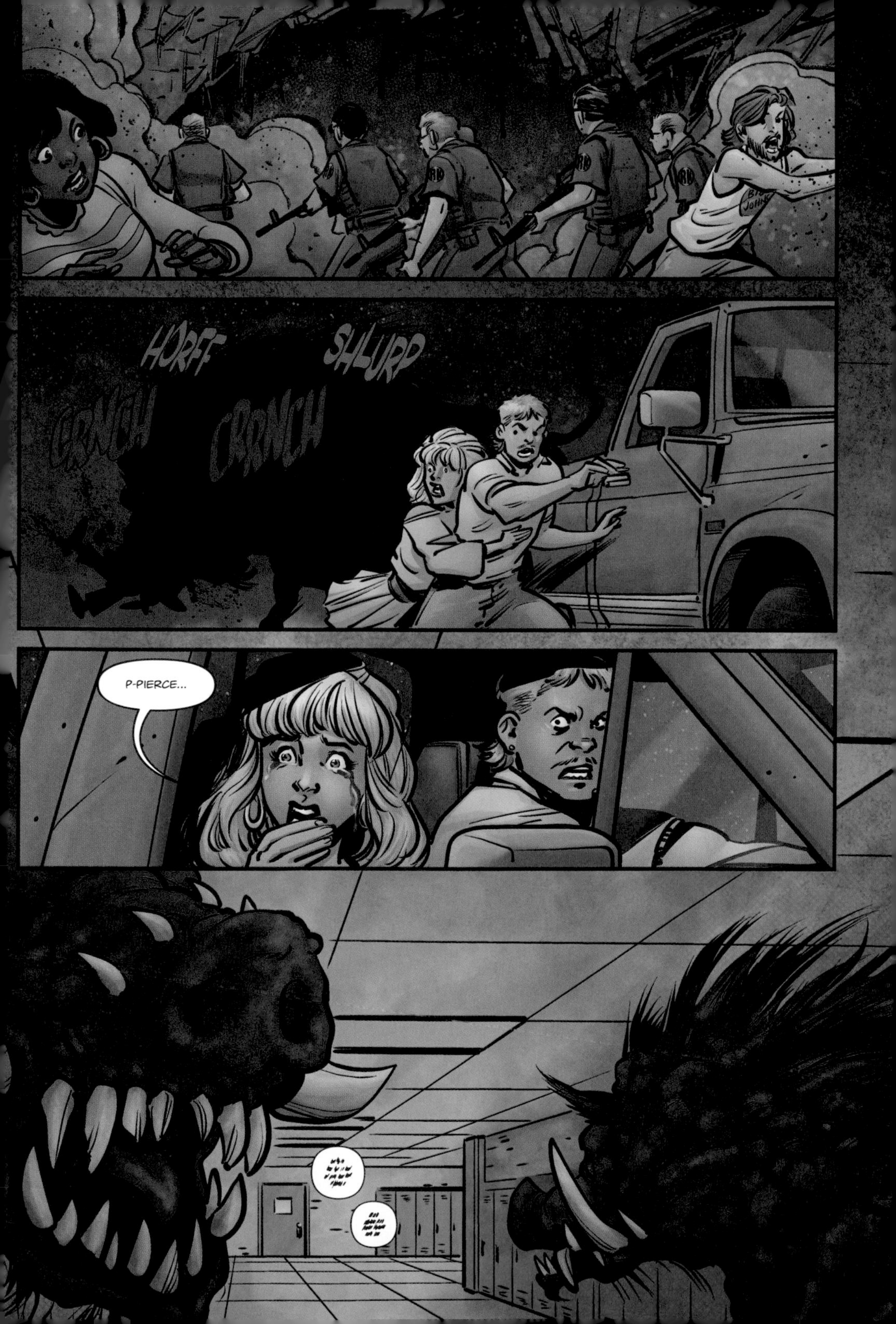
HORFF
CRNCH
CRRNCH
SHLURP
P-PIERCE...

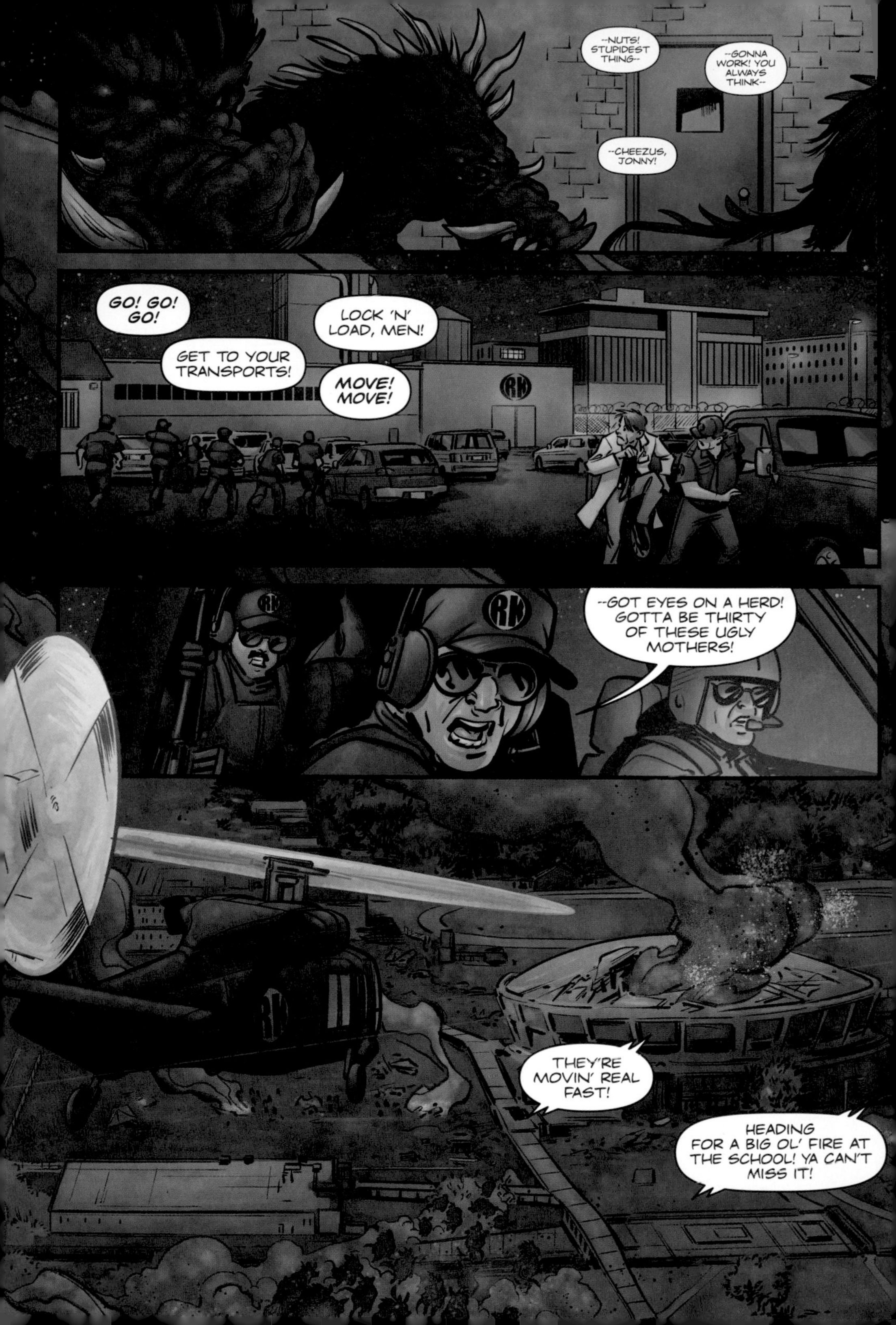
--NUTS! STUPIDEST THING--
--GONNA WORK! YOU ALWAYS THINK--
--CHEEZUS, JONNY!
GO! GO! GO!
GET TO YOUR TRANSPORTS!
LOCK 'N' LOAD, MEN!
MOVE! MOVE!
--GOT EYES ON A HERD! GOTTA BE THIRTY OF THESE UGLY MOTHERS!
THEY'RE MOVIN' REAL FAST!
HEADING FOR A BIG OL' FIRE AT THE SCHOOL! YA CAN'T MISS IT!

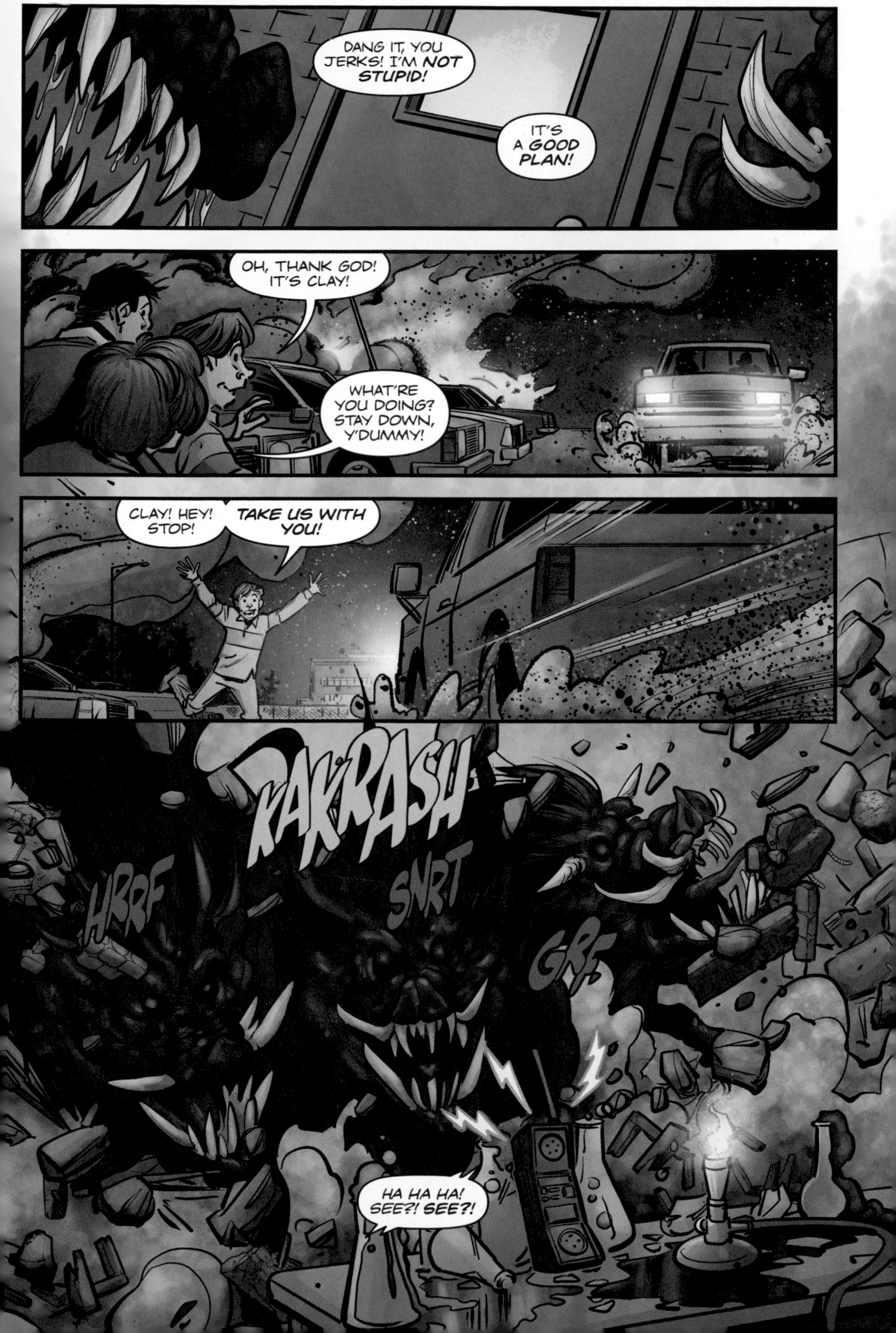
DANG IT, YOU JERKS! I'M **NOT STUPID!**
IT'S A **GOOD PLAN!**
OH, THANK GOD! IT'S CLAY!
WHAT'RE YOU DOING? STAY DOWN, Y'DUMMY!
CLAY! HEY! STOP!
TAKE US WITH YOU!
KAKRASH
HRRF
SNRT
GRF
HA HA HA! SEE?! **SEE?!**

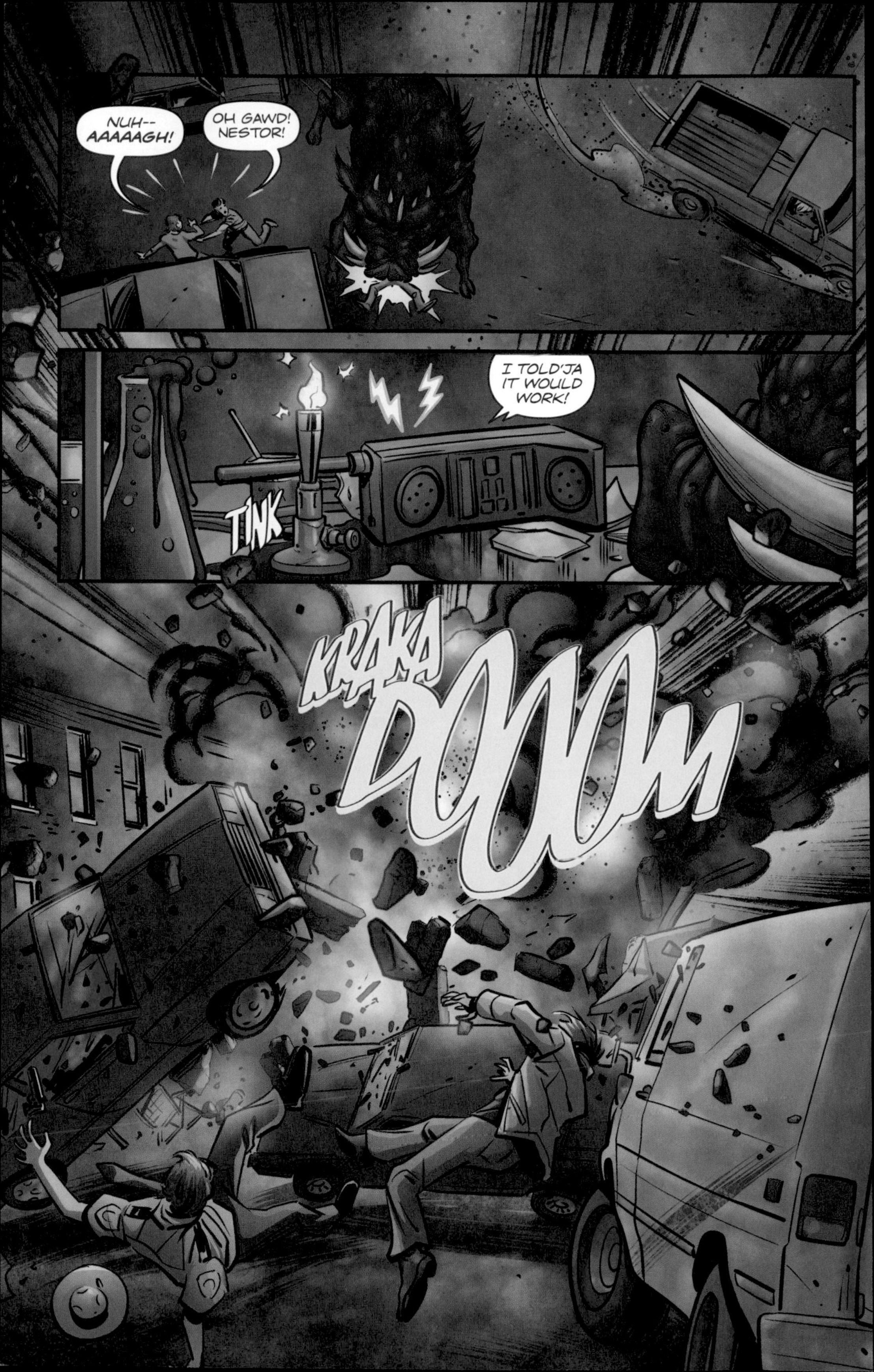
NUH-- AAAAAGH!
OH GAWD! NESTOR!
I TOLD'JA IT WOULD WORK!
TINK
KRAKA DOOOM

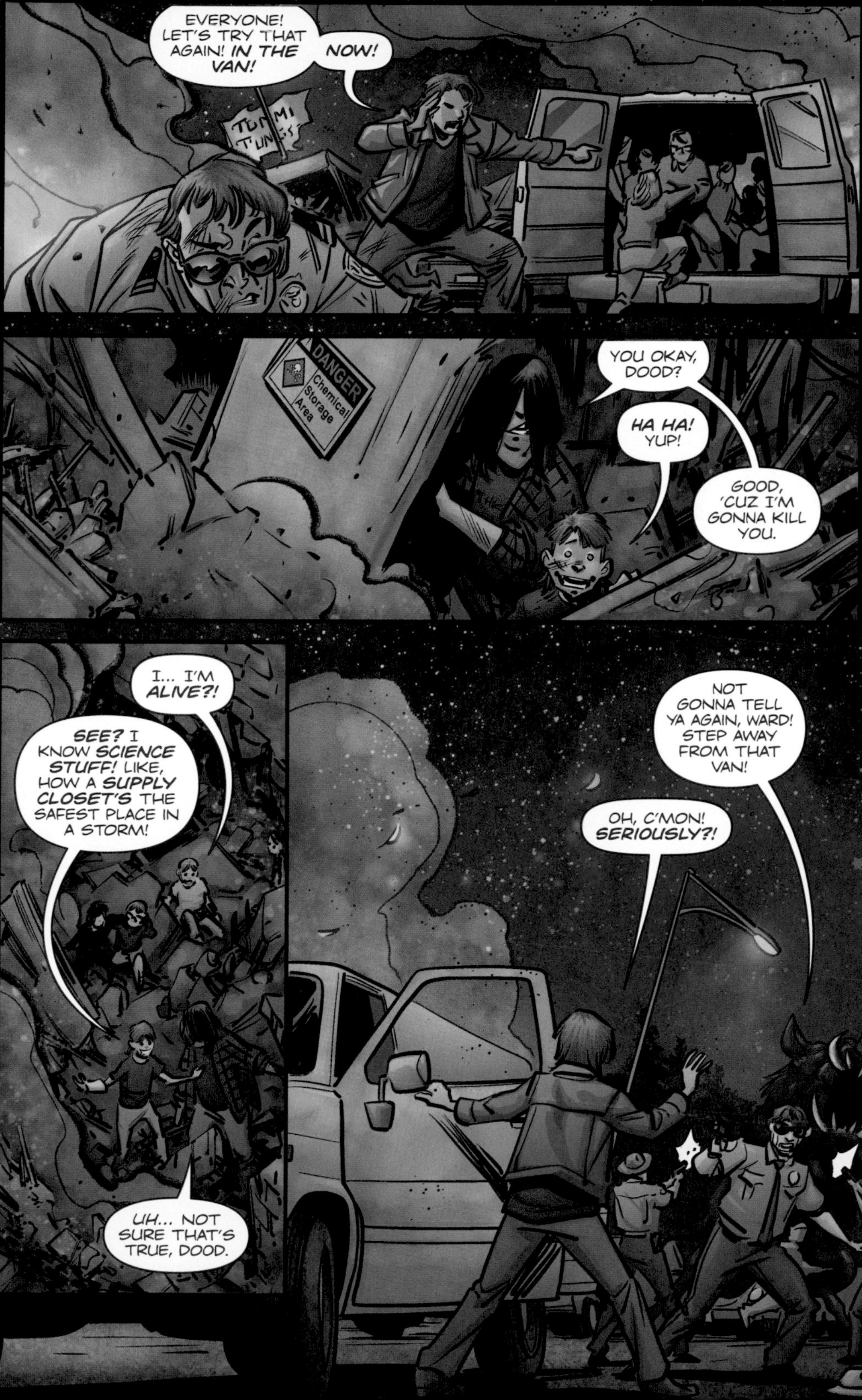
EVERYONE! LET'S TRY THAT AGAIN! IN THE VAN!
NOW!
TOMMI TUNES
DANGER
Chemical Storage Area
YOU OKAY, DOOD?
HA HA! YUP!
GOOD, 'CUZ I'M GONNA KILL YOU.
I... I'M ALIVE?!
SEE? I KNOW SCIENCE STUFF! LIKE, HOW A SUPPLY CLOSET'S THE SAFEST PLACE IN A STORM!
UH... NOT SURE THAT'S TRUE, DOOD.
NOT GONNA TELL YA AGAIN, WARD! STEP AWAY FROM THAT VAN!
OH, C'MON! SERIOUSLY?!

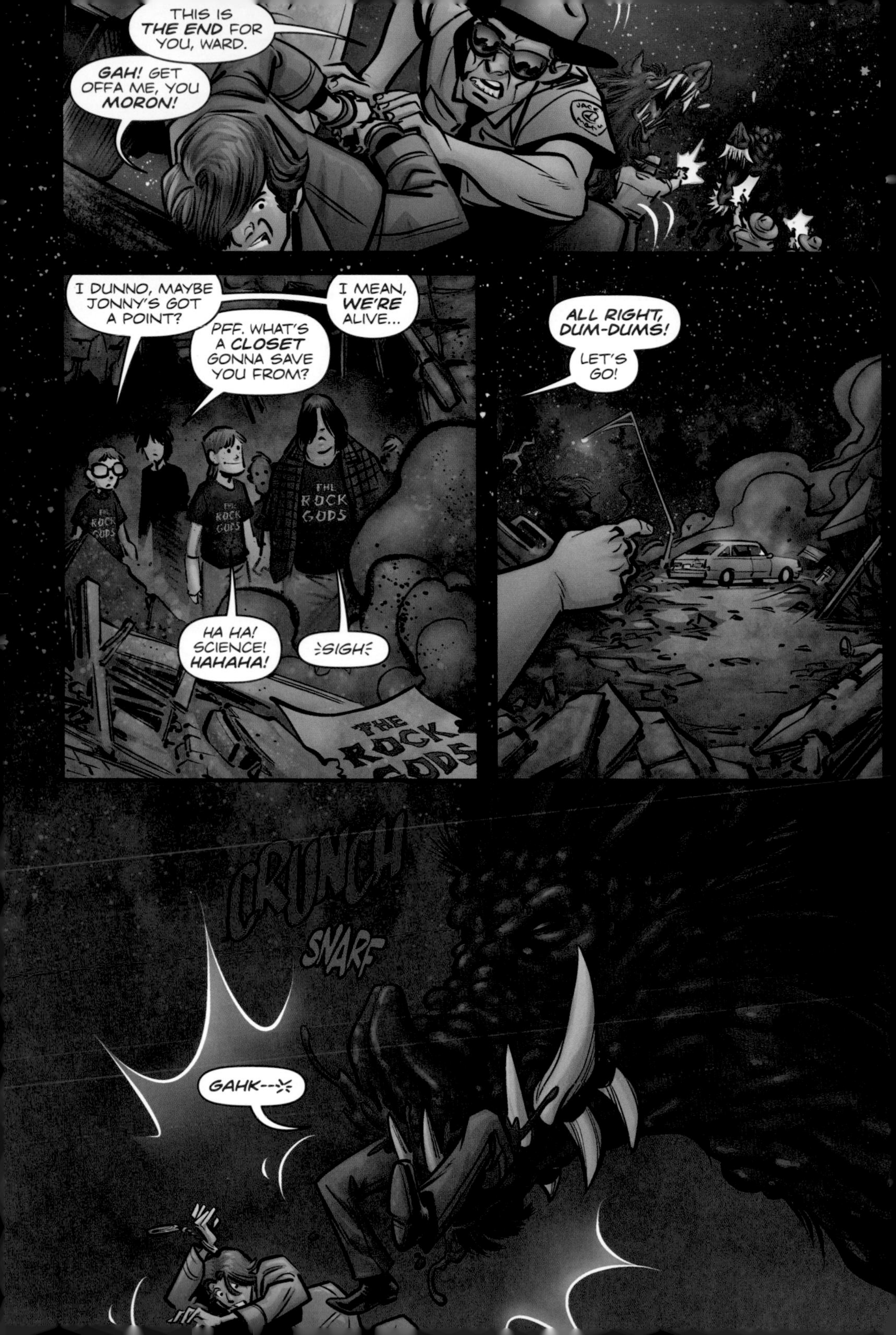
THIS IS THE END FOR YOU, WARD.
GAH! GET OFFA ME, YOU MORON!
I DUNNO, MAYBE JONNY'S GOT A POINT?
I MEAN, WE'RE ALIVE...
PFF. WHAT'S A CLOSET GONNA SAVE YOU FROM?
THE ROCK GODS
HA HA! SCIENCE! HAHAHA!
SIGH
THE ROCK GODS
ALL RIGHT, DUM-DUMS!
LET'S GO!
CRUNCH
SNARF
GAHK--

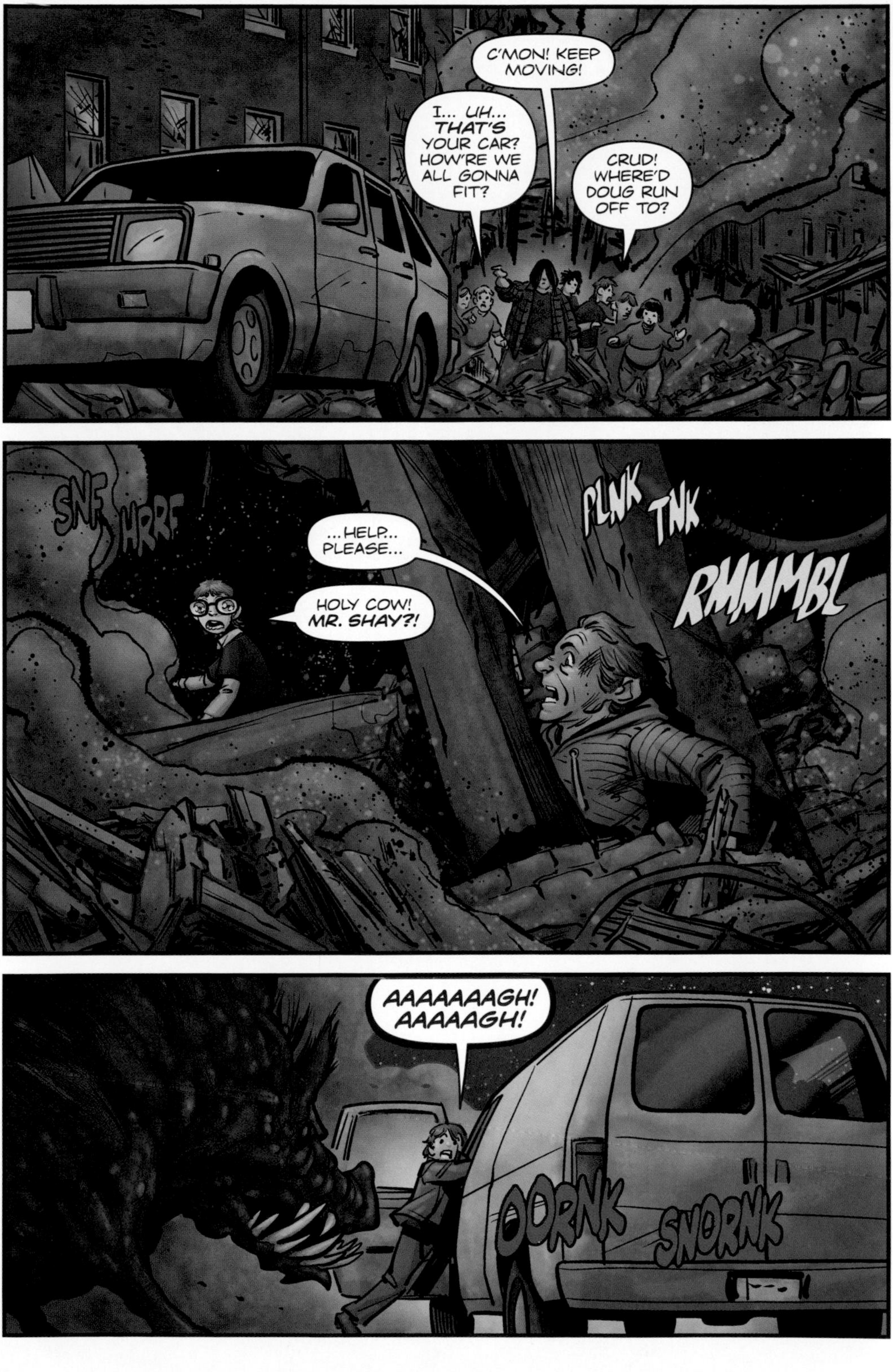
C'MON! KEEP MOVING!
I... UH... THAT'S YOUR CAR? HOW'RE WE ALL GONNA FIT?
CRUD! WHERE'D DOUG RUN OFF TO?
SNF
HRRF
PLNK
TNK
RMMMBL
...HELP... PLEASE...
HOLY COW! MR. SHAY?!
AAAAAAAGH! AAAAAGH!
OORNK
SNORNK

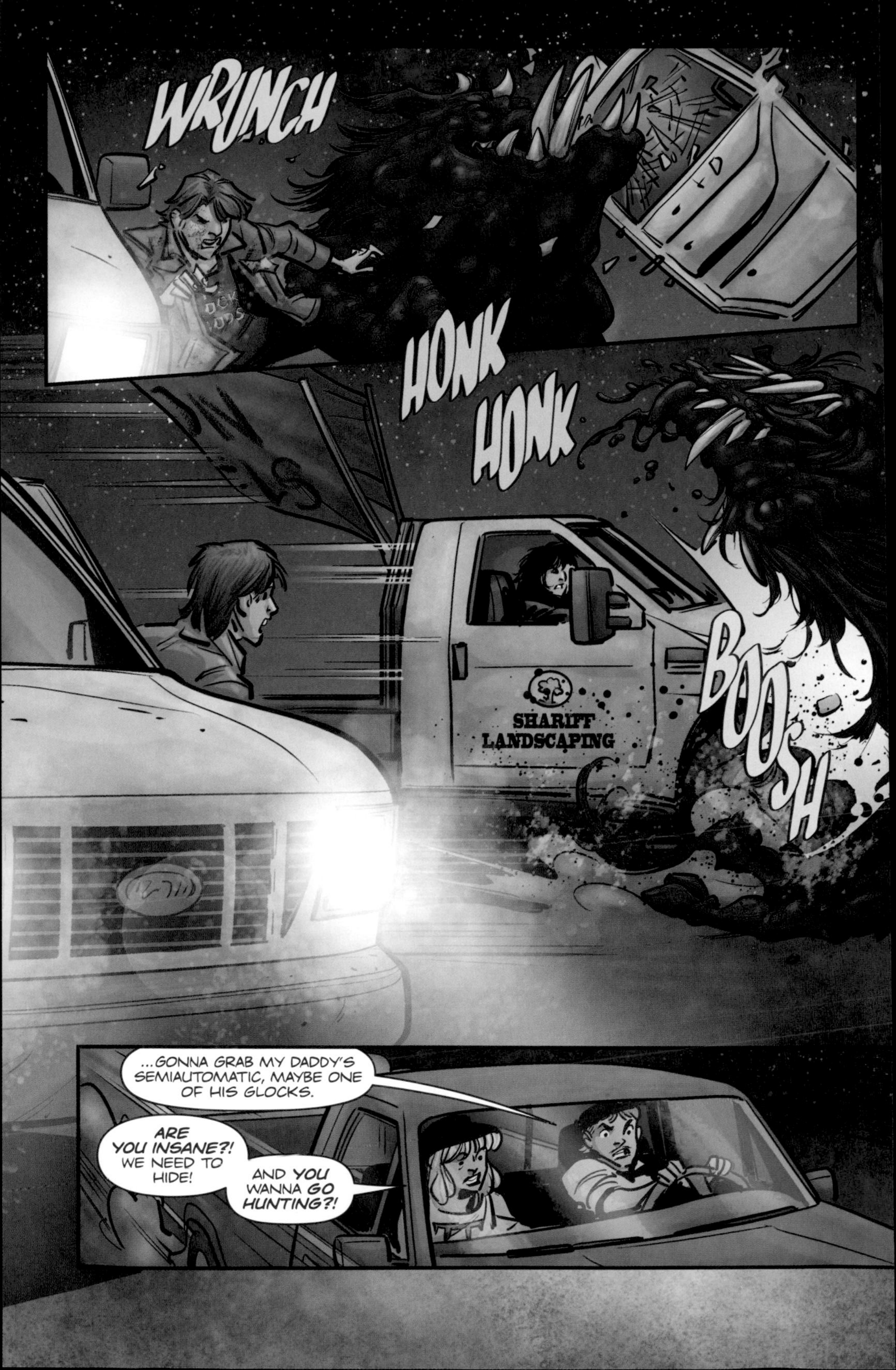
WRUNCH
HONK
HONK
SHARIFF
LANDSCAPING
BOOSH
...GONNA GRAB MY DADDY'S SEMIAUTOMATIC, MAYBE ONE OF HIS GLOCKS.
ARE YOU INSANE?! WE NEED TO HIDE!
AND YOU WANNA GO HUNTING?!

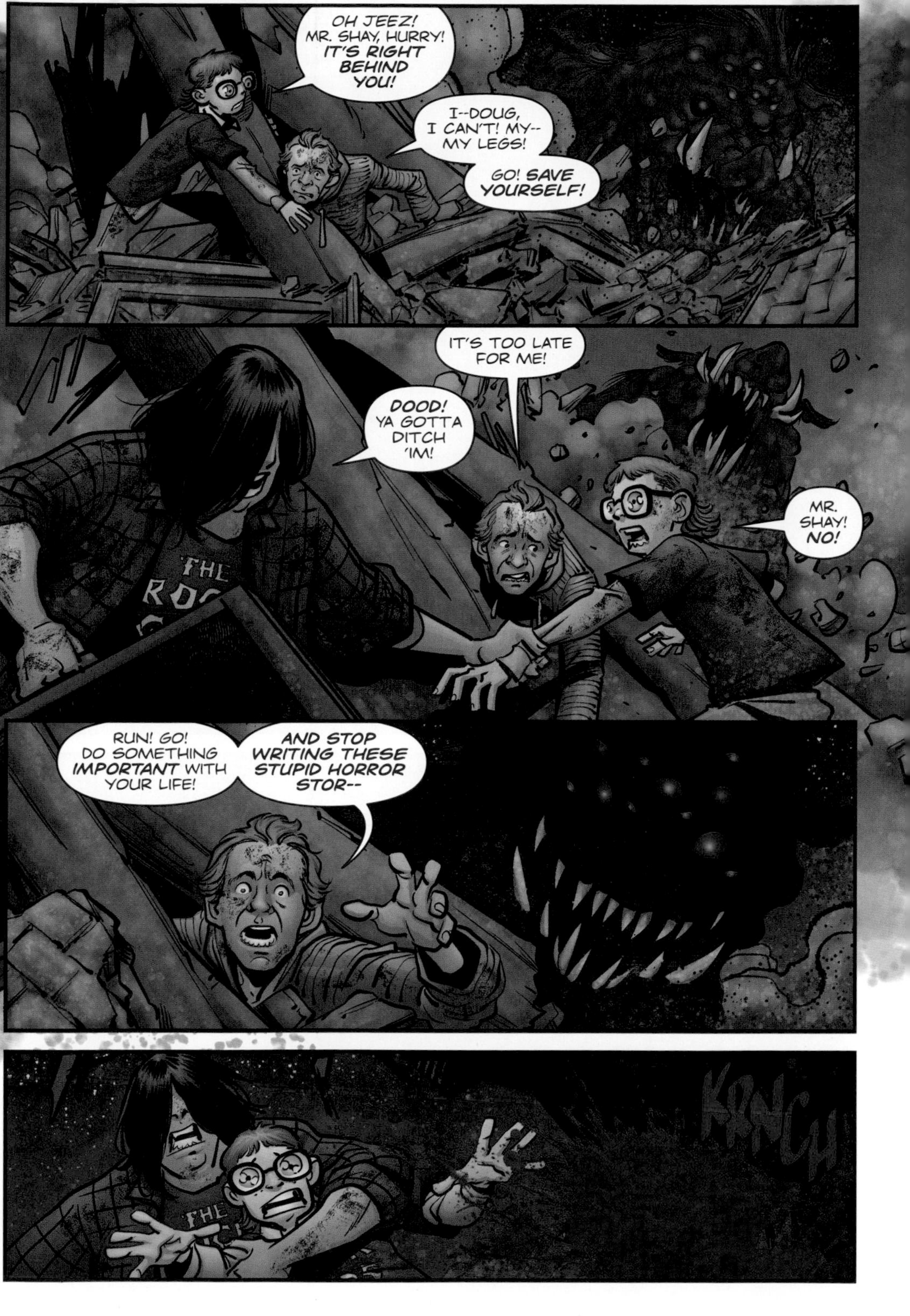
OH JEEZ! MR. SHAY, HURRY! IT'S RIGHT BEHIND YOU!
I--DOUG, I CAN'T! MY-- MY LEGS!
GO! SAVE YOURSELF!
IT'S TOO LATE FOR ME!
DOOD! YA GOTTA DITCH 'IM!
MR. SHAY! NO!
RUN! GO! DO SOMETHING IMPORTANT WITH YOUR LIFE!
AND STOP WRITING THESE STUPID HORROR STOR--
KRNCH

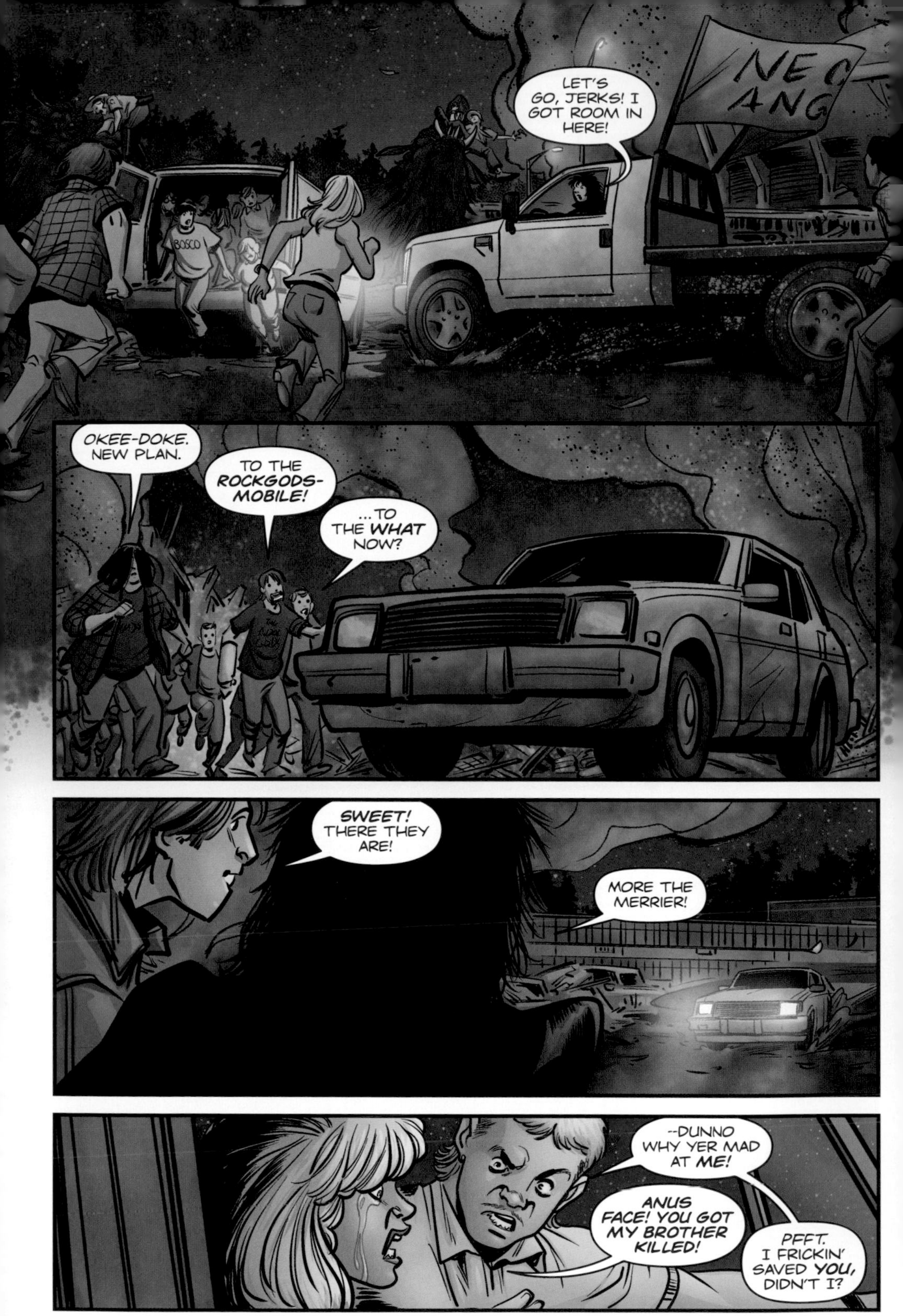
NEO
ANG
LET'S GO, JERKS! I GOT ROOM IN HERE!
BOSCO
OKEE-DOKE. NEW PLAN.
TO THE ROCKGODS-MOBILE!
...TO THE WHAT NOW?
SWEET! THERE THEY ARE!
MORE THE MERRIER!
--DUNNO WHY YER MAD AT ME!
ANUS FACE! YOU GOT MY BROTHER KILLED!
PFFT. I FRICKIN' SAVED YOU, DIDN'T I?

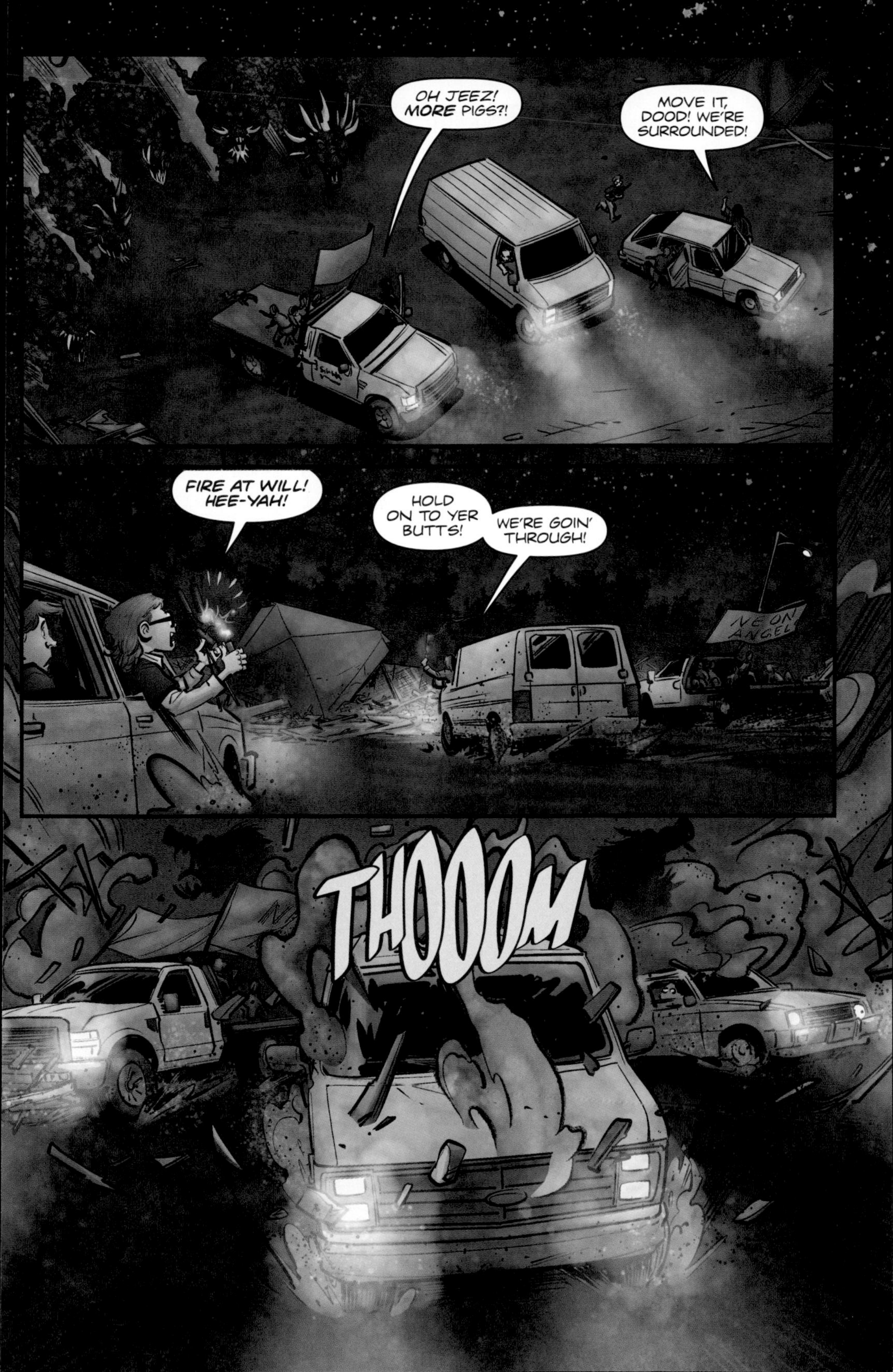
OH JEEZ! MORE PIGS?!
MOVE IT, DOOD! WE'RE SURROUNDED!
FIRE AT WILL! HEE-YAH!
HOLD ON TO YER BUTTS!
WE'RE GOIN' THROUGH!
THOOOM

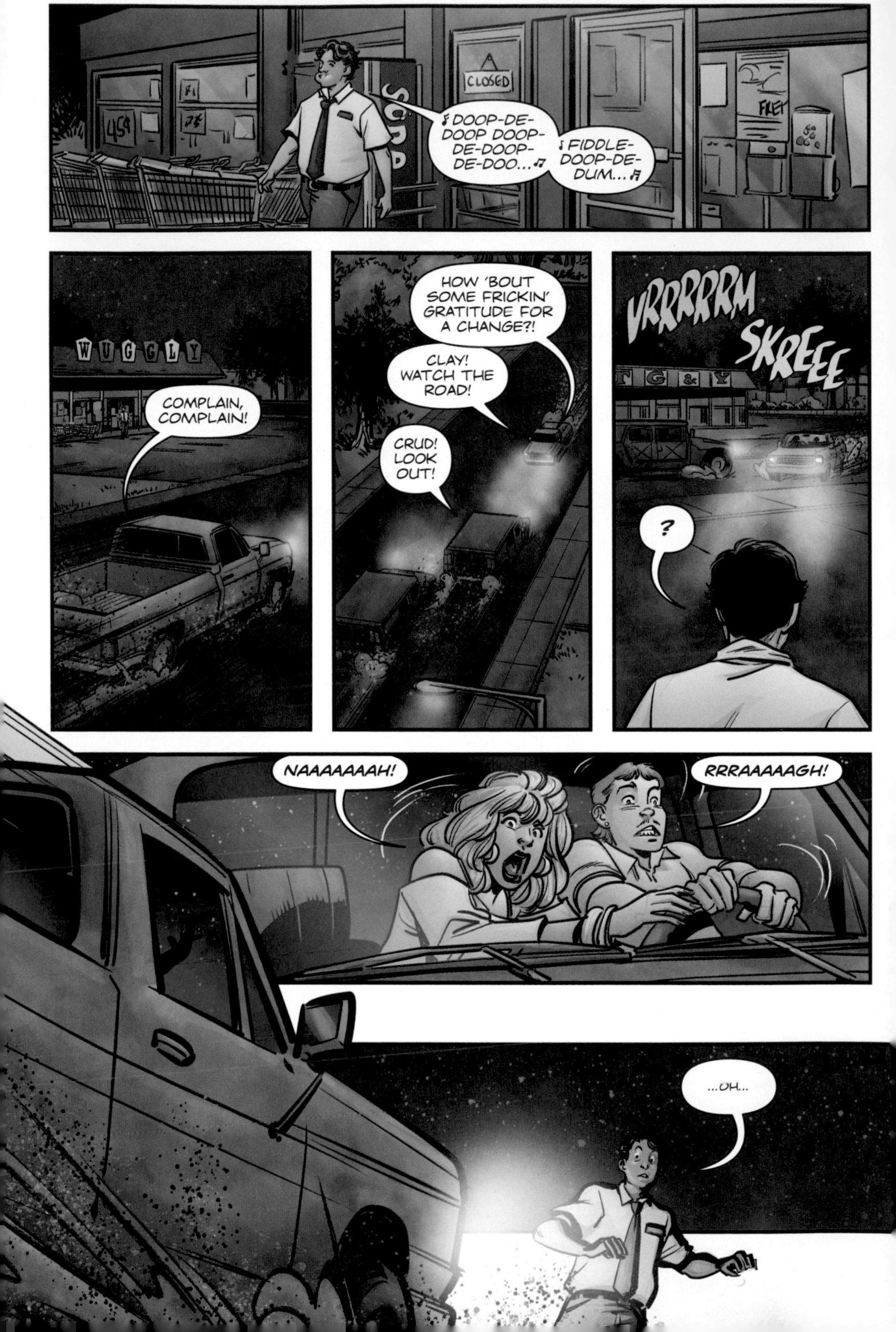
CLOSED
DOOP-DE-DOOP DOOP-DE-DOOP-DE-DOO...
FIDDLE-DOOP-DE-DUM...
WUGGLY
COMPLAIN, COMPLAIN!
HOW 'BOUT SOME FRICKIN' GRATITUDE FOR A CHANGE?!
CLAY! WATCH THE ROAD!
CRUD! LOOK OUT!
VRRRRRM
SKREEEE
?
NAAAAAAAH!
RRRAAAAAGH!
...OH...

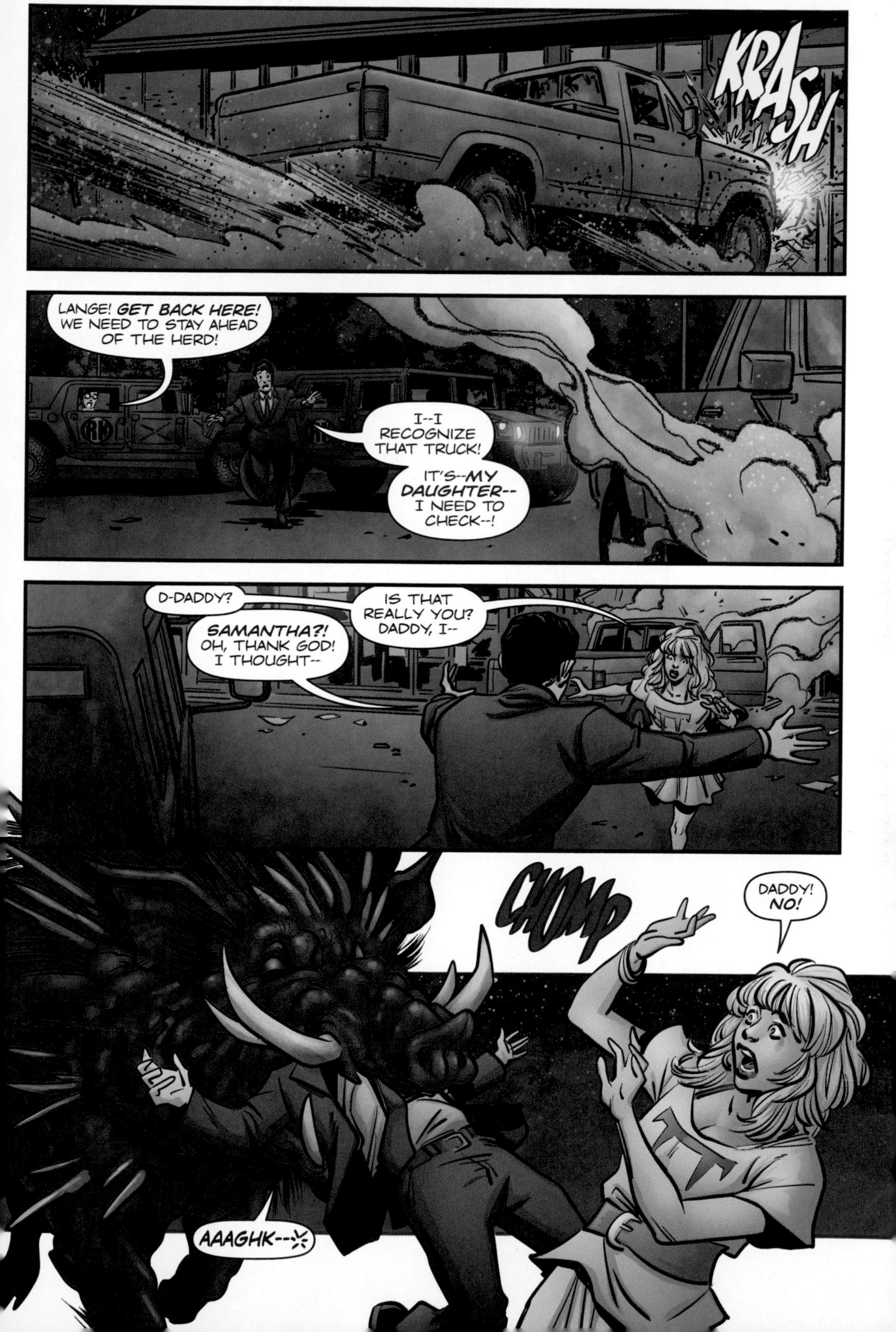
KRASH
LANGE! GET BACK HERE! WE NEED TO STAY AHEAD OF THE HERD!
I--I RECOGNIZE THAT TRUCK!
IT'S--MY DAUGHTER-- I NEED TO CHECK--!
D-DADDY?
IS THAT REALLY YOU? DADDY, I--
SAMANTHA?! OH, THANK GOD! I THOUGHT--
CHOMP
DADDY! NO!
AAAGHK--!

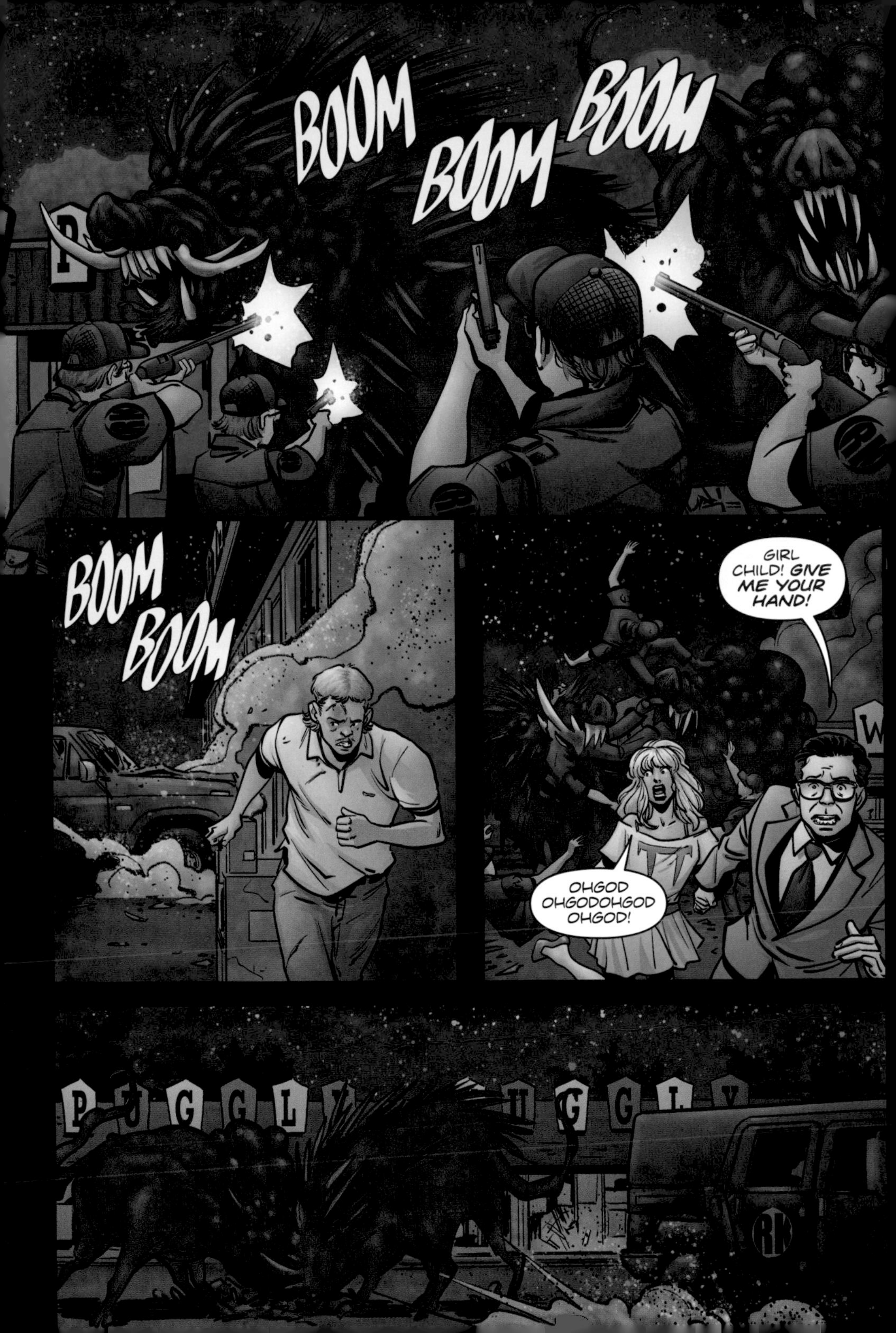
BOOM
BOOM
BOOM
BOOM
BOOM
GIRL CHILD! GIVE ME YOUR HAND!
OHGOD OHGODOHGOD OHGOD!

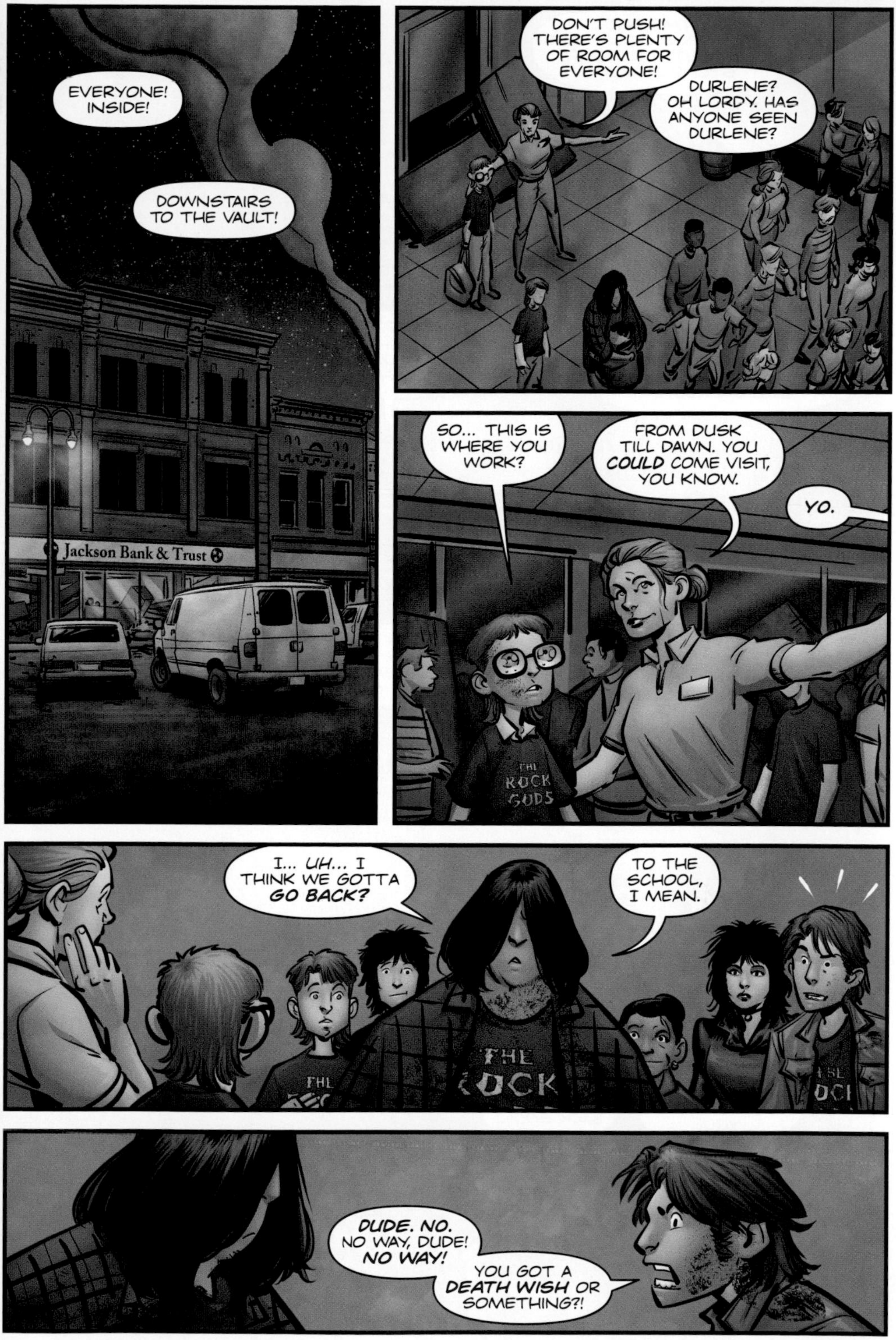
EVERYONE! INSIDE!
DOWNSTAIRS TO THE VAULT!
Jackson Bank & Trust
DON'T PUSH! THERE'S PLENTY OF ROOM FOR EVERYONE!
DURLENE? OH LORDY. HAS ANYONE SEEN DURLENE?
SO... THIS IS WHERE YOU WORK?
FROM DUSK TILL DAWN. YOU COULD COME VISIT, YOU KNOW.
YO.
THE ROCK GODS
I... UH... I THINK WE GOTTA GO BACK?
TO THE SCHOOL, I MEAN.
DUDE. NO. NO WAY, DUDE! NO WAY!
YOU GOT A DEATH WISH OR SOMETHING?!

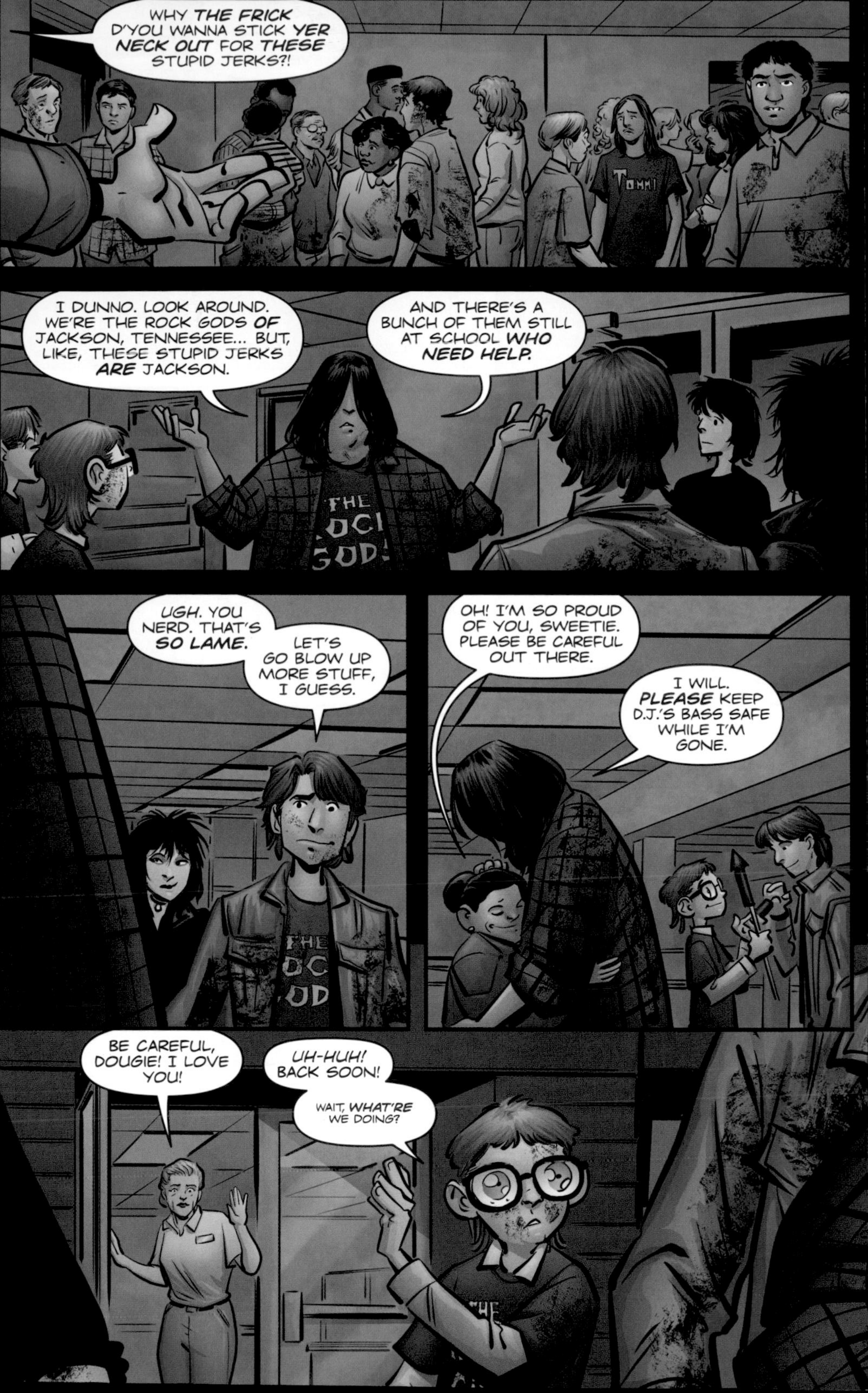
WHY THE FRICK D'YOU WANNA STICK YER NECK OUT FOR THESE STUPID JERKS?!
TOMMI
I DUNNO. LOOK AROUND. WE'RE THE ROCK GODS OF JACKSON, TENNESSEE... BUT, LIKE, THESE STUPID JERKS ARE JACKSON.
AND THERE'S A BUNCH OF THEM STILL AT SCHOOL WHO NEED HELP.
UGH. YOU NERD. THAT'S SO LAME.
LET'S GO BLOW UP MORE STUFF, I GUESS.
OH! I'M SO PROUD OF YOU, SWEETIE. PLEASE BE CAREFUL OUT THERE.
I WILL. PLEASE KEEP D.J.'S BASS SAFE WHILE I'M GONE.
BE CAREFUL, DOUGIE! I LOVE YOU!
UH-HUH! BACK SOON!
WAIT, WHAT'RE WE DOING?

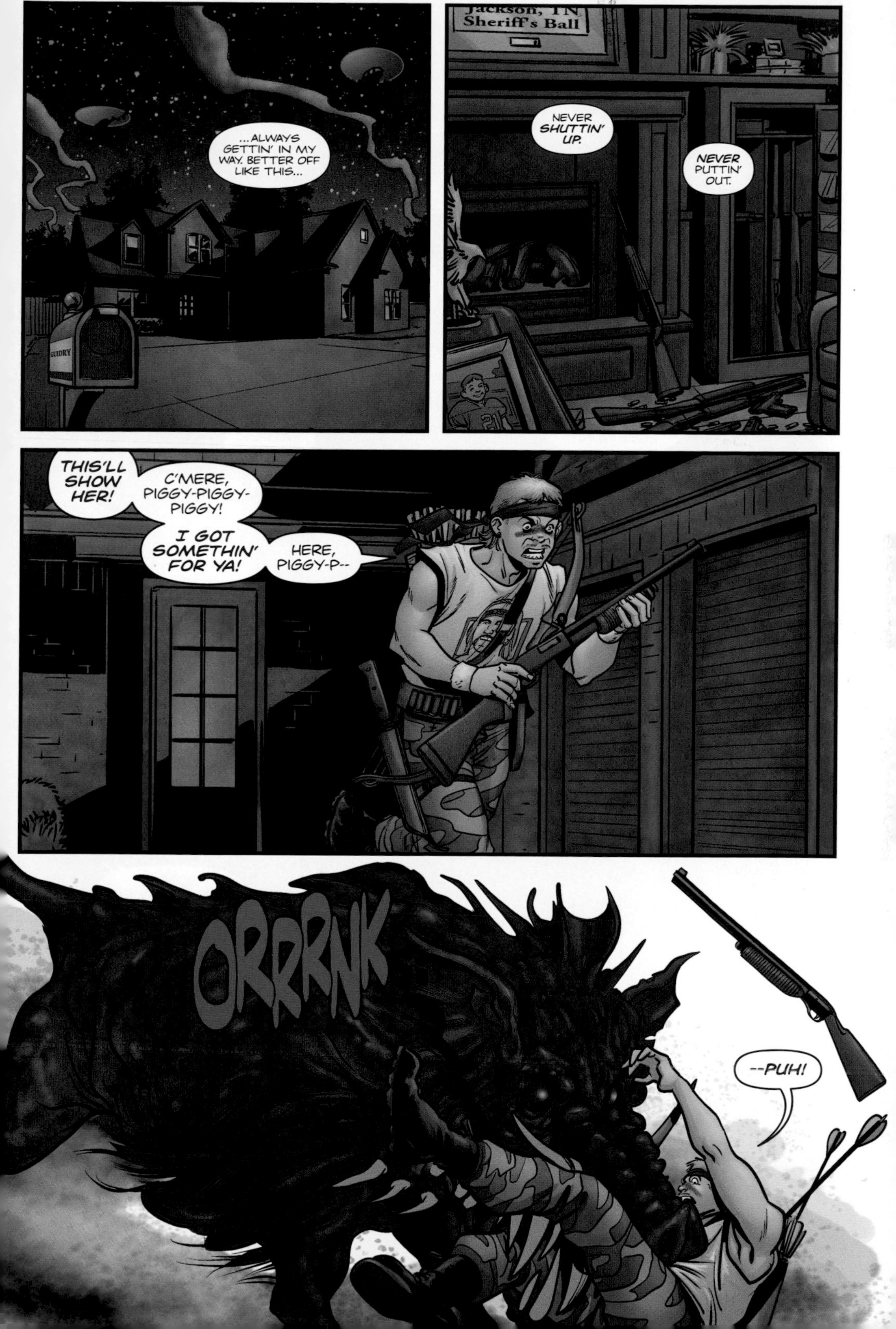
...ALWAYS GETTIN' IN MY WAY. BETTER OFF LIKE THIS...
GUIDRY
Jackson, TN Sheriff's Ball
NEVER SHUTTIN' UP.
NEVER PUTTIN' OUT.
THIS'LL SHOW HER!
C'MERE, PIGGY-PIGGY-PIGGY!
I GOT SOMETHIN' FOR YA!
HERE, PIGGY-P--
ORRRNK
--PUH!

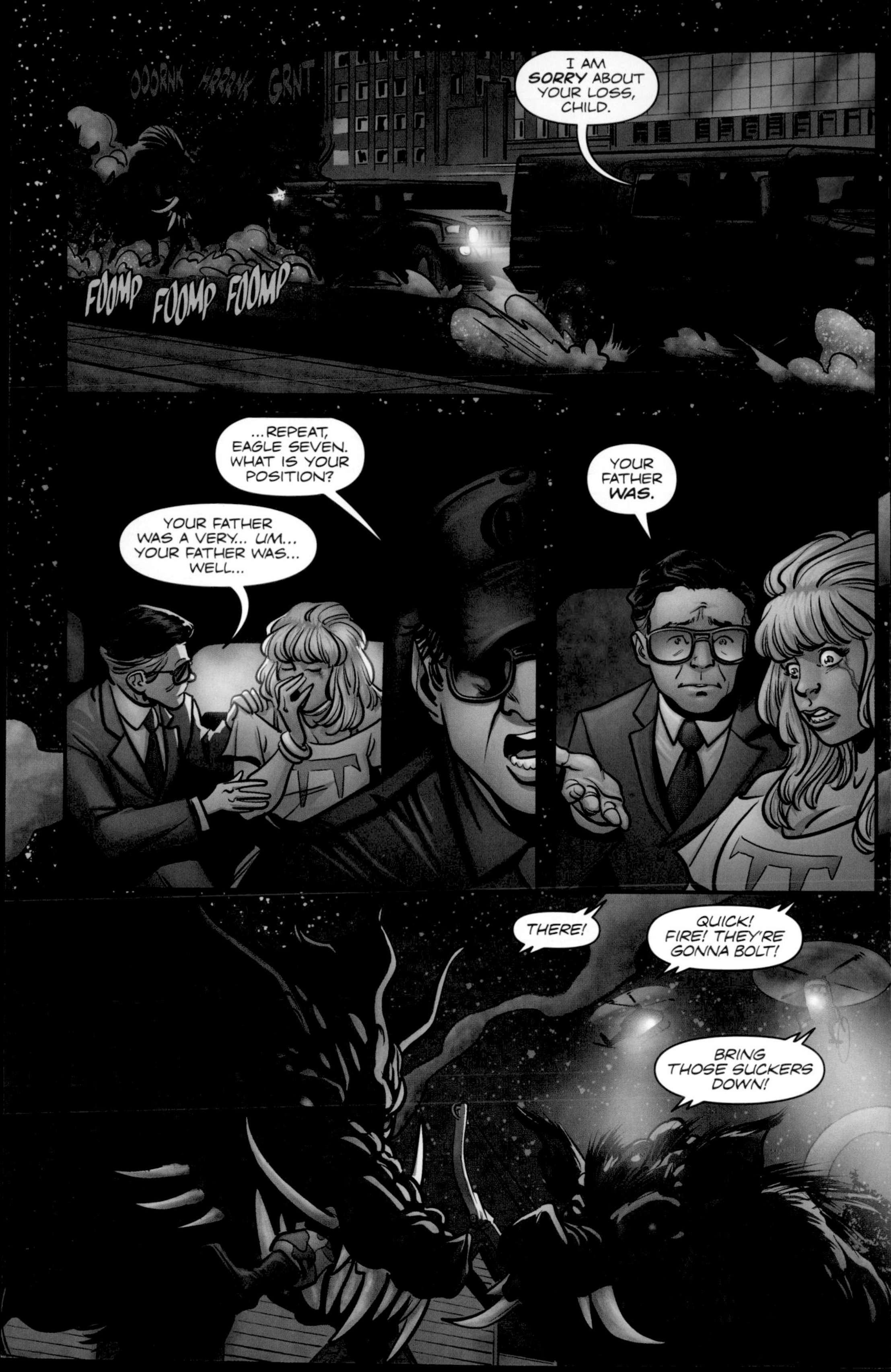
OOORNK HRRRNK GRNT
I AM SORRY ABOUT YOUR LOSS, CHILD.
FOOMP FOOMP FOOMP
...REPEAT, EAGLE SEVEN. WHAT IS YOUR POSITION?
YOUR FATHER WAS A VERY... UM... YOUR FATHER WAS... WELL...
YOUR FATHER WAS.
THERE!
QUICK! FIRE! THEY'RE GONNA BOLT!
BRING THOSE SUCKERS DOWN!

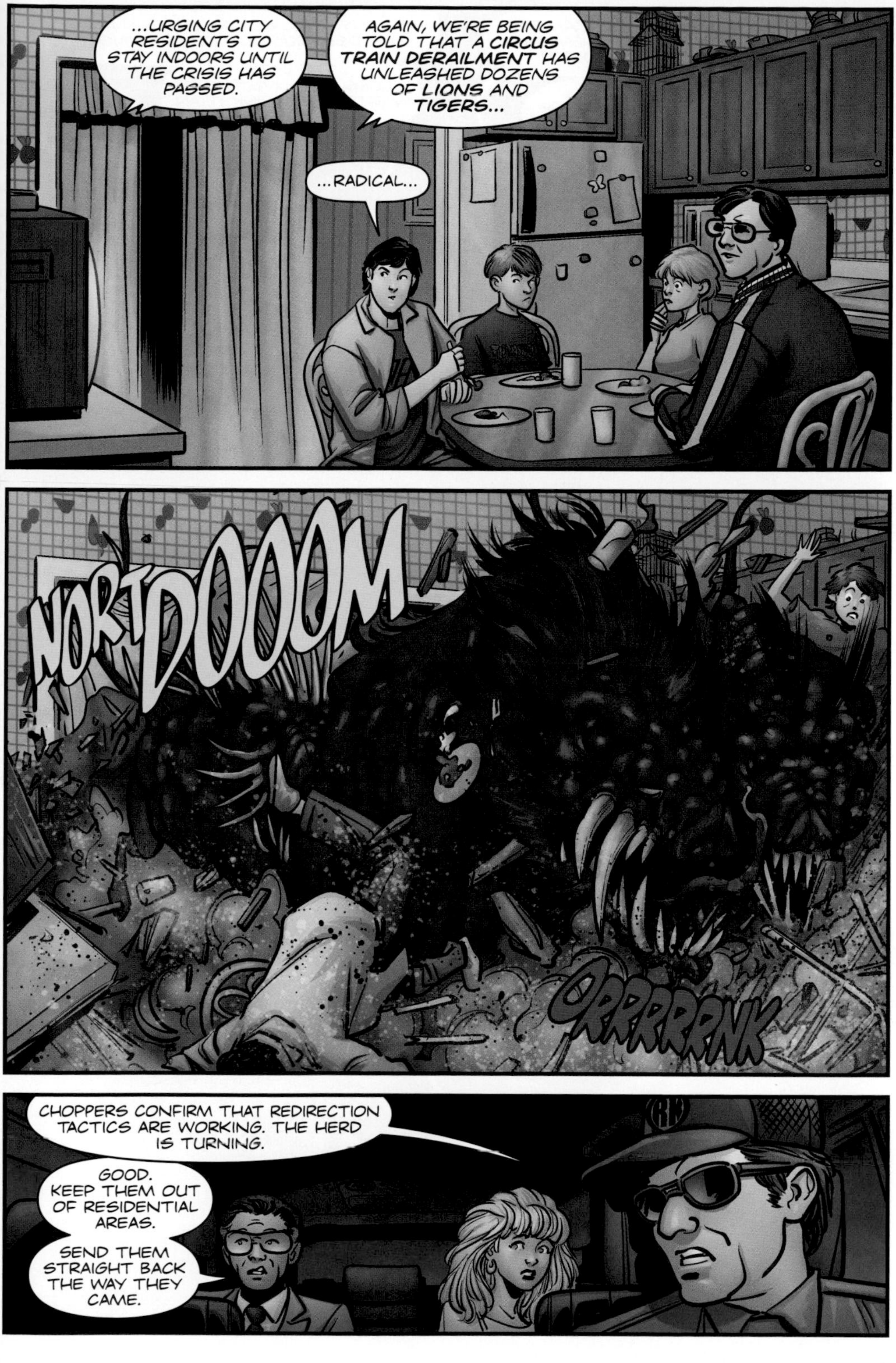
...URGING CITY RESIDENTS TO STAY INDOORS UNTIL THE CRISIS HAS PASSED.
AGAIN, WE'RE BEING TOLD THAT A **CIRCUS TRAIN DERAILMENT** HAS UNLEASHED DOZENS OF **LIONS** AND **TIGERS...**
...RADICAL...
NORTDOOOM
ORRRRRNK
CHOPPERS CONFIRM THAT REDIRECTION TACTICS ARE WORKING. THE HERD IS TURNING.
GOOD. KEEP THEM OUT OF RESIDENTIAL AREAS.
SEND THEM STRAIGHT BACK THE WAY THEY CAME.

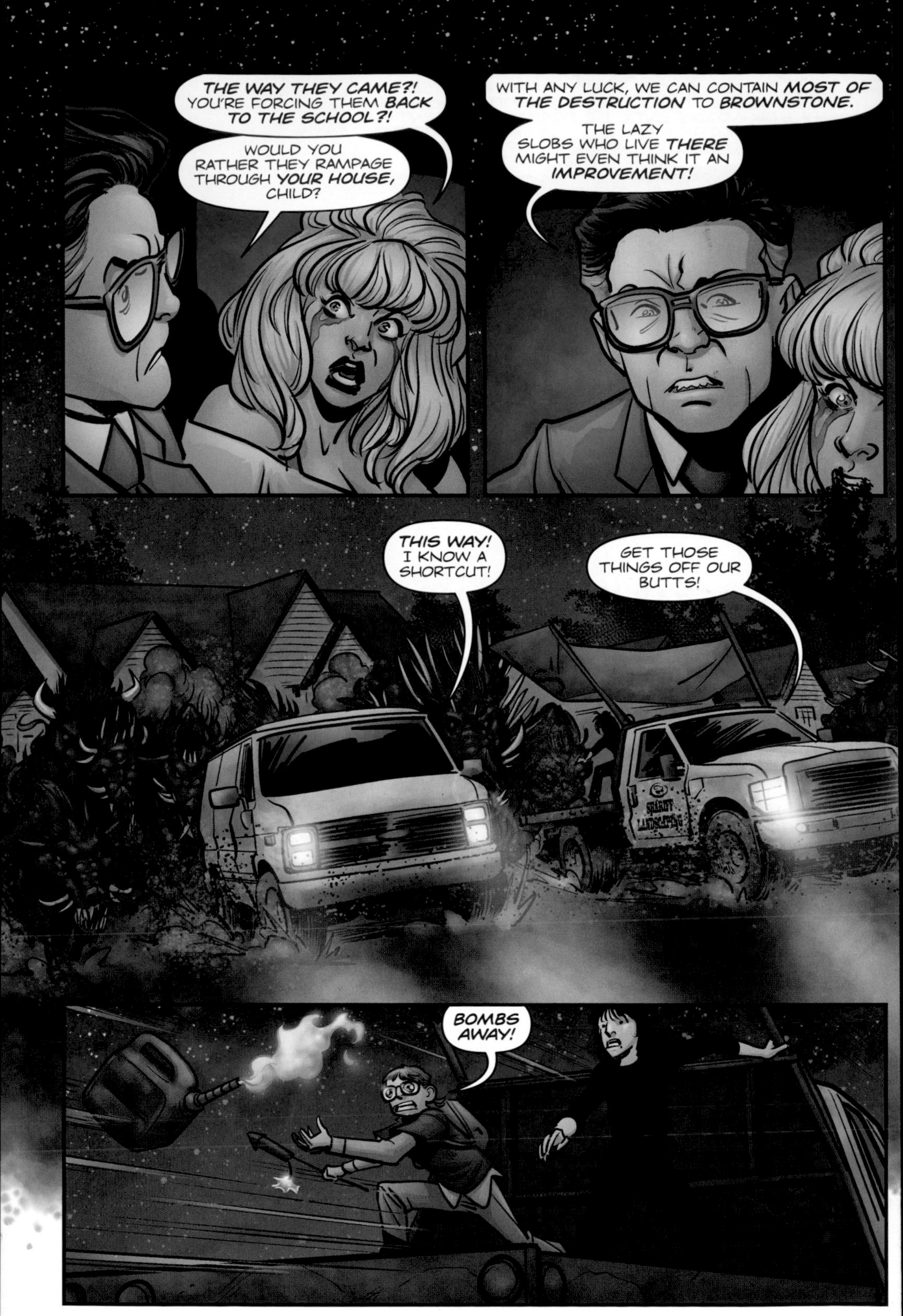
THE WAY THEY CAME?! YOU'RE FORCING THEM BACK TO THE SCHOOL?!
WOULD YOU RATHER THEY RAMPAGE THROUGH YOUR HOUSE, CHILD?
WITH ANY LUCK, WE CAN CONTAIN MOST OF THE DESTRUCTION TO BROWNSTONE.
THE LAZY SLOBS WHO LIVE THERE MIGHT EVEN THINK IT AN IMPROVEMENT!
THIS WAY! I KNOW A SHORTCUT!
GET THOSE THINGS OFF OUR BUTTS!
BOMBS AWAY!

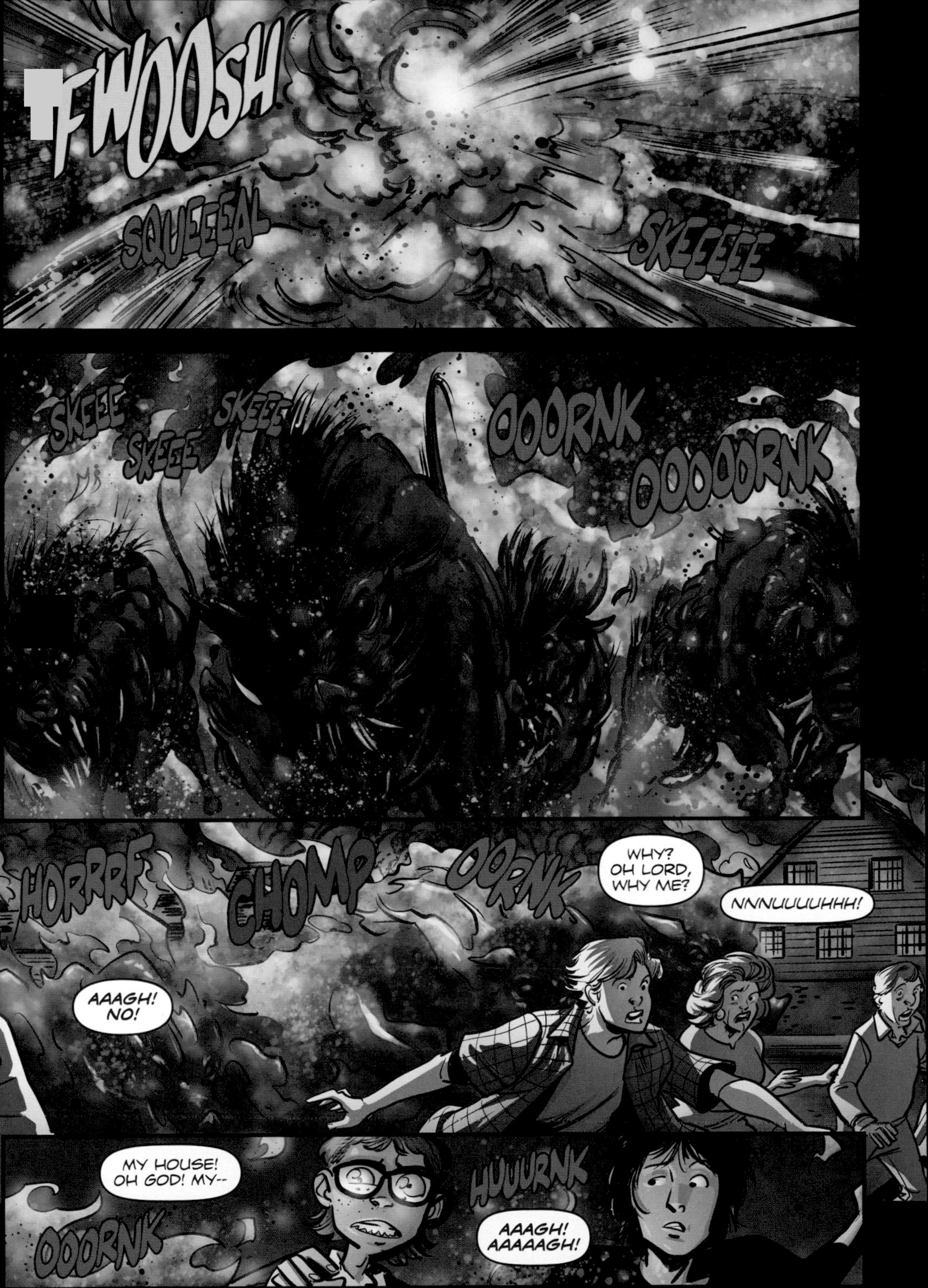
FWOOSH
SQUEEEAL
SKEEEEE
SKEEE
SKEEE
SKEEE
OOORNK
OOOOORNK
HORRRF
CHOMP
OORNK
WHY? OH LORD, WHY ME?
NNNUUUUHHH!
AAAGH! NO!
MY HOUSE! OH GOD! MY--
HUUURNK
OOORNK
AAAGH! AAAAAGH!

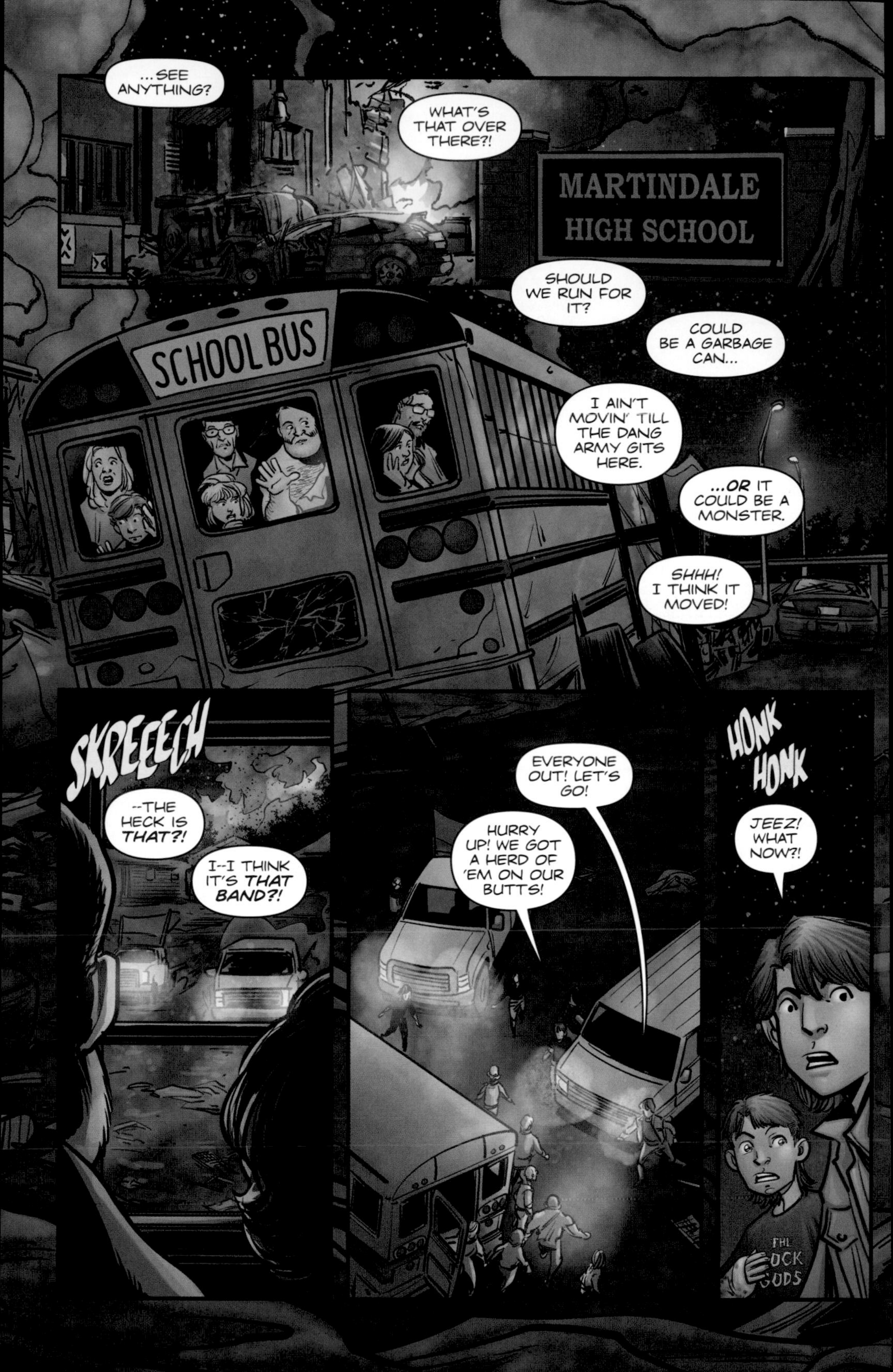
...SEE ANYTHING?
WHAT'S THAT OVER THERE?!
MARTINDALE HIGH SCHOOL
SCHOOL BUS
SHOULD WE RUN FOR IT?
COULD BE A GARBAGE CAN...
I AIN'T MOVIN' TILL THE DANG ARMY GITS HERE.
...OR IT COULD BE A MONSTER.
SHHH! I THINK IT MOVED!
SKREEECH
--THE HECK IS THAT?!
I--I THINK IT'S THAT BAND?!
EVERYONE OUT! LET'S GO!
HURRY UP! WE GOT A HERD OF 'EM ON OUR BUTTS!
HONK HONK
JEEZ! WHAT NOW?!

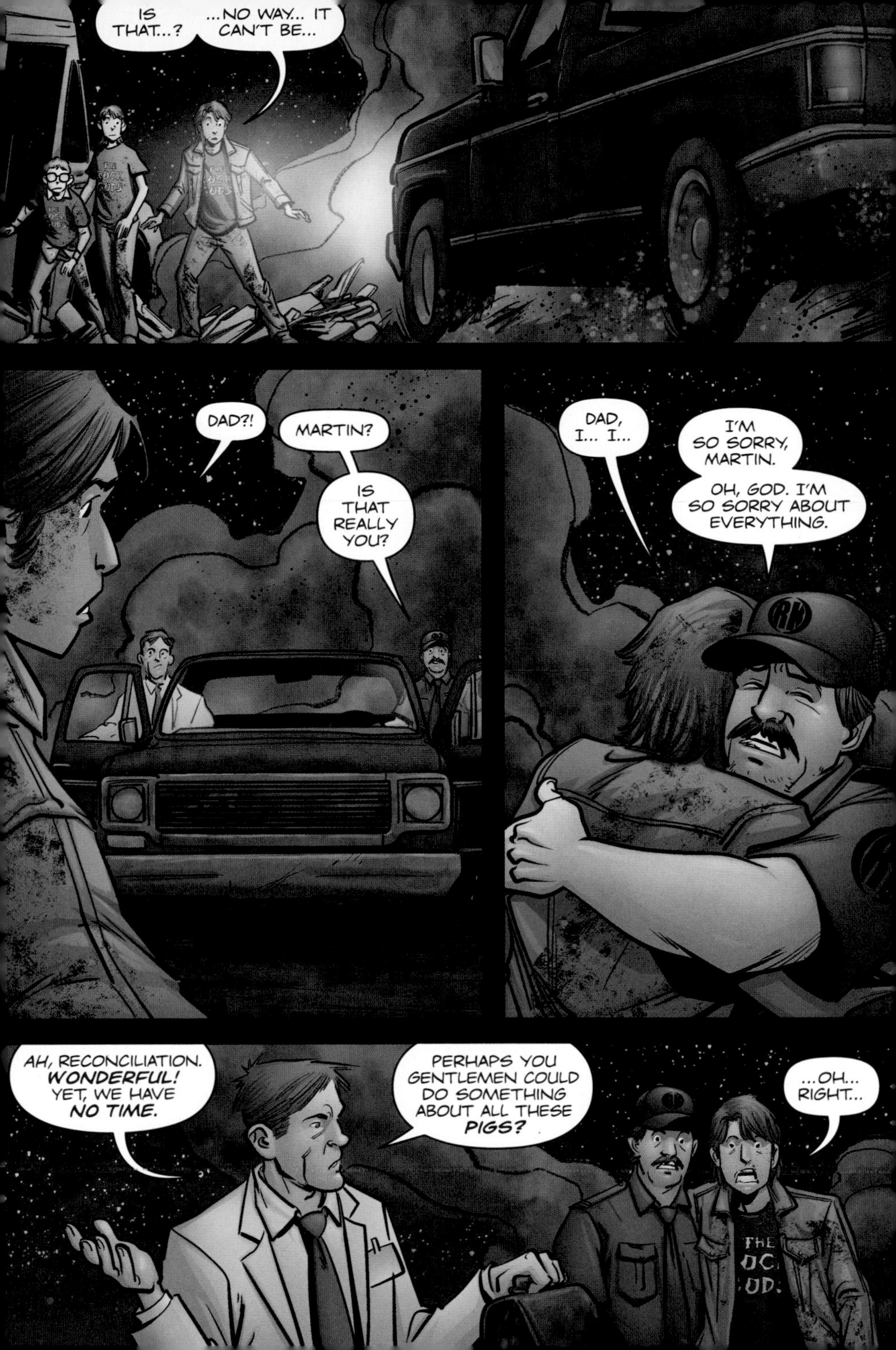
IS THAT...?
...NO WAY... IT CAN'T BE...
DAD?!
MARTIN?
IS THAT REALLY YOU?
DAD, I... I...
I'M SO SORRY, MARTIN.
OH, GOD. I'M SO SORRY ABOUT EVERYTHING.
AH, RECONCILIATION. **WONDERFUL!** YET, WE HAVE **NO TIME.**
PERHAPS YOU GENTLEMEN COULD DO SOMETHING ABOUT ALL THESE ***PIGS?***
...OH... RIGHT...

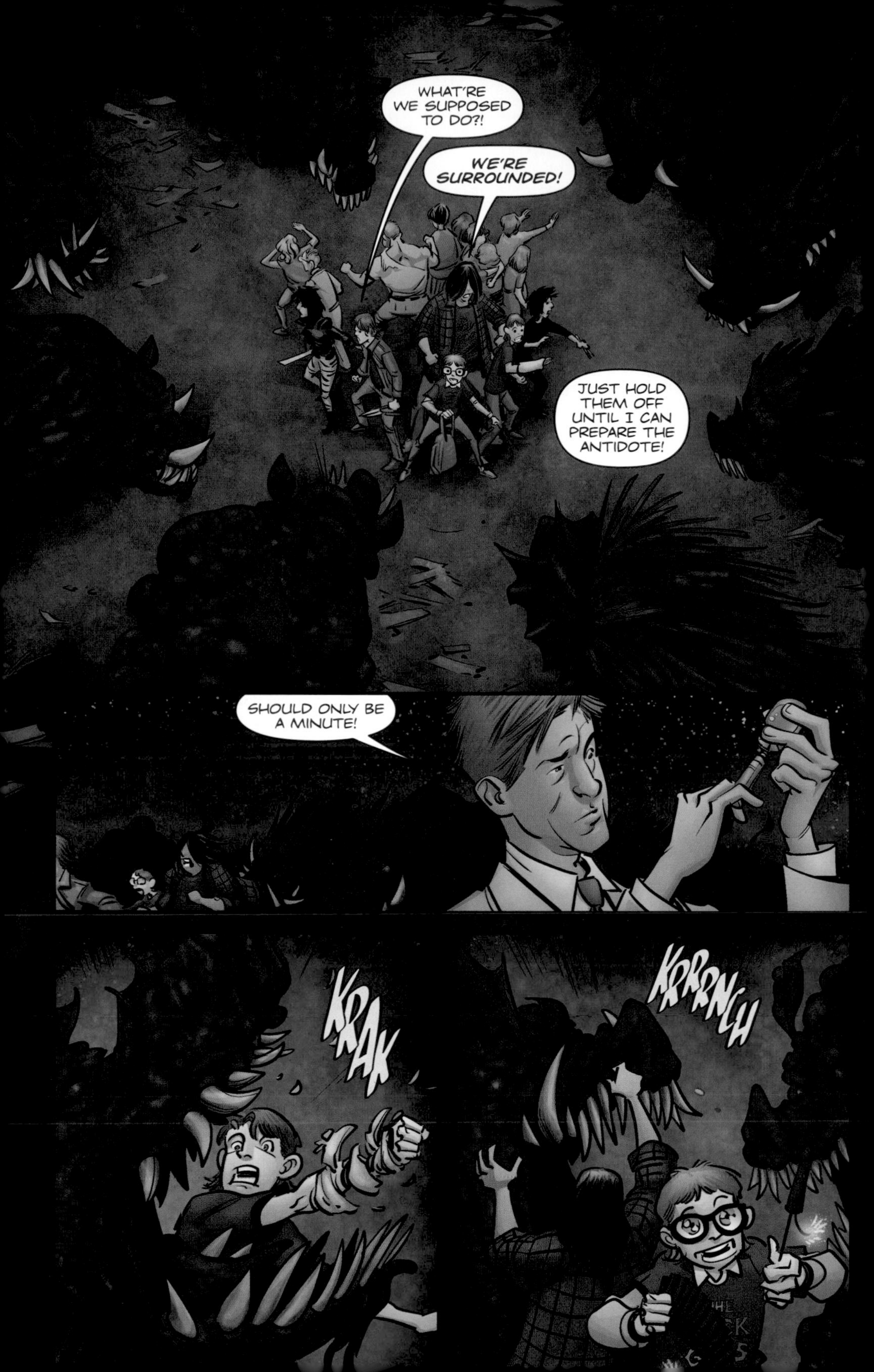
WHAT'RE WE SUPPOSED TO DO?!
WE'RE SURROUNDED!
JUST HOLD THEM OFF UNTIL I CAN PREPARE THE ANTIDOTE!
SHOULD ONLY BE A MINUTE!
KRAK
KRRRNCH

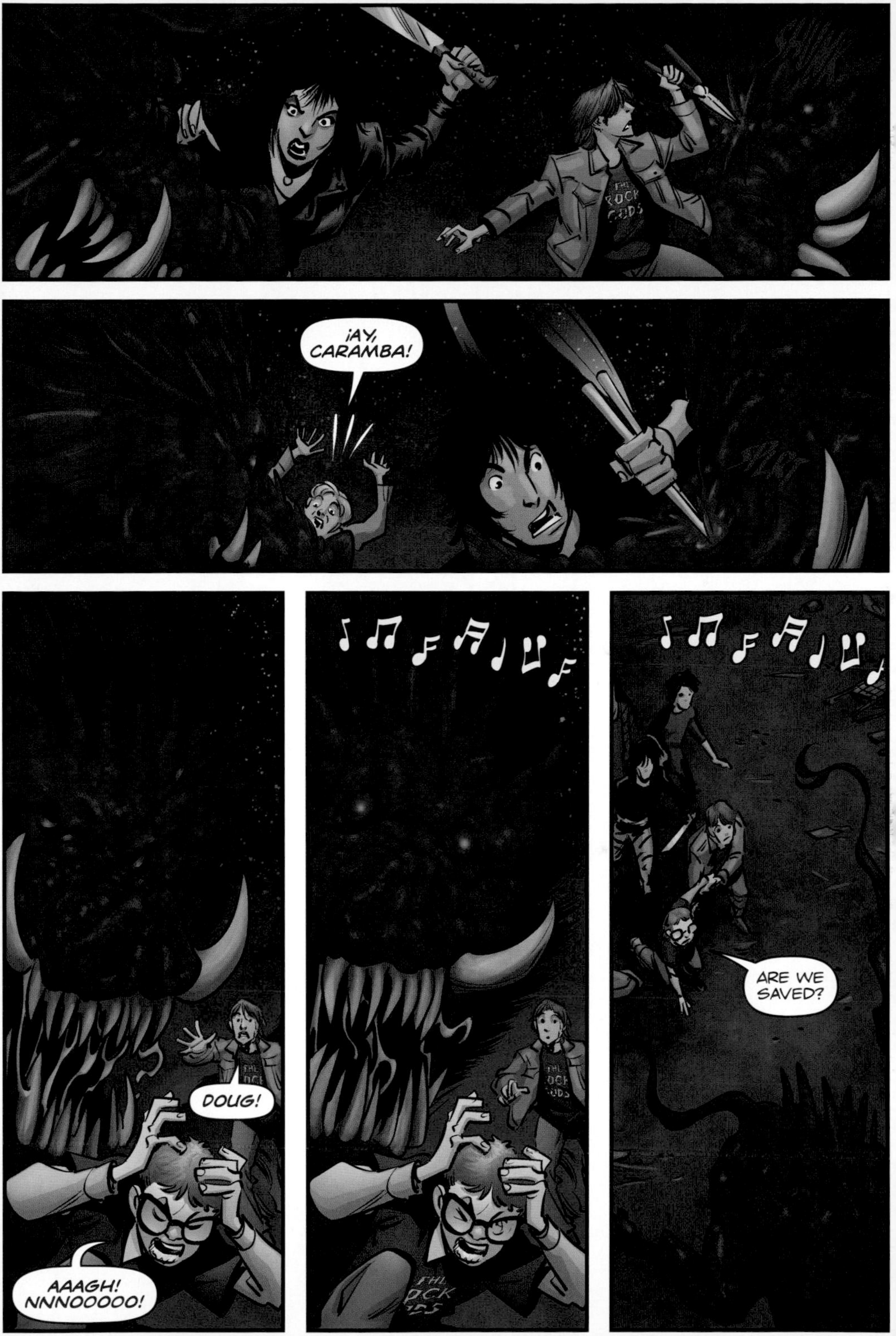
¡AY, CARAMBA!
DOUG!
AAAGH! NNNOOOOO!
ARE WE SAVED?

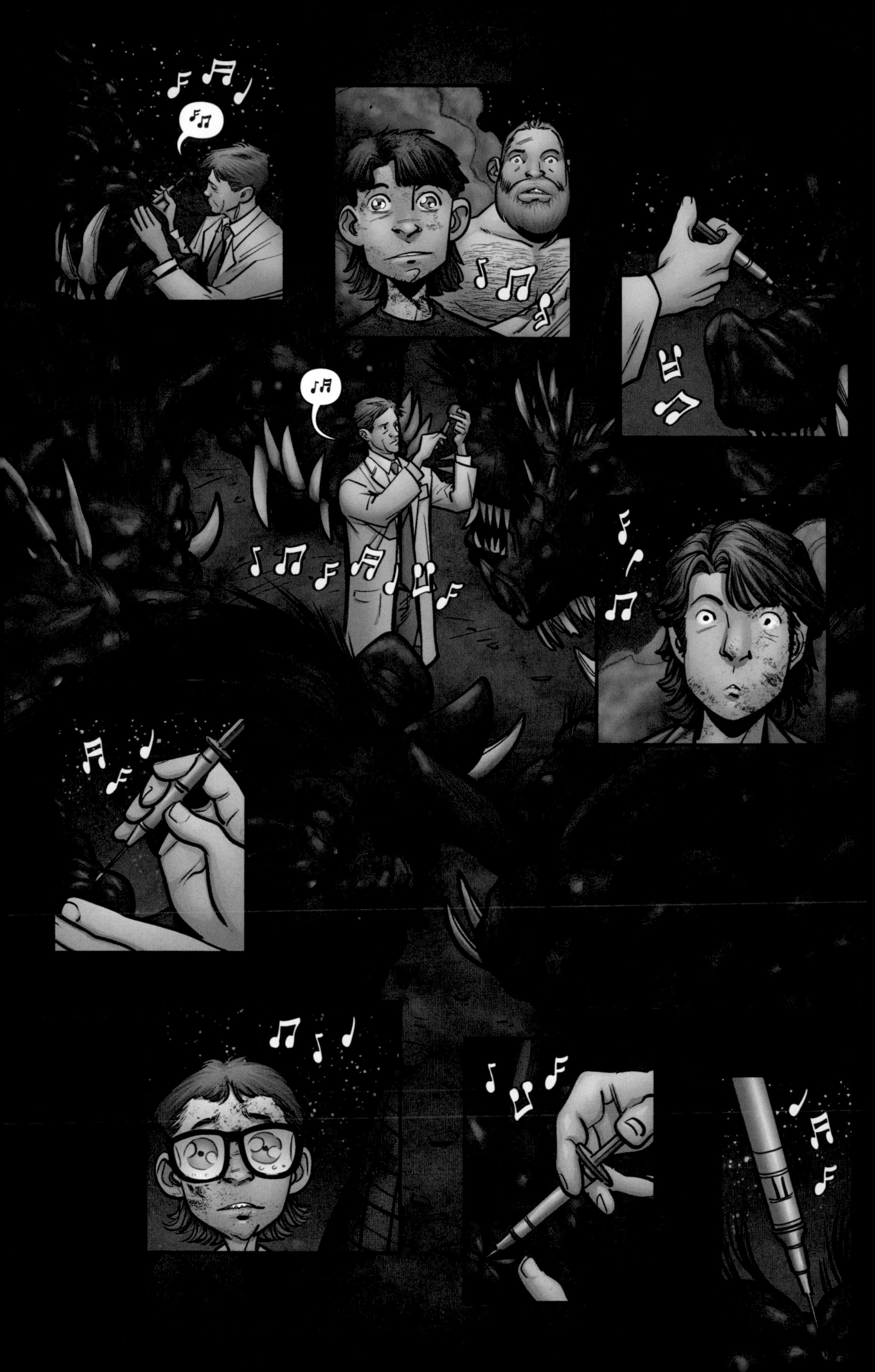

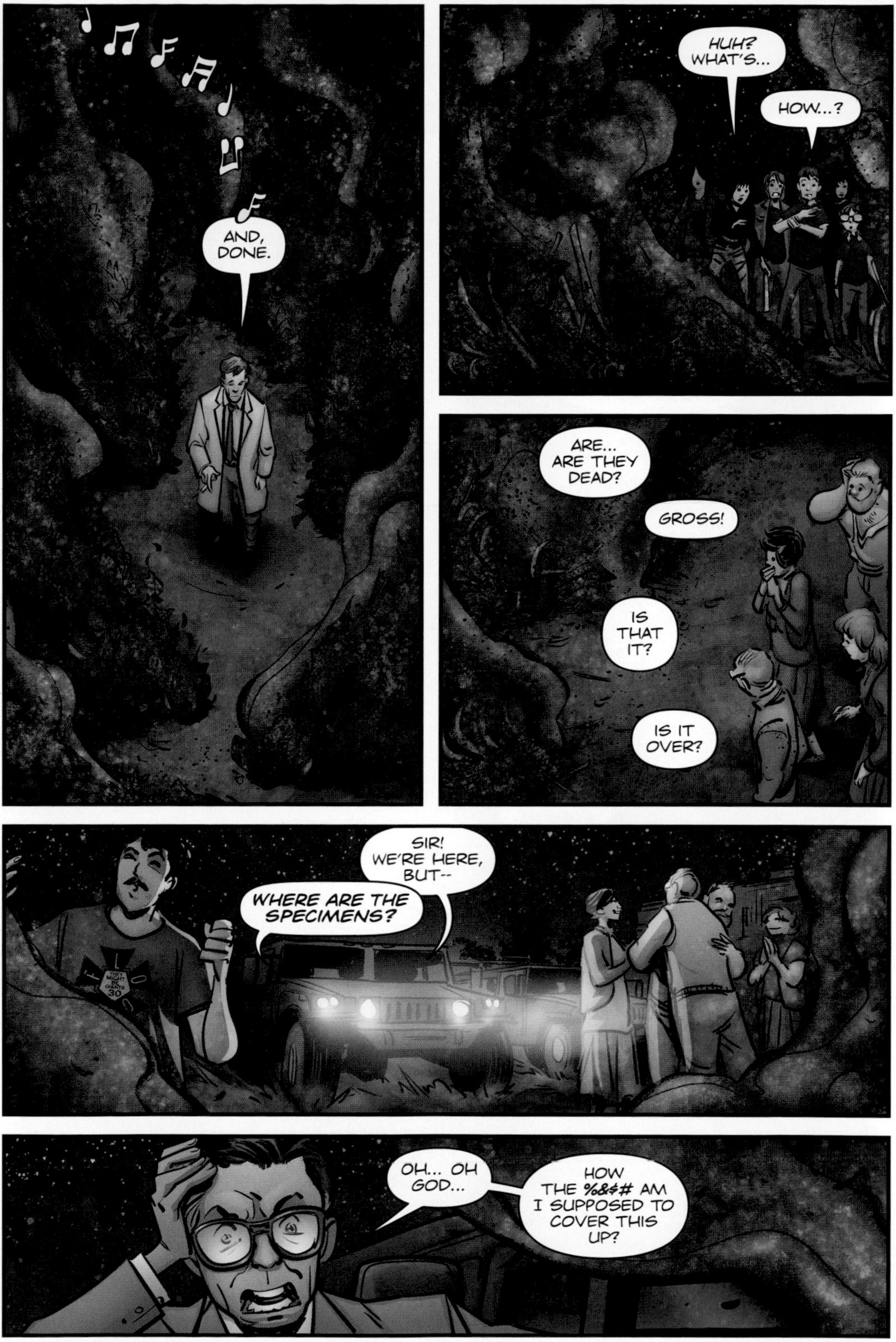
AND, DONE.
HUH? WHAT'S...
HOW...?
ARE... ARE THEY DEAD?
GROSS!
IS THAT IT?
IS IT OVER?
SIR! WE'RE HERE, BUT--
WHERE ARE THE SPECIMENS?
OH... OH GOD...
HOW THE %&$# AM I SUPPOSED TO COVER THIS UP?

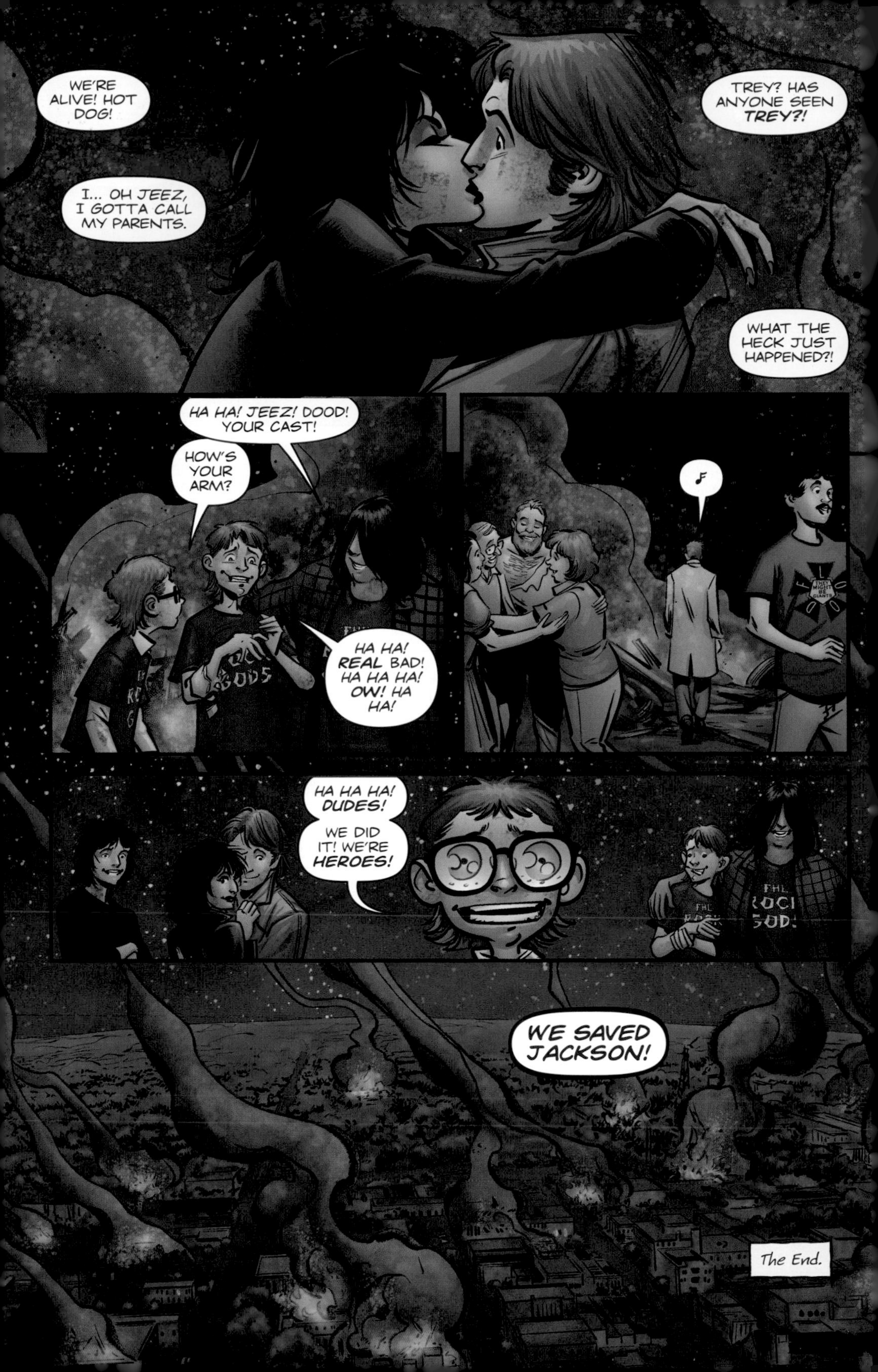

WE'RE ALIVE! HOT DOG!
TREY? HAS ANYONE SEEN TREY?!
I... OH JEEZ, I GOTTA CALL MY PARENTS.
WHAT THE HECK JUST HAPPENED?!
HA HA! JEEZ! DOOD! YOUR CAST!
HOW'S YOUR ARM?
HA HA! REAL BAD! HA HA HA! OW! HA HA!
THEY MIGHT BE GIANTS
HA HA HA! DUDES!
WE DID IT! WE'RE HEROES!
WE SAVED JACKSON!
The End.

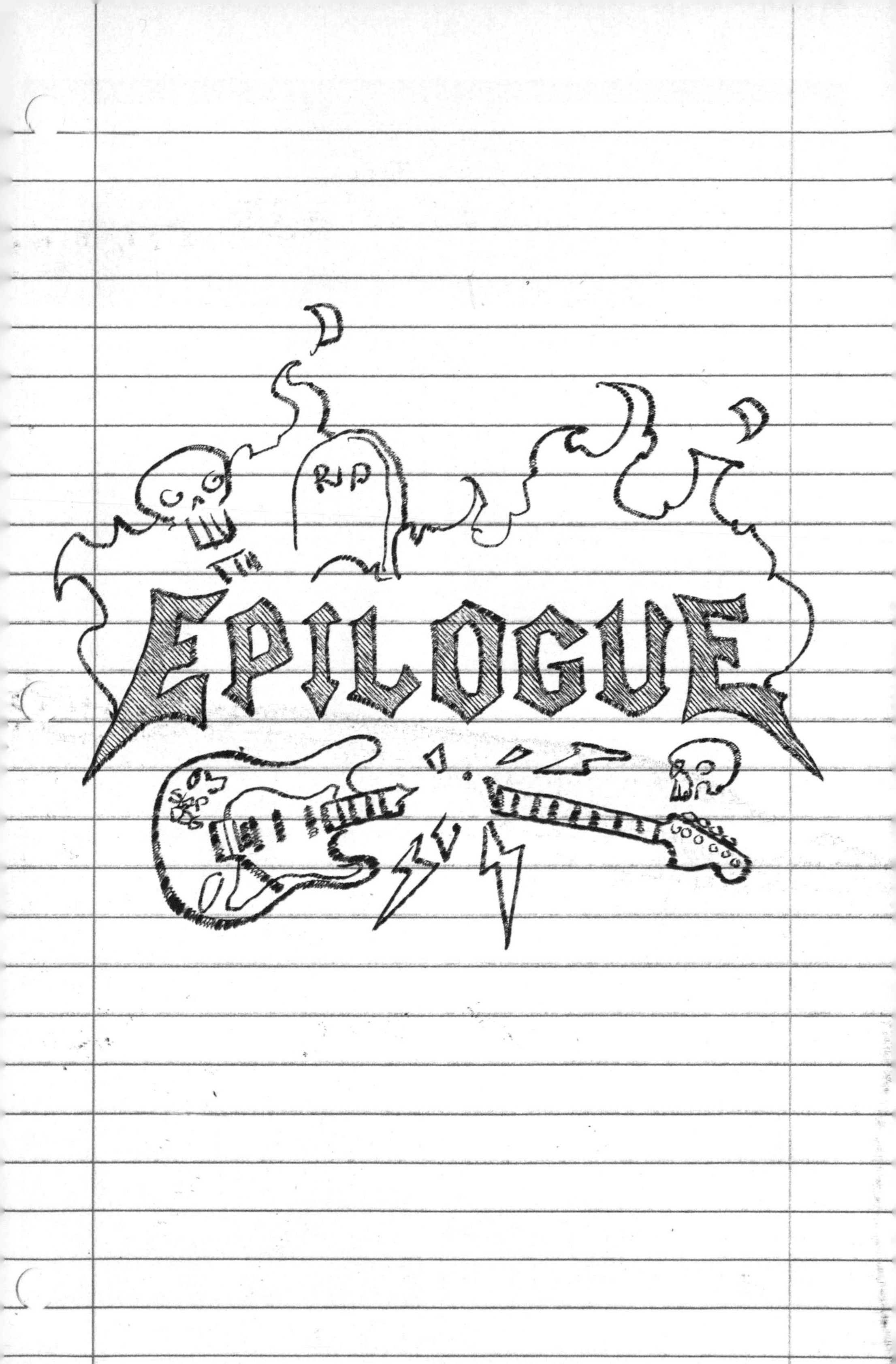
RIP
EPILOGUE

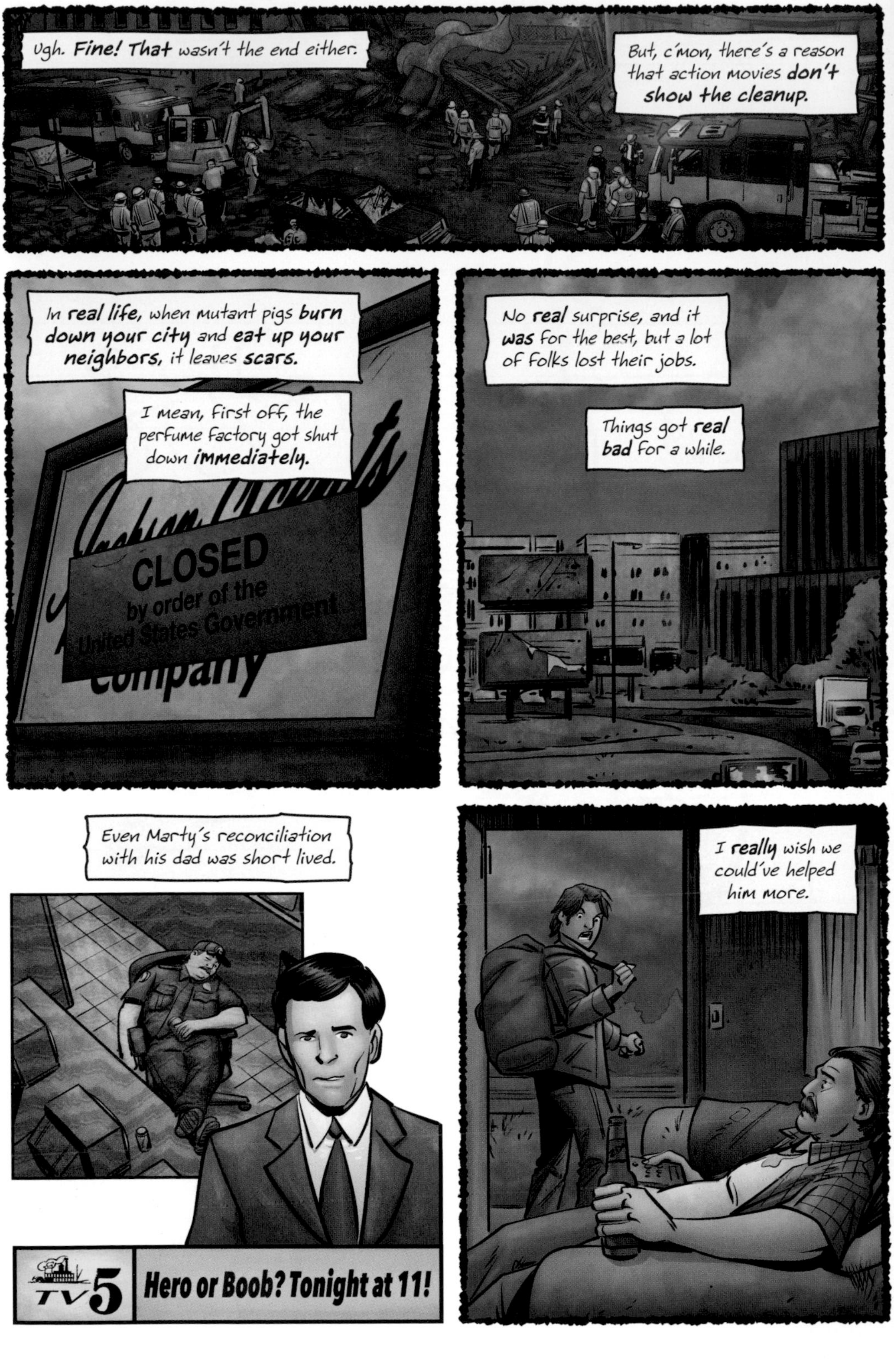
Ugh. Fine! That wasn't the end either.
But, c'mon, there's a reason that action movies don't show the cleanup.
In real life, when mutant pigs burn down your city and eat up your neighbors, it leaves scars.
I mean, first off, the perfume factory got shut down immediately.
CLOSED by order of the United States Government
Company
No real surprise, and it was for the best, but a lot of folks lost their jobs.
Things got real bad for a while.
Even Marty's reconciliation with his dad was short lived.
TV 5
Hero or Boob? Tonight at 11!
I really wish we could've helped him more.

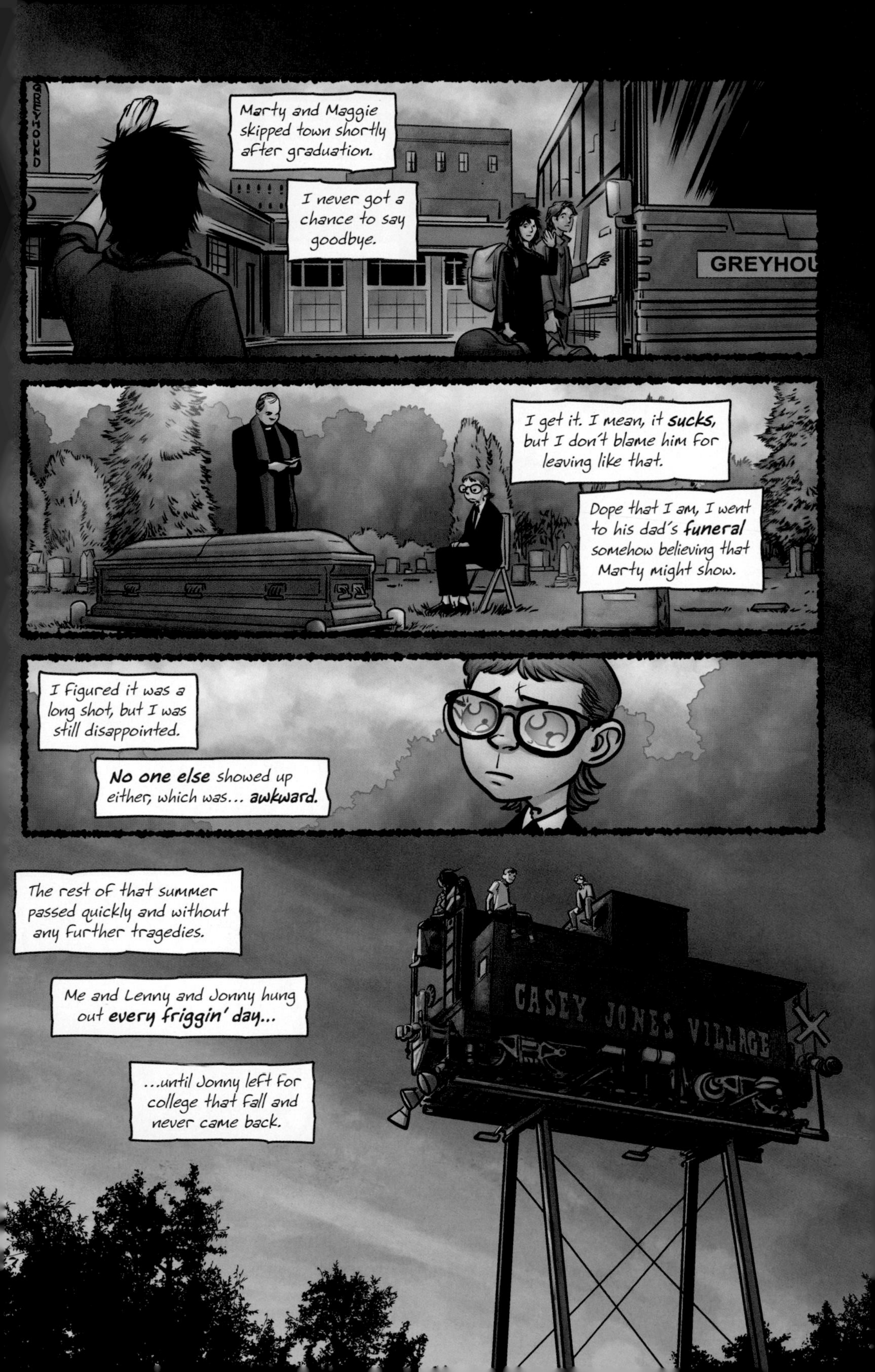
GREYHOUND
Marty and Maggie skipped town shortly after graduation.
I never got a chance to say goodbye.
GREYHOU
I get it. I mean, it **sucks,** but I don't blame him for leaving like that.
Dope that I am, I went to his dad's **funeral** somehow believing that Marty might show.
I figured it was a long shot, but I was still disappointed.
No one else showed up either, which was... **awkward.**
The rest of that summer passed quickly and without any further tragedies.
Me and Lenny and Jonny hung out **every friggin' day...**
...until Jonny left for college that fall and never came back.
CASEY JONES VILLAGE

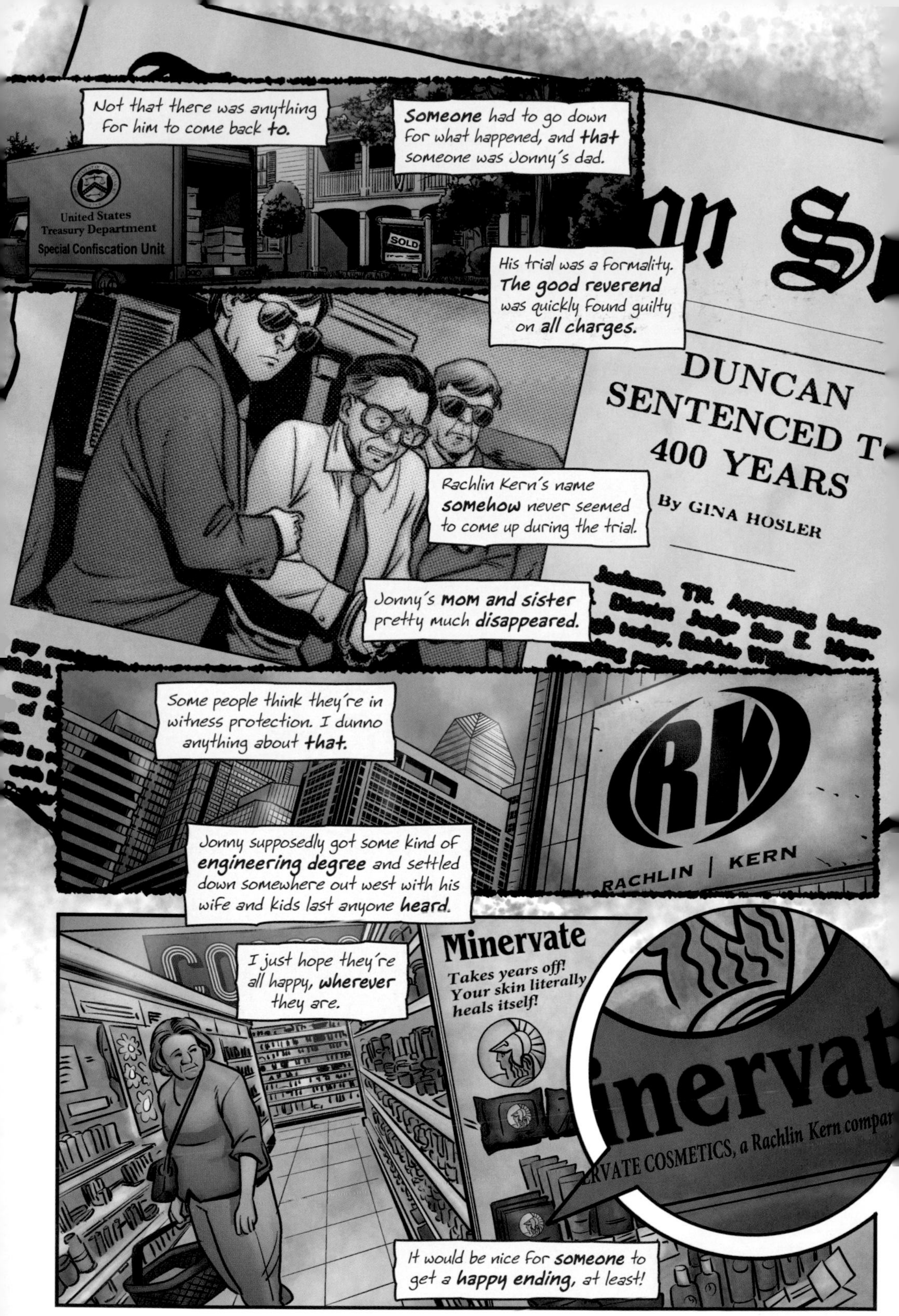
Not that there was anything for him to come back to.
Someone had to go down for what happened, and that someone was Jonny's dad.
United States Treasury Department
Special Confiscation Unit
SOLD
His trial was a formality. The good reverend was quickly found guilty on all charges.
DUNCAN SENTENCED T
400 YEARS
By GINA HOSLER
Rachlin Kern's name somehow never seemed to come up during the trial.
Jonny's mom and sister pretty much disappeared.
Some people think they're in witness protection. I dunno anything about that.
RK
RACHLIN | KERN
Jonny supposedly got some kind of engineering degree and settled down somewhere out west with his wife and kids last anyone heard.
I just hope they're all happy, wherever they are.
Minervate
Takes years off! Your skin literally heals itself!
inervat
RVATE COSMETICS, a Rachlin Kern compar
It would be nice for someone to get a happy ending, at least!

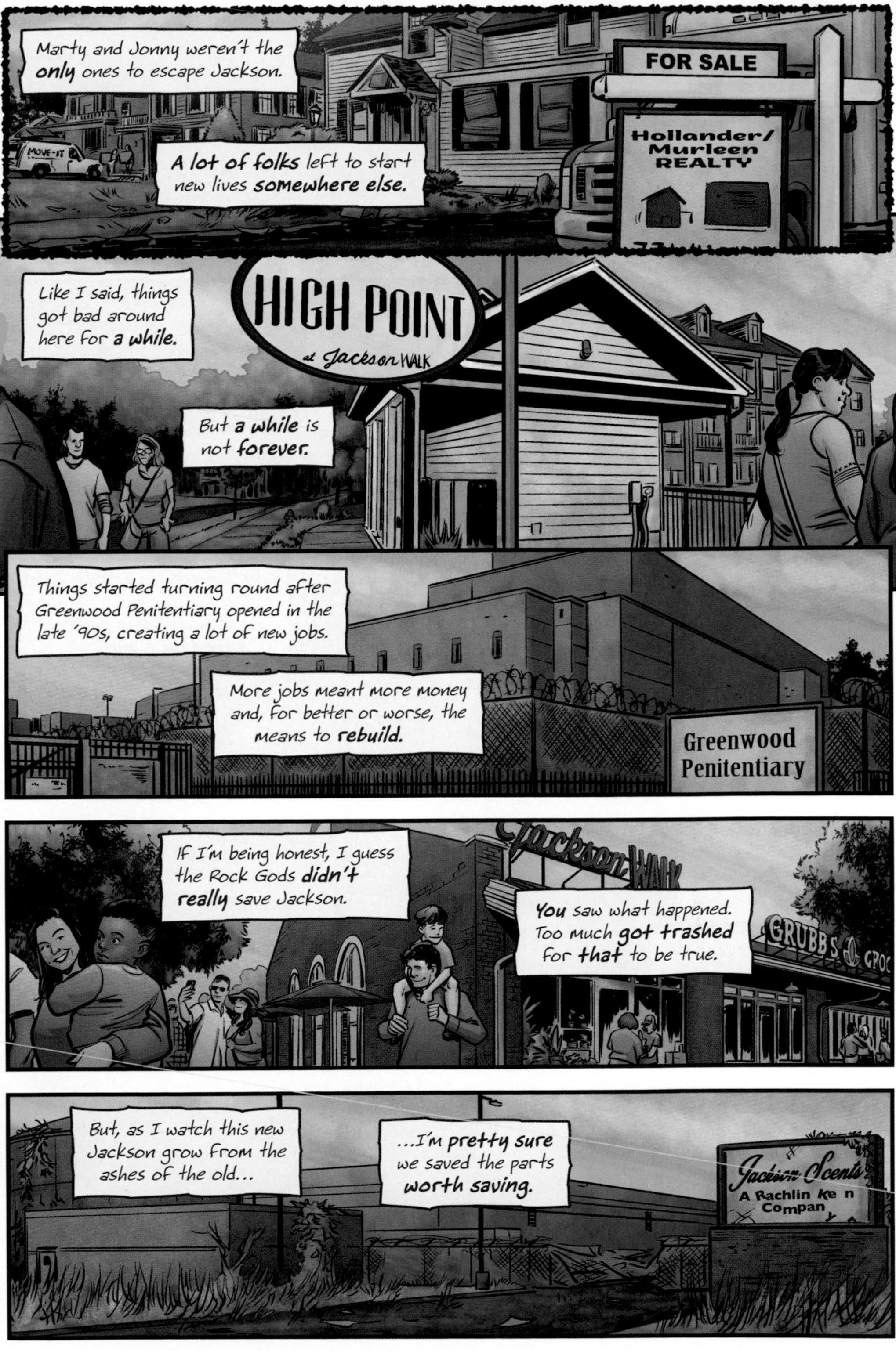

Marty and Jonny weren't the only ones to escape Jackson.
A lot of folks left to start new lives somewhere else.
FOR SALE
Hollander/ Murleen REALTY
MOVE-IT
HIGH POINT at Jackson WALK
Like I said, things got bad around here for a while.
But a while is not forever.
Things started turning round after Greenwood Penitentiary opened in the late '90s, creating a lot of new jobs.
More jobs meant more money and, for better or worse, the means to rebuild.
Greenwood Penitentiary
If I'm being honest, I guess the Rock Gods didn't really save Jackson.
You saw what happened. Too much got trashed for that to be true.
But, as I watch this new Jackson grow from the ashes of the old...
...I'm pretty sure we saved the parts worth saving.
Jackson Scents
A Rachlin Ke n Compan

I never left Jackson. Big surprise, right?

I got a job with the city, working in the public records department.

JACKSON BANK & TRUST

It's an okay-enough gig, but sometimes... sometimes I wonder if it's what Mr. Shay **meant** when he told me to **make something of my life.**

Re-Elect **Mayor** Samantha Lange-Shariff

HARTSFIELD'S

Trey Hollander & Durlene Murleen "Selling Jackson back to you!"

Like, I dunno, do I **really** have to live **my life** a certain way just because **some dude** got **eaten by a pig?**

That's a lot of pressure to put on a kid for a pretty random reason, y'know?

What else, what else? Oh, I got married once! **It didn't last.**

As usual, I **wasn't paying attention** and a lot of people got hurt.

JASPER CREMASTER MEMORIAL HIGH SCHOOL

Maybe I'll tell you that story someday.

That one has **aliens** in it!

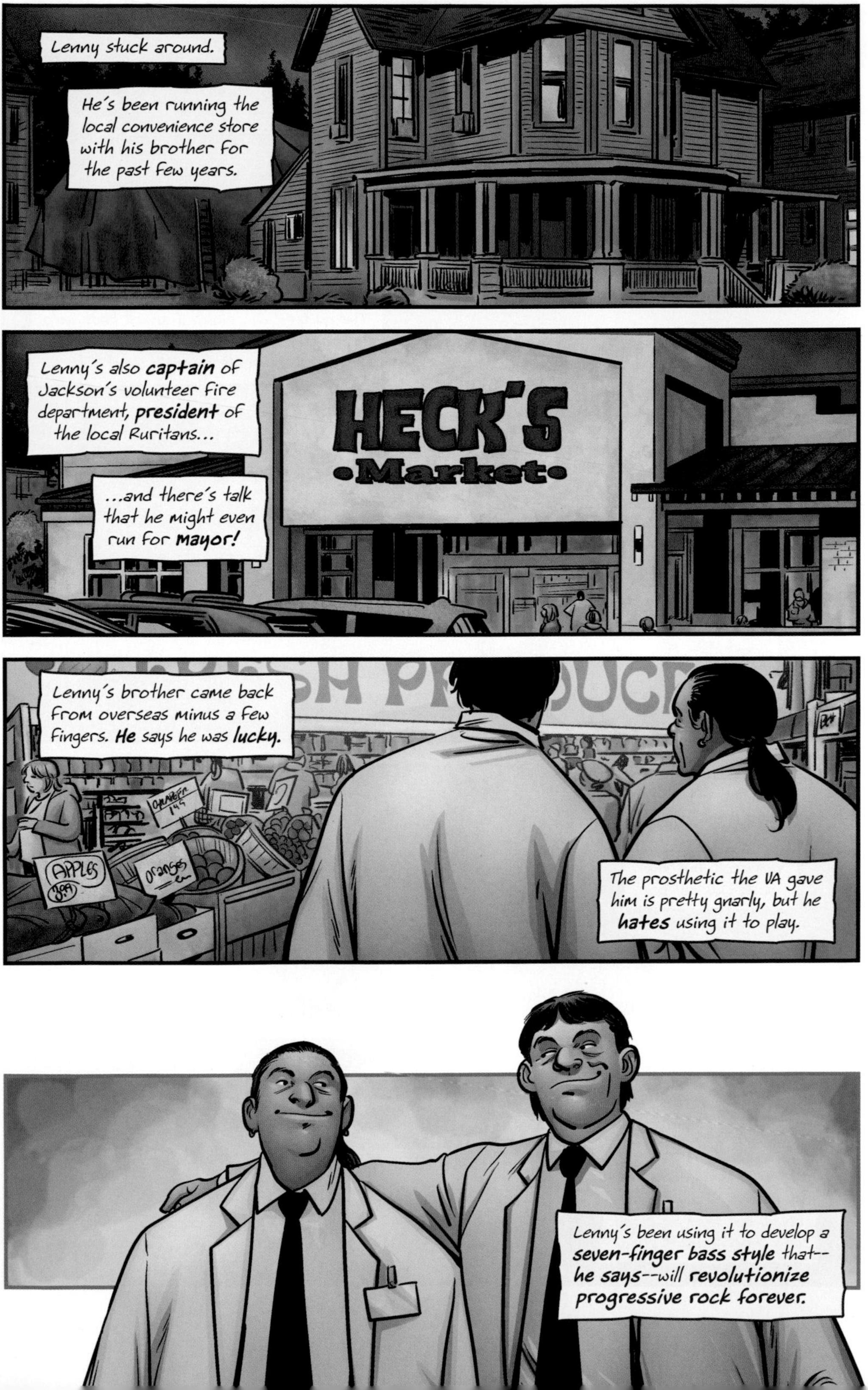

Lenny stuck around.
He's been running the local convenience store with his brother for the past few years.
Lenny's also **captain** of Jackson's volunteer fire department, **president** of the local Ruritans...
HECK'S
•Market•
...and there's talk that he might even run for **mayor!**
Lenny's brother came back from overseas minus a few fingers. **He** says he was **lucky.**
APPLES
oranges
The prosthetic the VA gave him is pretty gnarly, but he **hates** using it to play.
Lenny's been using it to develop a **seven-finger bass style** that--**he says**--will **revolutionize progressive rock forever.**

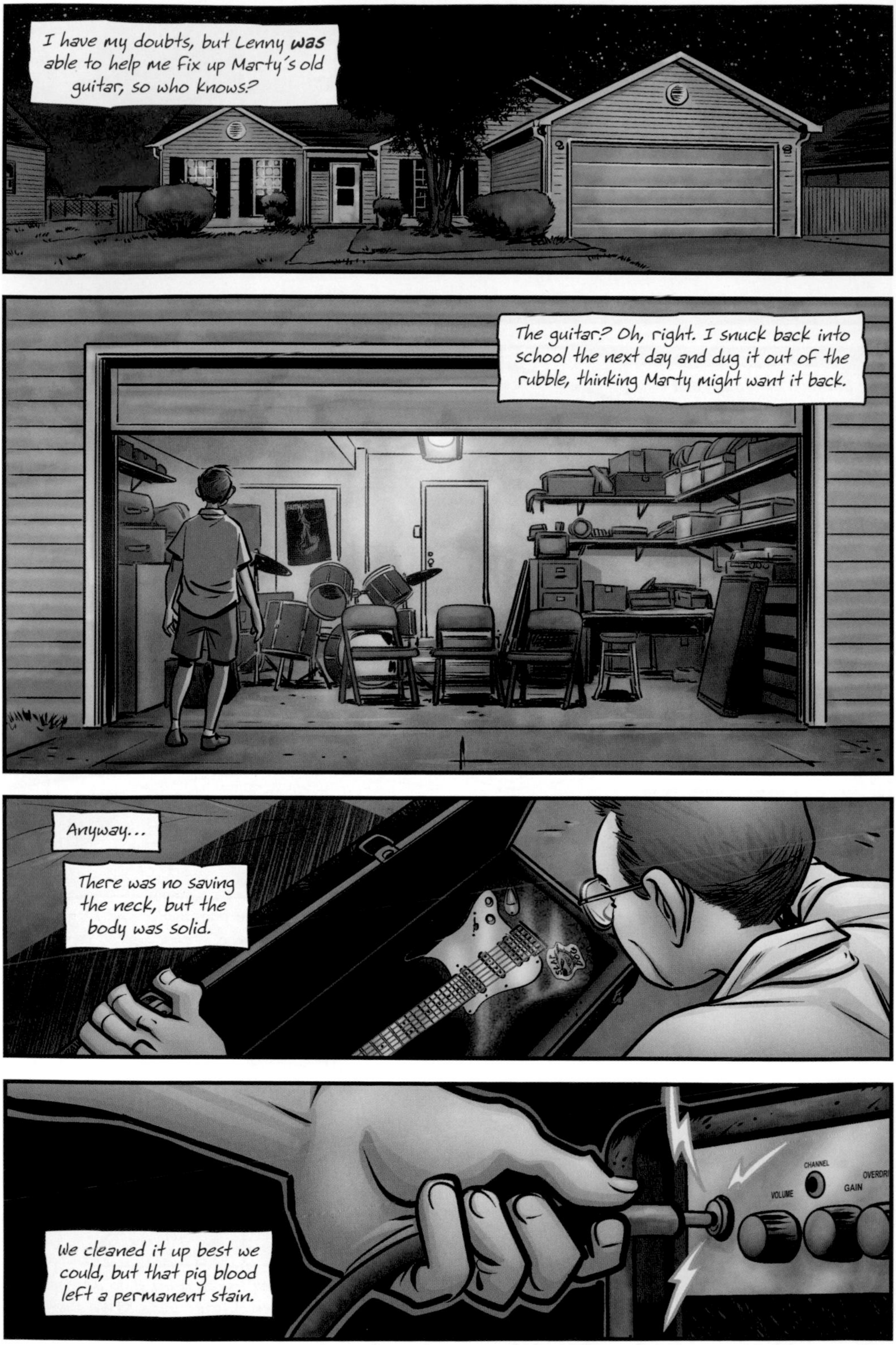
I have my doubts, but Lenny **was** able to help me fix up Marty's old guitar, so who knows?
The guitar? Oh, right. I snuck back into school the next day and dug it out of the rubble, thinking Marty might want it back.
Anyway...
There was no saving the neck, but the body was solid.
CHANNEL
VOLUME
GAIN
We cleaned it up best we could, but that pig blood left a permanent stain.

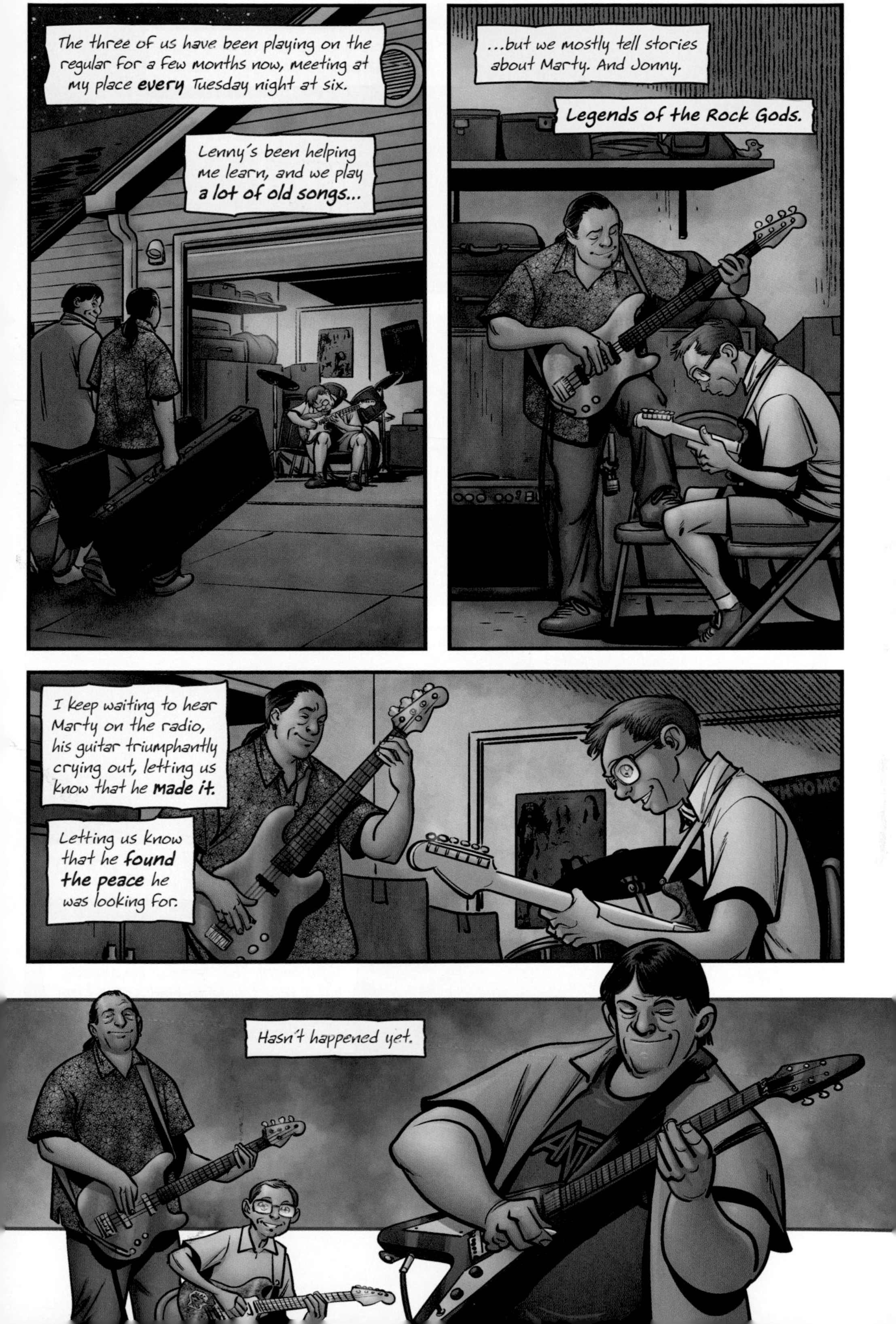

The three of us have been playing on the regular for a few months now, meeting at my place **every** Tuesday night at six.
Lenny's been helping me learn, and we play **a lot of old songs...**
...but we mostly tell stories about Marty. And Jonny.
Legends of the Rock Gods.
I keep waiting to hear Marty on the radio, his guitar triumphantly crying out, letting us know that he **made it.**
Letting us know that he **found the peace** he was looking for.
Hasn't happened yet.

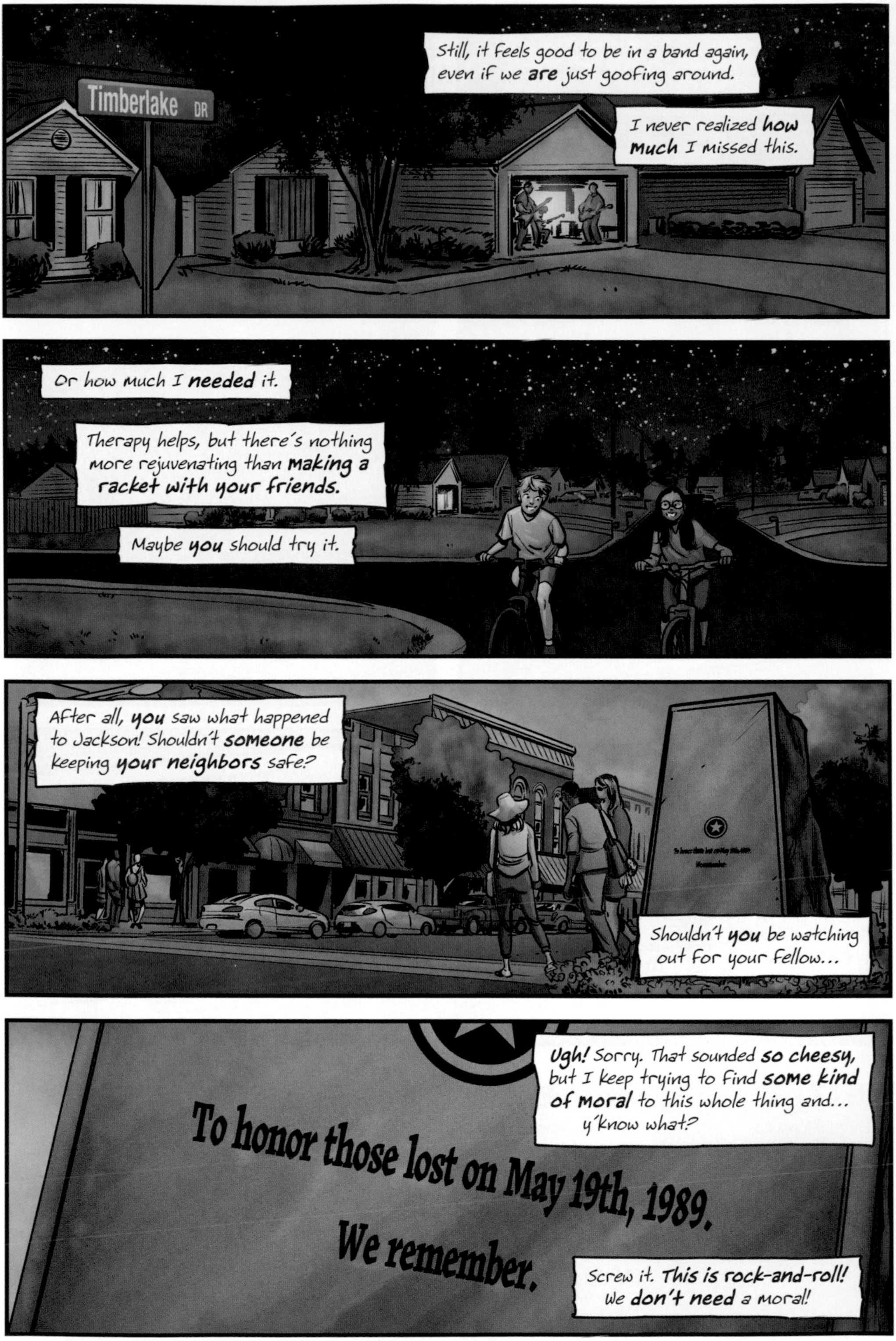
Timberlake DR
Still, it feels good to be in a band again, even if we **are** just goofing around.
I never realized **how much** I missed this.
Or how much I **needed** it.
Therapy helps, but there's nothing more rejuvenating than **making a racket with your friends.**
Maybe **you** should try it.
After all, **you** saw what happened to Jackson! Shouldn't **someone** be keeping **your neighbors** safe?
Shouldn't **you** be watching out for your fellow...
Ugh! Sorry. That sounded **so cheesy,** but I keep trying to find **some kind of moral** to this whole thing and... y'know what?
To honor those lost on May 19th, 1989.
We remember.
Screw it. **This is rock-and-roll!** We **don't need** a moral!

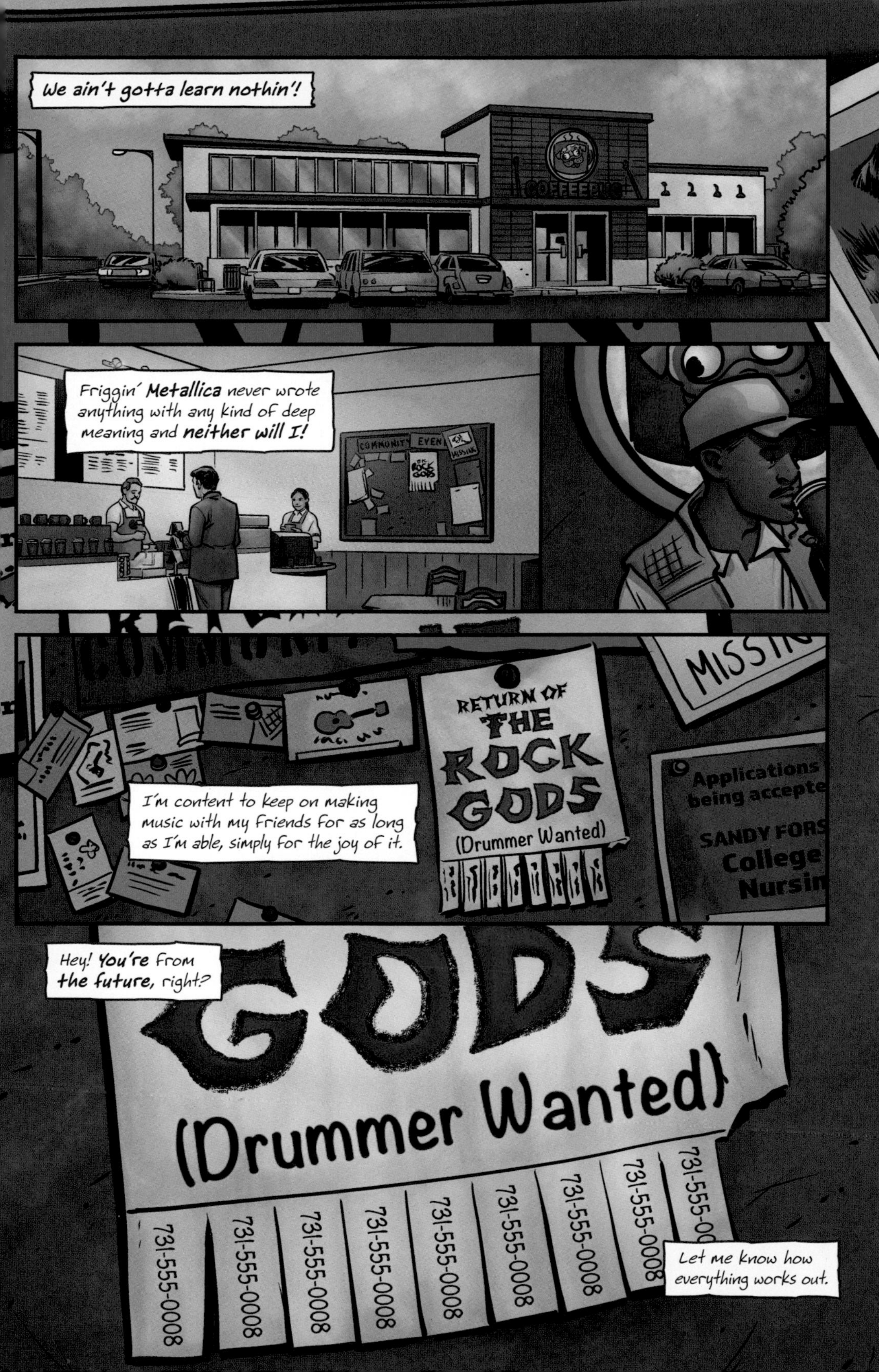
We ain't gotta learn nothin'!
COFFEEPUG
Friggin' **Metallica** never wrote anything with any kind of deep meaning and **neither will I!**
COMMUNITY EVEN
RETURN OF THE ROCK GODS
(Drummer Wanted)
MISSI
Applications being accepte
SANDY FORS
College
Nursin
I'm content to keep on making music with my friends for as long as I'm able, simply for the joy of it.
Hey! **You're** from **the future,** right?
GODS
(Drummer Wanted)
731-555-0008
Let me know how everything works out.

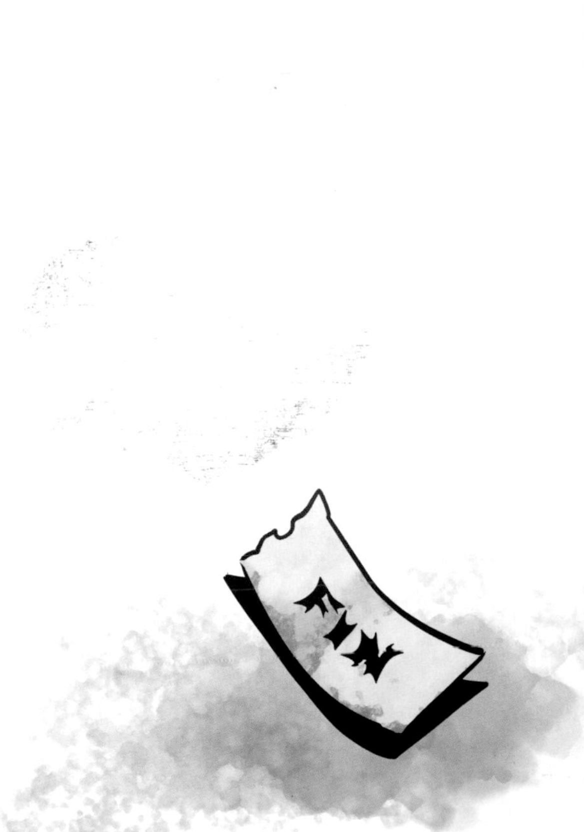
FIN

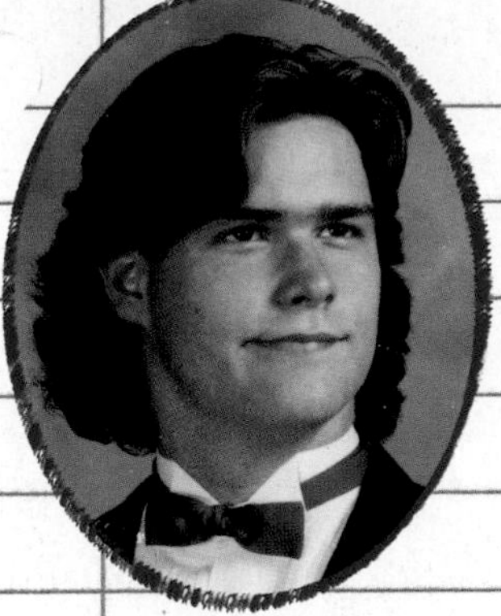

Mike Norton is the Eisner and Harvey Award-winning creator of the webcomic ***Battlepug***, and the cocreator and artist of ***Grumble*** and ***Revival***. He has worked for pretty much every comic company out there, drawing comics from ***Superman*** to ***Deadpool*** to ***Hellboy***. Mike is lead concept artist for ***Mystery Science Theater 3000*** season 13 on its indie streaming platform, the Gizmoplex. He currently lives in Chicago with his wife and some kind of animal or another.

Rafer Roberts is the writer and cocreator of ***Modern Fantasy*** and ***Grumble***. He's worked for ***Dark Horse***, ***Image***, ***AfterShock***, and ***Oni***, and even wrote a few superhero books for ***Valiant***, receiving two Harvey Award nominations for his efforts. Rafer's artwork appeared in the Eisner and Harvey Award-winning anthology ***Little Nemo: Dream Another Dream***, and he was founding editor of the Washington DC-based comics newspaper, ***Magic Bullet***. His self-published works include ***Plastic Farm*** and ***Nightmare the Rat***, among many others. Rafer lives in Baltimore, probably.

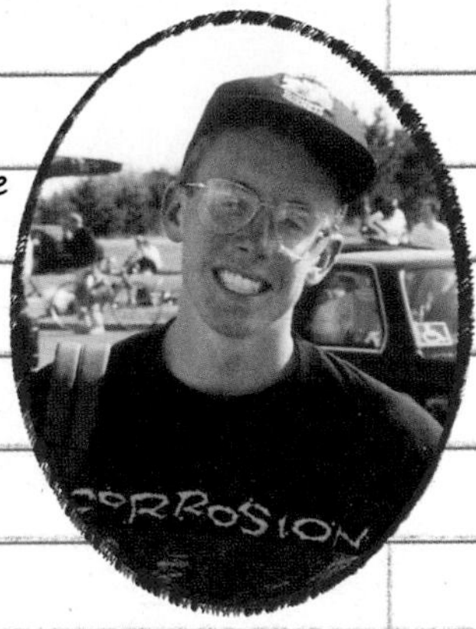
CORROSION

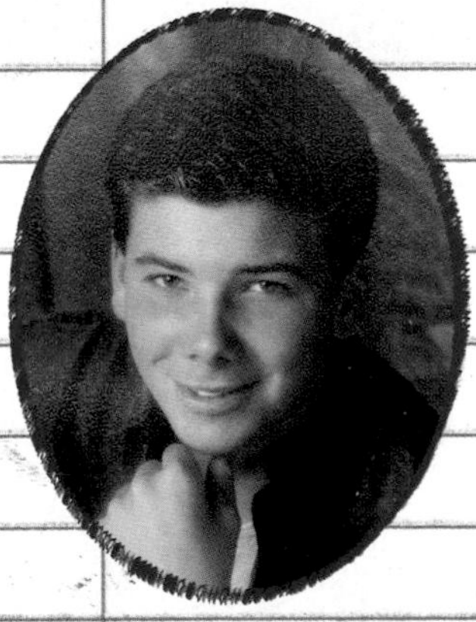

Allen Passalaqua is a professional comic color artist whose credits include ***Batman and Robin Eternal***, ***Justice Society of America***, ***Batman Confidential***, ***Detective Comics***, and the Eisner Award-winning ***Battlepug***. Allen has created artwork for several national parks, the San Diego Zoo, and the Grand Canyon, and storyboarded several Emmy Award-winning commercials, among various other projects. He is also a professor of digital tools for CCA's MFA in Comics program.

Christopher Crank (crank!) has lettered a bunch of books put out by ***Image***, ***Dark Horse***, ***Oni***, ***Dynamite***, ***IDW***, ***Albatross***, ***Vault***, and others. He has a podcast with Mike Norton and the other members of Four Star Studios in Chicago (***crankcast.com***) and makes music (***sonomorti.bandcamp.com***). Catch him on ***Instagram: ccrank_***

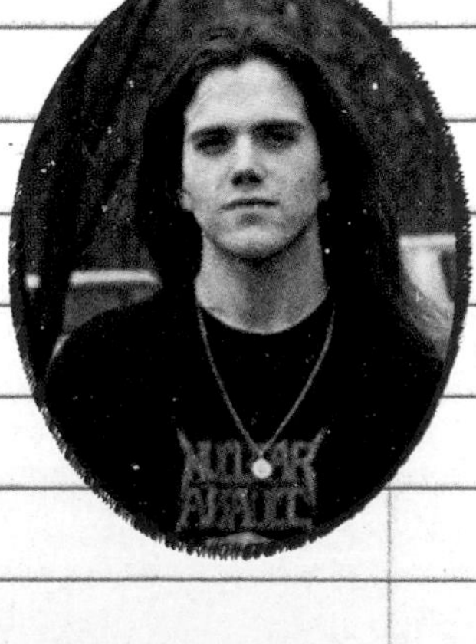

THE ROCK N GODS OF JACKSON TENNESSEE

COMMENTARY BY RAFER ROBERTS AND MIKE NORTON

This is the first drawing I did of the guys where I felt they captured the characters that were in my head. These are the kids I showed Rafer, and we went back and forth about what their personalities would be like. —Mike

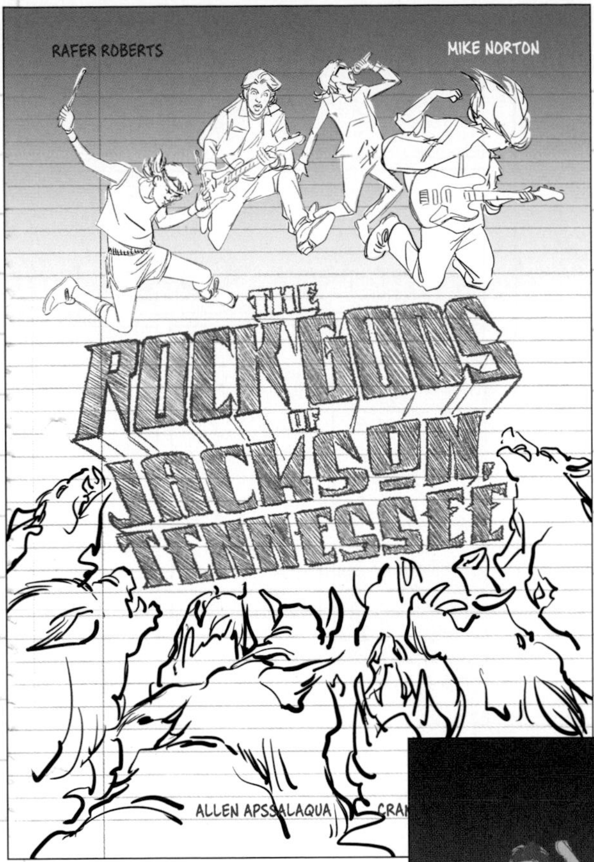
RAFER ROBERTS
MIKE NORTON
THE ROCK GODS OF JACKSON, TENNESSEE
ALLEN APSSALAQUA

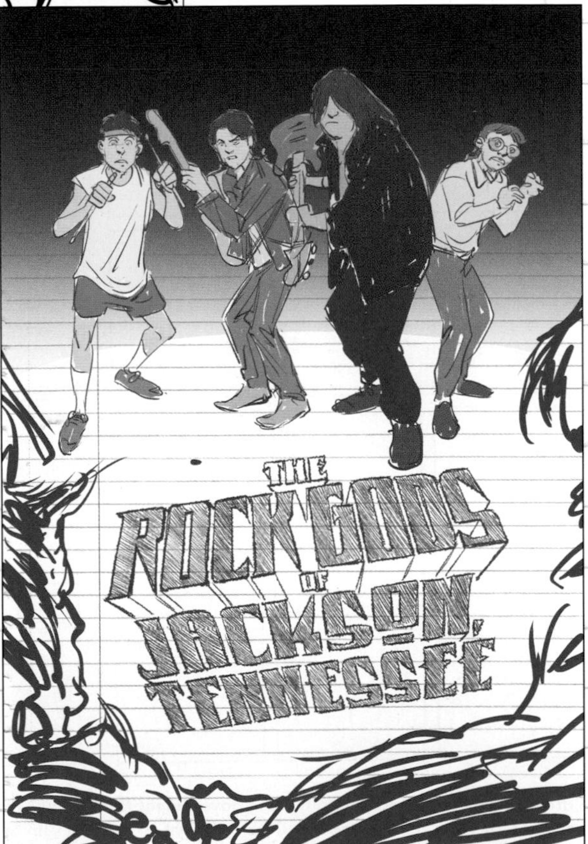
THE ROCK GODS OF JACKSON, TENNESSEE

Like most rock bands in the '80s, I wanted to design the cover around the logo. I wanted something that would remind you of that old notebook you had in high school that was just covered in doodles by the end of the year. Conversely, Rafer was feeling some Renaissance painting influences. I think I managed to combine them a little. I think? —Mike

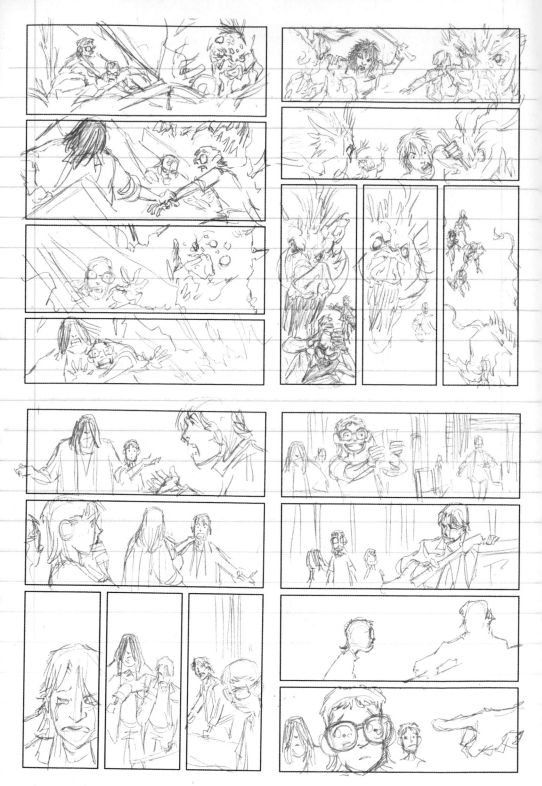

I draw most of my comics digitally these days, but for *Rock Gods* I did much of it on 8.5" × 11" sheets of copy paper first. I'd scan these rough pencils and then ink right on top with Clip Studio Paint. Really helped keep a more energetic feel for me. —Mike

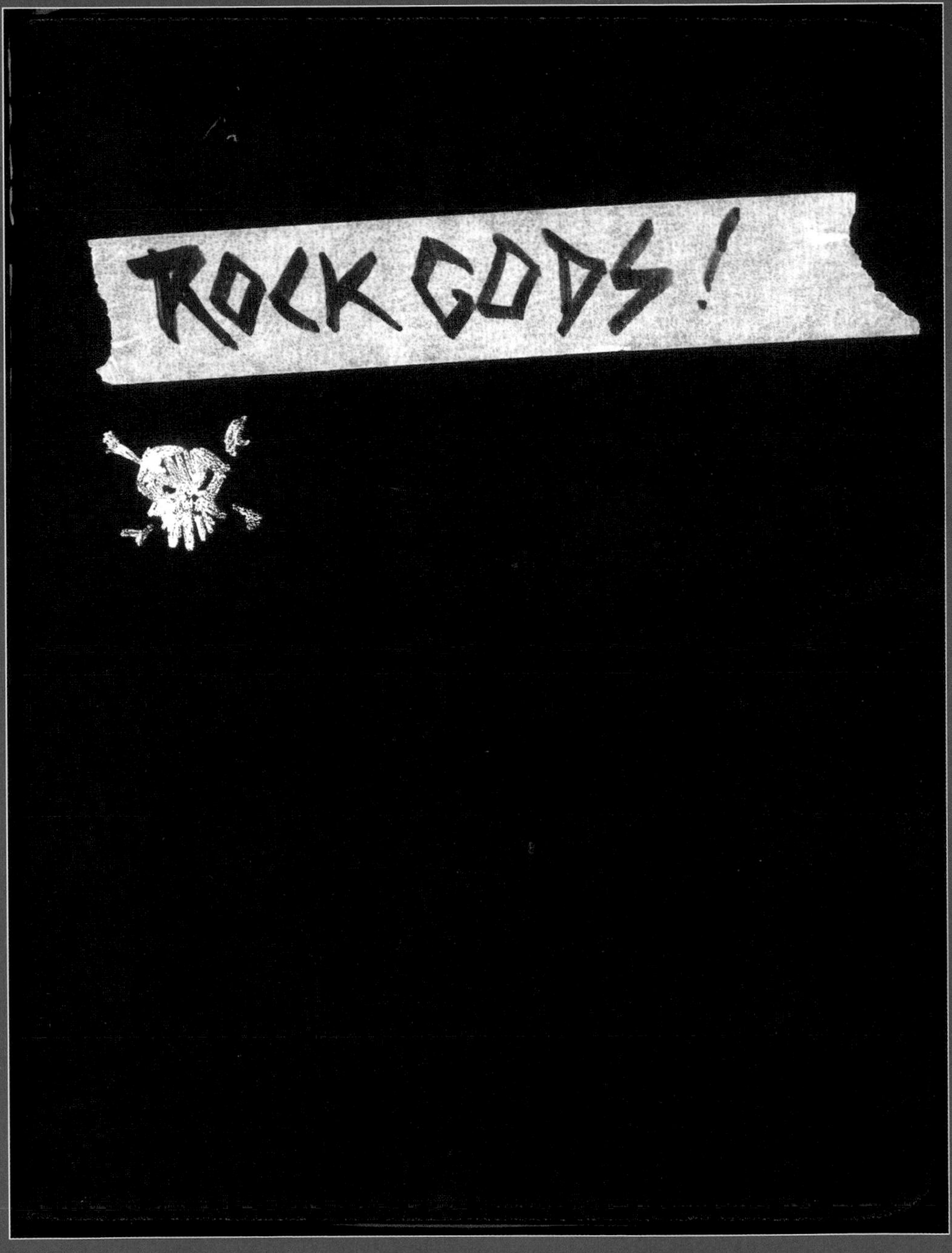
ROCK GODS!

Though I've previously written a bunch of ongoing comics and miniseries, *Rock Gods* was my first attempt at writing an entire graphic novel all at once. I decided to "do it right" and "not make it up as I go along" and started a journal where I could figure things out BEFORE trying to write the script. —Rafer

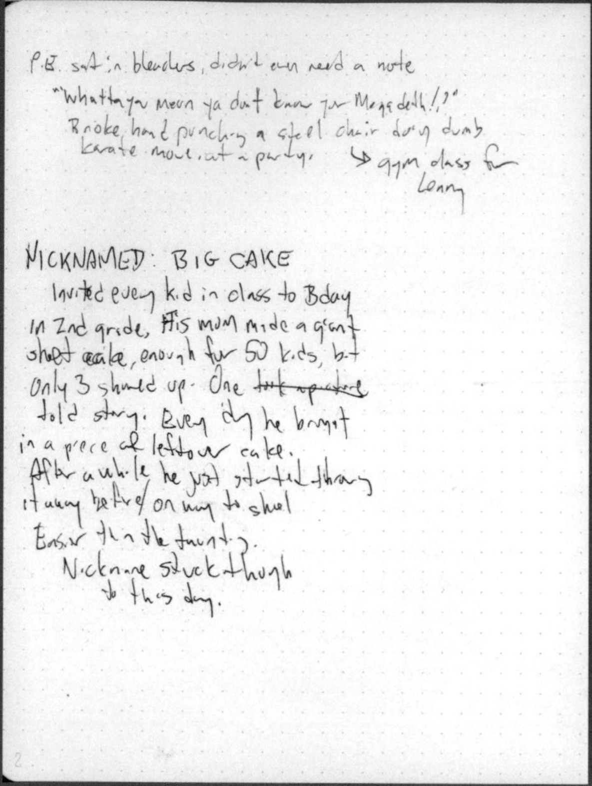

P.E. sat in bleachers, didn't even need a note

"Whattaya mean ya don't know for Megadeth!,?"

Broke hand punching a steel chair doing dumb karate move at a party. → gym class for Lenny

NICKNAMED: BIG CAKE

Invited every kid in class to Bday in 2nd grade, His mom made a giant sheet cake, enough for 50 kids, but only 3 showed up. One ~~took up~~ told story. Every day he brought in a piece of leftover cake. After a while he just started throwing it away before/on way to school. Easier than the taunting. Nickname stuck though to this day.

2

I can't write anything without knowing who the characters are and I had no idea who any of the Rock Gods really were, what their personalities would be, or even why they would want to be in a band. Mike and I talked a lot early on, trading stories of our own high school experiences and other kids we knew.
—Rafer

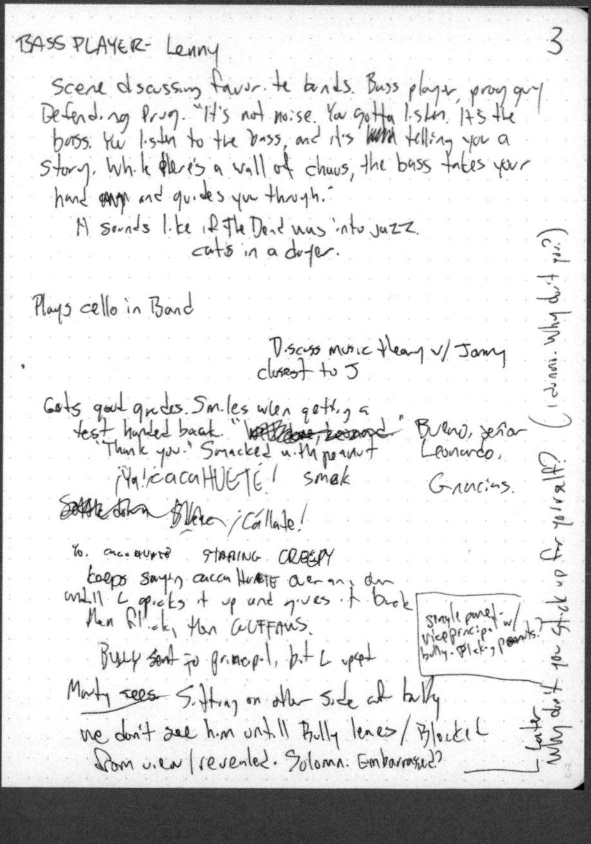

BASS PLAYER- Lenny 3

Scene discussing favorite bands. Bass player, prog guy Defending Prog. "It's not noise. You gotta listen. It's the bass. You listen to the bass, and it's ~~[illegible]~~ telling you a story. While there's a wall of chaos, the bass takes your hand ~~[illegible]~~ and guides you through."

M sounds like if The Dead was into jazz. cats in a dryer.

Plays cello in Band

Discuss music theory w/ Jamy closest to J

Gets good grades. Smiles when getting a test handed back. "~~[illegible]~~" "Thank you." Smacked with peanut ¡Ya! ¡cacaHUETE! smak

"Bueno, señor Leonardo. Gracias."

~~[illegible]~~ ¡Cállate!

Yo. cacahuete STARING CREEPY

keeps saying cacaHUETE over and over until L picks it up and gives it back then flick, then GUFFAWS.

Bully sent to principal, but L upset

single panel- w/ vice principal bully. flicking peanuts?

Marty ~~sees~~ Sitting on other side of bully we don't see him until Bully leaves/ Blocked from view/ revealed. Solemn. Embarrassed?

Why don't you stick up for yourself? (I dunno. Why don't you?)

Later